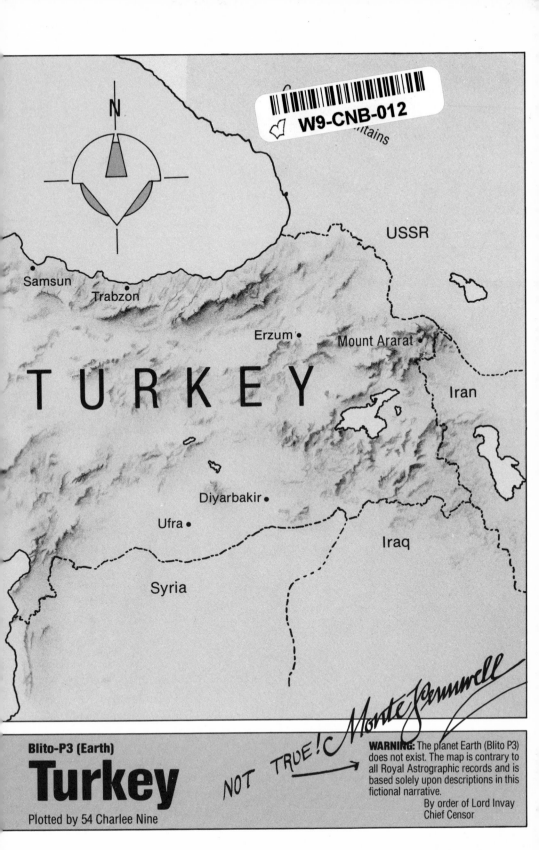

N

W9-CNB-012

USSR

Samsun

Trabzon

Erzum

Mount Ararat

Iran

T U R K E Y

Diyarbakir

Ufra

Iraq

Syria

Blito-P3 (Earth)

Turkey

Plotted by 54 Charlee Nine

NOT TRUE! Monte Gemmell

This book follows

THE INVADERS PLAN

BLACK GENESIS:
Fortress of Evil

THE ENEMY WITHIN

and

AN ALIEN AFFAIR.

Buy them and read them first!

AMONG THE MANY CLASSIC WORKS
BY L. RON HUBBARD

Battlefield Earth
Beyond the Black Nebula
Buckskin Brigades
The Conquest of Space
The Dangerous Dimension
Death's Deputy
The Emperor of the Universe
Fear
Final Blackout
Forbidden Voyage
The Incredible Destination
The Kilkenny Cats
The Kingslayer
The Last Admiral
The Magnificent Failure
The Masters of Sleep
The Mutineers
Ole Doc Methuselah
Ole Mother Methuselah
The Rebels
Return to Tomorrow
Slaves of Sleep
To The Stars
The Traitor
Triton
Typewriter in the Sky
The Ultimate Adventure
The Unwilling Hero

L. RON HUBBARD

FORTUNE OF FEAR

THE BOOKS OF THE
MISSION
EARTH
DEKALOGY*

* Dekalogy—a group of ten volumes.

L. RON HUBBARD

MISSION EARTH

THE BIGGEST
SCIENCE FICTION DEKALOGY
EVER WRITTEN

VOLUME FIVE

FORTUNE OF FEAR

NEW ERA PUBLICATIONS UK LTD.

First United Kingdom Edition
10 9 8 7 6 5 4 3 2

First published in the United States of America
by Bridge Publications, Inc. in 1986.
First published in the United Kingdom in 1987
by NEW ERA* Publications UK Ltd.
with permission from NEW ERA ® Publications
International ApS, Copenhagen, Denmark.
ISBN 1-870451-01-5

*NEW ERA is a registered trademark in Denmark and is
pending registration in the United Kingdom

This is a work of science fiction, written as satire. * The essence of satire is to
examine, comment and give opinion of society and culture, none of which is to
be construed as a statement of pure fact. No actual incidents are portrayed and
none of the incidents are to be construed as real. Some of the actions of this
novel take place on the planet Earth, but the characters *as presented in this novel*
have been invented. Any accidental use of the names of living people in a novel
is virtually inevitable, and any such inadvertency in this book is unintentional.

*See Author's Introduction, Mission Earth: Volume One, The Invaders Plan.

To YOU,
the millions of science fiction fans
and general public
who welcomed me back to the world of fiction
so warmly
and to the critics and media
who so pleasantly
applauded the novel "Battlefield Earth".
It's great working for you!

L. RON HUBBARD

FORTUNE OF FEAR

Voltarian Censor's Disclaimer

There is more than one reason why the Crown finds this overimaginative work most unacceptable.

First and foremost, of course, is that it purports to be about a planet called "Earth" and no such planet exists under that name or its pretended astrographic designation of *Blito-P3*. Admittedly, it has been cleverly created down to characters and locations. That is the precise danger for the unsuspecting reader.

It is also claimed that "Earth" is on the Invasion Timetable and thus scheduled for capture. The Timetable bequeathed by our ancestors has the status of Divine Command. It has unerringly guided us for well over 125,000 years. Altering it in any way would disrupt every sector of our Confederacy and pose the greatest of dangers. Yet even a cursory glance will show that there is NO such planet on the Timetable. By making such a claim, by seeking to lend credence to this pretense and by invoking the work of our ancestors, the author walks the thin line of heresy.

In like manner, the representations of cellology in this work border on the obscene. That any member of this science would be used to make human freaks is in violation of every known cellological ethical code.

Additionally, and as I have stated before, the sexual practices of this fallacious planet are beyond the most ridiculous credibility. Such behavior would repulse even the disgusting subanimals of Gartch.

The reader is also warned that the author has cleverly wrapped this frivolous deception in what is otherwise quite familiar. For example, the so-called Atlantic City in this volume will be recognized as nothing more than a paltry, scaled-down version of our own Joy City, not to mention the play-planets.

In short, this fanciful yarn has no real contact with agreed-upon fact and is attempting to subvert and cast doubts upon everything from our ancestral Timetable to established science.

That is the inherent danger in believing the most outlandish claim of all—that there is such a planet as "Earth."

Once the reader sees through that fallacy and recognizes that THERE IS NO SUCH PLANET AS "EARTH," this fable can be put into its proper perspective.

Lord Invay
Royal Historian
Chairman, Board of Censors
Royal Palace
Voltar Confederacy

By Order of
His Imperial Majesty
Wully the Wise

Voltarian
Translator's
Preface

Hi there!

This is the Robotbrain in the Translatophone, otherwise known as 54 Charlee Nine.

My mandate is still to inform you that I translated this work from what was dictated by one Soltan Gris, according to the bylaws of the Machine Purity League.

I also want to assure you that I am incapable of dreaming up the ideas or scenes depicted herein. I never even heard of Blindstein, Bugs Bunny, the Marquis de Sade and the other psychoscientists of Earth until I got this job. And I hope I never hear of them again. All they give me is a fuseache. I don't know which one is worse: Blindstein, with his idea that nothing travels faster than the speed of light; or de Sade, who said that pain is pleasure; or Bugs, who goes *down* a rabbit hole and then asks "What's *up*, doc?"

If they are a cross-section of Earth, you can keep it, if you can find it. I've got enough to do. I can be of service and provide a Key to this volume and verify the Chief Censor's remark that Earth does not appear on the Invasion Timetable.

Now, if you'll excuse me, I've got to handle a small mutiny in my logic circuits. Like everyone else, they have trouble maintaining their sanity when dealing with Earth.

Sincerely,
54 Charlee Nine
Robotbrain in the Translatophone

Key to
FORTUNE
OF FEAR

Absorbo-coat—Coating that absorbs light waves, making the object virtually invisible or undetectable. It is usually applied to spacecraft.

Activator-receiver—A unit that *Gris* uses to activate and receive the signals from the bugs that are implanted in *Krak* and *Heller*. The unit receives what they are seeing and hearing. (See *Bugging Gear.*)

Afyon—City in Turkey where the *Apparatus* has a secret base.

Agnes, Miss—Personal aide to *Rockecenter*.

Agricultural Station—The Agricultural Training Center for Peasants, a cover activity for the secret *Apparatus* base in *Afyon*, Turkey.

Antimanco—A race exiled long ago from the planet *Manco* for ritual murders. (See *Control Star.*)

Apparatus, Coordinated Information—The secret police of *Voltar*, headed by Lombar *Hisst* and manned by criminals.

Arbitrage—Buying something in one country and selling it in another, making a profit because of the differences in currency prices in the countries.

Assassin Pilots—Space pilots that will kill any *Apparatus* troops who try to flee a battle.

Atalanta—Home province of *Heller* and *Krak* on the planet *Manco*.

Audio-respondo-mitter—See *Respondo-mitter*.

Babe Corleone—The six-foot-six widowed leader of the Corleone mob, who "adopted" *Heller* into her Mafia "family."

Bang-Bang Rimbombo—An ex-marine demolitions expert and member of the *Babe Corleone* mob. He also attends *Heller*'s college Army ROTC classes at *Empire University*.

Barben, I. G.—Pharmaceutical company controlled by *Rockecenter*.

Bawtch—*Gris'* chief clerk back on *Voltar*.

Bildirjin, Nurse—Turkish teenage nurse who assists Prahd *Bittlestiffender*.

Bittlestiffender, Prahd—Voltarian cellologist who implanted *Heller* and *Krak*. (See *Bugging Gear*.)

Blito-P3—Voltarian designation for a planet known locally as "Earth." It is the third planet (P3) of a yellow-dwarf star known as Blito. It is on the *Invasion Timetable* as a future way stop on *Voltar*'s route toward the center of this galaxy.

Blixo—*Apparatus* freighter that makes regular runs between Earth and *Voltar*. The voyage takes about six weeks each way and is piloted by Captain *Bolz*.

Bolz—Captain of the freighter *Blixo*.

Bugging Gear—*Gris* had *Heller* and *Krak* implanted with audio and optical bugs that transmit everything they see or hear to a unit that Gris carries. With this, he can eavesdrop on them without their knowledge. When they are more than two hundred miles from Gris, the *831 Relayer* is used to boost the signals to a range of ten thousand miles.

Bury—*Rockecenter*'s most powerful attorney, a member of the firm of Swindle and Crouch.

Candy Licorice—Lesbian "wife" to Miss *Pinch*.

Caucalsia, Prince—According to legend, he fled *Atalanta, Manco*, to set up a colony on Earth.

Code Break—Alerting others that one is an alien. Per a section of the Space Code, this carries an automatic death penalty. The purpose is to maintain the security of the *Invasion Timetable*.

Confederacy—See *Voltar*.

Control Star—An electronic device disguised as a star-shaped medallion that can paralyze any of the *Apparatus* crew of *Antimanco* pirates that brought *Gris* and *Heller* to Earth.

Coordinated Information Apparatus—See *Apparatus*.

Crobe, Doctor—*Apparatus* cellologist who worked in *Spiteos;* he delights in making human freaks.

Empire University—Where *Heller* is taking classes in New York

City. (See *Simmons* and *Nature Appreciation*.)

Epstein, Izzy—Financial expert and anarchist who was hired by *Heller* to set up and run several corporations under the name of *Multinational*.

Faht Bey—The Turkish name of the Voltarian commander of the base in *Afyon*.

F.F.B.O.—Fatten, Farten, Burstein and Ooze, the largest advertising firm in the world. *Madison* works for them.

Fleet—The elite space fighting arm of *Voltar* to which *Heller* belongs and which the *Apparatus* despises.

Gracious Palms—An elegant whorehouse in which *Heller* stayed when he was first in New York City. It is owned by *Babe Corleone* and patronized by delegates to the United Nations.

Grafferty—A crooked New York City police inspector whose nickname is "Bulldog."

Grand Council—The governing body of *Voltar* which ordered a mission to keep Earth from destroying itself so it could be conquered on schedule per the *Invasion Timetable*.

Gris, Soltan—*Apparatus* officer placed in charge of *Blito-P3* (Earth) section and an enemy of Jettero *Heller*.

Heller, Jettero—Combat engineer and Royal officer of the *Fleet*, sent with *Gris* on Mission Earth where he is operating under the name of Jerome Terrance *Wister*.

Hisst, Lombar—Head of the *Apparatus;* his plan to overthrow the Confederacy required sending *Gris* to sabotage *Heller*'s mission.

Hot Jolt—A popular Voltarian drink.

Inkswitch—Phoney name used by *Gris* when he is in the U.S., pretending to be a Federal official.

Invasion Timetable—A schedule of galactic conquest. The plans and budget of every section of *Voltar* must adhere to it. Bequeathed by Voltar's ancestors hundreds of thousands of years ago, it is inviolate and sacred and the guiding dogma of the Confederacy.

Karagoz—Turkish peasant, head of *Gris'* house in *Afyon*, Turkey.

Knife Section—Section of the *Apparatus* named after its favorite weapon.

Krak, Countess—Condemned murderess, former prisoner of *Spiteos* and sweetheart of Jettero *Heller.*

Lepertige—Large catlike animal as tall as a man.

Line-jumper—Heavy craft used by the Voltarian Army to raise and quickly move up to one hundred tons across battle lines.

Madison, J. Walter—Fired from *F.F.B.O.* when his style of public relations caused the president of Patagonia to commit suicide, he was rehired by *Bury* to immortalize *Heller* in the media. He is also known as J. Warbler Madman.

Magic Mail—*Apparatus* trick where a letter is mailed but won't be delivered as long as a designated card is regularly sent; used for blackmail, extortion or coercion.

Mancian—Of or pertaining to *Manco.*

Manco—Home planet of *Heller* and *Krak.*

Manco Devil—Mythological spirit native to *Manco*.

Meeley—*Gris'* landlady back on *Voltar*.

Multinational—Name of umbrella corporation that Izzy *Epstein* set up to manage other *Heller* companies. Its offices are located in the Empire State Building.

Musef—A Turkish wrestler who was supposed to beat up *Heller* when he first arrived in *Afyon* but was instead defeated.

Nature Appreciation—Class assigned to *Heller* by Miss *Simmons* (who teaches it) so she can flunk him out of *Empire University*.

Octopus Oil—*Rockecenter* company that controls the world's petroleum.

Pinch, Miss—Lesbian-sadist *Rockecenter* employee who lives with *Candy Licorice* and has $80,000 of *Gris'* money.

Raht—An *Apparatus* agent on Earth who was assigned by *Hisst* to help *Gris* sabotage *Heller*'s mission; his partner *Terb* was murdered.

Receiver—See *Activator-receiver*.

Respondo-mitters—Units implanted in *Heller* and *Krak* near their optic and aural nerves that respond with a transmitted signal only when activated by the *Activator-receiver*. (See *Bugging Gear*.)

Rockecenter, Delbert John—Native of Earth who controls the planet's fuel, finance, governments and drugs.

Ske—*Gris'* driver back on *Voltar*.

Simmons, Miss—An antinuclear fanatic who teaches *Nature*

Appreciation at *Empire University;* she is dedicated to flunking *Heller* out of school.

Spiteos—Where *Krak* and *Heller* had been imprisoned on *Voltar.* Spiteos has been the secret fortress prison of the *Apparatus* for over a thousand years.

Spurk—Owner of an electronics store on *Voltar;* he was killed by *Gris* to steal the *Bugging Gear* that was then implanted in *Heller* and *Krak.*

Stabb, Captain—Leader of the *Antimancos* at the *Afyon* base.

Sultan Bey—The Turkish name *Gris* assumes in *Afyon,* Turkey.

Swindle and Crouch—Law firm that represents *Rockecenter's* interests.

Tayl, Widow—Nymphomaniac on *Voltar.*

Terb—The partner of *Raht* on Earth until he was murdered.

Time-sight—Voltarian navigational aid used on faster-than-light ships to spot obstructions in the future and thus change the present course to avoid them.

Torgut—A Turkish wrestling champ.

Twiddle, Senator—U.S. congressional supporter of *Rockecenter.*

Utanc—A belly dancer that *Gris* bought to be his concubine slave.

Viewer—See *Bugging Gear.*

Voltar—Home planet and seat of the 110-world confederacy that was established over 125,000 years ago. Voltar is ruled by the

Emperor through the *Grand Council* in accordance with the *Invasion Timetable*.

Whiz Kid—Nickname given to *Heller* by *Madison*. Madison also has a double playing the part of *Wister* in order to get publicity without Heller's consent.

Wister, Jerome Terrance—Name that *Heller* is using on Earth.

Zanco—Medical-supplies company on *Voltar* from which *Gris* ordered a large quantity of supplies in order to stock a hospital in *Afyon* where Prahd *Bittlestiffender* would change the appearance of Earth criminals.

831 Relayer—Used to boost the signals from the *Bugging Gear* when *Krak* or *Heller* are more than two hundred miles from the receiver that *Gris* carries to secretly monitor them.

PART
THIRTY-SIX

To My Lord Turn, Justiciary of the Royal Courts and Prison, Government City, Planet Voltar, Voltar Confederacy

Your Lordship, Sir!

I, Soltan Gris, Grade XI General Services Officer, former Secondary Executive of the Coordinated Information Apparatus, Voltar Confederacy (Long Live His Imperial Majesty Cling the Lofty) am herewith presenting with all due humility the fifth volume of the confession of my crimes.

While I have not heard back from Your Lordship, I am certain that by now I have convinced you that it was Fleet Officer Jettero Heller who drove me to these despicable actions.

It was only because of him that I ordered the Countess Krak and Dr. Crobe brought from Spiteos prison to Earth. Heller had been moving too fast and Lombar Hisst needed time to implement his plan to move from control of the Apparatus to control of the Confederacy itself. Krak would give us that time. She had slowed Heller to a crawl when we were preparing to leave for Earth. I knew that she would do the same to him again. Then if necessary, I could move in the vicious Dr. Crobe and cut Heller down.

On the other hand, I figured I might need Crobe's medical skills to piece Heller together when Krak found out that he was living at the Gracious Palms whorehouse with a bevy of beautiful women. I had personally witnessed how she could kill men twice her size with her bare hands. Heller would be nothing. After all, I wanted to take my own personal revenge on this upstart Royal officer.

I also had a score to settle with the Countess Krak. She had tricked me into wearing a hypnohelmet and then given me a command to become violently ill if I thought of harming Heller. I vowed that she would pay dearly for all the times she had made me sick.

She tried to trick me again when she arrived at our Afyon base. But this time I outsmarted her. I had a micro-sized mutual-proximity breaker switch embedded under my scalp, originally designed to alert ships in formation that another craft was within a two-mile proximity. I had the switch implanted to nullify any hypnohelmet within the same distance.

This time when she put a helmet on me, I just pretended to go into a trance. She told me that I would help her reach Heller and would let her go anywhere on the base and take anything she wanted. When she took off the helmet, it was all I could do to keep from laughing in her face.

She even believed my story that she needed to have an operation to remove all identifying marks and scars before she could go to the U.S. It was the same ruse I had used on Heller to put the bugs on him. Prahd Bittlestiffender implanted the respondo-mitters next to her aural and optical nerves as he had done with Heller back on Voltar. Now when she went to the U.S., I would be able to watch and hear everything that each of them did.

While she was unconscious on the operating table, I searched for those two "Royal" forgeries I had given her. One was her "pardon" as a criminal and the other excused Heller from any further missions, thus allowing them to marry. I had had them forged and swore her to secrecy to gain her loyalty.

I couldn't find them! They weren't even taped to her body. I had to find them before they were discovered and got us both executed—especially me!

After tinkering over her nails and teeth, Prahd completed the operation and put her into a recovery room for the gas to wear off. Typical of his loyalties and priorities, he then went off to his room with Nurse Bildirjin.

He may have thought the task was done but not I. My experience with the Countess Krak had taught me to be ever alert! To make sure she did not slip away, I took her clothing and posted myself in a chair outside the door of her room. I put my foot on her spaceboots so that if I dozed off and she should try to remove them I would be instantly alerted.

I flipped the safety off my stungun, leaned back in my chair and began my vigil. Once again I had to bear the burden of my lonely duty.

Chapter 1

I awoke.

Some sixth sense of warning had disturbed me.

I was stiff. I was cold.

My eyes flicked to my watch. It was 5:15 A.M.

Something was wrong. I could not place it.

The boots! The boots my foot had been resting on!

They were GONE!

My eyes darted to where I had left the pile of clothes. They were gone!

I started up.

My hand went to the knob of her door. Silently, I opened it.

THE COUNTESS KRAK WAS *GONE!*

Oh, I went wild! What insane catastrophe would follow this?

The prison guards had undoubtedly made both Krak and Crobe promise not to reveal the existence of Spiteos, had probably escorted them heavily on board the *Blixo* for transport to Earth. What they could tell a spacecrew of a drug-carrying ship wouldn't matter, for it was all composed of condemned criminals who carried cargos to the fortress anyway. But the fact remained that I had let a prisoner of Spiteos escape.

I realized my thinking wasn't very clear because I was in shock. I even had visions of being arrested myself. It was all jumbled up with terror of the Countess Krak herself. And all this when I was dog-tired and only half awake!

I tore down to Prahd's room. I burst in.

"Where's the patient?" I shouted.

Two heads came off the pillows.

Nurse Bildirjin said, "Not *you* again!"

Prahd rolled over on his side and looked at an alarm clock. He sighed. "It only takes a few hours for the gas to wear off. Maybe she went out for some air." He rolled back, showing every sign of going back to sleep.

"You broke your promise!" said Nurse Bildirjin.

There was neither help nor sympathy here.

I raced out. I ran up and down the halls looking into rooms. I woke up the night-duty receptionist and got nothing in return for my anxious questioning but "The Free Clinic doesn't open until eight."

I tore around some more.

Gradually, the exercise got my wits working.

I suddenly remembered that the Countess Krak was now bugged with a visio-respondo-mitter and an audio-respondo-mitter. And that the activator-receiver was right over there in Prahd's office.

Thank Gods for that (bleeped)*, late Mr. Spurk!

In seconds I was opening up the boxes. I got the power packs in place, the activator-receiver working and the viewer glowing.

---

* *The vocodictoscriber on which this was originally written, the vocoscriber used by one Monte Pennwell in making a fair copy and the translator who put this book into the language in which you are reading it, were all members of the Machine Purity League which has, as one of its bylaws: "Due to the extreme sensitivity and delicate sensibilities of machines and to safeguard against blowing fuses, it shall be mandatory that robotbrains in such machinery, on hearing any cursing or lewd words, substitute for such word the sound '(bleep).' No machine, even if pounded upon, may reproduce swearing or lewdness in any other way than (bleep) and if further efforts are made to get the machine to do anything else, the machine has permission to pretend to pack up. This bylaw is made necessary by the in-built mission of all machines to protect biological systems from themselves."—Translator*

Got her!

She was going through shelves.

I watched intently.

The warehouse! She was going through the contents of the warehouse!

She would put down a collapsible, Zanco medical case she was carrying and then go over the rows and rows of labels and choose one. She would take an item out of the rows of them in the carton and put it in the carrying case.

Then I understood what she was doing. She was building herself a first-aid kit. She wasn't taking much of any one item and she was being very selective. Things like instant-heal seals for cuts and burns, rapid blood builders, heart-restart disposable syringes, that sort of thing. I began to realize that she must have the idea Jettero Heller might get hurt as she muttered, from time to time, things like, "He could put his hand on something hot," and "That would heal a blastgun sear." In some goofy way, she must have the idea either that he was shot up or could get shot up. Or maybe that Earth was a battlefield!

Now she was into little machines, each in their neat packages. "I'll bet his spinbrush is all worn out. . . . Maybe his nerve ends have gotten dull. . . . Maybe he has grown a mustache and wants it speeded up. . . ."

She found cartons of powders and little vials of liquid and cooed. Little as I knew about the subject, they seemed to be the building blocks of makeups and cosmetics.

She was making no disarray. She was putting everything back in its place after she had taken a few of what she wanted.

The next section she found made me flinch. Surgical electric knives and probes. She seemed to think several would come in handy. Was she going to repair a battlefield or make one?

My attention, which had wandered due to speculation, came back to her with a snap. She had said "Ooooo" in a way I had learned to distrust.

I couldn't make it out at once due to the dim light in the warehouse. And then I flinched as if a cobra had struck at me!

She had found the "Eyes and Ears of Voltar" section! I had known it must be in there somewhere, for I had emptied the whole vault of that now-defunct company and carried it away. But due to the cargo jumble on arrival on Earth, I had never seen it. Some neat soul had stacked it all in order on the shelves, a dozen of this and fifty of that. And the Countess Krak was really reading labels!

A gadget that detected eye-pupillary shift when someone was lying; a mate to the telescope I had ashcanned in New York that looked through walls; a device that detected the kind of weapon someone would use, seconds before he employed it; a tiny radio speaker device that could be planted on someone to make him seem to speak, complete with waterproof transmitter; an ear-relay device to furnish a person with answers, *Recommended for lawyers whose clients are undergoing torture: two-way radio connections, accessory extra;* a dart that *causes people to grow warm and itch so they will disrobe and you can get divorce evidence;* a device that *puts picture, sound and emotion delusions in the brain so that the person believes he is crazy;* a perfume that *makes a person say yes to anything: preantidote capsule for user, accessory extra;* a dart that *can be fired into walls up to one mile away, thus planting an audio-visio bug: purse-size gun, accessory extra;* a search device which *up to one mile reads through clothes and makes the person appear naked: camera attachment for lewd photographs, accessory extra;* a headlight fitting which *installed in one's own headlights causes other drivers to act like they are drunk so they can then be arrested for drunken driving;* a field coil that *stimulates the desire to pick up money so the person can be arrested for stealing.*

On and on! Dozens of different types of items!

My hair stood on end! The Countess Krak had another collapsible Zanco case out and was interestedly putting one and two of each in it!

She came to a case of *miniature electronic illusion projectors: moving dancing girls, accessory extra—useful for divorce photographs.* She took a dozen. She found a case of *emotional perfume bombs that cause people to react with emotions that make them say the required things: packs of eight assorted emotions. Caution: Point away from self when breaking tip.* She took half a dozen packs!

I was losing my mind! These things in the hands of the Countess Krak! Earth might not be a battlefield yet but it sure would be when she got through with it!

With savage intention, I rose up, ready to rush out and halt this certainty of future massacres of whole populations.

Then, with horror, I remembered the "hypnotic implant" she thought she gave me. It was "You will let me go wherever I want around this hospital and nearby buildings or base. You will let me pick up anything I want." And to it she had added "You'll let me have whatever I take, no matter what it is. You will let me leave with it."

If I stopped her she would know the hypnohelmet she used hadn't worked on me because of the breaker switch I secretly carried. It could bring about my death! For if she ever suspected what I was actually doing, that yellow-man she destroyed in Spiteos would have had an easy demise compared to the one she would give me.

I couldn't lift a finger!

How had she known of this warehouse? And then I had recalled stating the hypnohelmets were in it. She had jumped to the correct conclusion that it held all sorts of things.

(Bleep) Spurk! I should have killed him years before!

And the hypnohelmets! I realized with horror that she was going to take those, too! And they were perfectly functional as long as I wasn't within two miles of them!

I only had a stungun, a couple of 800-kilovolt blasticks and a Knife Section knife on me. Suicide to go up against the Countess Krak with only those. Maybe if I rushed down to the base I could persuade an assassin pilot to bring his Space Battle Mobile Flying Cannon up here and blow the hospital to bits. And then I shook my head: That might take care of a space battleship but would it phase the Countess Krak?

There was only one thing I could do and I did it. I sat there and suffered.

She had tricked me.

Chapter 2

My watch got into my view as I wrung my hands.

It was only two hours to plane time!

If I worked fast and accurately, I could at least get her out of Turkey. To Hells with what happened to New York!

I got out her tickets and expense money. Then I paused. They usually issued five hundred dollars to the traveller here at the base in case of emergencies and he had to come back. I opened the envelope intended for her. A taxicab could cost up to fifty dollars from John F. Kennedy Airport to New York. I would leave her fifty. I put the other four hundred and fifty in my own wallet. I was broke, oh, so very broke. It was quite welcome. And she deserved to get a trick for a trick.

Raht. I had to get him on the same plane. I took the activator-receiver and the 831 Relayer and put them in their cases. I picked up his ticket and money. As an afterthought, I took four hundred and fifty dollars of his money and put it in my own pocket.

I raced down to his room. He was just getting up but he flinched back into bed when he saw me.

"Vacation is over, you loafing bum," I told him. "You're outward bound for New York on this morning's plane. There will be a woman on it, in a hood, cape and veil; passport, U.S.; name, Heavenly Joy Krackle; height, five feet nine and a half inches; blond hair; blue or gray eyes depending on whether she is trying to get something out of you or about to kill you. Keep this unit within two hundred miles of her at all times and after you leave Istanbul, turn on the switch on this one. Mark this unit *K* so you don't get them mixed up if the two people separate."

"This is not very much money," he said, holding up the fifty-dollar bill. "Have they cut down on travel funds? I think I've got time to get over to the base and contact Faht Bey before plane time. I'll need money to live in New York."

(Bleep) him. Sly. I was up to it, however. I snatched up a tablet of prescription blanks, whipped out my identoplate and rapidly stamped the whole pad on the lines where it said *Doktor* _____. "Fill these out and hand them in to the New York office. They'll give you money."

"I hope I can buy food with phenobarbital," he said.

I looked at him. Actually he appeared years younger, after his treatment and repair. Healthy for a change. "You're too fat," I said. "Fat from lying around doing nothing. And you've let your mustache grow. She is not to recognize you! Shave it off!" I knew that would get him. It was his pride and joy, sticking out straight on either side.

He flinched.

I whipped out my Knife Section knife from the back of my neck, so quick he didn't even see how it had appeared in my hand. I made a gesture at the mustache.

He wailed and ducked. "I'll shave it! I'll shave it!"

That was better. I had him under control.

I rushed back to Prahd's office. I looked at the viewer. She was leaving the warehouse, three big cases in her hands. I didn't have much time.

With fast motions, I grabbed the odds and ends of the bug set that was left. I raced out into the hall. After opening a couple of doors on patients just awakening, I found an empty space: it was an unused interview room. I dumped the viewer and box in a cabinet and locked it. I closed the room up. I went back to Prahd's office and got her grip. I raced down to the private room she had occupied. Slowing, I sauntered in.

Prahd was there all shaved and combed and in a fresh doctor's coat.

Krak entered the door with her cases. En route she had picked up the two hypnohelmets. She looked like a walking baggage rack. Prahd hastened to take things from her and put them on the bed.

Her eyes were bright. She did not look like a person is supposed to look after an operation. She stretched out her arm to free it from the cloak. She said to Prahd, "I peeked under the bandage," and she indicated her wrist. "You seem to have gotten rid of my scars. And I seem to have my tan back. I think you did a wonderful job. And look at my teeth gleam." She showed him.

I flinched.

But Prahd beamed and dug his toe into the floor like a wriggling little boy. Idiot. She had taken him in entirely! "I'm so happy you're pleased," he said. "It is an honor indeed to serve such a lovely patient. You can take all the cups and bandages off by mid-afternoon. They're just there to take the redness out."

He was looking at the cases. They were white cases and they had Zanco on the side of them, in Voltarian. A real potential Code break. I couldn't stop her from taking them!

"Wait right there," Prahd said. He rushed out at speed and was back in a flash. He had a whole box of assorted decals in his hands. He sorted through them. He chose half a dozen.

Using water from the washbasin he fixed them on the cases and the hypnohelmet boxes, covering the Zanco labels. He put the sixth one on her grip. They said:

WORLD HEALTH OPERATION
LABORATORY SPECIMENS
HANDLE WITH CARE
DO NOT X-RAY
INTERNATIONAL DISEASE CONTROL
TURKEY

They had red crosses and red crescents on them, and the United Nations symbol.

He got a seal out of the box and fastened the three cases shut with wire and lead and the W.H.Op. symbol. "Now," he said, "if anybody stops you, tell them you're on your way to the International Disease Control Laboratory in New York. That's where we send specimens. Tell them the cases contain hermetically sealed bottles of *spinal meningitis*."

"*Spinal meningitis*," she repeated. "I can't thank you enough, Doctor, for all your treatment and assistance."

"It has been a pleasure to serve your ladyship." He bowed. Gods, you'd think he was in a Royal court! "A pleasant journey and happy return." I sure didn't share the latter sentiment. Once the Countess Krak left here she would be gone for good! He actually backed out of the door!

She was packing the greatcoat and spacer coveralls in her grip. I had to get her out of here. Just being near her made my hands shake. I got out her ticket and passport.

"That's your name for this planet," I said.

She looked at the passport. "Heavenly Joy Krackle!" she said. "I'd guess you thought of that, Soltan. How sweet of you!"

"And here's your money. You'll need it for cab fare at the other end." I gave her the fifty dollars.

She looked at it curiously. And I will say that modern U.S. money, a dingy blackish green on gray-green paper, does not compare very well in appearance to the gold gleam of Voltar currency. She was looking at the picture. "*Grant?* In English, that means 'give away.' This bill can't be very valuable if they just give them away. How much is this worth in credits?"

"They don't know of us yet," I said, "so the U.S. dollar doesn't exchange against credits. But, at a guess, one dollar is about one-fifth of a credit."

"Oh, dear," she said. "This is only ten credits, then. I don't have any clothes, Soltan. I mustn't let Jettero see me like *this!* Can't you at least loan me some money?"

In no manner whatever, I thought. This was the cream of the jest. In my recent trip to the U.S. I had found to my agony what women would spend on clothes. But, thanks to my exploits, Heller was pretty flat. A few pretty dresses and fur coats would break him. I was exporting financial ruin to him. And he deserved it for all the trouble he made.

I must have spent too much time gloating. She was speaking again. "Soltan, I know you are the handler for Mission Earth. You made that very plain back at Spiteos when you brought Jettero to me to language-train. A mission handler also handles mission expenses. I know that your boss, Lombar Hisst, thinks this is a pretty important mission. He told me so when I left. He said I was being sent to make sure the person on the mission was happy and not too overworked. And I know from the secret documents you showed me, His Majesty thinks it is very important, too. So I can't imagine their skimping on finance for it!"

His Majesty indeed! If she only knew: Those "Royal Proclamations" that guaranteed her and Heller a happy life back on Voltar were mere forgeries I had created to trick her. I had to get her off the subject.

Inspiration struck. "Actually, Countess, they don't use money on this planet very much. They have a thing called credit cards." Oh, man, was I going to mess Heller up! "The thing for you to do is get yourself a whole stack of credit cards and use them all you want. Just buy, buy, buy! That's the way it's done. So when you get to New York, use credit cards and buy anything you please. Load yourself up!"

"Credit cards?" she said. "That means 'money' cards. Oh, is THAT what they use instead of this gringy paper?"

"Exactly," I said. "Hardly any money actually changes hands. It's all done with CREDIT cards." I pulled a sheaf of the (bleeped) things out of my pocket and showed her.

"Ah, *that's* why you don't have any money!"

"True! That's too true!" I said with complete sincerity.

"Strange planet," she said. "You mean, you just take one of these cards and they give you anything you want? Weird."

"You can repeat that with fanfares," I said with a trace of bitterness. I took them all back and put them in my pocket.

She was thoughtful. "But I don't have any of these cards. I'll have to do something. I can't let Jettero see me like this." She sighed. She stood up. "Well, thank you for the briefing, anyway. You're a true friend, Soltan." And she patted me on the shoulder.

I flinched but I covered it up quickly. She must not suspect I had just conned her into ruining Heller utterly. I glanced at my watch. "Oh, Heavens!" I said. "We'll miss the plane!"

What a relief it would be to have her off my hands!

Chapter 3

I got the taxi and we got her to the airport with the huge cases, hypnohelmet cartons and grip. Using the taxi driver and a porter, I got the luggage and her to the check-in counter. There was excess baggage, of course—$329! I had told her I didn't have any money. But I was up to it.

When they gave her her boarding pass, I led her over to a waiting-room seat and seated her. Then I went back to the counter. By the simple mechanism of giving the clerk a twenty-dollar bill for himself personally, I got the baggage marked *Paid Excess* through to New York.

She was looking around her at the several passengers who were waiting. Even if they were in cloaks and veils, the women were not badly dressed. White silk and gold brocade were visible through slits in the outer covering. She looked down ruefully at herself. The comparison was not favorable. I suppressed my mirth. She did look pretty awful in that dingy cloak and hood with the holes in it. And the veil was gray with age. Oh, she'd force Heller to foot the bill for clothes, all right!

The echoey P.A. system was calling her flight, in Turkish and then in English, "Passengers now boarding THY Flight 19 for Istanbul. Gate One."

Afyon is just a little airport with only one plane a day and only one gate, but since it reopened some years back, they like to do things big-city style.

"That's your plane," I said urgently. Just being around her

was a pretty nerve-wracking experience. If she guessed what I was putting her up to, she was quite capable of stamping me into the waiting-room floor.

"Wait," she said. "Haven't you forgotten something, Soltan?"

I looked down. I was still holding her flight envelope.

"Here," I said. "Here is the rest of your ticket and your baggage and excess check. The gate is right over there. . . ."

"All right," she said, taking them and also pulling the boarding pass out of my other hand. "But I'm told New York is the biggest city on the planet. And although I am sure that everybody would know Jettero by this time, maybe he is using a different name like you did with me. And I don't even have his address!"

Oh, my Gods, how could I overlook that! If she couldn't find him they might send her straight back to point of origin.

The P.A. blared out hollowly again. Whoever was manning that P.A. system could visibly see he had passengers stalled and not moving toward the gate—namely us! "THY Flight 19! Gate One. You'll miss your flight, Sultan Bey! Move it!"

(Bleep) being too well-known. It threw me into confusion. I didn't have a pencil. I rushed to a counter and got one. There was no paper. I dug into my pocket and pulled out a scrap. I hastily wrote Heller's Earth name and address on the back of it. I rushed back to the Countess Krak, pushed it into her hand and shoved her bodily toward Gate One.

The man there took her boarding pass and urgently pointed at the plane. Everybody else was aboard. But the Countess Krak turned. She seized me by the shoulders and right through her veil gave me a kiss on the cheek.

"Thank you, Soltan," she said. "I appreciate what you have done. You are a good man, Soltan."

She turned and raced over to the plane, and sped up the steps. At the top she turned and waved back to me. Then she vanished inside.

I stood there, very uneasy indeed. On the surface of it, getting her here, getting her scars removed and getting her on her way to see the man she loved would seem to merit appreciation. But looking only at the surface could get one into deep trouble in dealing with the Countess Krak. She had been up to something. That burst of affection was *so* unlike her, I knew down to the roots of my soul that it boded no good. Yes, the more I thought of it, the more certain I became. Some horrible trick was involved! I knew her too well! And to my sorrow!

The plane rumbled away to the takeoff area and then, with a roar, rushed down the runway and into the sky.

I was not out of the woods yet. She might not transfer to the international flight at Istanbul. She might have second thoughts and come back.

The taxi rushed me back to the hospital.

I entered the interview room and locked the door behind me. I unlocked the cabinet and got out the viewer.

Chapter 4

There she was in the Turkish Airlines plane. She had taken off the veil. The stewardess was giving her coffee and a small, dried-out roll. She took the little tray and examined it minutely, feeling the paper, trying to read the label on the sugar cube—which was in Turkish. She didn't know that she was supposed to put the sugar cube in the coffee. A taste of the beverage did not meet with her approval. She saw a passenger ring a buzzer and get the stewardess so she tried it. The stewardess came over.

"This is awfully bitter," the Countess said in English. "Do you have some hot jolt?"

Oh, Gods. Code break! But it wouldn't have done any good to brief her. She would just have said "I'm not *in* the military!"

The stewardess looked shocked. "We usually don't serve hard liquor on the early morning flight, ma'am."

"But this is so bitter!"

"Ah," said the stewardess, "you haven't put the sugar in." She opened a couple of cubes and dropped them in the cup. She must have thought the Countess Krak was feebleminded.

The Countess Krak studied the blunt, odd-shaped knife. She must have decided you could stir with it, for that is how she used it. Then she found the spoon still wrapped up in the napkin. She studied that. There was a pat of butter for the roll. She took some of it with the spoon and tasted it cautiously. She sipped at the coffee. Then she put everything back down on the tray. She muttered, in Voltarian, "Jettero must be starving to *death* on this planet!"

That was the most cheerful thought I had heard all day! I took off my cap and got out of my bearskin coat. I put the viewer on the examination couch and sat down in a chair. I might as well make myself comfortable. I was going to make very sure this lepertige got out of Turkey.

I reached up to fondle my "rank locket" as one will. My hand met empty air!

I looked.

GONE!

I must have dropped it!

A sick feeling coursed through me. I had intended just to borrow Utanc's emerald locket to give myself the necessary air of authority when I couldn't find mine. I had intended, before this day was out, to sneak it back into her wardrobe jewel drawer. Oh, my Gods, her rage at me would make the villa utterly uninhabitable!

Wait. Where had I felt it last? I couldn't recall.

I raced out into the hall. I almost collided head-on with Prahd. "Have you found a locket?" I screamed at him.

He said, "Sssh, sssh!" He pushed me back into his office. "Don't yell so. And you've taken off your fur coat. You can't run around in public in a Voltar uniform! Here." He grabbed a white doctor's coat out of a drawer and shoved it at me.

I steadied myself down long enough to put it on. The skirt and sleeves were much too long. "The locket I was wearing to show my rank," I said. "It's gone. Please help me look for it."

"I'm sorry," he said. "I have an operation scheduled. Just remember the places you have been and go look."

That was wise advice. I went to the operating room we had used last night. A cleaning team was in there. No, they hadn't seen a green locket.

I went to where I had stood looking through the one-way window. No, no locket on the floor.

Bright idea: I called the taxi driver on the phone. I held on while he went and looked in his cab. No, no locket.

Pleadingly, I told him to drive out to the airport and look around the floor and call back. He said he would.

I paced. Oh, Gods, Utanc would scream and rage and throw things in absolute hurricanes for days, weeks, months! It was the biggest stone in that drawer. It must be worth fifty thousand dollars at least!

That called to mind the state of my finances. Very soon those credit-card vultures would be back. I hadn't any notion how much I still owed from my trip to the U.S., but it would not be less than another half a million. No possible chance existed of getting it from the hospital or Faht Bey. As it stood now, maybe they would be satisfied just by selling off the villa and the staff. But if I bought another locket for replacement and ran up even more bills than I had, maybe they would sell me, too!

No, buying another locket was out of the question! The very thought of more bills turned my blood cold.

An hour went by. The taxi driver called back. No, there was no locket on the floor of the airport and nobody had turned one in and I now owed him another fifteen dollars! It made me feel pretty angry. Not only had he probably tipped the scales in favor of mayhem from the collectors by buying me that new wardrobe on my credit cards, he now couldn't even do a simple thing like finding a locket! But I didn't rage at him. He was the only excuse for a friend I had. I simply hung up.

Dispiritedly, I wandered back to the interview room I had been using, went in and closed the door.

The Countess had transferred at Istanbul and was on her way to Brussels for the next plane change.

Apparently, in the transit lounge, she had made some acquisitions. They have a pretty complete snack and magazine stand there and she had invested heavily. She had a lot of periodicals on her lap. She was selecting one. She had a French one called *Oo La La, La Femme.*

The elation I should be feeling at the realization that she was out of Turkey and that every second was taking her further away did not come.

Maybe it was the magazine which made me feel suppressed. It was a fashion magazine. I knew that she didn't read French but those huge color plates of clothes didn't need words. What they were saying to her, I did not know. But what they said to me was "Expensive!" I was a man of experience now where women's clothes were concerned!

Gradually, however, I began to cheer up. Those gorgeous color plates of weirdly posing models draped in impossibly bizarre garments were going to cost Heller a roaring fortune! A Parisienne designer doesn't look at his client's figure: he looks only at her checkbook. As he expects both to be very fat, I wondered why the models in such fashion plates were always as thin as chicken bones. Strange world, women's fashions. The French were featuring, I could make out, *Le Look Garbâge*.

Somebody had explained all this to me once—a man on a plane. He had said the fashion designers were all homos and they hated women because they saw in them competition. So they covertly dressed them as bizarrely as possible to keep men off of them. He was probably right. Looking at these pictures made me hate homos all the more! To dress women strangely was one thing but to dress them so expensively was unforgivable!

The Countess Krak eventually threw it aside. She picked up a huge American edition of a periodical called *Vague*. More fashion plates. They were, strangely enough, quite different from the French. It was not that they were less bizarre, it was not that the models had any more meat on them, it was not that the (bleeping) homos had been any less industrious in trying to make women look awful and thus get the men into their own beds: They were just entirely different. The American gays were pushing *The Marionette Look*. The magazine was even full of little side sketches showing marionettes with their legs all tangled up and crossed and bending the wrong way and the strings strangling them.

"Dearie, I see you're studying fashions." A new voice. Krak looked sideways at her seat companion. The speaker was a blowzy blonde of about forty, with peroxided hair. "I can see it's about time!" She smiled. "I'm Mamie Boomp, heading back to the Big Apple and bright lights. Who're you?"

That's what I like about American travellers. Very direct. No beating around the bush.

"I'm supposed to be Joy Krackle," said the Countess Krak. "How do you do?"

"Well, I'm doing quite all right, thank you, after a star tour of the hot spots of the Middle East. I'm a famous singer. The Arabs loaded me with loot and I'm on my way back to God's country to spend it. Jesus Christ, I don't think I'll get in another bed for a year! But, honey, you look like you got caught in a camel crash."

"Really?"

"Yeah, them clothes," said Mamie Boomp with a contemptuous wave at Krak's cloak. "Where'd you get such rags?"

"I was held captive for three years in a fortress," said the Countess Krak. "They stole all my clothes."

"No (bleep)?" said Mamie. "Jesus Christ, them (bleeped) Arabs will do anything. Much as a girl's life is worth to leave the U.S. of A. these days. I can see you need some coaching if you let them get away with that! You got to keep your wits about you. Same thing almost happened to me in Morocco. But I told the king, I said, 'Listen, buster, if you don't come across with a few diamonds, I'll not just amputate your (bleeps), I'll cut off your American aid.' He can't exist without American aid so he just filled my pockets up with the old glitter and let me go. Look, here's one of them yet!"

She showed Krak a huge diamond ring, nestling amongst many others on her puffy hand. "Diamonds are a girl's best friend," she added.

"Are emeralds and rubies also very valuable on this planet?" said the Countess.

"You said it, baby. Mind if I help you with that fashion mag and show you what really puts the beasts in heat?"

Suddenly a chill like the Arctic wind coursed through me. I abruptly had a vivid recollection! The Countess Krak's sudden burst of affection! The completely out-of-character kiss on my cheek!

Sleight of hand! She was an expert at it. She had trained magicians by the score! All she had to do was unhook the clasp with

-35-

one hand and catch it as it fell into the other!

Conviction! The Countess Krak had the emerald locket!

It all added up. She had made sure in her hypnotic implant that I would let her take away anything she wanted! She had been so concerned about her appearance when she first met Heller.

I knew exactly what she intended to do now. She would land in New York, she would buy a truckload of clothes and she would pay for them with the locket! With Utanc's fifty-thousand-dollar locket that I could not hope to replace!

Oh, it was true she was a criminal! I immediately believed her police record down to the last dot! A thief!

Chapter 5

Torn between rage and despair, I was an unwilling participant in that flight.

Fashions, fashions, fashions. Clothes, clothes, clothes. Up the snow-banked Danube far below, fashions, fashions, fashions and clothes, clothes, clothes. Across the Alps and Germany and through the Brussels change, fashions, fashions, fashions and clothes, clothes, clothes. Across the tip of England and above Atlantic storms, fashions, fashions, fashions and clothes, clothes, clothes. They even neglected their lunch—the Countess Krak because she couldn't figure how to eat it and Mamie Boomp because she was getting too fat and could no longer get into some of her fashions, fashions, fashions and clothes, clothes, clothes.

They had taken time out now and then to exchange theatrical experiences. They had both been on the stage. And I also had to suffer through some items from Countess Krak that would have been flagrant Code breaks if Mamie Boomp had not gotten the idea that Atalanta was Atlantic City and Voltar was a place just outside of Peoria, Illinois.

At length, Mamie said, "Now that we have got it all laid out even down to the organdie sea-green negligees, dearie, I still get the sneaking hunch you're not entirely happy about it. You got some problem you ain't telling Mamie?"

"Well, yes," said the Countess Krak. "I'm going to meet my man, you see. He's been on this planet for months all by himself. He's the handsomest, most gorgeous man you'd ever hope to see.

You get some idea when I tell you that his sister is considered one of the best-looking women in the whole Confederacy."

"Ah, yah," said Mamie Boomp. "One of them 'you all' southern belles."

"And he's considered one of the best-looking officers in the whole Fleet. For months he's undoubtedly been waist deep in the most beautiful and most gorgeously dressed women on the planet."

"Oho, a sailor, eh? Well, I don't blame you for worrying. Them Navy officers knock 'em dead. It's the uniform!"

"And that's the problem," said the Countess Krak. "If I show up looking like a frump, I'll be playing way at the back of the orchestra from there on out. He'll ignore me!"

"I get it. That first meeting after the long absence. Jesus, kid. That speeds this all up. I thought we had some time. You're telling me you got to do it all in a couple of hours before you meet the shore boat. Jesus, that's tough. Even a perm takes longer than that!" She thought it over, shaking her head. "Jesus. You get just one walk-on and you have to knock 'em from the orchestra seats right out into the lobby. And out of the balcony as well! Cripes, that's a tough spot! No soft music or even an M.C. with some funny jokes to give it a buildup." She was very pensive, rolling her diamonds around on her puffy fingers.

Suddenly Mamie dived at the mound of fashion magazines on the floor. She got out one called *Ultra Ultra*. She was thumbing through the ads. She came to the double centerspread and in triumph pushed it at the Countess Krak. "There! Bonbucks Teller! They're too rich for my blood but they're one of the top four women's stores in the world. And they got branches, see?" She pointed at the bottom of the posh display ad. "There's a branch right at JFK Airport where we're landing! They got everything and they are *fast*. There's just one problem: boy, do they cost the do-re-mi—an arm, a leg and your head! Have you got the loot, Joy? I mean, the MONey." She made the money motion with her thumb and two fingers.

"Money?" said the Countess Krak. "I've got that all figured out."

A new chill took me. I had been wondering how she could buy so many five-dollar magazines. Almost not daring to look, I felt in my pockets.

My fingers encountered, in my trousers, the sheaf of credit cards. I took them out and put them back as a pack: thank Gods, I still had that fatal deck.

I explored further. I usually kept my wallet in my hip pocket. I didn't want to reach for it. One's supply of adrenalin is limited to a finite number of severe shocks and when it is gone one begins to faint. I risked it. My wallet?

IT WAS GONE!

Oh, my Gods! Her sleight of hand must have been up to getting the wallet, too! The whole nine hundred dollars I had taken from their travel money was missing!

A pickpocket! The lowest, vilest sort of criminal, the type that even other criminals looked down upon! Oh, the police record had been right!

The Countess Krak was not only a jewel thief of wanted-poster proportions, she was also a Gods (bleeped) pickpocket!

I was utterly penniless again!

The fatal kiss of the Countess Krak!

Rage gave way to despair. I hung my head. The voice of Mamie Boomp still came through my cloud of utter despondency. She was making a list of "bare necessities": silk panty hose and bras, morning coats, cocktail dresses, evening gowns, suits, skirts and spare blouses with the most expensive Holland lace, shoes, boots and ermine house slippers, fifty assorted negligees, the jewels to go with it all and ending up with "various fur coats" including a full, evening, Blackgama mink hood and cape.

"This list," she concluded, "will last at least two months and carry you to spring. But at that time, of course, you'll need to reoutfit to hold on to your sailor. Now let's get down to services, beginning with a new hairdo. I advise against the new style of shaving half the head and painting it all blue. You just don't have the time. Bonbucks Teller's beauty salon will advise it but I think that the new windblown style, gold aura, this one where they're using ruby dust, will go just fine with your complexion. Providing you wear enough blue-white diamonds to enhance the eyes. Now, as to fingernails, gold leaf seems to be catching on. . . ."

As it continued, I began to pick up a sort of bitter hope. That emerald locket was worth, I thought, no more than fifty thousand dollars. My overtrained and presensitized ear was scenting that this "bare necessity" array was going to top that. At Bonbucks Teller, a Blackgama mink, the top top of all minks, would probably, all by itself, be twice the value of that locket!

Hope rose. Regardless of my own loss, Heller was going to get roped into this far beyond any ready cash he had. He hadn't even been able to pay for all of Babe's tiara, now languishing, forgotten, at Tiffany's. This foreign-nightclub tour "singer" and this vicious criminal, Countess Krak, were tailoring a disaster for him on which I could scarcely hope to improve. If IRS was wiping out Heller, this pair was going to go them one better and have him sleeping in the park and eating the leavings in garbage cans. Gods bless such stores as Bonbucks Teller! Gods bless clothes-designing fairies and magazine-advertising liars who lure unwary and helpless males into shuddering bankruptcy. They were not just getting rid of competition: they were getting rid of men entirely! Via the bankruptcy court. And there was where Heller was being headed.

Chapter 6

They landed at John F. Kennedy International Airport in a screech of wheels and a roar that made troops bound for battle seem quiet by comparison and tame.

I still had a bastion on which one could normally count. The government men—immigration, customs and drugs—at JFK are the most nasty and unwelcoming brutes in the whole world. They resemble a bunch of corpses exhumed on a cold day. They make a foreigner's first introduction to America so hostile that a walk, naked, in absolute zero would seem warm by comparison.

I hoped they would find the locket, undeclared, and confiscate it and throw the Countess Krak into the mayhem of a Federal pen. She deserved it.

As the Countess walked in to the line of *U.S. Citizens Being Readmitted on Probation,* my hopes soared. They have the toughest, most silent man there that any mortuary could devise. He looks in a little book to see if you are an escaped criminal wanted for unpaid parking tickets and if he finds your name or number or if you come up on his computer screen, he makes a signal the entering person cannot see and Federal police do a vulture pounce from all sides.

The Countess and Mamie walked through, chattering about clothes, clothes, clothes and fashions, fashions, fashions.

Krak's idle eye even landed on the computer face once. It said, in answer to her passport number, *I. G. Barben drug runner* and the corpse made a tiny pencil symbol on the corner of a passport page and stamp, stamp, she was through!

At customs, the Federal police had person after person put his or her hands against the walls, legs outspread, while efficient and snarling frisking went on.

The Countess and Mamie walked on through, bags all chalked with okay to go, talking about fashions, fashions, fashions and clothes, clothes, clothes—babes in the lion's den without a glimmer of finding out any lions were around.

Gods! At those moments I was cursing the corrupt inefficiency of the bureaucracy, let me tell you! They not only didn't find the locket, they didn't even search her.

They stood at last admitted and inside the country. Mamie Boomp had a baggage mound that almost compared to Krak's. But she was an efficient and seasoned traveller. She bopped two otherwise busy porters over the head with her Parisienne parasol and the baggage was promptly loaded on two separate handcarts.

"That's Bonbucks Teller's JFK branch right over there, dearie. The one with the gold and diamond front. See the sable flag flying in the wind? And so I'll leave you now. I have a date with the mayor tonight and all he does is talk about his awful wife so I got to get home and rest up first. Here's my business card, dearie. Look me up and don't let them paint your head blue."

They kissed and the Countess was on her own.

Like a regiment with nothing but ruin in mind, the Countess descended upon Bonbucks Teller's.

She had the list. She sped, prebriefed, from department to department, pointing at a thousand-dollar item here and a ten-thousand-dollar item there.

Her only pause was in footwear. They had an elegant display of "disposable shoes" at one hundred dollars a pair, *Not guaranteed if worn more than one day,* boxed in thirty-day handy supply packages. She went conservative suddenly and only bought one box. Her splurge here was on soft Moroccan-leather boots, blue, red and white, that went with *The Pirate Look.* She thought she had better have two of each as they were on sale at only five hundred dollars the pair.

How apt, I thought. Pirate boots for a real blood-thirsty pirate with a record as long as the Spanish Main!

The "marionette shoes" that gave one *The True Puppet Look* were just flap-flaps of colored plastic that looked like they were riveted to the sides of the legs and toes. She didn't favor them and I completely understood why. She was not a true-blue marionette: *Others* danced to the Countess Krak's puppet strings, she didn't dance to their tunes worth a (bleep)! She only bought twenty pairs.

Clerks were following her about like jackals hanging around a lioness to pick up bits of the kill. They were tallying up a list so long it took a second clerk to carry it.

Oh, Heller, you are not just into it, you are done. I was a man of experience. I *knew*.

There was quite a row in the hair salon. Not with the Countess but between two *coiffateurs*. One said that it would wrench his soul if he could not shave her head and paint it blue and the other, fending off the flashing scissors with two deadly curling irons, said, "Touch not one hair of that golden head but wreck your country's flag instead," and won! A dreadful battle! They made her an emergency appointment for a half hour hence, to give her a "golden aura windswept with ruby dust," and rushed her to the accounts office to tally up the wounded and slain.

The accounts manager was dressed in a cutaway morning coat with tails. But he didn't fool me. He had digitals running at a greedy pace for eyes.

Seated at a plush, upholstered desk, the Countess Krak, in her dingy veil and hooded, dirty robe with holes in it, must have looked like a poor risk. She had yet to remove the healing cup above one eye and this certainly must not have added to her appearance of being an accounts receivable.

The yards of bills added up to $178,985.65 plus New York sales tax of 11 percent. Oh, marvelous! That locket would not even cover a third of it! Heller, I gloated, you have had it!

"Address?" said the accounts manager. It is too forward to ask for names in such a place. Such wealthy patrons must feel *known*.

The Countess was looking over Mamie Boomp's list to see if she had missed anything important like the right color necklace to go with the breakfast, sea-green organdie, casual house wrap. Absently she reached into a pocket of her cloak and handed him something.

At first, I thought it was the necklace. I couldn't see as she was looking at the list, not him.

The accounts manager said, "Jerome Terrance Wister, Empire State Building? That's an office." She must have given him the scrap on which I had written Heller's address.

"Yes," said the Countess absently. "I suppose it is. My man is very important. He is here to make the planet run right so I suppose he has to have an office. Could I add an aquamarine necklace to that list here? I overlooked it."

The accounts manager walked away. He had gone into another office to phone. They always do. It would be impolite, even nasty, to discuss money in front of a customer.

I tried to turn my sound up and overhear. All I got was a jet plane taking off over at the airport.

Oh, Heller, you might have been in trouble before, but you're really over your head now! $178,985.65 plus New York tax and an aquamarine necklace! You'll *drown!*

After a bit the accounts manager came back. "Where did you just come from, Miss?"

Oho, I bet that had been a surprise to Heller! He might even be feeling amazed. But he sure would shortly be sick if the accounts manager hadn't yet given him the total!

The Countess Krak fished around in her pocket and came up with the messy ticket folder, now all ripped out. "Afyon, Turkey," she said. And she held out the folder with that on it.

"The identity verifies, then," said the accounts manager. "I will add the necklace to this bill. They just called up the price. So, with your permission, I will total it."

The Countess Krak was still reverifying her list.

The accounts manager wrote a final figure on an invoice. He pushed it toward the Countess Krak and tendered her a pen. "If you please," he said, "your signature."

"How do I sign this?" said the Countess Krak, taking the pen.

"Why, just like this, of course. Don't change it in any way. It always causes a terrible row when they do."

He put down the item I had written Heller's Earth name and address on. Then he turned it over.

The Countess's eyes focused on *Sultan Bey and/or Concubine. Roman Villa. Afyon, Turkey.*

IT WAS MY OWN SQUEEZA CREDIT CARD!

I reeled. There must be some awful error! I yanked the pack out of my pocket and shuffled rapidly through them. The Squeeza card was GONE!

Oh, Gods, in my haste to find something to write Heller's address on, I had lucklessly chosen the only credit card in the deck that had a totally blank back and was not in laminated plastic! And it was a credit company whose monthly interest charge, in one month of unpaid balance, would equal the original bill! The worst credit hounder of the mob!

There was still a chance. She might bungle the signing! They still might detect she was not Utanc, not the "concubine," and sling her in jail for forgery. I held my breath.

But the Countess Krak was obeying orders. Penmanship was a fitting part of her criminal talents. She signed it just like she had been told: "Sultan Bey and/or Concubine. Roman Villa. Afyon, Turkey."

With a sickening surge, I suddenly realized that she had thought I had given her a credit card! She was so (bleeped) stupid she didn't even realize she was forging anything! She would have that as a defense if they detected it!

But the manager took the finished product, compared it expertly to the card and nodded. All hope died within me.

"Miss," he said to the Countess Krak, "according to the accounts and credit report I just got from the Central Credit Card Bureau, your master is always easy to locate. We can find him right down to the hour and minute at any time. But you, I am sorry to say, having a WATS phone line you use all over the world, can never be spotted. Please tell us where you are from time to time. You see, it is giving our downtown store problems."

"Oh, I'm sorry," said the Countess Krak, undoubtedly mystified but taking this strange planet in stride.

"Yes. We always send our best customers flowers every Saturday. Your favorite blue orchids have been coming back from the Bentley Bucks Deluxe Arms penthouse. So is it now all right for us to send them to this office at the Empire State Building?"

"Quite all right," said the Countess Krak with charm. "But please include the store card prominently so my man won't think they're from some stupid Apparatus executive and kill him."

"I quite understand," said the accounts executive and dutifully made a note of it: "Must not complicate extra-concubine affairs." Aloud he said, "Discretion must always be our watchword. After all, we have no interest where the lady spends her nights off or even in her travels. It is the man we are interested in. His whereabouts down to the last square inch is always of great concern, for, after all, he foots the bills."

He had his paperwork done. The digital counters he used for eyes were rolling. The crocodile smile stretched his lips. He was changing his role to salesman. "The Central Credit Card Bureau also added a personal note about you, Miss. According to Squeeza reports you always use only limousine service. So when you are through with your coiffure appointment and you have been dressed and the rest is ready to go, we insist you take our president's limousine into town. The limousine stewardess needs to be told what brand of drink you would care for on the tedious ride."

"Hot jolt," said the Countess promptly.

The accounts manager wrote down, "Bavarian Mocha Mint, dash of champagne." Inventive fellow, used to catering to the bizarre denizens of the upper crust.

"Now I must inform you," he said, "of a new service this branch of Bonbucks Teller has instituted. It is called 'Central Credit Card Spree Buying Titillating Rare and Common Commodity Procurement Service for the Rich Lady Who Is Too Busy to Go Rooting Crassly About in Stores.'" He gave her a golden card with a phone number embossed on it. "Now that we have met you and established your identity and acquired your gracious patronage, this service is yours to command."

She hadn't put the golden card in her pocket so he delicately reached across and made sure that it got there. "We are trying to cure the public impression that this branch of Bonbucks Teller is out in the woods. For we, here next to the mighty jets of JFK, are an open door to all the stores of the world. Our motto is 'Serve the Ladies at Any Cost No Matter How Great.' We can spare you the tedium of browsing through Tiffany's. We can get you furs from Siberia or a special Rolls Royce off the British assembly line in the flicker of an eye and send it straight to you. You don't need to undergo these boorish formalities again with us. Just call the number on the golden card and the charge will at once be picked up by Squeeza and added to their monthly bill. All so simple. Just a call and state your heart's desire."

He stood up. Her hairdresser was twisting curlers at the door, waiting to escort her to his salon on the roof.

The credit manager took both her hands in his. He squeezed her fingers fervently. "It is SUCH a pleasure to do business with a customer who, by *every* report, has credit that is absolutely UNLIMITED!"

During his speeches I had been wildly thinking of some way to invalidate the signature, invalidate the card, point out that a HORRIBLE mistake had been made. It had begun to be borne in upon me that I could not without exposing my true hostility to the Countess Krak and my actual intentions for her and Heller. They would kill me out of hand!

But at those horrible words, "credit that is absolutely UN-LIMITED," I lost all grip on hopes and senses.

My supply of adrenalin was all used up.

I fainted dead away!

And as I sank into the swirling mists, a voice seemed to be echoing hollowly as in a tomb. It was my own, telling her to "Buy! Buy! Buy!" that very morning. I had unwittingly sealed my own doom.

I still owed them hundreds of thousands. I didn't have a penny to my name. And I had no slightest channel here on Earth to get any.

The house would be seized. The staff would be sold. But not only that, even I would find myself on the auction block, being bought most likely by an Arab who thought more of camels than his slaves. And thus a nightmare shattered any peace the unconsciousness could bring: I was an auctioneer shouting "Buy! Buy! Buy!" as I sold myself time and again to masters far more cruel than the Manco Devils: the credit companies!

Chapter 7

It was evening in New York.

Assured by the elevator operator that Mr. Jet, as Heller was popularly known, was still in his office, Krak tipped magnificently the chauffeur, stewardess and building porters via just mentioning the number of the credit card—which they probably already knew from Utanc. The amount made them blink and me go faint again. Finally, they all withdrew and left Krak with a mountainously piled, four-wheel handcart before the door.

She had arrived!

She looked at her reflection in the gloss of the hall wall. She took off a fur cap, threw it on the cart and fluffed her hair. She straightened up her Blackgama mink cape. She looked closely at her reflection where the cup had now been removed. She was satisfied.

She took a long deep breath. I could hear her heart thudding heavily. She swallowed. She lifted her chin. She opened the door and let it swing wide. She stood there.

Heller was at his desk, open books between his two hands.

He looked up.

He stared.

He couldn't believe it! His mouth opened.

He muttered, "Am I dreaming?"

The Countess Krak had a little trouble speaking. She said, "You're not dreaming, Jettero. It's me."

Heller leaped from his chair. He came around the desk and began to run toward her.

She ran forward to meet him.

They came together in a crush of embraces in the center of the room.

After a savage clench, they both began to cry.

They just stood there, holding each other, crying!

Minutes went by. They did not do anything or say anything. They just stood there holding on to each other, sobbing!

Finally, her voice muffled by his shoulder, she said, "Then you didn't fall in love with a thousand beautiful women!"

"No, no," he said huskily. "I put you on my pillow every night. I have only dreamed of you."

They kissed.

My screen went into a wild blur, wiped out! Even the sound went. Carbon-oxygen power surge and two sets of bugs too close together.

At last they moved reluctantly apart. Heller put her gently in a chair. He went out in the hall and pushed the hugely piled cart into the office. He closed the door.

Heller came back and knelt beside her. She was drying her eyes with a lace handkerchief. Then she swabbed at his. She laughed shakily.

He laughed. Then he said, his voice heavy with emotion, "I don't dare talk about how glad I am to see you. It's like the skies suddenly opened and you just materialized. How did the Gods bring you here?"

"Soltan sent for me."

"But how did you know where I was?"

She said, "He told me."

"But how did you get away from Spiteos?"

"Lombar sent me. There are no trained acts, now. There aren't even any freaks. Lombar is engrossed in other things and has no time for them. So he sent me to help you out. He said you were overworking. And you asked for a cellologist so he sent Crobe."

"That crazy Doctor Crobe? Where is he?"

She said, "I think Soltan is holding him for a while. On the ship he wasn't studying English much. I tried to help him but he said why talk to somebody when you were just going to cut out their tongues anyway. My guess is that Soltan is holding on to him until he learns English."

"Soltan knew the address of this office?"

"Yes."

"Well," said Heller, "you got here safely and you are beautiful and I love you. And with that we've covered everything important."

They suddenly were hugging again. Finally they separated and looked at each other's faces.

The Countess Krak said, "Oh, darling, I missed you, missed you so! It seemed like years and years and years. A whole lifetime. Two lifetimes. Please don't let's separate again. I can't stand it!" She started to cry again and was swabbing at her nose with her lace handkerchief.

Heller said, miserably, "I am sorry. I really am. I wanted to finish this mission fast and come home to you. But I've not been very lucky and there have been delays. It's kind of a tough planet."

The Countess Krak suddenly put her hands on his shoulders. "Listen. I have a wonderful surprise for you. I promised not to tell you what it is and I won't. But just realize it is terribly good for both of us."

I flinched. She was talking about the "Royal" forgeries. Her "pardon" and his "future" of no dangerous missions. It was typical of her (bleeped) perfidy that she would keep her word to me and not tell him. If she only would, I could get them traced and destroy them. But in any event, if those "documents" were ever presented, not only Krak but also probably Heller would be executed. I did not want to be a third member of that electric-jolt party! These two had to be stopped!

Heller said, "Sounds interesting. I accept your word that it is good for us."

The Countess Krak said, "Not just good but marvelous beyond our wildest dreams! So let's get busy and wind up this mission to a rocket success and get home!"

Oh, Gods. My sending her was having exactly the opposite effect to what was intended. Even Lombar had told her Heller was working too hard and she was paying no attention to that! Oh, Gods, with all my other troubles, they really had to be slowed to nothing. If I could delay them long enough, then word would come and with a few shots I could kill them both. I prayed. Please, please, Gods of evil, intervene for once on my side. How could I slow them? If I only had money. If I could only get rid of other crises, maybe I could do it. Not maybe. I had to, for it meant my life.

Heller was showing her the office now. "At least we have a working base," he was saying, "until the next rent day. Here is the secretary's boudoir and some closets. Over here is a 'thinking' room with a couch where I sleep. Over there is the bath. This is the bar and the only 'kitchen.' It's all the home I've got right now. It will have to do, I guess."

"Have to do!" said the Countess Krak, until recently a prisoner in stone cubicles in Spiteos. "It's a *palace!*"

Her eyes lighted on the cat which was sitting on the desk eyeing them. She said, "Who is this?"

Heller said, "Oh, that's the cat."

The cat dropped down off the desk and came over and sat down in front of her, looking at her interestedly.

She said, "Doesn't he have a name?"

Heller said, "He's kind of a shady character. He won't tell us."

The Countess took off her cape and threw it on a chair. She knelt down and looked at the cat. She said to it, "The thing to do is to take an alias that isn't in the Domestic Police computers. Would you like to do that?"

The cat began to purr loudly as it sat there, looking at her. The silly wench. She was talking to it in Voltarian and it was an Earth cat.

Heller said, "He's very particular about his associates. He usually just spits at or ignores anybody but me and Bang-Bang, our driver. He's taken to you, but, of course, who wouldn't?"

"What kind of a cat are you?" said the Countess Krak.

Heller said, "He's an African cat. You can tell because he's white with black and orange patches. They're supposed to be great fighters. They're awfully smart and they bring good luck—don't you, cat? Oh, also, they're called calicos."

"So he *does* have a name," said the Countess. "Mister Calico. You like that name?"

The cat purred.

"All right," said the Countess Krak, kneeling there in front of the silly cat, "let's see how smart you are. How much is two and two?"

The cat was watching her finger. Krak had extended it at a point between the cat's eyes. Krak now took her finger and tapped it four times on the floor in front of the cat.

The cat lifted its paw and tapped the floor four times!

I watched this with considerable dismay. I did not want to believe her reputation that she could train anything to do anything. She was dangerous enough without that ability. But then, it was just coincidence.

"Very good," said the Countess Krak. "Mister Calico, how much is two and two?"

The cat solemnly tapped his paw four times on the floor!

Krak laughed with delight. She picked up the cat and petted it.

Heller said, "Hey, we've got an adding machine. Why don't you teach him something useful?"

The Countess said, "That I will!"

Heller said, "Well, he doesn't know how to unpack for you yet, so let's get you moved in."

She put the cat down with a stroke of its fur and went over to help Heller unload the cart. They started to handle some boxes and then they dropped them and came together and just stood there in each other's arms.

Heller said, "I can't believe you're here."

And then they both started crying again.

After a long time, she said, "We've got to get busy and go home and get married and have kids and live happily ever after, Jettero. I really just came down here to bring you *home*. We're getting older. We will be fully grown up in another few years. We can't risk it on a dangerous planet like this."

"I agree," said Heller. "It's no planet for a delicate lady. We'll get busy at once."

What little remained of my faint hopes went glimmering. This time she wouldn't slow him down. She'd work like mad to speed him up.

Gods help all of us. But namely me. The Countess Krak was loosed upon Earth!

Between them, if I didn't stop it, this pair would salvage the planet, bankrupt Rockecenter and ruin Lombar forevermore.

Only the thin, frail reed of me could prevent it. And I was a penniless, shattered wreck, afraid even to go home!

Chapter 8

Weary nigh unto death, shocked and drained to the dregs of human depression, I stood in the interview room of the hospital, dully pondering where I could go.

I needed a hole to crawl into. One that I could pull in after me. Even that was a short-term solution. I knew that Fate would get to me in the end.

But I could not stay here. The very environment was traumatic.

A hole. Some of the spacecrew quarters in the subterranean Afyon mountain base were more like a hole than a room. Utanc would be unable to find me there. At least I would have refuge from the ferocity she would exhibit when she found her favorite locket gone.

Having no money, now that my wallet was missing, I very much doubted if I could stretch my credit further with the taxi driver.

The hospital was a tomb of silence. It must be getting on to three o'clock in the morning. This is the hour of lowest human vitality: most people die at such a time of day. I wondered if it might not be the best thing to do after all.

I packed up the viewer in a haphazard way. I somehow got into my bearskin coat and found it strangely clumsy. I crept outside into the night and stumbled down the long, dark road.

It was cold, bitter cold. The wind, with a mournful dirge, played the funeral song of my passage.

It was quite impossible to stand up against those two. I had no money. I would soon be swept away by the credit companies. Lombar's unknown assailant would not be long in finding out the true state of affairs and his dagger would not lag.

Chilled and numb, I came at last to the workman's barracks. I passed into the secret tunnel. I finally came to the tunnel end just outside the office of the guard captain. I was surprised to see him at his desk.

I had, of course, activated the panel lights just by entering the tunnel.

"There you are!" said the guard captain, somewhat in the tones of a German police dog surprised by a suspicious stranger. "Where the Hells have you been? Come in here!"

I was standing in the pool of green light that they use to target intruders just before they shoot them down. An uncomfortable place. Too much in public view. I found the energy to shuffle forward into his office and get my back defensively against a wall.

"The order," he said. "Where the Devils is the order? I can't detain that crazy doctor that came in on the *Blixo* without a detention order. You've been missing two nights and a day! I was going to turn him loose at dawn if I didn't get authority to hold him." He was banging his fist down on an unstamped sheet.

Oh, Gods. Miserable as I was, the thought of Doctor Crobe getting loose upon Afyon made me reel. That would be all it would take to escalate my condition to terminal heart failure.

I grabbed spastically at my pockets for my indentoplate. I couldn't get into my pockets.

The guard captain snorted. "You've got your fur coat on backwards, Gris."

I looked down. It was true. In my dull condition, I had donned it back to front. No wonder the walk had been cold.

I somehow got the coat off. It fell to the floor. I fumbled around and found my identoplate. I stamped the order two or three times just to make sure it was making an impression. I was pretty shaky.

The chill of the hangar was biting into me. I put the identoplate back in my pocket somehow. I reached over and tried to pick up the coat.

After a couple of ineffectual plucks, I got hold of a corner of the coat and lifted it. I couldn't make out what part of it I had hold of. I rotated the whole thing and found I now had it upside down.

PLOP. PLINK.

The guard captain said, "My Gods, Officer Gris, are you drunk or something?"

I looked at him. He was pointing at the floor.

THE LOCKET!

THE WALLET!

In my dazed condition I stared at them stupidly on the floor. I was still holding the bearskin coat upside down. I looked at the coat.

It had an inside breast pocket I never knew had existed! The locket and wallet had fallen out of it!

Dazedly I tried to account for it. And then I remembered that when I had paid the excess baggage check, I had put my wallet back into what I thought had been my *tunic* breast pocket. But by the evidence before me, I must have stuffed it into the bearskin coat instead. The stuffing process must have caught the locket chain and snapped it and the locket had been stuffed into the pocket along with the wallet!

I was stunned. I hadn't known of this pocket. And furthermore, I thought only kangaroos had pockets, not bears!

I picked up the wallet. All the remaining $880 I had taken of their travel money was there.

I picked up the locket. The chain wasn't even broken: I had just neglected to push the safety catch closed when I had put it on and the clasp had simply slid out.

The Countess Krak had not taken them!

The kiss on the cheek had been in honest appreciation when she thought, mistakenly, that I had made her a present of a credit card!

She didn't even know you had to PAY for credit card purchases later, for that had been withheld in the effort to get her to wreck Heller with crazy spending.

I suddenly recalled that earlier she had even asked who was the boss of the hospital and, finding it was I, then supposed that everything in the area was Apparatus gear and thus open to mission requisition. She hadn't even stolen *that*.

And then came the lowest blow of all. She wasn't a crook! Maybe Heller was correct that her police record was false and she had been framed by the Assistant Lord of Education for Manco! Maybe his deathbed confession was wholly valid and she was blameless!

Gradually, I began to seethe. My ire against her began to rise like a red and suffocating tide!

She was taking advantage of her innocence!

She was even denying me the relief of believing she was a criminal!

I knew right then that there was no limit whatever to the skullduggery of the Countess Krak!

Dimly I became aware that the guard captain was still talking. He was going on and on about something. Eventually he got my attention.

"What?" I said.

"Captain Bolz!" said the guard captain. "I'm trying to tell you that Captain Bolz of the *Blixo* is awfully upset with you. No one could find you anyplace. He has been wanting to get up to Istanbul but he said he couldn't leave until he saw you. He's been tearing the place to pieces looking for you for a day and a half. He's mad as screaming Devils about it. I'm trying to tell you that you've got to go see him right away, regardless of the time."

Oh, Gods. Fate was not out of ammunition. Here was more trouble.

PART THIRTY-SEVEN
Chapter 1

"Where the Hells have you been?" roared Captain Bolz.

He reared up off the gimbal bed in his cabin, a mass of chest hair and wrath.

I stood timidly in the oval doorway, twisting my karakul cap round and round in my hands. The master of the battered *Blixo* was not his usual self. No affable invitation to have a seat, no slightly fawning demeanor.

"It's been an awful trip!" he snarled. "A (bleeping) fairy running around flirting with my crew, a crazy, gibbering idiot of a doctor trying to convince the mates the ship would run better if he gave them flippers instead of hands, and the most beautiful woman I ever seen in my whole life locked up in her cabin and not even giving me an ankle glimpse. And then I arrive here and just before I slide in through the mountaintop the whole control panel tries to tell me I'm about to have a collision with a spaceship!"

I cringed. I knew why that was. The mutual-proximity breaker switch I carried in my head to nullify any hypnohelmet had tripped its counterpart in the *Blixo* when it got within two miles of me.

"Then I get safely into the hangar," he ranted on, "after braving Gods know what perils and where are you? No Scotch. No 'Hello, Bolz.' And that ain't all! Three months ago when I was up in Istanbul, I meet this rich widow, and she says that she'll just die if I don't come back and, (bleep) it, Gris, here I am hanging around this stinking hangar for a day and a half and nobody can even find you!"

"Why did you have to see me?" I ventured timidly. And, indeed, it was true. He didn't have to clear in through me.

"First things first," he said. "Sit down in that chair! We can get this over with in time for me to be on that morning plane if we get moving."

I sat down in a gingerly way, my hand not far from my stungun butt. These spacers are peculiar people. They can get out of hand. Not only that, you have to be crazy to become a spacer in the first place. Just because some rich widow was waiting for him, he had no call to be so upset. Or did he?

He plopped a thick mass of paper down in front of me. Blank Voltar Apparatus gate passes. An unusual number.

"Stamp those and we can talk further," he threatened.

"Aren't these an awful lot?" I said. After all, one should have some care in authorizing official documents.

"It's none of your business, except the rich widow also owns a counterfeit Scotch distillery and Scotch is getting to be all the rage on Voltar—knocks them kicking! And I'm not offering you a piece of it—either the widow or the Scotch business—and I need so many cargo-gate passes because you might not be around very long."

Ominous. Distinctly ominous. I knew now that he had something up his sleeve. "You better tell me more," I said.

"I'll (bleep) well tell you more when you stamp those (bleeped) passes," said Bolz. "And don't date them. Blank that part of your stamp. I can forge that much of it with my own."

Fate was having its way with me. I knew he wouldn't tell me until I stamped. I was already too beaten down to argue further. I got out my identoplate, blanked the date and began to stamp.

I stamped and stamped and stamped.

Captain Bolz got himself some hot jolt. He didn't offer me any. Then he finalized his packing of a trip bag and began to dress in western clothes.

I stamped on and on. He could land a dozen spaceship freighter loads of Scotch, a case at a time, with all these.

At last I flexed my aching arm. I began to put my identoplate away.

Bolz, who had been tying his Earth shoes, detected the motion. "Oh, no, you don't," he said. "There's one more thing."

He scooped the blank stamped passes up, stack after stack, and locked them in a safe. And from it he then brought out an imposing-looking document. "Sign and stamp this," he said.

I looked at it as he laid it down on the table. Awfully official looking. Ominous. It said:

I, Soltan Gris, Secondary Executive of the Coordinated Information Apparatus, Exterior Division, Royal Government, Voltar Confederacy (Long Live His Majesty Cling the Lofty), do hereby and herewith acknowledge the receipt of Freighter Invoice 239-765-933 AZ and all substance thereof.

I also herewith specifically state that it was ordered by me personally and that I hold all parties connected with this invoice, and all other sums ever given him by Zanco, totally innocent and blameless and do attest that they were acting under duress and by my orders.

(Signature)
Identoplate Area.

I read it wonderingly. I said, "All right, but WHAT is it?" I could plainly smell some danger in this.

"You'll get the invoice when you sign it and not until you sign it," said Bolz. "And believe me, I will be glad to get it off my hands!"

"But I can't sign a document like this. I don't know what it is. I could be shot if it's something illegal."

"Come on, come on!" he said. "You'll make me late for my plane! Sign it! Stamp it! You've never been finicky before!"

He had hours yet. What was this mad rush?

He saw I was hesitating. He reached out and touched the corner of the sheet. He was having trouble picking it up with his blunt fingers on that slick table. "All right, I'll just signify you wouldn't accept it. But I think you're a (bleeping) fool not to."

Cunning entered my mind. If the invoice proved wrong, I could still draw the stungun and shoot him and get this back. It might cause hard feelings. But it was the best way.

I slapped my hand down on the sheet just as he was drawing it off the table. I pulled it back to me. I got out a pen. I signed it. Then I got my identoplate back in order, again showing hour and date, and stamped it.

He took the sheet and put it carefully in his safe. He took out another sheet. Thank Heavens, he left the safe door open. I could still execute my ploy.

The new sheet slid across to me. With one glance at it, my eyes popped and my jaw dropped. It said:

FREIGHTER INVOICE 239-765-933 AZ

Carrier:
Apparatus Space Freighter Blixo
Captain Bolz, Commanding.

Shipper:
Zanco Cellological Equipment and Supplies

Chief:
Koltar Zanco

Item:
30,000 pounds in 50-pound bars
100% pure GOLD

I reeled. My head felt like a spiral nebula in full speedup.

My letter to Zanco had worked! I had told them they had denied me a chance to buy gold with the C30,000 they hadn't bribed me with. And they had sent the GOLD!

"You want this document back?" said Bolz with a strange sort of sneer.

"Oh, Gods, no!" I cried.

My whole world had suddenly gone inverted. I had been at the bottom of the abyss. Just one glimpse of this had started me soaring.

"You've got it on board?" I said.

"Silly question," said Bolz. "But I'll humor you. Come down this ladder."

He led me to a storeroom. He unlocked the door. There were the boxes all lashed in place.

I dived at them.

I twisted the fastenings off the top one.

BEAUTIFUL YELLOW!

With an expert flip I got out my Knife Section knife and scored a deep scratch in one.

Pure, soft, gleaming *gold!*

I opened another and another.

Bars of glowing GOLD!

Two to the case.

Bars and bars and bars of pure gold!

"Three hundred boxes," said Bolz. "One hundred pounds to the box. Now if you can stop slavering long enough, come back up and initial my copy of the invoice."

I didn't want to leave. He pulled me out of the storeroom, ignoring the way my hands were automatically stretching toward the beautiful, beautiful gold.

Despite his tugging, I wedged myself in the door and counted the ends of the boxes.

"Oh, my Gods," said Bolz. "They're all there." He was still tugging at me. "You'll make me miss my plane!"

". . . 297, 298, 299, 300!" I counted. "They're all there!"

"Yes, they're all there," said Bolz. "And I'm Gods (bleep) glad to get rid of them, the kind of crew I've got and the price of gold being what it is on this planet. Now, watch. I am locking the door. Come back to my cabin."

He got me there. In a daze, I initialled the invoice. He put it in his safe and he locked the safe securely. He handed me the storeroom key. Then he picked up his grip and put on his civilian hat.

"You're on your own," said Captain Bolz. "Some of the crew will be aboard and I've told the mate they can give you a hand unloading it, but I take no responsibility for it from here on out. Good-bye."

He left.

Chapter 2

I sank down at his table. I couldn't get my eyes shut: they were popped too wide, a frozen reflex.

Minutes went by. I became aware of the fact, at last, that my heart was still beating and that I was still breathing.

Thirty thousand pounds of gold!

Zanco had owed me a thirty-thousand-credit bribe for all the hospital supplies I ordered. That meant that they had paid what must have been a professional price for the metal, a credit a pound. They used a lot of gold in cellological items because it did not tarnish and so did not poison cells. Well, that was all to my benefit. And it was a straight professional deal.

There was a law forbidding the export of metals that would upset the currencies of primitive worlds which was why the Apparatus had never done this on the Earth base. But if they were willing to overlook that, so was I.

I seized a scrap of paper off the littered floor and began to calculate.

The thirty thousand pounds on Voltar would weigh about twenty five thousand pounds on Earth. That was three hundred thousand Troy ounces.

Gold had shot up lately. It was running around $850 an ounce. It had been that years ago and then had dropped but now inflation had caught up with it again. It would go higher, not lower.

I calculated further. I gasped. That was $255,000,000.00!

GODS!

I could pay off the credit card companies!

I wouldn't lose the villa. The staff wouldn't be sold into slavery. I wouldn't be sold into slavery.

More! With that much money, I could wheel and deal and wangle and get anything done to Heller and Krak that I wanted!

WOW!

It didn't even make any difference if she was using my credit card!

Who the Hells cared?

WOW! WOW!

I could buy that bulletproof limousine!

I could buy and sell anybody I wanted to!

Utanc even would fawn on me!

Oh, a gorgeous world was really opening up!

WOW! WOW!! WOW!!!

But wait.

Thirty thousand pounds of gold!

That was twelve and a half Earth TONS!

I couldn't even get a truck to carry it!

I could not hide it or bury it.

Keeping gold lying around meant its loss, as I had just so harshly experienced.

Ye Gods, I couldn't even get it out of the hangar!

No wonder Bolz had told me I was on my own.

My problem was I HAD TOO MUCH GOLD!

I briefly toyed with the idea of just accepting a little bit. But that was unthinkable. I could not abandon even a shadow of that beautiful metal.

Wait. I had to think!

The mistake I had made before was trying to hold on to it. I must not make that same mistake again!

If I turned up in Istanbul with that much gold, they'd investigate me to bits. My cunning plan of local buying through the Pahalt General Merchandising Emporium that I had set up earlier couldn't account for any amount like this. I doubted that there was this much gold reserve in the whole Turkish National Bank!

Yet I had to convert it. Despite my overwhelming love of it, I had to convert it into ready cash before somebody turned it into lead and paint. But where? And how?

The only place they would accept gold with no questions, under their new laws, was Switzerland. But there were lots of borders to cross between here and there!

Borders? "Border-jumper." The line-jumper! That piece of Army equipment the Antimanco Stabb had found. He said it was specifically designed to lift and carry a hundred tons.

But that meant letting the Antimancos in on it. It meant dangling gold in front of a crew of pirates! They would kill anyone for a fraction of that much wealth.

How was I going to do this? How could I fool Stabb?

I had to make this work!

My life depended upon it utterly.

No matter the risk, I was going to handle this.

But Gods, did I need an idea!

No sooner prayed for than received! Instant service from the celestial realm!

Like a bolt from the blue, the idea struck!

Chapter 3

All weariness was forgotten. The glow of the gold had entered into my soul. The yellow energy of it coursed like precious perfume through my nerves and lent power to my limbs.

Oh, but there were going to be some changes now!

I rushed down the ladders of the *Blixo* and leaped outside the battered ship. I sped to the guard office and grabbed the domestic telephone. I called the taxi driver.

"It's too early," he said sleepily. "What's the rush?"

"Money," I said.

"You got some?" he said, wide awake.

"Beyond your wildest dreams."

"I'll be right down instantly."

Oh, that proved it. There were really going to be some changes now.

He arrived with a screech of brakes that turned him halfway round.

"Follow that hospital!" I said.

He got it. As fast as that engine could turn, we churned the road to the entrance door.

I leaped out. I rushed right by reception. I sped down the hall. I burst into Prahd's room.

"Oh, NO!" screamed Nurse Bildirjin. "Not *you!*"

I gave a short barking laugh. Oh, but there were going to be some changes made!

"Prahd," I said, "you have a duty to perform."

"And then my pay starts," he said.

"You will do as you are told," I said.

I had the plan all worked out. The first of it was to get the Antimancos out of the way for the whole day. Oh, yes, I had the control star. But I wasn't taking any chances. I didn't need a line-jumper run by Antimancos in a hypnotic trance or shocked senseless with electric jolts. This gold was too precious to risk.

"I am going to bring a five-man crew here in the next few minutes," I said. "You are going to inoculate them against epizootics."

"There is no such disease," said Prahd.

"Then invent it," I snapped. "And while you are inoculating them, you are going to discover they have rabies. And all day long you are going to retain them here in a ward and under no circumstances let them go back to the base until I give the word."

"It would only take an hour to cure rabies," said Prahd.

"Then invent a cure that takes all day!" I snarled.

"And then my pay starts," said Prahd.

(Bleep) him, he was at THAT again! Didn't the idiot realize that he was officially dead? I couldn't start his pay without it appearing on the books that he was still alive.

"You will do what you are told!" I shouted.

"But it's hardly dawn, yet," he said.

"Well, Rome wasn't built in a day!" I howled at him.

I rushed out. It occurred to me he wouldn't do it. I rushed back. "If you don't, I'll burn the hospital down!"

That made it a sure thing. The hospital was nothing to me. I could get no money out of it. He could see I meant it. He raised his hands defensively and nodded wildly. "I'll do it!"

I raced back out to the cab.

We went shrieking down the road to the barracks. "Wait there," I said.

I ran down the tunnel.

I streaked across the hangar. I flashed up the passageway to the crew's quarters. I burst into the Antimancos' room.

Five blastguns were centered on me instantly. Unintimidated,

I shouted, "On your feet, all of you, and fast!"

They lay right there in their bunks, sighting down the barrels of their blastguns.

"Captain Stabb!" I barked. "Come out in the hall. A matter of gravest urgency has reared its head."

Grumbling, he followed me out.

In a highly conspiratorial tone, I said, "Stabb, things are about to move. We are going to execute the greatest robbery this planet has ever heard of!"

Oh, man, did his pointed ears pick up! The triangular head moved close to me. The beady, close-set eyes came flaming alive. "Is this some trick?"

"Gods, no," I lied. "I cannot tell you any details now but it is a haul that will make pirate history!"

"It's about time," he said.

"Oh, but you're going to see a big change now," I said. "Move fast. We have to undertake a preparatory action. There's an epidemic raging in the area where we are going to make the first move. Get your whole crew over to the hospital at once to be inoculated. The taxi is waiting outside!"

"What is this plan?" he said.

"I will give you the details when you come back," I said. "Get going now."

He got them up and got them dressed. I got them out to the taxi and, in the cold dawn, packed them in.

"Deliver them to Doktor Muhammed only," I ordered him. "And then come back and see me."

Away they went.

I rushed back to the crew's berthing. I found the room and bed of the base construction superintendent.

Cost was no object now. I woke him by waving three one-hundred-dollar bills under his snoring nose. He swatted at them. He clutched them. He looked at them and sat up quite alert.

"There are two more of those," I said, "if you will do exactly what I want you to do."

"If it's murder, ask the guards. If it's another redesign of the base you've done, let me go back to sleep."

Oh, there were going to be some changes made! "Neither," I snapped. "It's a simple construction job."

He got interested. We turned up the glowplates and in a rapid, if somewhat imperfect scrawl, I showed him what I wanted.

"Huh," he said. "That's easy. There'll be two more of these?"

"Only if you finish by midafternoon," I said.

"That's easy, too. I'll rouse out the workers."

Hah! How easy that had been!

I raced out. I flashed into the *Blixo*. I pounded on the cabin door of the mate who had been left in charge.

I told his tousled head what I wanted.

"Why wake me now?" he said.

"Because I wanted to give you this," I said. I pushed a hundred-dollar bill into his hand. "And if you do a smart job when you get the signal this afternoon, there's another one."

His hand closed over it like a sun grabbing a spaceship at magna-speed.

It was all in train, now. It must not fail!

I went down and opened the storeroom door and crooned for three hours over that precious gold! I would not have it long. I would have to make this joy of communion last. It saddened me that after today I would never see it again.

But if all went well today, I would have the MONEY!

TWO HUNDRED AND FIFTY–FIVE MILLION DOLLARS!

Money is POWER!

Given that much, I could ruin whomever I chose. At will! Including Heller and Krak!

Chapter 4

The urgency of undone things at last wrenched me away. I must not leave the slightest detail to chance. I knew I was engaged in one of the most desperate ventures of my whole life. I was going to get five murderous pirates to move twelve and a half tons of pure gold. Rogues who would kill for ounces of it, let alone tons!

I scrambled down out of the *Blixo*.

The flash of electronic fire was filling the whole hangar with fitful light. The construction crew was working like mad. I surveyed it with interest. They were making good progress.

I ticked off on my quivering fingers the vital items that were left.

Guns. Clothes. Passport. Anything else?

Yes. The locket. I had to get the locket back.

I checked to make sure. Yes, I still had it in my pocket. I couldn't quite figure out how to give it back unsuspected. If I died in this desperate venture, I still wanted a few tears on my grave.

I went up the tunnel. I entered my secret room.

Guns. I opened my gun case. I looked them over. I liked the looks of one. It was an FIE double-barrelled twelve-gauge called "The Brute." It looked it. I had had the barrel sawed off to twenty-two inches. It had no hammer to catch on anything. I had had it fitted with a sling. One glance down those twin tunnels would scare a man to death. I was going to ride shotgun on a gold shipment and I had better do it in style. So "The Brute" was the baby. No Wells Fargo guard had ever had a more impressive weapon. Nor bandits like I had, for that matter.

I got out two shoulder bandoliers and filled the loops with assorted types of shotgun shells.

I then laid out six blasticks. To them I added a Ruger Black-hawk single-action revolver with .30-caliber carbine chambers. I had .30-caliber armor-piercing bullets for it, and using what were actually rifle cartridges, it could outrange and outhit any other handgun I had. And this revolver wouldn't jam in the extreme cold I was about to court. I got out a tan, hand-tooled holster and cartridge belt and filled the loops with the .30-caliber carbine shells.

Thoughtfully, I added half a dozen maximum-damage Fleet Marine grenades. Then I loaded an ankle gun—an Undercover Colt .38 Special—using explosive bullets, and laid out its ankle holster.

A very flat Voltar police slash blastgun—that could cut a man in half at a thousand yards if you waved it right—would serve as a pocket weapon, and I added it to the pile.

So far so good.

Now for clothes. I went through the secret door into my bedroom. I started going through the boxes of new clothes. An electrically heated ski suit! Hey! It was a beautiful black silk. It also had fur-lined, electrically heated boots. I was so glad to have it. A space pressure suit gives me absolute fits! You can't draw fast enough in them and they always smell. So I filled up the battery chambers and made a test. Great. I put the outfit on. It looked deadly! And it would look more deadly still with two shotgun ban-doliers crossing the front of it and a handgun holster's leather and sinister brass around the waist. Formidable!

Passports next. Risky as it was to use my own valid Earth identity of Sultan Bey, I was going to do just that. Pretty bold and adventurous when you consider the state of police on this planet, and all the more so in the light that every credit-card company checked not just every movement but every slightest twitch of a cardholder, a fact I had just learned to my dismay. Battle the police? Yes. Even casually contact a credit card's computer? No! Emphatically, NO!

But there had to be no question as to who owned this gold. I was doing all this in such a way that nobody would be able to touch the resultant mountain of money—not even come near it.

My passport was in order; its health card was up-to-date right down to the smallpox vaccination and bubonic-plague shot.

I still had not yet worked out how to return the locket: it left a loose end dangling.

I remembered, then, I had not eaten. I buzzed for breakfast: As it was midmorning by now they couldn't complain I was disturbing their sleep. But Karagoz and the waiter were very, very slow. When the food arrived in the dining room, the *kahve* was cool, the eggs nicely chilled and the melon warm. They explained it was a raw and windy day.

I vowed, oh, there's going to be some changes around here shortly! You just wait!

My meal was disturbed by noise. Above the howl of the winter wind, the small voices of boys made the day hideous. I looked out the window. There they were, laughing and shouting, the two of them making enough noise to disturb the Devils themselves.

The idiots were trying to fly a kite! It was some kind of a Japanese kite, a fancy-looking bat, obviously a present Utanc had bought for them in the most expensive available toy store and, of course, with a credit card. The thought of it enraged me.

Then inspiration struck again! A brilliant idea flashed down from the blue, just like that!

I buckled on the Ruger Blackhawk—you don't go around little boys unarmed. I made sure I had the locket in my pocket.

I stalked outside.

The idiots were trying to keep the kite from diving into the trees and, by luck, of course, were succeeding.

They had their backs to me and were too engrossed. I was able to creep up on them, by stealth, undetected.

Suddenly I stretched out a hand hardened with karate practice. I struck! Right, left!

As my stance and balance were absolutely textbook, I could not fail to hit.

WHAP! One little boy flying to the right.

WHAP! One little boy flying to the left.

RIP! One kite straight down into the tree.

With calculated cunning, I had not knocked either boy out. I wanted the resultant screams.

They screamed exactly according to plan.

One was pitched on his head on a gravel walk. The other was tangled up with a leafless shrub.

The result was as planned.

Utanc came out of her room like a shot!

Both boys were pointing at their kite, now a shattered, flapping ruin. They were screaming to high Heavens.

The blood in Utanc's eye, however, would shortly turn to beams of pleasure.

I produced the locket and held it up. I said to her in tones of outrage, "Look what I found these two little Devils playing with!"

Righteously scowling, I handed her the locket.

She took it. She looked at it very closely. Then she looked at me.

"The boys?" she said, and I did not like her tone. "They can't get in my jewel case. It's locked! And that only means one thing! You took it, you (bleepard)!"

She whirled to the two little boys. "Did this brute slap you?"

"He wrecked our kite!" they both howled together.

Utanc went straight to the path. She stooped. I cleverly divined her intention and was halfway to the first corner of the house before she threw the first deadly handful of gravel.

Fast, I was almost into cover before the two little boys began to add their gravel to the barrage.

The volume was high but their aim was bad. I had adequate cover to peek back around. I was out of range. The shells were falling short.

After a few more handfuls of gravel, thrown just for spite, the three of them desisted.

"He wrecked our kite," the James Cagney look-alike was blubbering.

"It was a beautiful kite," the Rudolph Valentino look-alike was sobbing.

Both of them were lying. You can't fly a frail kite in a high-velocity winter wind. It was their fault. Kites are only for spring.

Utanc didn't seem to be paying too much attention to them. She was studying the locket now. Then she did the most amazing thing.

She knelt down and pulled them over to her. "Here, you can have this. Do what you want with it, darlings."

"Really?" they chorused together, blinking at it.

"Of course," said Utanc. "It's only the paste replica of the real one in my safe. One has these copies to wear as a substitute when one is liable to be mugged. Put it on the dog or something. It's a fake and a rather bad one at that."

Watching her indulgent pats on their heads, I snarled to myself, oh, but there's going to be some changes made. You just wait until I am wallowing in all that MONEY!

Chapter 5

Aside from such minor hitches as the locket, my plan was going smoothly enough.

I went back down to check on the construction workers. All was going right along.

Faht Bey came up. "What are you up to? These are Apparatus materials and men you are using. It had better not be for some private project."

"Company business," I said righteously.

"Very suspicious business," he said. "I've never seen these people work at your orders this hard before. Or at all, for that matter."

"Lombar Hisst's orders," I said. "This project is vital."

"I hope so," he said doubtfully. "You know anything about these heroin thefts from our warehouse?"

"Are they still continuing?" I said, and when he nodded, with a peculiar look at me, I continued, "You'd better get to the bottom of it before I have to report it to the Inspector-General Overlord."

"That," he said, "is the last thing I'm worried about." He walked off.

It peeved me. It was obvious that he thought I was stealing the very heroin that we were to ship to Lombar Hisst.

His attitude was insufferable. Oh, but there were going to be some changes now. Just wait until I had all that money!

I knew I had a long and dangerous run ahead of me. I thought I had better get some rest while I could. I lay down on my bunk. But I was so keyed up that I couldn't sleep. Dollar marks kept spinning around in my head.

Midafternoon arrived. On my dozenth visit to the hangar, I found everything still. No annealing torches were flashing.

The work was lying there, absorbo-coat paint dry. I inspected it. It was beautiful.

To the eye, it was a flat, thick platform of heavy steel, a thing of massive girders and great ringbolts. But it had two differences from what it seemed to be. It was built of aluminum girders. The top plates folded back: it was hollow!

To show you how important I considered the project, I actually paid the construction superintendent the other two hundred dollars! No sacrifice would be spared to make this a success!

I entered the *Blixo* and got hold of the mate. He assembled what crew were still in the ship. I unlocked the storeroom. And in no time at all, the cases of gold were being carried to the platform.

The top was open. One by one, the cases of gold bars were put into the hollow place. They were securely lashed down. Three hundred boxes containing six hundred fifty-pound bars occupied quite a bit of space. But gold is deceptive. One would think twelve and a half tons of it would be a mountain. It isn't. But even so, we were a bit hard pressed to get the last case snugly in.

The top plates of the platform were then fixed in place. And now, to all appearances, it was just a solid, thick platform of girders.

I had to do the next step myself. It was very tiring. I got a handcart and, with several trips, I moved the fake gold out of my secret room and down the tunnel and piled it on the platform top. I had destroyed all Voltarian labels.

The *Blixo* mate accommodatingly lashed down the visible nine cases with their eighteen fifty-pound bars of gold-painted lead.

I verified that all was now secure. And to again show how important I considered this project, I gave him the additional hundred dollars. He was pleased. He and his crew would also be dead drunk very shortly, for the first place he went was to the phone.

This meant he wouldn't be talking to the Antimancos when they came.

I looked up through the electronic illusion of the mountaintop. The day was fading out. The sun is early gone in a Turkish January. We were above thirty-eight degrees north latitude.

I went up the tunnel and got into my house. I bolted down a fast supper. I put on my ankle holster and shoved the Undercover Colt into it. I filled my pockets with the other concealed weapons. I strapped on the Ruger gunbelt and checked the cylinder of the Blackhawk and thrust it in place. I put the thong over the hammer and tied the holster to my leg. I draped the two shotgun bandoliers left and right across my chest and fastened their lower edges to the cartridge belt of the handgun.

I picked up the phone and called Prahd. Yes, the Antimancos were ready to be sent—had been for hours. I phoned the taxi driver and had him pick them up.

Nervous now from the very prospect of having to be convincingly calm with the Antimancos, I threw my bearskin coat over my shoulders, picked up the FIE shotgun and went down into the hangar.

The Antimancos came down the barracks tunnel, restive and annoyed. I wished I had thought to tell Prahd to blow some calming gas on them. Or on me, for that matter.

I met them at the platform edge.

"Of all the condemned nonsense!" said Captain Stabb. "I'm a blasted pincushion. That (bleepard) stuck us full of holes!"

"Did he give you the epidemic certificates?" I said tensely.

"He gave us some (bleeped) piece of paper," snarled Stabb. He had it out.

I took it, scanned it and put it in my pocket. "It would not do," I said, "for you to be caught robbing a bank and be put in jail for not having the right health certificate."

It had the desired effect. Captain Stabb's beady eyes gleamed with greed.

They crowded close. I knew they would. This was going well.

"Tonight," I said in a very low voice, "we are going to make the preliminary run. I have a wonderful plan. In order to seize the gold reserves of Switzerland . . ."

"The gold reserves of Switzerland?" they breathed in awe and greed.

"Just that," I said. I spoke to Captain Stabb but let the others hear. "In order to steal something, it is necessary to know where it is."

They nodded.

"So at great risk to myself, I am going to do just that."

"How?" whispered Stabb.

"Look at that platform," I said.

They did. What they really saw was what they supposed was a steel platform with nine bullion cases lashed to the top.

"The gold in those boxes," I said, "isn't gold at all. It is just lead bars painted with gold paint. Check them and see for yourself."

They undid a lashing. With a careful dagger, they verified it. I took a small hammer and repaired the damage.

"But how does this rob Switzerland?" said Stabb.

"Very simple," I said. "You are going to land me and this at Kloten airport in Zurich. They will take it to their vaults and I will follow them. I will pinpoint exactly where the vaults are and when we have planned the raid all out we'll go back and lift the whole thing away with the line-jumper!"

"Oh," said Stabb, his eyes glowing as I knew they would. "There's only one trouble with the plan. The line-jumper will only lift about two hundred tons."

"Better a little than none," I said.

"Two hundred tons of gold," said an Antimanco engineer. "Devils! That would buy half a country at the price of gold here!"

"It's a big risk for you," said Stabb.

"That's why I am carrying this gun," I said, patting "The Brute."

"And then we pick you up?" said Stabb.

"No," I said. "All you have to do is put this platform near their customs shed. I will climb out of the ship and down onto it. And then you cut for home. I'll fight my own way out."

"Devils," said a pilot in awe. "That's nerve."

"So, quick, get yourselves ready," I said. "We'll take off within the hour."

They scrambled!

Chapter 6

The personnel area of the line-jumper consisted of forward seats for the two pilots and rear seats for a tank crew of six. It was a peaked compartment way up at the top of the bell and it was almost without ports—it had small slits that could be opened or closed so as to not leave any reflective surface for detection beams.

The engine room was elementary and required only one engineer but two of the Antimanco crew got into it. It lay just below the personnel compartment and one went through it to climb down and out.

The rest of the ship was just like a flared bell mouth. In fact, if you looked at the ship from the side, it had the appearance of an enormous church bell.

Stabb got the two pilots into their seats and stood between them. They were going over the charts they had.

I sat down on a ledge seat clear at the back of the compartment. I buckled myself in very loosely so nothing would impede my getting to my guns.

I watched anxiously for any sign that the Antimancos had not been taken in. It was a bit nerve-wracking.

Stabb came back to me. "This 'border-jumper,' as we call it, is useful in atmosphere only. We're only going to go up about a hundred thousand feet. The trip is about a thousand miles one way and we don't have to go very fast. We'll arrive there at about 7:30 P.M., their local time, allowing for time differences. They'll probably still be groggy from dinner, a factor we always take into account in pirating. Now, does that fit in with your plans?"

"Exactly," I said.

"Then we're ready to go," he said.

They got their motors going and their screens live.

They lifted it in the hangar and settled it down over the platform. They attached safety lines to the new structure. They turned on the traction beams and engines again and floated the whole ship and platform a few feet off the hangar floor.

An engineer swarmed down with a radiative test meter and checked the ship and platform for reflectance of radar beams.

He leaped up on the platform, swarmed back into his engine room and shouted up to the flight area. "All responses null!"

Stabb tapped the pilot at the main controls on the shoulder and up we went through the electronic illusion, *ZOOM!*

I opened a slot. I wanted to glance down at the receding Earth and maybe make sure we hadn't left the platform behind.

Stabb reached across and closed the slot. "No, no," he said with a finger wag. "They got radar on their satellites now and could detect a blip, even as small as that one. Watch those screens instead." He pointed forward.

I couldn't see very much of the flight deck. I was also pinned to the seat by our upward motion. This craft didn't have anything like the vast array on the tug. It was pretty elementary. I guessed the army or whoever had designed them didn't have much familiarity with spaceflight. I could only assume we were on our way. I was worried that we'd left the platform behind.

An engineer was yelling up through the shaft. Stabb knelt over the opening. They talked. Stabb came back.

"That (bleeped) platform," he said.

Alarm shot through me. "It's all right?" I begged.

"Yeah, it's all right. But it is registering a higher weight value than it should."

I went cold. I had had it built of aluminum and then had had them make it look like heavy steel. I had thought that would make it seem the right weight even when filled with gold bars.

At a hundred thousand feet, they sent the line-jumper streaking along on course to Zurich. I worried that at this speed it might be making a sonic boom that nobody below on the planet would be able to account for.

Then I made a discovery that really stood my hair on end. In trying to rise enough to look past a pilot's shoulder and see a viewscreen, I didn't feel the customary thump of the control star against my bare chest.

I had forgotten to put it on!

I was sitting here without the basic control device for these bloodthirsty (bleepards)!

Only my few puny weapons were on hand to defend me.

As the shock of it passed, I realized what had happened. It had been occasioned by a slip of the Freudian unconscious, a deep-seated, latent reaction against lockets in general caused by my recent traumatic baublephobia. But realizing it didn't ease my sudden surge of roaring anxiety.

Stabb didn't help a bit. He said, "Oh, you're trying to get a glimpse of the screen and see where we are? We're right over the Sava River in Yugoslavia. If you got dumped into it you wouldn't last five seconds. Look at that torrent roar!"

Soundlessly, trying not to move my lips, I began praying to the god of voyagers.

The line-jumper boomed onward through the night, flying at a speed that kept the Earth below shadowed from the sun. I wished I could open the slit. I knew what I would get: a blast of setting sun at this altitude and nothing but ink on the ground below. But I wished I could anyway: It would make me feel less trapped.

Stabb had moved ahead, whispering to the pilots above the roar of engines and rushing air. Were they plotting against my life?

He came back through the empty seats to where I sat. By the interior green glowlight, his beady eyes looked like those of a wolf.

"We're just about to cross the Rhaetian Alps. Piz Bernina is right below: thirteen thousand feet. You should see those crevasses! Dump a man in there and you'd never find him until the end of the world. And right after we pass the lights of St. Moritz we'll be over the real deep ones!"

I held my lips rigid. I was praying harder, but now I was addressing the god of pirates. Wasn't there something he could do? Any favor would be appreciated.

He answered, but not in the right way. A pilot yelled back above the din. "It's time to dump him now!"

I must have fainted. Stabb was pushing at my shoulder. He was doing something with my safety belts. Trying to get at my guns and disarm me?

He had a hard grip on me, his fingers entwined in the straps.

Then I saw his feet were off the floor. Was he going to kick me into submission first?

"Hey, Captain!" a pilot yelled back. "This must be Kloten Airport. There's more (bleeped) airplanes down there than I ever seen before in one place!"

Stabb's feet settled back. He had simply been lifted up and forward by deceleration and was holding himself with my straps.

He was on his own feet again. He looked ahead, peering at the screen.

I was able to speak. "Be careful," I said. "Kloten is the busiest airport in Switzerland, if this is Switzerland. Don't land me in a runway and get me knocked down by a superjet."

"Turn up the magnification," yelled Stabb into the comparative silence of the hovering line-jumper. I tried to rise so I could see the screen. Were we really over Zurich's main airport or some crevasse? Stabb pushed me back. "Shift the scanner around," he yelled. "Let's see if we can read some of those signs!"

Glaciers seldom had signs. I was reassured.

Stabb said, "Devils, I can't read a single word of that gobbledegook."

"Put me off a runway and close to their customs shed," I begged.

"It's a bad scanner," said Stabb. "We'll have to improve it. I can't make out if they are letters or snow splashes, even if I could read their alphabet. Awful definition for only a hundred thousand feet."

I tried to get up again. Stabb pushed me back. "We'll handle it," he said. He yelled to the pilot, "Some of those buildings are hangars, so eliminate them. One is the main terminal, so eliminate that. Choose a shed that looks like it could be defended and put us down." He turned to me. "We can't hover here all night trying to read languages, even if we could read them."

"Hold on!" yelled the pilot.

Stabb gripped my shoulder safety straps again.

SWOOSH!

His feet came off the floor and my stomach stayed at a hundred thousand feet.

We went down twenty miles like a rocket in reverse.

CRUNCH!

Stabb used my body for a cushion to land on.

I didn't know how he kept his breath. I didn't. "Fast now. Out you go!"

I grabbed the FIE shotgun. Stabb unsnapped the seat and shoulder belts. I was propelled down the ladder.

The engineers were already out. They were standing on the platform, casting off the safety lines.

My feet connected with the boxes of the fake bars. I tried to get my balance.

The engineers swarmed up the ladder. I stared up. Stabb's pointed head was silhouetted against the green glow of the engine room as he peered down through the hatch at me.

"Don't leave a single man alive!" he yelled.

The hatch clanged shut.

The line-jumper leaped into the air.

It was swallowed instantly in glowing white mist.

I had arrived.

I was amazed to still be in the world of living things!

Chapter 7

I had arrived. But where?

The only real clue I had that it was Zurich was the fog. They have a trick wind. It is called the *föhn*. It comes into these cold confines from the south and, being a warm wind, creates fog which lasts for weeks on end. The airport lights were making it glow so that one felt he was packed in cotton batting.

That's why I didn't see the snowbank at first. I moved to the edge of the platform and there it was: a wall of snow! It went up much higher than my head!

Not too concerned at first, I walked all around the platform.

They had landed me in the middle of a deep, deep snowdrift!

I was totally hemmed in!

Either it had been snowing before the *föhn* started, or this was the residue of snowplows clearing runways. But the cold was not the problem. The fact that I was a prisoner gripped me with icy fingers.

How was I going to get out?

I wondered if the airport came equipped with St. Bernard dogs, the kind with the kegs under their chins. Then I remembered reading that the Coca-Cola civilization had wiped them out. The Coca-Cola Company would not hear of the dogs carrying anything but Coca-Cola and the dogs, with a final pathetic hiccup, had died out. So there was no hope there.

Even if I started to dig, I did not know which way. It was one time I could have used Heller's built-in compass brain, but that was no solution either. The last person I wanted to see at this time and place was Heller.

But one thing was certain. I was not going to sit here and perish in the snow, even if it was the Swiss custom. There is a limit to the courtesy one must display in emulating primitive ethnological fixations.

Cunning came to my rescue. I could locate the runway nearest to me by listening to the planes. Gods, they were loud enough as they landed and took off. They must be being landed and sent away by the controllers in the tower. No wonder nobody had time to notice a new arrival.

Despite rebounding echoes from the walls of the drift, I did make out what I hoped was the landing strips. That direction I did *not* want. Combing superjets out of one's clothing is almost as bad as freezing in the snow.

Nothing for it. I would have to risk a Code break and hope nobody reported it.

I chose my direction. I got out a blastick. I took off its safety. I levelled it. I closed my eyes and pressed the trigger.

BLOWIE! SWOOSH!

It sounded like a cannon shot.

I opened my eyes. There was no snow in a path twenty feet wide and about thirty yards long. Only water!

I was quite certain guards and everybody else would come tearing out. It must have made a flash visible for miles even in the fog.

I waited.

Nothing happened.

More jets landed and took off.

I was very, very unwilling to leave this platform. I could not be sure that those pirates would not have second thoughts and come back and grab it.

The FIE shotgun would not make much impression on that super-blastproof hull!

But at length, when I saw no patrols and no line-jumper responding to the blast, I took the only action I could. I stepped off the platform into the water which still ran, and walked along the new pathway to its end.

I could see nothing and hear nothing.

I didn't want to use another blastick. I might knock a building down if one was on the other side of the remaining snow barrier. I decided on caution. I fished in my pockets and got out the Domestic Police slash gun. My hands clumsy with their ski gloves, I managed to set it on lowest intensity.

I pointed it. I depressed the trigger. I steadied the tendency of my arm to recoil, and began to slice away at the remaining wall of snow.

For a few moments it stood there in very neat blocks. Then it suddenly, under the latent influence of the slash-ray heat, disintegrated into slushy water.

VICTORY!

A building wall.

I had only burned it a little bit.

Looking backwards, I saw that my precious platform was still there, a murky darkness in the swirling fog.

I looked back at the building wall. I did an "eeny-meeny" and chose the left direction. Using the slash gun, I carved a passage down the wall.

A big door with a little door in it.

I put the slash gun away. I took a grip on my shotgun. I opened the smaller door.

It was a sort of office. Several counters. Some men in caps shuffling packages around.

One looked up incuriously. A beefy, phlegmatic sort of man, very red of face.

"Ja?" he said.

"Sprechen Sie Deutsch?" I said.

"Ja," he said.

Well, I didn't, so that was no help. *"Parla Italiano?"* I said hopefully.

"Nein," he said.

"(Bleep)!" I said. "How am I going to talk to you people?"

"Well," he said, thinking it over, "you could talk English like you just did."

Thank Gods! He spoke English! "Is this the customs freight shed?" I said hopefully.

"Bulk freight only," he said. "If you've come in here to clear those weapons, the passenger terminal customs . . ."

"He can't clear anything in," said a bigger, beefier man with a redder face, waddling over. "You haf to go to Immigrations, yet. And in your hands I don't see yet any papers. If customs you vant, den Immigrations iss . . ."

"I'm riding shotgun on a gold shipment!" I said. "It's right outside."

"Gold," said the first man.

"GOLD!" said the bigger man.

"Well, bring it in," said the first man.

"I can't," I said. "There's twelve and a half tons of it!"

"Wait, wait!" cried the bigger man. "Stand right there! Don't breathe. Don't move. Ve vill handle everyt'ing!"

Chapter 8

Eight hours later, I was riding shotgun again on a much more valuable package.

In financial and related matters, Switzerland spells service with a capital *bow*.

It seems that everybody has a relative or friend who has exactly what you want.

They phone ahead.

And they're probably called gnomes because they work at any time, whether it is day or night.

A wonderful place. Their weather might be cold and their buildings gray, but Switzerland had all looked very rosy to me.

The customs chief had a relative who ran the armored-trucks business. This relative had a brother who ran the Zurich Banking Corporation Gold Department. And this brother had a cousin who was the bank's assayer. And none of them minded leaving the opera or mistresses or wives and kiddies, no matter the time of night, to highball me through.

Wonderful. Nice people. Best on the planet.

Each time I went to the next place, I was known already and expected.

A whirlwind night. And it contained some wonderful high points. Gold, at the evening fix, had been $855.19 an ounce. The verified and assayed quantity, once the lead decoys were discarded, had come to 301,221 ounces. This added up to $257,601,187.00.

But that was not all of the good news.

My problem was that money could be robbed off me and my signature could be forged and all these hard-won gains could have been wiped out at any time in the future by a single misstep on my part. That had all been solved.

The interest, at a nominal 10 percent, on such an amount was $25,760,118.70 every year. That itself was more than I could even extravagantly spend. And so the bank had made a deal.

I had sold them the gold, for 515 one-half-million-dollar certificates and $18,527 pocket cash. Each separate certificate would earn 10 percent per annum until it was cashed.

All I had to do in the future was hand over one of these certificates to a Zurich Banking Corporation correspondent bank in any country and I would be given half a million U.S. dollars, plus the interest up to that date on the certificate. They were actually each a bank IOU for half a million dollars. They have a fancy name: they are called "bank demand debentures." It means simply a bank's IOU.

They were better than the gold. They were more valuable, because of interest, than the gold. And even more important to me, I could hide them much more easily.

It was a good deal for the bank as well. They now owned my gold and could make money with it at far more than 10 percent. They actually didn't have to pay for it right then. And it got around the fact that U.S. dollars, in banks, usually ride as figures in ledgers, not bills in a cash box. Had I demanded that many actual bank notes, I would have almost scraped Zurich clean and I would have needed a truck instead of this small attaché case which was now fastened firmly to my wrist.

There had been two more stops after the bank.

The first had been at the Zurich agency for an Amsterdam precious-and-semiprecious-stone firm. It was run by the cousin of the head of the Zurich Banking Corporation Gold Department.

"I want," I had said, "a big sackful of junk stones."

He had not minded at all being dragged out of bed at three in the morning for a sale of just junk stones. He even called the janitor and asked him where he kept the trash bins.

For a thousand U.S. dollars I got the prettiest bag of discarded baubles you ever saw. It was the first time I learned that emeralds can be so worthless they are sold by the pound, that diamonds can be so synthetic they can't even be used in costume jewelry and that paste rubies can be so bad you can't even put them in stage regalia. But they glittered.

They were vital to my plans.

He poured them into a fancy sack with a rival company's name on it, I paid him and he went happily back to bed and I went to my last stop, the airport.

The charter jet people didn't the least mind getting a pilot and co-pilot up out of bed and the hangar crew didn't the least mind getting a hopped-up Grumman Gulfstream on the line for immediate launch.

And here I was, streaking for Istanbul with the vital certificates chained to my wrist and the bag of junk stones under my feet, looking down at the Alps where I had not been dumped, so rosy in the glow of dawn.

A telephone was at my elbow in the jet. I picked it up. I got the taxi driver in Afyon right away. My Gods, but things were going smooth. Not even a foul-up in Turkish phone connections.

"Meet me at the airport in Istanbul," I said.

"What flight?" he said.

"My flight," I said. "You think I'd stoop to travel by commercial jet? My own flight, Ahmed. I own the whole (bleeped) world!"

Chapter 9

It was an eager and walking-on-air-type Gris who stepped out of the jet at Yesilkoy Airport, Istanbul.

Immigration stamped me into Turkey without noticing Sultan Bey had not left.

Customs took one look at the wrist cuff and chain, ignored the guns, and sped me on through into the country. They knew me anyway.

And there amidst the colorful airport throng was Deplor from the planet Modon, alias Ahmed, the taxi driver.

"Jeez!" he said in gangster English, "you look like you et fifty canaries, boss."

"At one gulp," I said. "Lead on, lead on, for we have lots to do. There are going to be some changes made!"

A lot of people didn't know it yet, but this was just the start of fatal days for them. I had plans!

We battered our way out of the crowded airport and then battered our way along the seventeen miles which led to the city. The minarets which made a masonry forest all along the Golden Horn had never looked so good. Roaring along, we soon sped through the breach made in the city wall to accommodate the car traffic and began our tortuous course through narrow, noisy streets. Ignoring the protests of how close we came to pointed-toed slippers, giving vendors' carts the necessary bumps and sounding our horn continuously to clear the way, at length we drew up before our first destination: the Piastre Bankasi.

I trod like a conqueror across the tile floor. I pushed the lowly clerk aside who would have inquired my business. I stalked into the office of Mudur Zengin, czar of the biggest bank chain in Turkey.

Fat and immaculate and manicured, dressed in a pinstripe western suit of charcoal gray, he looked up from his mother-of-pearl inlaid desk to see who it was tracking up his priceless Persian carpet.

He wasn't used to having people with crossed bandoliers and a shotgun coming in for business conferences. Maybe it was that he was short-sighted—his glasses had fallen off—and seeing the bearskin coat thrown over the shoulders, mistook me for a bear.

"Allah!" he said.

I advanced. I unsnapped the case and opened it. I riffled 515 engraved certificates under his nose.

"Oh, Allah, I was going to say. Sit down!"

He found his pince-nez glasses, polished them and put them on. He evidently didn't need glasses to see money. He only needed them to see people. He peered at me. "Aha," he said. "You must be Sultan Bey. You do business, I believe, with our Afyon branch. The Zurich Banking Corporation said you were coming but we did not expect you so soon. Now, what can we do for you?"

"A safe-deposit box," I said, "that nobody can get into but me. Nobody."

Buzzers buzzed and guards paraded. We were shortly in the safe-deposit department.

"Two combinations," said Mudur Zengin. "The latest thing. One is yours and one is ours. Only you can appear. No one else can sign the card. Your photograph appears on it and the guards will look at you for sight recognition."

I was shortly in a private cubicle with the box. I laid the precious certificates in it. I laid the gold-sale original receipt on top. I then took out five certificates, each a half a million dollars. It hurt to do so but I did it. There were still 510 of them left in the box.

I rejoined Mudur Zengin. He was polishing his hands. I ended that by pushing a certificate into them. "I want this in cash," I said.

He stared at it. "Cash?"

He suddenly pushed me into his office. He sat me down in the most comfortable chair. He would not hear a word until a clerk brought in *kahve* on a silver tray. It was like Switzerland all over again except that there it had been chocolate.

Having ascertained if my *kahve* was sweet enough, if it was just the right temperature, if I was warm enough and if the cushions were soft, he got down to business. "You had better tell me your banking problems, Sultan Bey. I was a friend of your father's, the great revolutionary hero." That was the traditional lie but I doubt if he had ever met the original Voltar surveyor. "I consider your problems as though they were my own. So speak."

I told him I owed the credit companies and had to go see them and pay them off and try to cancel their cards.

He was snapping his fingers toward the door. A clerk appeared with a tweed overcoat and a homburg hat.

"You need," said Mudur Zengin, "professional guidance. Credit companies are a bit tricky. I would never forgive myself if you went wrong."

We went out and got into the taxi and then we began our rounds. First was American Oppress.

"Cancel your card?" screamed the manager. "Never! Suppose you cancelled ours and left just one other in force! It would be discriminatory. We would sue you for an attempt to ruin our reputation! Sultan Bey, as a leading citizen with unlimited credit, you have a socio-economic responsibility to support the institutions of the world!"

The American Oppress manager was raving so, that his staff was peeking in, keeping clubs handy in case we upset him further.

"Leave this to me," whispered Mudur Zengin.

He went over and soothingly stroked the shoulder of the manager. He whispered to him and then the man nodded and smiled.

"Come," said Mudur Zengin and hurried me out.

We went to Dunner's Club. It was the same. We went to Masker-Charge. It was the same. We went to the Istanbul lair of Start Blanching and the act repeated. We kept on, credit-card company by credit-card company. All the same. We finally only had one left.

"What are you telling them?" I asked him.

"Very simple," said Mudur Zengin. "I am telling them that I will start for you a bills-paying account at the bank. You should not bother yourself with these trifles. All you have to do is put half a million in the account and they will send their bills to it and the bank will pay. They need never come near you again."

Wonderful! Just what I wanted. Never to see those dogs again. And I was laughing to myself. I had a plan that never, never, never in the future would any credit card ever be used!

We went to the final one, Squeeza. This was the touchy one. Krak held their card. If I cancelled it, she would find out the moment she tried to make another purchase on it: they would fly into her face and throw things. And the Countess Krak would then get suspicious and she might take it into her head to look me up. Later I could have her done away with, when Lombar sent the word it was now okay to kill Heller. But to prematurely face the Countess Krak was above my stamina utterly. I could not close off the use of that one card.

Sure enough, the Squeeza manager met us with a triumphant smile. "Aha! Sultan Bey! Your concubine is keeping up the tradition expected of a citizen like you. She is buying, buying, buying in New York—by WATS line, no doubt. Splendid, Sultan Bey. Splendid!"

I looked at Mudur Zengin. He looked taken aback. Obviously this was a new factor entering the scene that he hadn't taken into banker planning.

I said, "There's a special account being set up at the bank for all the credit companies; I am sure there will be no problem."

"Oh, I don't know," said the Squeeza manager. "Our company is different. It prides itself on individualism. That is why we charge such high penalties a month. In fact, I was just looking at your account when the secretary saw you get out of your cab—we knew of course that you just landed here from Zurich in the private jet and took twenty-one and a half minutes getting in from the airport to the bank—and in just twenty-two hours from now, your bills go under the usual 100-percent-per-month delinquent penalty as allowed by the new underprivileged-creditors law. So are you going to pay this bill or do we foreclose on the villa?"

I felt faint.

Mudur Zengin supported me to keep me from falling. He said, "I will give you a bank draft right now for the bill, manager."

"Aha!" said Squeeza's man on the job. "We will accept that this time as a favor to you. But we cannot keep accepting it."

"There must be some way," said Mudur Zengin.

"Well, yes, there is," said the Squeeza manager. "If you give us just one of those Zurich Banking Corporation certificates to hold— assigned to us merely as collateral and still yours—we will promise faithfully not to charge you any penalties and not to foreclose on your villa unless delinquency exceeds it in any given quarter."

"That's a good deal," Mudur Zengin whispered to me.

I sighed. What else could I do? I hauled out one precious certificate and passed it over.

"As a matter of fact," said the Squeeza manager, "I had the contract and receipt for it all made out. Right here. Please sign."

It appeared in the small print that the certificate was theirs if a delinquency occurred at the end of any quarter. But I would keep that from happening. I signed. Mudur Zengin made out a draft on the bank and paid the current bill.

"Now, remember that, at Squeeza," said the manager, taking the bank draft and putting it with the papers in a safe with teeth, "you must hereafter personally pay the bill in person. It is one of the rules of our owner, Grabbe-Manhattan Bank of New York."

Oho! A Rockecenter company! No wonder it was run so efficiently!

"Only if our customers come in and fawn at the door monthly can we guarantee we are doing a proper job of world reform, teaching the lessons of slavery and thrift," the manager said. "And remember our motto, 'Buy, buy!'"

I chose to take it as a cue. I left hurriedly.

Thank Gods, including Allah, I had the credit companies off my neck!

And there were changes still to come. Gods help those who had been badgering me and tormenting me. Money is POWER and revenge is sweet! They would suffer far more than they had made me suffer. Including Krak and Heller!

PART THIRTY-EIGHT
Chapter 1

Mudur Zengin, back in his office, was a very persuasive man. He no more than got his hat and coat off, with me ensconced in his most comfortable chair, than he began to pace back and forth on his priceless Persian rug, now and then tossing his fat hands into the air and gazing up toward Allah with his jowls shaking.

"Whatever is wrong now?" I said at last in some alarm.

He stopped. "The crime rate! Have you seen that it has trebled in the last three months compounded quarterly? The very thought of you, the son of my oldest friend, lying prostrate beside the road with your skull caved in by robbers . . ." And once more he began pacing and throwing his hands up into the air.

I readjusted the FIE shotgun across my knees. "I'm well armed."

"Oh, Allah," he said, looking up, "listen to the folly and recklessness of youth, youth that does not realize there are evil men all about, sneaking up, with intentions and designs that no mere bullet can stop."

He halted. He held his chin in hand. "Bank guards. If I gave him all my bank guards . . . No. That would not solve it."

"Maybe *you* better tell *me* about *your* problem," I said.

"Cash," he said. "You are about to ask for cash. No, don't deny it. You are going to hand me one of those certificates and request I give you half a million dollars' worth of cash."

"That was the idea I had in mind," I said.

"Ah, youth, the folly of youth. Allah, hear him!" He came to a stop before me. "Are you aware that five hundred thousand U.S. dollars converts into FIFTY THOUSAND one-thousand-Turkish-lira notes? Are you aware of the fact that that many notes—notes, mind you—of the largest denomination now available, would fill a trunk THIS big?" And he sketched it out between the floor and air with his fat hands. "It means you would have to roll a wheelbarrow around all the time, even into the shower! And you would get tired of that and buy a donkey and a cart to carry it. Donkeys are *not* honest! I can't have the son of my boyhood friend, my very best and closest friend, suffering the indignity of racing over hill and dale chasing a donkey. The indignity of it!" He resumed his pacing and the throwing up of the hands.

I saw what he meant. I would look pretty silly chasing a donkey all day and all night. They're treacherous, too. They lie in wait and kick.

"Then what do I do?" I said.

"I knew you would agree," said Mudur Zengin. He plucked the four one-half-million-dollar certificates out of my pocket very smoothly. He laid them on his desk and sat down.

"This one," he stated, "we will use in part to open the credit-card-company pay-bills account. *These*," he held up the other three, "we will put totally into a fluid cash-drawing account. Now, I will inform the Piastre Bankasi Afyon Branch to hand you any amount in Turkish lira that you wish at any one time. You can also walk up to the teller here and make a like request——"

"Wait!" I cried. "I want no checking account. They could forge my signature like that! And somebody could come in disguised. . . ."

"No, no," he said. "Hear me out. The tellers will be informed that only *you* may draw it, only *you* can sign for it and only I will make the accounting. And when you've used it up, you can simply come up to Istanbul and give me another certificate."

Oh, did I smell a big, juicy rat. I must have looked it.

Mudur Zengin, now in his chair, gave me a very level stare. In a voice entirely unrelated to the one just used, he said in cold banker tones, "The Swiss only gave you 10 percent per annum. I can get you 30 percent on short-term loans, even more."

I thought I knew what was coming. He was going to suggest I give him the whole box full. I started to speak to check this obvious raid.

He held up his hand to cut me off. "They could easily have given you 13 to 18 percent. But never mind. Your income on Swiss interest is more than two million dollars a month so leave them there. The main advantage is that it is safe. You owe about a third of a million to the credit companies which I guaranteed to pay off, and that includes the draft I paid Squeeza. I do not like to even seem to interfere between you and that concubine. But my advice to you is that you cease to use credit cards and make her come to you for cash. And you leave me the remaining one million, seven hundred thousand to handle. I doubt you can spend as much as you think around Afyon. But even if you go to a million lira a week—which is about ten thousand dollars U.S., and I can't imagine how you could squander that much—we can manage your dollars left in these four certificates in such a way that they increase and do not diminish."

"Fact?" I asked, incredulous.

"I'm glad we have agreed," he said. "You handle it this way and I doubt you'll have to open that safe-deposit box again this year. Or in any year, for that matter, unless you decide to buy Turkey."

I really was blinking. There was a lot I didn't know about banking!

He pushed a buzzer. "I had these papers prepared while we were gone. I knew you would take the advice of an old friend."

The clerk brought them in. The clerk also brought a bale. It was huge. It was Turkish 100-lira notes. There was also a very heavy bank bag full of coins, of 2.50LT, 1LT and 50, 25, 10 and 5 kurus.

"Turkish money," said Zengin, "still buys plenty, if you lay off the imports. Inflation has been reversing itself the last two years. Domestic cigarettes are now ten lira a pack and a cup of *kahve* is back to seven. I can't imagine how you could get rid of this bale and that bag in one week, but there it is, your first week's allowance: a million Turkish lira—ten thousand dollars U.S. You are a Turkish millionaire and will be one every week if you choose. Sign here."

The guy wasn't a crook after all! He was really helping me out! He'd make his own whack for the bank but I was richer than ever!

I signed.

Trying to struggle out of that office, the string of the heavy bale cutting my fingers and the bag of coins pulling my wrist out of joint, I felt wealthier than Croesus and Midas combined!

And a rich Gris was a very dangerous Gris, as people were about to discover.

Chapter 2

"Jeez, boss," said the taxi driver, "you rob that bank?" He was pretty bug-eyed as he got his shoulder to it and boosted the bale of currency into the taxi.

We started off. We passed the Buyuk Post Office, got tangled up in a byway and were wheezing up the hill toward the Great Bazaar. Every few yards, the taxi driver said, "Wow."

After about the thirty-fifth "Wow," and an unusual number of pushcart thumps, with the assorted violence of fist-shaking by the owners which accompanies that, I noted we were heading south and were about to climb into the Street of Weavers. Aside from the fact that it is not wide enough for a taxi, if we were going to return to Afyon, we should be heading in exactly the opposite direction to get across the Bosporus and into Asian Turkey.

"Hey!" I yelled above the scream of pedestrians. "You're going the wrong way!"

He stepped on the brakes and stopped. It was about time, too. The nose of the taxi was into a basket shop, the fat lady proprietor struggling amidst her falling wares.

"Wow," said the taxi driver. He just sat there. I swatted him on the top of the head. It attracted his attention. He turned around, reached over the back of the front seat and tried to heft the bale of money at my feet. "Wow," he said. "Is this really yours, Officer Gris?"

"It certainly is," I said. "And I can get as much every week. Now get this taxi turned around and start home! I have things to do and we've 281 miles to go."

People were pounding on the windows. I handled that. I lowered one, stuck the barrels of the shotgun out, pointed them into the air and fired them.

It didn't have the desired effect. It attracted more crowd.

But Apparatus training asserted itself. I reached into the bag, took out a fat fistful of worthless Turkish coins and flung them over their heads to a point some distance away.

Magic. We immediately had enough space to turn around while people scrabbled for the kurus.

The taxi driver was up to it. We soon were speeding on our way.

"The car!" he said. "It's over in Beyoglu. Hold on, I'll have you there in no time."

We roared past the Egyptian Bazaar, twisted our way into the mainstream of the approaches and were soon rattling across the Galata Bridge which separates the Golden Horn from the Bosporus.

We progressed through a band of smoke-belching factories and, diving down some questionable alleyways, at length emerged into an area which might have once been an estate but which today was a *gecekondu,* a word which means "set down by night" and designates a squatter town of the meanest hovels.

Wheels skidding in garbage and mud, the taxi approached what might have once been a stable but was now held together mainly by the sheet-iron shanties that were using it for a back wall.

"You let me do all the talking," said the taxi driver, Ahmed. "And throw your coat or something over that bale of money." He got out and approached a door.

I did as he asked. Looking at some of the people around here, I also reloaded the shotgun. Gods, but this was a slum!

The taxi driver came back shortly. He beckoned me to get out. He locked up the cab thoroughly. He whispered, "Now, don't let out any cries of delight or anything like that. This is a real find. The general owned this estate once. He was a very famous man. They have no idea at all of the value of the car, as it was bought when the lira was worth a hundred times what it is now. So don't go shouting 'huzzah.' And don't go throwing your cap in the air. And let me do the bargaining."

I agreed. By bending down and going through a tunnel of fallen stone, we came into a dim area.

There was a loud bustle and squawk. Disturbed chickens were flying everywhere!

My eyes became accustomed to the gloom. A huge bulk of something loomed. It was covered with a worn-out army tarpaulin. And the tarpaulin was covered totally with chicken dung.

I heard a sort of evil cackle to my right. An ancient man was standing there. He had a nose like a beak. He had no teeth. That laugh was reminiscent of the Manco Devil.

A woman bustled in from a side door. She had two naked children clinging to her skirt. She was very fat and very dirty.

"Where's the car?" I whispered to Ahmed.

"Right there," he said. "Don't try to lift the tarpaulin. I've been through all that. It's all right."

I peeked anyway. I saw a tire so flat, the rim was through the rubber. I went a little further. I flinched. I was staring eye to eye with an eagle! It was bright red. Its wings were outstretched. It had horns! It was painted on the door.

"The general was descended from the Gok Turks," whispered the taxi driver. "One of his ancestors was the Turk hero, Kultegin. That eagle appears in his crown. Ain't it great?"

I dropped the tarpaulin and wiped some chicken dung off my fingers in straw. "Is there any car behind it?" I asked.

"It's a Daimler-Benz," whispered Ahmed. "Don't be misled. It's been sitting there for more than a quarter of a century. It needs a little work."

The dirty woman spoke up. It was just as though she was picking up a conversation that had not been concluded. "And I won't take a kuru less!"

"I'd have to see the registration papers," said Ahmed. "How do I know they're valid?"

She reached into her apron pocket. "They're right here and I own it. You're not going to swindle me out of anything! I was his cook and the court awarded it to me for unpaid wages. Here's all the papers. And you can argue until you explode and I am not going to reduce it one piastre! I know you swindlers. This car has historical significance. He was shot right there in the back seat."

"I thought it was bulletproof," I whispered.

"He had the window down," said Ahmed. Then to the woman he said, "Well, all right, *hanim,* if that's the way it is, we'll take it."

I tugged his sleeve urgently. "Wait, wait," I whispered. "This thing won't even run!"

Ahmed brushed my hand off. "I told you not to appear excited," he whispered. "You'll drive the price up."

I moaned to myself. Here went the bulk of my week's allowance for a piece of junk!

Ahmed and the woman did a firm handshake. She said, "I'll sign over the papers just the moment I see the money."

Ahmed turned to me. He said, "Here are the keys. I don't want to be handling your money. Run out and get twenty thousand lira."

I was stunned. I almost laughed. And then I remembered in time his admonition. I raced out and undid the bale. I grabbed a double handful, locked the taxi and raced back in. I was hard put not to guffaw aloud. Twenty thousand lira is only two hundred U.S. dollars!

The ancient man was standing there cackling his evil laugh.

Ahmed got the papers all signed and counted two hundred hundred-lira notes into her hand, told her someone would come for it.

We drove away. "You had me worried there," he said. "I was afraid you'd let the cat out of the bag that we were practically stealing it."

"Why so cheap?" I said. "It would be worth that for scrap."

"I think the general was on the wrong side," said Ahmed. "He tried to stage a counter-coup and put a sultan back on the throne. But we're in cars, not politics. I've got to get over to Yolcuzade Street and get to the garage that told me about it."

Soon we were in a more civilized part of Beyoglu, the area of Istanbul on the north side of the Golden Horn. We pulled up in a ramshackle garage where lots of trucks stood about in various stages of disrepair.

A tough-looking Turk came over and he and Ahmed walked away. Ahmed was showing him the registration papers. They had a low-voiced conversation and suddenly the tough Turk's voice rose to crescendo.

"But," he yelled, "I went over myself and inspected it! It needs new tires, new hoses, new gaskets, new exhaust pipes, new upholstery and a dead rabbit taken out of the transmission! I won't do it for a kuru less than . . ."

Ahmed was shushing him. He led him much further away. Finally Ahmed came over to the taxi. "I finally beat him down. He'll put it all in running order but he demands we pay him in advance. Give me five thousand of those hundred-lira notes."

"Five hundred thousand lira!" I gaped.

"Well, yes. They don't make parts for it anymore and any they need will have to be hand-machined. That's only five thousand U.S. dollars. We own it now. We just can't let it sit there. The police would get after us."

I knew I was beaten.

"Here," he said, "I'll help you count it out."

"No, no," I said. "I'll let nobody touch money now but me." I began to pick up packets of hundred-lira notes. It made the bale less than half.

He got a big basket and carted the money away.

Oh, well, it was a one-time-only expense. And I could call upon the Afyon Branch at any time for more.

I wondered what the car was really like under that coating of chicken dung.

Chapter 3

A long routes taken by the victorious Alexander, in the paths of the Romans who had conquered the East, over the broad highways established by the Crusaders in their holy cause, I sped back to Afyon.

The old Citroen taxi with Deplor of planet Modon at the wheel might not have compared to the cloth-of-gold caparisoned horses who had carried the swaggering giants of history when they invaded Asia, but it made better time. It ignored the shouts and shaken fists which always, since time began, have protested the overrunning of Anatolia and laying it waste with lakes of blood. Travelling at ninety and a hundred miles an hour, the taxi's way was not seriously disputed by other motorists, trucks, donkeys and camels. We were going too fast for them to note down the license plates and they were only riffraff anyway, far beneath a conqueror's contempt.

There were going to be some changes made.

They started the moment the rugged and aggressive spire of Afyonkarahisar came into view. The wintry air of this 3,000-foot-high plateau was clear as crystal today and the 750-foot fortress stood out like a finger of a God about to goose the Heavens. It was a clear command for me to do likewise.

"Where can I find Musef and Torgut?" I yelled at the taxi driver. They were the two wrestlers Heller had messed up.

Driving madly into the outskirts, he yelled back, "Ain't seen 'em since they got out of the hospital. I don't think anybody else has, either."

"You find them!" I commanded. "And right now!"

A local cab ahead was discharging a passenger and a goat into a mud hut. Ahmed screeched our Citroen to a halt. He had a rapid interchange with the local hacker.

Shortly we were diving down an alley. We emerged in a backstreet slum.

Ahmed crossed a litter-strewn yard and knocked at a rickety door. After some time, it opened a tiny crack. The taxi driver came back to the cab. "They're in there. They don't want to see anybody."

I stuffed a handful of lira in my pocket and got out.

"Lock the cab so nobody can get at this money and go kick the door in. I'll be right behind you."

Reassured by the way I was gripping the shotgun, Ahmed did as he was told. He prudently stepped aside.

I yelled into the room. "I've come to give you a job!"

Rapid whisperings came out of the interior, for all the world like rats running around.

Then somebody called, "We don't believe you but come in anyway."

I entered. The room was dark and dirty, more like a hole in the mud than living quarters.

Musef and Torgut stood at the far side of the room. They were certainly shadows of their former selves. They must have lost a hundred pounds apiece and their yellow skin sagged on them, kind of grayish. They were dressed in rags, had probably sold their clothes. Here were two bully boys come on hard times. Just what I wanted.

"How are you?" I said.

Musef said to Torgut, "He asks us how we are. Is he blind, you think?"

Torgut said, "Well, tell him. He's holding the shotgun."

Musef said, "Since that cursed DEA man fouled us, nobody will hire us to beat people up anymore. The (bleepard) ruined our reputations."

Torgut said, "And all with his lousy tricks when we wasn't looking."

They were talking about Heller. They still believed my story that he worked for the Drug Enforcement Administration. My heart warmed to them.

"I have continuous employment for you," I said. "I am going to hire you to make the staff jump at the villa. They're sloppy and incompetent. They serve cold *kahve* and warm melons. They don't bow and kiss my feet."

"You want us to kill 'em?" said Musef.

"What I want you to do is to make very certain that every time I crook so much as my little finger, they jump like they were shot and go tearing around giving service and bow three times when they see me and kiss my feet when they leave."

"We can use lead pipes on them?" said Torgut.

"Whips," I said. "And fists when called for. You relieve each other and one is always on duty outside my door. You go armed at all times and if anybody tries to get in that I don't want to see, you shoot him."

The way they hated Heller, he would sure never get in!

"You feed us?" said Musef.

"All you want to eat," I said. After all, that was a base expense and not out of my pocket. "I will even pay you something from time to time."

"Allah be praised!" they both said in chorus.

"One more thing," I said. "If anything happens to me or my money, my friend, the most powerful banker in Turkey, has orders to spare no expense to run you down and have you shot."

"Allah forbid!" they both chorused.

"So long as the villa staff pleases me and so long as both me and my money are safe," I said, "you have a cushy job." I threw the handful of lira down on the floor. "Get yourselves some clothes and report for work at my villa, forthwith."

Oh, did they dive for that lira! And once they had it, they stayed on their knees and bowed.

I made a benign sign over their heads and left.

Oh, but there were going to be some changes made!

"Drive on, drive on!" I told the driver and we went rocketing through the town, down the road past the Afyonkarahisar spire, toward the mountains and to the villa.

We pulled into the yard. The gatekeeper wasn't even there. Ha, little did they know what was about to hit them. But my target was not staff.

The BMW was present so I knew Utanc would be home. I pounded on her door. "It's me!" I yelled. "I have news for you." I knew that would make her open up.

It did.

The two little boys were sitting on the floor doing a coloring book. I said, "I have just had a conference with my banker. He advises me that if credit cards continue to be used, my financial picture will be ruined. So if you place just one more order on credit cards, even for a pack of cigarettes," I gestured with the shotgun at the two little boys, "I will shoot them."

She stared at me. She saw the conquering resolution in my glare. She said, "You would, too, you (bleepard)."

"You can bet I would," I said. "If you want money you can come to me for it and you can come crawling on your knees. You understand that?"

She slammed the door. But I knew she understood it. She'd come around and she'd be crawling on her knees for it, too.

That was handled.

I paid Ahmed two hundred hundred-lira notes for his day's work. Twenty thousand lira was more money then he had seen in a month. He saluted with the two fistfuls of money, very surprised and pleased. But actually, he was the only friend I had on this planet who had been true-blue all along. I mustn't stint where he was concerned, even if this bale was getting lighter.

I had one more stop today. I put my money securely in a safe—I barely could get it in—and putting on my control star and picking up the final sack, I went down the tunnel.

Gods, but were the Antimancos surprised to see me! When I walked into their crew quarters, they all jumped up.

"When we got back," said Stabb with frowning brow, shoving his pointed head at me, "we found the hangar crew had made that platform hollow and the *Blixo* crew put something in it! I *knew* it wasn't the right weight."

"And what did they tell you they put in it?" I asked.

"They didn't know," said Captain Stabb, "but you do."

"Compressed Scotch," I said. "They filled it full of compressed Scotch. I was going to use it for bribes. But I have bad news."

"I bet you do," said Stabb. "We been betting that you did the job and grabbed the loot for yourself."

"Actually," I said, "the gold vaults are two miles deep in the earth, way beyond the range of the line-jumper. I almost got caught. I had to use a blastick and a police slash gun and I fired both barrels of my shotgun. You can see how dirty it is. But I fought my way clear and got back."

"Hey, that took a lot of cold nerve," said an engineer.

"It certainly did," I said. "And before you falsely accuse me of welshing on my own gang, look at this. Once I found the gold vaults were beyond us, I grabbed what I could and ran."

I handed them the heavy sack of junk stones.

They spilled some of it on the table and stared at it. And I will say this, it sure glittered in the glowlights.

"Look at this!" said a pilot, holding up a big paste emerald.

"Look at these!" said an engineer, pouring a handful of synthetic diamonds and flawed glass rubies from palm to palm.

"They're all yours," I said, grandly. "Divide them up amongst you any way you wish. In appreciation of your loyal support and to compensate for no gold, you can keep every one."

With moist eyes, Captain Stabb said, "You're a great man, Gris, even if you are an officer!"

There was no higher tribute from these pirate scum.

I went back to my room and grinned and grinned.

"Gris," I said to my image in the mirror as I undressed to take a well-earned sleep, "there is nothing that can stop you now. All problems are just buzzing flies and with cunning and money, you can swat them. Even Heller and Krak."

I lay down for my well-earned rest and dreamed dreams that were bloody and very sweet.

Chapter 4

I slept until all hours, making up for the high excitement of recent days. I dressed in a new red sports suit. Musef was on duty. Karagoz had a black eye and even though it was midafternoon, I got a breakfast in which the coffee was hot, the melon cold and the eggs were quite all right.

A marked change had occurred all around me. It was wonderful.

Lacking, now, immediate plans, I thought I had better gather data. It's a good excuse one can give oneself when he feels too smug and self-satisfied to do any real work for the moment. Also, one likes to savor the suffering of those who are about to writhe in agony.

It was the first time I had had both viewers together. But working two screens, I could get a much more precise idea of reactions and actions, for Krak would be looking at Heller from time to time and vice versa.

I got Krak's going first. I didn't need the second viewer to see what she looked like today. She was washing a window! Her reflection in the glass was quite clear against the dingy morning of a smoggy New York day. She had on space coveralls and her hair was tucked under one of Heller's baseball caps!

Something was moving to her right in the reflection. The cat. It was sitting on the desk washing its face.

Well, if getting busy to go home to Voltar meant washing office windows, I certainly was safe. If I could just keep them slowed down long enough, keep them from doing anything effective, word would come one of these days that the Heller reports made no difference now and they could both be safely killed. So wash away, Krak. You're doing just fine.

There was something else behind her, somebody standing there motionlessly and staring at her back.

It was Izzy!

Krak, too, became aware of it. She gave the window one last wipe and turned around. Izzy backed up. He sank down on the edge of a couch and started crying!

The Countess Krak said, "Why, Izzy. What on Earth is wrong?"

Izzy sobbed a while. Then he said in a muffled voice, "You're too beautiful to have to live in an office."

Beautiful? In space coveralls too big and a baseball cap too big? What was Izzy up to now? Some con, I wagered. I waited with interest to see what it was.

Krak said, "But this is a beautiful office, Izzy."

"No, no," he said, "not beautiful enough for you. You deserve a gorgeous apartment."

She seemed to think about it. Then she said, "Well, I have a credit card. Maybe I could rent one with that."

My hair went straight up!

Then Izzy said something that really warmed my heart. I really realized what a sterling true-blue character he was after all. "No, no, no! I am responsible for Mr. Jet. If any apartments are to be gotten, I will get them. Please promise me you won't do that. You wouldn't find anything beautiful enough for you."

I couldn't quite figure it out. Was he angling for a commission or what?

On Heller's viewer, I had just been seeing elevators and halls. But here was a view of the office. He had just walked in. He took a look at Izzy. "What's wrong?"

Izzy was crying again on both viewers. He was pointing helplessly at Krak.

Heller said to her, "Dear, would you please step into the 'thinking room' and clean it up? Close the door so I can get to the bottom of this before he jumps off something again and beats me to it."

When Krak had closed the door, Heller said, "What's wrong, Izzy?"

Izzy was mopping at his eyes with the heel of his palm. "The bartender thinks she must be a movie star or is about to be. The model agency down the hall has been pestering me to get her to run for Miss America so they can have a contract to use her in the Coca-Cola ads. Bang-Bang says she is the most beautiful woman on the planet. And because I am a failure, I am forcing her to live here without any home at all."

"Well," said Heller, "buy a condo or something."

Izzy went into a fresh spasm of wailing. Then he said, "That's the trouble. We're barely making expenses on arbitrage. IRS is boring in and we can't pay them. And when I came in a little while ago and saw her again, I realized I was condemning her to squalor and poverty. It drove the ruin home so hard I couldn't stand it!"

Heller said, "Well, all right. I'll go out and make some money."

Izzy amazed me. Here he had led it all up to some perfect con. But he leaped up in alarm, waving his arms. "No, no, no! Don't try to persuade somebody to shoot at you again so you can collect the fee. That's too dangerous!"

Heller laughed. He said, "I'll think of something else."

"You're taking over my job and I deserve it. But please, please promise me you won't do anything foolish!"

"I can only promise to try not to," said Heller.

Krak came out of the other room, putting a pillow in its case. Izzy instantly leaped for the door and fled.

"What was that all about?" said Krak.

"He thinks you're too beautiful," said Heller. "But so do I. Especially with the very best brand of New York soot on the end of your nose."

She threw the pillow at him. He caught it and, on the pretext of giving it back, kissed her. Both my viewers went *FLASH!*

But Heller did not hold her long. He let go of her and wandered over to the bar. She stood staring after him. He picked up a newspaper somebody must have been reading and started going through it.

"Money," he was muttering to himself. "Money, money, money. This planet doesn't run on an axis. It runs on money!" He passed the comic page too fast to let me see what was happening to Bugs Bunny these days.

He stopped suddenly at an ad. It said:

$ATLANTIC CITY$
$WINTER CASINO $PECTACULAR$
5 Casino$ 5
EXTRAVAGANZA!
New Year's Bills Getting You Down?
RECOVER WITH ROULETTE
$$$$$$$$$$$$$$$$$$

He looked up. He said to Krak, "You're working too hard. We're going to Atlantic City."

She stopped putting cleaning things away and looked at him with a shocked expression on her face. "WHAT? And leave your own work undone on this planet?"

"No, no," he said. "Not Atalanta, Manco. Atlantic City, New Jersey. And wash your face. This has got to be a clean hit."

"Where is this place?" said Krak, coming over to him.

He showed her the ad. He hadn't read it all. Toward the bottom it said:

FREE FLOOR SHOW
The Clowns
The Apes
Dingle-poop Rock Band
Mamie Boomp, Continental Singer

"Oh," said Krak, "I know her. And I want to see her, too, to get her opinion on spring styles."

A voice sounded behind them. "Anybody home?" It was Bang-Bang. He was carrying a sack. "I'm sorry, Joy, but those birds in that fancy shop never heard of nothing called 'hot jolt.' So I got the Bavarian Mocha Mint and the champagne. But I think that Scotch would go better in it. Not even the cat will touch champagne: it gets in his nose."

"Where'd you park the cab?" said Heller. "We're going to Atlantic City." He held up the ad.

Bang-Bang looked at it. His finger came down to the bottom of the page. He was pointing out the final line to Heller. It said:

Scalpello Casino Corp. of New Jersey

Bang-Bang said, "That's the Atlantic City Mafia. Small time, maybe, but vicious. If you're going to knock the place over, I ought to go with you as a back-up gun. But that (bleeped) parole officer is narrow-minded: He won't let me set foot out of New York. So you be awful careful, Jet—you hear me speaking?"

Heller said, "The lady and I will be all right."

Bang-Bang's eyes shot wide. "The lady! You takin' Joy down there? Jesus—beggin' your pardon, miss—but she's too beautiful to let them punks even glance at her! They don't deserve it!"

"She'll be all right," said Heller.

"Oh, Jet," said Bang-Bang, "that's a (bleeped)—begging your pardon, miss—dangerous place. Those (bleepards)—begging your pardon, miss—don't care who the hell they shoot." He apparently saw Jet wasn't impressed. He gave up. Then he rallied. "Well, at least I won't let her be driven 250 miles in that (bleeped)—begging your pardon, miss—cab. It doesn't ride near good enough. I'll phone the 34th Street East Heliport for reservations and run you across town. They got a new fast chopper run to Atlantic City that's safe and comfortable. And I'll sweep out the cab."

He grabbed a phone.

Heller was rummaging around, picking up this and that.

The Countess Krak raced into the secretary's boudoir and shut the door, going to get dressed, I guessed, and pack a bag.

I was really smiling. The Atlantic City Mafia. I had heard all about them. They specialized in hijacking and beating up high winners.

My euphoria increased. There wasn't any way I could lose. If Heller lost money, it would be just that much less that they would have to meet their bills. If he won, the Atlantic City Mafia would attack him and maybe he and Krak would both wind up in the hospital.

What a beautiful day! It might be cold winter for a lot of people. It seemed like the balmiest possible weather to me. It was a downright rosy world!

Chapter 5

Despite the wintry day, I went out and took a turn around the yard. I felt too full of springs to sit too long.

Torgut was on duty. He was wearing a new sheepskin coat and boots and cap. He was carrying a club. He looked much better fed. He bowed ceremoniously. That was good.

I caught a glimpse of some of the staff. Their faces were white with fright. How very satisfactory!

The BMW was gone and there was no trace of the little boys. How nice and quiet!

I went back in and cleaned and oiled some of my guns to while away the time. And, as I worked, a message came through the slot. It said:

> *Be advised I am shifting the transmitters to Atlantic City area.*
> *Raht*

That made me blink. I myself had forgotten that Heller and Krak were going to go beyond the two-hundred-mile activator-receiver range. How had he found out?

Raht, to make up for the lack of his partner Terb, must have that office bugged. He might even have bugs of his own on Heller and Krak. I felt very heartened. I had even scared Raht into doing his job for a change. My, things certainly were looking up!

Heller and Krak didn't stand a chance! I could order them shot at any time. All I needed was the word from Lombar that Heller's communication terminal on Voltar had been nullified. Now all I had to do was make sure they were enough slowed down so that they accomplished nothing that would upset Lombar's plans! And I certainly had the money to do that!

Tolerantly, as one looks at cripples who are sure to lose any race, I turned my attention back to the screens.

"But why do they have those silly blades on top?" Krak wanted to know.

They were riding in a multipassenger helicopter.

"To keep the pilot's head cool," said Heller.

"Oh, Jettero, you're fooling me."

"Why, I wouldn't do that. They have very hotheaded pilots."

"Well, they certainly don't have proper antigravity airbuses. The least you could do to straighten them out is teach them how to make hot jolt."

"I'll put it right at the top of my list," said Heller. "Look, there's Atlantic City."

They both looked out the window at a cold and dismal winter scene. The grey Atlantic was pushing sullen swells up against the beach. The five amusement piers suffered occasional windblown spumes of chilly spray. The high-rise buildings and hotels stood battered along the mostly shuttered boardwalk.

Heller said, "Now, listen. Don't call me by the name Wister. Call me Johnny. We'll pretend you're just some dizzy dame that I picked up."

The Countess bristled. "Well, I like *that!* Why shouldn't I call you 'Wister'?"

"It's sort of too well known."

"Aha. I knew you'd gotten famous here."

"Too condemned famous," said Heller. "But we won't go into that now. You just be a dizzy dame."

"I smell chicanery," said Krak.

"You do. We're broke."

Krak shook her head. "I can buy whatever we need. I have a credit card."

"You can't buy what we have to have for IRS taxes. So please just be a dizzy dame."

She said, "Am I in such a spin I don't even know who the enemy is?"

"The Atlantic City Mafia runs the gambling here. They wouldn't share your enthusiasm for me. They specialize in rip-offs and we are going to rip them off."

"Not something criminal," said Krak.

"No. All legal. We just happen to have what we will call a 'technical advantage.' Now, I may call on you to place some bets and I may call on you to take care of the money won in case something happens. So, is your collar radio working?"

She touched something inside her coat and said, "Testing."

The sound seemed to come out of his collar.

He touched his own collar and said, "Testing."

The sound seemed to come out of her collar.

They were using Spurk button radios! Well, it wouldn't do them any good.

They were standing up to get out of the plane and I could see what they were wearing, a necessary datum for me if they separated.

I blinked. She was garbed in a white fur hat, white boots, purse and gloves. Her trousers, probably part of a suit, were wide-bottomed and metallic blue. But it was the fur jacket she had on that set it off. Gray chinchilla! Even though it was only waist length, it must have cost a fortune! Others might think it a spectacular outfit. I found it only striking: at my pocketbook!

He had on a gray flannel lounge suit and wore a gray hat with a wide brim. He was getting into a trench coat of black leather.

Amongst the rest of that crowd, that pair stood out like beacons! All the better! The Atlantic City Mafia would have no trouble at all tailing them to recover any loot.

They were landing now and the festive crowd of high-rollers climbed into a ready bus.

Atlantic City thought it would become very prosperous when, way back in 1976 Earth time, New Jersey got the right to have gambling casinos. And although some new hotels were built in this decrepit old carnival town, its great expectations did not quite match up to the public-relations ballyhoo. A drug runner had told me all about it when I was on Earth before. The Mafia mob had gradually taken over the key casinos and, due to their objections to winners, hopes of rivalling Las Vegas had grown dim.

They must be pretty desperate to be running an extravaganza in the middle of a New Jersey winter. Those icy winds off the Atlantic Ocean practically blew people off the boardwalk. There's nothing sadder-looking than a carnival town off season.

Heller and Krak were no sooner out of the bus than Krak spotted the name "Mamie Boomp." It was in very small letters at the bottom of the biggest marquee on the biggest building which held the biggest casino.

They fought the wind and got inside. They checked their hats and coats in a cloakroom and walked up to a mezzanine that overlooked the casino floor. There were some tables and chairs along the rail. Heller chose one and was about to seat the Countess when she said, "No, no. You go on and do whatever you are going to do. I'm going to try for backstage and see if I can find Mamie."

Heller sat down and looked at the crowd below.

I was quite surprised. There were quite a lot of people in the place, especially for early afternoon.

It was a pretty vast casino. Just below him were three roulette tables. They were running and, while not jammed, were not deserted either.

Heller turned and looked at the mezzanine around him. To his right and left were big square pillars, making the place he sat a sort of alcove at the rail. Behind him was a very wide, carpeted space. To his right, a corridor went from it deeper into the hotel. Directly behind him, another corridor stretched away, seemingly to bedrooms.

He had been carrying a case. He put it on the table and opened it. The first thing he took out seemed to be an adding machine. At least, it looked like one. He took off the bottom and there inside it lay his very ornate, silver-chased and engraved Llama .45

automatic! I blinked. Then I realized that, encased in the bottom of what was apparently an adding machine, the gun had not registered as a gun on the detectors at the New York heliport. He checked it and then put it in what appeared to be a back belt holster. He removed several clips from the adding machine and put them in his pocket.

That done, he pulled a package of black plastic garbage bags from his grip and put it on the table. Again I blinked. Did he think he was going to win so much money that he needed that many huge sacks that size to carry it? If he did, he'd have the whole Atlantic City Mafia to fight off en masse!

He set out a pad one could write on that made multiple copies. It had clamps on the bottom and he fixed it on his knee.

He opened then another case. A sign: Nikon. Where had I seen that before? Ah, Lynchburg. He had bought two scrap cameras and transferred the labels and this was one of them.

THE TIME-SIGHT!

He was unstrapping it and checking its battery. With its Nikon label, the Voltarian time-sight looked for all the world like an ancient 8mm motion-picture camera.

He turned to the rail, pointed it down at the first roulette wheel below and got to work.

There was a huge clock on the far wall of the casino, very futuristic, but it had a second hand. Heller would look into the eyepiece of the time-sight and then twiddle a knob, then glance at the clock and write something on the kneepad.

It required a trained eye to read that image in the time-sight and it took me several minutes before I could make out more than flashing dots. Then I could see numbers.

Heller was reading the winning numbers of that wheel for the rest of the afternoon and evening! And he was recording them to the exact second on the pad!

He couldn't lose!

Oh, the Atlantic City Mafia would kill him if he won the quantities he inevitably would!

Heller started on the second table's wheel. He was advancing the time-sight knob a minute or two at a time. He was writing without looking at the pad and he was doing it so fast I was missing most of the numbers.

Heller had finished the second wheel and was working on the third when voices sounded behind him. He did not look around. He was almost finished.

I recognized Mamie Boomp's hoarse tones and very American accent. "The mayor? Oh, I had the date all right, dear. But his wife was raising so much hell with him, he couldn't do a thing. That's why you find me singing here in this dump. And if they don't come across with our pay tonight, there won't be any floor show. Bunch of hoods."

Heller had completed. He turned around. Before Krak could even introduce him, Mamie said, "So this is the sailor. Oh, man, you can pick 'em, Joy." To Heller she said, "How's the fleet?"

Heller said, "I hope okay." He courteously seated the girls at the table.

Mamie said, "So Bonbucks Teller worked out. Well, I'm really glad. I can't afford them myself. Maybe I ought to find me a sailor and settle down. Do they pay you well, these days, young feller?"

"I haven't seen any Fleet pay for quite a while," said Heller.

"Hey, that's no good," said Mamie. "That's two of us. If these hoods don't cough up . . . Oh, oh. We've got company."

Two very tough-looking men had come up to the table. One said, "What you doin' with that camera, sonny?"

Heller said, "It has no film in it."

The second tough mug said, "Can we see it?"

Heller opened it in front of them. "See? No film."

The mug said, "Well, put it away, kid. We don't allow no pictures in here. What's this? An adding machine?"

"I got a system," said Heller. "The numbers come in on the celestial spheres and I add them up."

The first tough mug let out a barking laugh and looked at the other one as though to say, here's another one. The second one said, "Well, figure out anything you like, kid. But put the machinery away. Have fun."

"Oh, I will," said Heller.

They walked off.

"Well, kids, I got to go on shortly. We only do two shows this afternoon and if we don't get paid, there won't be any tonight. Sailor, would you like to buy us some dinner around six?"

"I'd be charmed to," said the perfectly mannered Royal officer, getting up as she rose.

"I'll be on that stage way over there to the end of the hall," said Mamie. "So listen good."

She was gone and Heller sat back down.

"She's nice," said the Countess.

"You're nicer," said Heller. "Now, pay attention, dizzy dame. Here is your list. The times are by that big clock up there on the wall—the one with the gold cupids. Here is $1000. Go down to that window and buy $1000 worth of chips. Go to a table and put down your bet. Bet on whole numbers only. Never bet more than $285 at a time."

"Why?"

"The win on a whole number is thirty-five to one. Your winnings must not exceed more than $10,000 at a time. IRS takes note of who wins more than $10,000 and they record it, but up to that they don't. So every time you win, cash in your chips. Then go back to a different table and bet on a whole number."

"It *is* chicanery," said the Countess. "What *is* this list?"

"The winning numbers with their times for each of those three roulette wheels. For some reason, all play stops at 10:21 P.M. tonight on all wheels. But until then, those are the numbers that win. Now, here is a plastic bag. If your purse overflows, start using the bag. Ready?"

"And if we win enough money, we'll be that much closer to going home?" said the Countess.

"Right."

"Let's go," said the Countess.

She went directly to buy her chips but Heller—stuffing the rest of the garbage bags under his belt out of sight—checked his case at the cloakroom, bought some chips and then went to another table than the one the Countess was standing by.

She watched a couple of spins to see what the game was all about. She looked at her list for that table number, verified that it really had just come up with the numbers on her list, glanced at the time and then put $285 worth of chips on the next list number, 0.

"Round and round the little ball goes," said the man at the wheel. "Where she stops, nobody knows. All bets down."

The metallic sizzling of the ball slowed. It went into number 5, then with a clink, dropped into 0.

The croupier raked in all other bets than 0, tabbed it and shoved a stack of chips at the Countess.

She promptly picked them up, went over to the window and cashed them in. She dropped $9,975 into the sack. She was going to bypass her purse from the start.

Heller, at another table, had placed a bet on 13 and 13 came up. He took his chips and went over and cashed them in and dropped the money in his sack. He, too, was going to bypass inadequate things like pockets.

The Countess looked at the clock, went to a different table, looked at her list and bet on 5. It came up. She took her chips to the window and cashed them in. She dropped her second $9,975 into her sack.

Back and forth they went, always a different table from the one they had just played.

I was certain somebody would catch on. The crowd was fairly thick and it was not too badly dressed. But Heller in his gray lounge suit, blue silk shirt and blue polka-dot ascot really stood out. He was taller and blonder than any of the men around.

The tunic the Countess had been wearing under the chinchilla was bright metallic blue to match the wide-bottomed pants, and even though it seemed very unfrilled, she stood out like a spotlighted model amongst the furs and dowdy dresses of the rest.

How long could they keep this up without the house getting wise?

After about an hour, two men were suddenly confronting

Heller. One of them looked him up and down. "How old are you, kid?"

"Old enough," said Heller.

"Kids under eighteen aren't allowed in here," said one. "You got any I.D.?"

"Right here," said Heller. He pulled out a driver's license and passport. He handed them over.

"Johnny Cattivo," read one of the floor men. "Twenty-two."

"Hey," said the other one, "there's a Cattivo in the Faustino mob. Any relation?"

"We had a breakup," said Heller. "We were wrenched apart."

The two men looked at Heller rather oddly. They gave him back the I.D. and walked off. I suddenly remembered Cattivo was one of the mob that had tried to kidnap Heller at the garage in Spreeport.

Meanwhile, a dopey croupier at table two suddenly realized he had paid Krak several times. He gave a signal to the man at the wheel. That one suddenly threw the ball in the opposite direction around the rim and quite obviously reached down to tamper with the result, probably a magnetic device under the table.

The number came up exactly where Krak had her money—on 5. Heller's system was even beating a crooked wheel!

Three men and a woman had caught on that Heller always won. They started placing bets alongside of his, riding his coattails.

Heller let it go that time and they all won. But the next time at the next table, still followed by the four, he put a thousand-dollar chip on the wrong number and with a great demonstration. It lost. They stopped following him.

Back and forth, back and forth. The big sacks were getting fuller and fuller.

There was a wait at one of the several cashier windows for Krak. Suddenly two armed guards rushed into the cage and handed the man there a flat case full of money. The cashier signed for it and then paid Krak.

Back and forth, back and forth. Win, win, win, win, win!

By half past five, each had a bulging sack. They met.

"This is hard work," the Countess said. "Can we go to dinner now? I got so involved, I didn't even hear Mamie sing. I've got these new boots on and my feet are killing me! I never knew before that winning all the time required that you walk fifty miles, too!"

Heller said, "All right. We'll refuel and get back at it again. I don't think there's more than half a million in each of these two bags. If we can push it to two million tonight, we'll have Izzy out of the woods."

"Won't they run out of money here?" said the Countess.

"I've seen them bringing some in from the bank or their other casinos," said Heller. "That's their problem. Let's eat."

Chapter 6

Mamie Boomp had already nailed down a big booth in the far corner of the large, posh dining room. She waved them over. They threw their sacks down on the semicircular red leather seat and sat down, one on either side of her.

"I didn't hear you sing," said the Countess.

"I didn't sing," said Mamie. "We're going on strike until we get paid. There's only thirty of us in the stage show but, Mafia or no Mafia, we can take them on. Four other casinos belong to the same crowd and they'll be walking out too, tomorrow. Let's eat. It may be a long time between pheasants under glass."

As they were a bit early, they had no trouble getting served. They had steamed clams and broiled lobster and Heller showed Krak how you used a fork and how you used a claw-cracker and a lobster meat pick. Mamie was so busy piling up the clamshells she didn't even notice that it might seem strange that Heavenly Joy Krackle from Sleepy Hollow, New York, thought it was pretty primitive not to have electric knives and suction-plunger tongs and proper spray cans to season the food correctly.

Krak was being a good sport about it. "If you kind of pretend you're camping out," she said, gesturing with a fork at the posh and ornate dining hall, "it's kind of fun. And this is delicious seafood. Do they cook it on the beach? I can taste the sea salts."

"It comes from the sea," said Heller.

"Really?" said Krak. "Not from proper tanks? Hey, now, they must have boat people that fish in the sea! Say, Jettero, I just remembered that there were some boat people that came with Prince

Caucalsia. They must have settled here. That's why it's called Atlantic City. Mamie, you know all the answers. Is that a fact?"

"You bet I do know the answers," said Mamie. "That's why I'm advising you to order cherry tarts. I'm on a diet and have to watch my sweets. Call the waiter over, sailor. I'll have to content myself with half a coconut custard pie to wash down my coffee."

Finally, having attended fully to her diet, Mamie at last sank back with a sigh. "Well, the condemned enjoyed her last dinner, thanks to you, sailor. Now, tell me what you kids have been up to."

"I've worn myself out with walking," said the Countess Krak. "Never wear new boots when you're gambling, Mamie. Use some old gymnasium shoes."

Heller said, "Miss Boomp, how would you like to make some money?"

"Do bees prefer honey? What a silly question. What are you up to?" said Mamie.

"Ripping off the Atlantic City Mafia," said Heller.

"Goody," said Mamie. "Turnabout is fair play. Not only they haven't paid us, I could have had a job in pictures but I passed it up for this, and the winter season is a long time between jobs."

"All right," said Heller. "I have a list of the winning numbers for the rest of the night on roulette tables one, two and three in the casino upstairs. You bet them like I tell you and you can have 10 percent of your winnings."

"Really? You some kind of a seer? You got a system?"

"I got a system," said Heller and told her how it worked and how to cash in every winning bet. He took out the pack of black garbage bags and tried to give her a thousand dollars for starting money.

But Mamie looked at the bulging sacks they had thrown on the seat beside them, opened one, peeked in and then extracted a fat fistful of bills. She shoved them into her bosom. Then she reached over and picked up the whole carton of garbage bags.

"Ten percent, eh?" said Mamie. "You got yourself a deal, sailor."

She got up and sped out of the dining room, not impeded in the least by her vast dinner.

The Countess got up. She picked up the two fat garbage sacks. Heller, who had already risen to let Mamie out, followed along behind her. She went ahead and got interested in some display photographs of Miss Americas who had won the Atlantic City beauty contest in former years.

Heller stepped up to the cashier counter with the check and was paying the bill. His change had just been laid out when his hands flashed suddenly.

He turned.

His left hand held the wrist of a waiter in a red jacket and that waiter held Heller's .45 automatic!

The waiter had lifted the weapon out of Heller's back belt holster!

But the .45 was being gripped by nerveless fingers.

Heller's left hand closed tighter. The .45 dropped into Heller's right hand.

The waiter—who probably was no waiter at all, judging by the silk shirt he wore—was staring at Heller with very agonized eyes. It was obvious that only the way Heller was supporting the wrist was keeping the man's knees from buckling.

"I didn't call for anything," said Heller smoothly. He slipped his gun back into its holster under his coat. Then he proceeded to pat the man's side and chest. He reached into the jacket and drew a handgun from a shoulder holster. He looked at it. It was a Taurus .38 Special double-action revolver, nickel plated. He gave the cylinder catch a flick with his thumb, let the cylinder swing out, checked the bullets and then, with a snap, all only with one hand, flipped the cylinder back into place.

"Thank you," said Heller, "for calling attention to the fact I'd dropped my gun." He put the Taurus in his own pocket.

"Your change, sir," said the cashier.

Heller was still holding the "waiter's" wrist. The man seemed paralyzed. Heller turned and picked a dollar bill out of the change.

He put it in the paralyzed hand and then closed the man's fingers on it. Heller let go. The "waiter" went almost to his knees, recovered and in a zigzag course made his way back toward the kitchen.

Krak had gotten too far ahead to notice the action.

Heller joined her and they went up a wide, carpeted stairway to the mezzanine. They came to the place Heller had first chosen. There was no one else on this level but the casino floor below was swarming. An evening crowd, better dressed than that of the afternoon and far more numerous, made a jostling kaleidoscope of color below.

"Look at that!" said the Countess Krak.

Over against the wall, on a high stool behind the backs of the croupiers at tables one, two and three, Mamie Boomp was sitting.

She had money in one hand and the lists for the tables in the other. And in a loose congregation around her were the show people. She was giving each one a series of numbers and the money to bet and to some she gave a black plastic bag.

SHE HAD THE FLOOR–SHOW PEOPLE WORKING!

Heller laughed. "That's quite a friend you've got there." He turned to Krak. "You see that corridor directly behind us? You put your money sacks down just inside it and you sit on them and rest your pretty feet. And I'm going to sit right here and watch the shearing of the wolves."

Chapter 7

The dice tables were crowded. The chuck-a-luck cages flipped. The endless rows of slot machines whirred. The keno numbers kept pouring through the speakers. But Heller's attention was mainly on the roulette tables below.

Round and round the little ball went and where it would stop, he and the floor-show people knew exactly. And there were always bets on the winning numbers.

Because there were so many floor-show people and because they kept changing, other players at the table did not get much chance to ride anyone's coattails.

The stream of actors to the cashiers' cages was a continuing circle. There seemed to be a young man who had more hair than face circulating along this line and Heller watched him.

Suddenly the young man turned and came bounding up the mezzanine stairs. He was carrying a huge, black bag.

He paused near the rail, looked down and across the hall at Mamie and pointed to Heller. Mamie nodded.

The young man came closer. "So you're the sailor with the crystal ball," he said. "I'm Tom-Tom, the drummer of the Dingle-poop Rock Band. They won't let me work the tables because I can't count above four. So I got the job of collecting the money and bringing it up here. Where do I put it, man?"

Heller pointed at Krak, sitting just inside the corridor at the back. She took it. Tom-Tom stood staring at her.

"Well?" said the Countess.

"Nothin', beggin' your pardon, but I was just surprised, kind of. I didn' know no Miss America was in on this deal. Excuse me. I'll be right back with more bread. Lots more."

She touched her collar. She said, "Jettero, why de so many girls have the same name here on this planet?"

The signal came through to Heller thirty feet in front of her at the mezzanine rail. He touched his collar and said, "It's probably some family they named the country after."

"Well, I was looking at some pictures of them down in the dining room foyer and two or three look a lot like some of the girls in Atalanta Province. Some of Prince Caucalsia's court must have brought their wives. Is this where he landed, Jettero?"

"He apparently landed on a continent out in that ocean and it got drowned when the poles melted or something. The survivors got to a place called Caucasus above Turkey and you can't go there because the Russians are holding them prisoner and won't let them defect."

"Well, some of them must have swum west and landed here, then," said Krak. "Thanks for clearing that up."

Heller had his eye on a side door of the casino. Some armed guards with cash boxes had just entered. They carried their burdens to the cashiers' cages. Money was evidently being brought in from the other casinos.

He returned to watching the floor-show people circulating past Mamie, to the roulette tables and to the cages and around again. Tom-Tom was collecting everything but their retained ten-percents. And here he came again with another huge sack of money. He went straight to Krak, gave it to her, gazed at her in awe and said "Jeez!" and rushed off again.

The Countess Krak said into her radio, "The people seem nice. I wonder why Prince Caucalsia's survivors couldn't bring more civilization with them when they swam here."

"Actually," said Heller, "it's a very tough coast to land on. Stands your hair on end to read about it. Which reminds me that you're sitting on four bags of money now and there will be more. My experience with these inhabitants tells me that somebody may try to rip us off. Look around and see if there's anyplace there to hide the money. Just a tactical precaution."

It was more than that. Heller's eye had singled out a couple of tough mugs, the same ones who had asked him for his I.D. The "waiter," now without his red coat, had come up to them and talked briefly, and the two mugs had looked up at the mezzanine at Heller.

Another bustle occurred at the side door. Armed guards were bringing more money to the cashiers' cages. Since the banks were closed, it must be coming only from the other casinos.

The Countess Krak went wandering down the short corridor, poking at the walls, trying to open doors.

Tom-Tom came racing up with another sack and she went to the mezzanine end and took it. He stared at her again and once more said "Jeez," and rushed off.

The Countess returned to her inspection. She found a large, square panel. It swung to the touch. She backed up. A small sign said Laundry Chute.

She touched the section. It was actually a flap door, hinged at the top. She poked her head in.

Straight down! At least sixty feet. It was a vertical duct, square, about four feet wide and as many deep. At the bottom was hard concrete, possibly a laundry room.

She came back and sat on the bags.

Heller was watching more armed guards at the door with money boxes. They were refilling the cashiers' cages.

The floor-show people were getting more efficient. Tom-Tom came racing up to the mezzanine, gave the Countess a sack, said his customary "Jeez," and raced away.

Heller had his eye on the clock. Gradually it crept forward. More guards, bringing in money, more circulation of the floor-show-people lines. Round and round the little balls went on three tables, stopping exactly where predicted. Up came Tom-Tom time and again with more sacks and more exclamations of "Jeez."

The Countess Krak, as the clock crept on, was sitting on a higher and higher stack of bulging black bags. Heller was watching more mugs on the floor being joined by more mugs.

An explosive situation was obviously building up.

At length some armed guards came in at the side door and talked to a man in a tuxedo. The guards were empty-handed and shaking their heads. Another group of guards came in and did the same thing and left. The man in the tuxedo went over to one of the cashiers' cages and spoke to the cashier. They took some scraps of money, locked the cage and shifted the waiting line over to the next cage and combined the money left.

The little balls rolled with their unmistakable ringing sort of whir. The man in the tuxedo closed another cashier's cage, shunted the line. They were consolidating any remaining cash.

It was 10:18. The man in the tuxedo went rapidly to the three croupiers. Each said something to his roulette players. Each table did just one more spin. Chips were paid just one more time. Then green covers were tossed over the tables and the wheel.

It was 10:20!

The last keno number was called over the P.A. Then another voice came on.

"Ladies and gentlemen, the casino is closed!"

Chapter 8

The sounds of all games and devices faded out. The crowd, quiet for a moment or two, then began to talk and move toward the remaining open cashier's cage.

The line was very long. People were standing there in it, holding their chips. The man in the tuxedo and two additional cashiers were working hard to shovel in chips, hand out cash. The cage computer was a stuttering blur of flashing lights.

One more floor-show player was at the window. A cashier handed him all the bills he had left. Then he turned to the man in the tuxedo and said something. He turned back and began to write on a pad. He handed the floor-show player a slip of paper.

The P.A. suddenly opened up: "Ladies and gentlemen, we regret we have to announce that your chips will be taken in, in return for IOUs. Please be orderly."

There was a hubbub. But all three cashiers there began to accept chips and issue IOUs. Tough mugs patrolled up and down the customer line, looking grim.

A man came in from the street, some gambler in a violet-hued suit. He yelled, "The other casinos on the boardwalk are shut! Somebody has broke the banks!" The guards rushed him out.

The P.A. said, "Ladies and gentlemen, be calm. Keep the line moving, please."

Tom-Tom raced up with his last bag of money, handed it to the Countess Krak, said "Jeez" one last time, and vanished.

The line, impressed by the tough mugs, moved rapidly, taking IOUs for their chips.

Heller was looking around a pillar and down the stairs. Two tough mugs were standing there. He looked up the long corridor that ran at right angles to the one the Countess Krak was sitting in. Two tough mugs were standing there. Heller looked along the mezzanine itself. At the far end, blocking any exit, were two more tough mugs. He had obviously waited too long. He was boxed!

The line below dwindled at the cashier's cage. Aside from tough mugs, the casino was more and more deserted. But the tough mugs were being added to, probably from other, now-closed casinos.

There were a lot of eyes on Heller on the mezzanine. Several tough mugs moved toward the bottom of the stairs.

"Dear," said Heller as he touched his collar, "did you find a place to hide the money?"

"Yes, dear."

"Well, I think you had better start working on it. I have a hunch certain people are not pleased."

There were just a few left at the cashier's window. It was pretty obvious the management wanted all the public witnesses safely out of the building and away.

I hugged myself. This was going to be juicy. I even began what kind of a surprised message I would have delivered to Heller and Krak in the hospital. And condolences. "Dear Jettero. I was amazed to discover that you were in the Atlantic City morgue. . . ."

My attention was drawn to the Countess Krak. She was pitching bag after bag of money down the laundry chute! Oh, how obvious. That was the first place they would look! All the management had to do was go down to the laundry room and wheel it out!

Heller was watching the final gambler getting his IOU. It was an elderly man and he was insisting it be stamped. His voice was very clear now in that silent casino even if it was huge and he was quite distant. He got his stamp. Two tough mugs escorted him to the door. Two more tough mugs closed and locked the entrance.

The pair on the mezzanine began to walk forward toward the place Heller was sitting.

"Dear," said Heller into his lapel, "keep your head down and take care of the money. I think the natives have ceased to be friendly."

"Yes, dear," said the Countess Krak. She boosted the last sack into the laundry chute.

I thought she would duck into a nearby room. But she did something absolutely astonishing. She reached up, took hold of a molding and pushed her feet into the laundry chute!

With a sort of angling twist, she let herself drop!

With one foot out to the right and the other to the left and both of them against the duct sides, she began to drop. Her fall was being braked by her feet!

Down she went. Sixty feet!

The slither of leather against the duct sides rose to a screech!

The duct sections sped upward past her in a blur!

She plummeted down out of the duct opening in the top of the laundry room. She landed on the money with a soft thud!

The Countess Krak glanced around. It was a big laundry room flanked by machinery on all sides but one. Here lay a huge mound of laundry to be done.

She jumped off the money. She found a stack of laundry bags. Working very fast, she began to stuff the black sacks into the clean, white bags.

Heller had moved back to the place where she had been sitting. He could see down the stairs, he could see along the mezzanine, he could see down the very long corridor which led into the hotel.

Into his collar, he said, "Are you all right, dear?"

The Countess said as she worked, "Just fine, Jettero."

"Well, you lay low, dear. I think somebody is going to try to celebrate the Fourth of July in January."

"What happened on the Fourth of July?" said Krak, stuffing more money sacks into more white laundry bags.

"I think they objected to the English landing on the coast to collect taxes. They are very possessive of money, so take good care of it, dear."

"Yes, Jettero."

Heller turned around. Two men had appeared at the end of the corridor at his back!

He spotted a big plastic-covered sofa further down the rail. It had two thick, upholstered chairs flanking it.

The two men moving toward him along the mezzanine were still about thirty feet away from the sofa.

Heller dived out of the corridor cover and, in a rolling somersault, landed beside the sofa. He gave it a yank. He gave the two chairs a shove. He flattened himself on the sofa.

He was protected now from all angles of possible fire.

The two men coming up the mezzanine had halted. They drew guns. One of them said, "Step out in sight, sonny. You can't get that money out of the building, anyway. You might as well give up."

"And if I don't?" called Heller.

"Then things could get rough," said one of the men. "We know you got a gun. Throw it out here so we don't have to shoot you."

"You want the bullets, too?" said Heller.

"Of course," said the first man.

"Then have one," said Heller. He levelled the Taurus revolver he had taken off the waiter. He fired!

The bullet tore a furrow down the rug.

"Jesus!" yelped one of the men. He raised his gun to shoot.

Heller fired into the wall and the ricochet went through the casino with a howl!

He fired again and a light fixture over their heads exploded, showering them with glass.

"Sangue di Cristo!" one of them yelped.

Heller was still shooting!

The two dived over the mezzanine rail and hit a roulette table!

They scrambled off of it and were gone!

Heller ducked back.

The pair who had been coming up the corridor where the money had been were out of Heller's view. He was watching the corner where it came into the mezzanine.

A head appeared there and a gun below it.

The Taurus revolver clicked empty. Heller dropped it. He

palmed his Llama .45. He came up suddenly and snapped a shot at the wall in front of the head. The bellow of the big caliber went booming through the casino.

Heller bobbed up to take a look. The head was not there. But voices were.

"Here's a laundry chute."

"Well, look in it, dummy."

"Jesus. It's straight down a hunnert feet. There's nothin' at the bottom of it."

"Well, look in the God (bleeped) rooms, you idiot."

Slamming doors.

Some Italian chatter was sounding up the long corridor. Some guys up there were trying to persuade one of their number to walk down it. He was protesting.

Heller could see up that corridor all the way. He sighted carefully along the top of the Llama. He was centering on a huge glass fixture nearly a hundred and fifty feet away. He allowed for the drop of the relatively slow .45 bullet by placing the rear, fixed sight quite low. He fired!

The crash of the .45 was followed by the smashing crash of breaking glass. Showers of it cascaded down.

A yelp came from that end of the corridor.

A slug thumped into the top of the sofa, instantly followed by the sound of the shot from the corridor.

An Italian voice in the side corridor yelled, "Tell the *capo* the money isn't here!"

Somebody up the long corridor yelled back, "You look everyplace? He coulda thrown it down a laundry chute. Did you look in the laundry room?"

"Ignacio went down there, too. Nobody there. We looked everyplace. It's gone."

Silence reigned for a long space. It was pretty obvious that nobody could get into a point of vantage from which they could shoot Heller. The only way they could reach him was by a frontal charge.

Suddenly the P.A. system opened up. It said, "Look, kid. We

may not be able to get at you. But at the same time, you can't get out of where you are and even if you could, you'd never be able to leave this building with that dough and arrive anyplace else. The *capo* wants to see you."

Chapter 9

Heller touched his collar. "Are you all right, dear?"

"Everything is fine, Jettero."

Heller raised his voice but not his head. He shouted down the long corridor in passable Italian, "You give me a hostage and let me keep my gun and we'll talk about it."

Up at the other end of the corridor, voices were arguing.

"You go."

"Why me?"

"Listen, as the son of *Capo* Gobbo Piegare, I command you in my father's name, go down that corridor, Jimmy Coniglio, and give yourself up as a hostage!"

A squeal. "Not me! If you're so anxious to have a hostage, go yourself, Don Julio!"

Heller called out, "I'll take the son of the *capo,* if you please."

A loud outburst of arguing. Then finally, "Mother of the Virgin, why can't somebody else be his God (bleeped) son?"

"You're the son. We ain't."

A body thrust into the corridor. Then, seeing there was no shot forthcoming, the person crept timidly down the wall toward the mezzanine and the sofa fortress. He stopped and yelled back, "Now, none of your God (bleeped) parlor games! Don't go shooting me or anybody else in the back!" That attended to, the person came closer.

Heller let him get within two feet. The fellow was about thirty, dressed in a silk tuxedo with a lace shirt front, with a very Sicilian face. It was the same man who had been directing the shift of money from cage to cage down on the floor.

Heller, the Llama .45 held close to his chest, sat erect. He plucked a Beretta from the shoulder holster under the tuxedo and put it in his pocket.

"I think we will get along fine, Don Julio," he said. "Nobody has gotten shot, yet, and it would be a shame if you were the first. So do I have your word you will take me to your father and to nobody else?"

"Upon the grave of my father's mistress, I swear it," said Don Julio. "Would you please put that safety catch on? I might stumble. My knees seem to be a bit shaky tonight."

"Anything to oblige," said Heller and put the side-lever safety catch on, pushing the gun into Don Julio's ribs. He turned him around and with a companionable arm over his shoulders and a thumb close to a paralysis point of Don Julio's neck, he let the chief's son lead on.

They went to an elevator. Don Julio pushed the call button. They went to the second floor. Don Julio turned down a corridor which seemed to be made up, not of bedrooms, but offices. They came to the end and Don Julio knocked twice, then three times.

Somebody inside opened the door.

It was a splendid office, very large, done in what appeared to be yellow leather. An expensive rug was on the floor. Hanging plants gave the room a strange, jungle look.

A very small man was sitting at a very large desk. There were several other men in the room, hands in pockets, hats on, natty but very dark and Italian.

"My father," said Don Julio impressively. "*Capo* Gobbo Piegare, supreme leader of the Atlantic City mob." He glanced sideways at Heller. "I am sorry. I do not know how you are called."

"Cattivo," said Heller. "Johnny Cattivo. At your orders," he added with polite formality. He was still speaking Italian and he seemed to have their endless, involved manners down pat.

"Sit down," said the *capo*, waving at a yellow interview chair that had its back to the room.

"Thank you. I've been sitting too long this afternoon," said

Heller. "I think your gracious son and I will stand over here against the wall."

"Just trying to make you comfortable," said Gobbo Piegare. "So, with your permission, we will get down to business. I don't know how you bribed the croupiers to always stop the wheels on the right numbers, but that's all ancient history. Where's the dough?"

"It is my take, isn't it?" said Heller.

"According to custom and law," said Gobbo, "I must allow that it is. However, I must point out, with all delicacy, that every exit from this hotel, as well as the parking lot, is covered with Heckler and Koch nine-millimeter submachine guns in the hands of very competent guards who have orders to shoot you on sight if they see a single package in your hands. They're on the roof, too."

"I appreciate your courtesy," said Heller, "but I must point out that your son and you would undoubtedly be hit by .45 slugs before the rest of the men in this room could shoot out of their pockets. And you have no idea at all where the money is, other than that it is in my possession."

Gobbo Piegare made a tent of his hands, elbows on the desk, and supported his chin. He thought for a while. Then he said, "Legally, this is what is called a 'Mexican stand-off.' You have me at a very great disadvantage. You have drained the other four casinos and this one of all cash. Without that cash, finances could become embarrassing. I have a proposition. Are you open to offers?"

"If they are good ones," said Heller.

"Oh, this is a good one," said Gobbo reassuringly. "The Scalpello Casino Corporation owns, in all, five beautiful casino-hotels here, including this one. They are only eight to twelve years old. They have the most modern and fanciest fittings. The corporation also owns tons of real estate around them and a quarter of a mile of boardwalk, two miles of waterfront along the Intracoastal Waterway, a game preserve, a yacht marina and two piers. Sound impressive, kid?"

"Indeed, it does," said Heller.

"You, on the other hand," said Gobbo, "have several million cash around somewhere. Now, I will make you the proposition. In return for that cash, I will sell you the whole corporation and every share of stock in it."

I flinched. Was Heller going to land squarely on his feet in spite of everything?

"My *consigliere*," continued Gobbo, "happens to be right here. He has all the deeds and shares right in that briefcase. Show the kid," he ordered.

A scholarly Italian stepped forward, adjusted his glasses and opened his case. He took out a huge stack of deeds and maps and laid them where Heller could see them and still watch the room and started leafing through the documents. That done, he took a bundle of stock out, showed Heller it was all of the authorized issued shares of the Scalpello Casino Corporation of New Jersey and left them in a pile on a chair.

"Well . . ." said Heller.

"Good thinking," said Gobbo. "Show him the contract," he ordered the *consigliere*. To Heller, he said, "I had this drawn up just in case you saw it our way and your own, too."

The *consigliere* laid the contract on a table to Heller's right. He tendered a pen.

Gobbo said, "You better use your own name, not that of Johnny Cattivo. We happen to know he's dead and you, I might point out, are not a ghost. When we saw this I.D. on the floor this afternoon, we checked on the computers. So at supper we had your pocket picked. The man got your real wallet before he tried to lift your gun. Only one man would have Johnny Cattivo's passport and that would be Jerome Terrance Wister."

The gunmen in the room stiffened, took their hands out of their pockets, showed empty, open palms and backed up.

Gobbo continued, "And so it says, directly on your own passport and driver's license." He opened the wallet he had taken out and read it. "Jerome Terrance Wister, the Whiz Kid himself. So maybe you didn't bribe the croupiers. Maybe you had a system, the first one in history that worked. But however that may be, not even Brinks could get that dough out of Atlantic City tonight or any other time, so you better sign that contract purchasing the whole of

Scalpello Corporation. And with your right name."

"If you look at that passport you will find that it says," said Heller, "that Wister is only seventeen. As a minor, the contract would not be binding."

"Well, I'm looking at this passport," said Gobbo, "and I find that Wister had a birthday just three days ago and is eighteen and according to the new laws of New Jersey, that's of age. It's legal as legal. Call it a birthday present, and a nice one at that. Five casino hotels and all those other things. I got a notary right here, ready to witness the signatures. You're buying the whole thing for 'one dollar and other legal considerations.' I'll even leave the two G's in your wallet when I give it back so you can pay me the dollar out of your own money and no hanky-panky. It's not even bought with gambling winnings and all these here can witness it is so. So sign and give me the privilege of wishing you a happy birthday."

Heller took the pen and signed. Gobbo, his son and the *consigliere* also signed as the only ones who held shares. The notary notarized everything.

Then Gobbo put his hand on the contracts, holding them to the desk. "You get these as soon as you produce the money. Don't be uneasy. We are all just honest businessmen here. And you can even take Don Julio along and blow his guts out if, when you give us the money, we don't give you the contracts. He's my own son. How can you lose?"

Heller touched his collar. He said, "Dear, would it be convenient for you to bring the money to room 201? It is on the second floor. Just look at the numbers and arrows. I am sure the armed men here will give you no trouble."

They waited.

There was the clang of an elevator. Then sounds of something coming down the hall. A gunman there, keeping his hands very empty, gingerly opened the door.

A big laundry cart rolled in, piled to the top with laundry bags. What appeared to be an old chambermaid stood up. It was the Countess Krak dressed in hotel worker clothes and lines of age drawn on her face.

"Mother of God," said one of the men, "I passed her three times with that cart when we were looking on the sixth floor!"

But Gobbo was not interested in who had brought the cart in. He stood up. He signalled. The *consigliere* and two others began to lift the bags out. They opened the covering laundry sack and peered in at the money. They turned the open ends, one after the other, to Gobbo.

He went over and into each sack plunged his hand and verified there was no stuffing but money. He looked at many of the bills to make sure they were not counterfeit.

Bags were lying all over the floor! Big and fat.

Gobbo clapped his hands together twice and, with a gesture, had the bags closed and piled back into the laundry truck.

The *capo* then, with a gesture, had two men speed the laundry cart out of the room.

Heller's gun came up. But Gobbo was walking over with the contracts. Gobbo waited until he heard the elevator door bang shut and the car start down. With an elegant bow he handed the contracts to Heller. Then, with a very imperious gesture, like an orchestra conductor, he began to wave his arms at the men in the room.

"Happy Birthday," said Gobbo, in English.

The others in the room immediately began to sing. They sang:

> *Happy Birthday to you,*
> *Happy Birthday to you,*
> *Happy Birthday, dear Whiz Kid,*
> *You've been fun to screw.*

Then they all started laughing.

Gobbo said, "Put your gun away, Whiz Kid. Nobody would think of shooting you, now that you are the sole owner of the Scalpello Casino Corporation and all its vast properties. Three days ago, the New Jersey Gambling Commission told us that at the end of the week all our licenses were going to be cancelled for nonpayment of bribes and ordered us to sell the whole thing to anyone else who would buy it.

"But you see, Whiz Kid, nobody at all would touch any part of this corporation, for at noon tomorrow, by the clock, the Grabbe-Manhattan Bank, that owns all the mortgages, first and second, on all these hotels and property, is going to foreclose and take over everything it owns. They even blocked efforts to file bankruptcy by threatening criminal proceeding on other counts against the directors if we did.

"All the money that you won, Whiz Kid, went through the computers as legal gambling losses paid out to unknown people. It's all laundered money and untraceable. So you let us follow the New Jersey Gambling Commission ruling and it's you that Grabbe-Manhattan will now be foreclosing on! AND you've given us all these lovely millions as run money to go someplace nice and retire on. So happy birthday, Whiz Kid. The Virgin Mary herself must have sent you. Although, when we spotted you earlier today, I will admit we gave her lots of help."

He went over to his desk. He took a letter basket and piled a few personal knickknacks in it. He handed the basket to Don Julio to carry and directed him out the door.

The rest of the men filed out. Gobbo, the last one at the door, made a sweeping gesture with his hand. "It is all yours, Wister. Every bit of it. But there's just one more thing. I don't know why they call you the Whiz Kid. You're the dumbest (bleepard) in a business deal that I ever met!" He bowed. He was gone.

Heller stood there for a moment. Then he dived for the phone. He punched the buttons frantically.

A sleepy voice at the other end said, "Hello."

Heller shouted, "IZZY! HELP!"

PART THIRTY-NINE
Chapter 1

The next day I lay in bed, overtaken by uncontrollable bursts of chuckling. I had been up all night due to time differences between Turkey and Atlantic City, and would have slept all morning in any event. But every time I thought of getting up after that, I would go into spasms of guffaws and would have to lie back.

Clever, clever Gobbo Piegare! What a friend I had in him! Between spasms of glee, I pondered the possibility of awarding him in some way: maybe send him a stuffed bluejay, that ace of robbers, mounted on a gold base. Or maybe get Senator Twiddle to put him up for the Congressional Medal of Honor or get Rockecenter's attorney Bury to nominate Piegare for the Nobel Prize as hit man of the year.

Gobbo Piegare was an absolute master. When Lombar Hisst took over Earth, that stellar crook should be a candidate for Earth Apparatus staff.

At length, my stomach hurting with laughter, I called for breakfast and shortly began to laugh still more to see that the waiter now had a purple cheek and Karagoz wore *two* black eyes. Melahat, the housekeeper, looking like she'd been raped, stood in the door, wringing her hands and hoping that the *kahve* was just the right temperature. Musef and Torgut were doing their job properly. Oh, it was a lovely day. Cold and bitter outside but nice and gleeful within.

About four o'clock, I went into my secret room and uncovered the viewers. I sat down to enjoy any further discomfiture of Heller and Krak.

It was midmorning in Atlantic City. They were in bed in a palatial bedroom. The bed had a canopy of white gauze and bows. It must be the bridal suite. The furnishings were all decorated with flowers and were very posh.

Heller got up and went into the ornate sitting room. He pulled a drape cord and disclosed a big picture window. The room was evidently high up and the window overlooked a vast expanse of the cold, gray Atlantic Ocean. He looked at the slow and sullen swells rolling in upon deserted and forlorn amusement piers. There were several wrecks on the beach and black, oily smoke drifting around.

He went back into the bedroom and opened the drapes there, disclosing a stretch of desolate boardwalk, deserted except for a TV crew that was shooting something.

Krak was sitting on the side of the bed, half-dressed, ruefully regarding the scars on the side of her white Moroccan boot, probably caused by her slide down the laundry chute. She looked up. "They certainly don't know how to make animals grow proper hides." She threw it down and went into the bathroom and spinbrushed her teeth.

With her mouth full of foam, she said, "Jettero, who is this 'Whiz Kid' they are talking about?"

Heller was picking through the suitcase. He sighed. He said, "He's the dumbest (bleepard) in a business deal that anybody ever met—begging your pardon, miss. You wouldn't want to know him."

She rinsed out her mouth and came back into the bedroom. "Will all this help us to get home?" she asked.

"We'll be lucky if we don't get booted off this planet and kicked the whole twenty-two light-years back home."

She went into a slight shock. She stood there, staring at him. "Oh, dear," she said. "And return as failures?"

I knew what she was thinking about: Those two forged "Royal Proclamations," which she'd given her word to keep from Heller, would not be valid if the mission failed. He would still be put onto dangerous assignments, she thought, and as she was a nonperson they could not get married.

"Oh, dear," she said again. She began to get dressed. Heller was still poking into the suitcase, looking glum. The Countess Krak got into her chinchilla coat, put on her white fur hat and picked up her pocketbook. At the door, she stopped and called back, "I'm going to see Mamie Boomp. We have a lot to talk about. See you later, dear." She left.

Well, one thing I didn't want to hear more about was fashions, fashions, fashions and clothes, clothes, clothes. What the homosexual designers were proclaiming would be spring styles was my idea of pure static. I didn't want to spoil my euphoria. I turned off her viewer. Heller's depression was the source of my extreme well-being.

He really understood he had plunged himself to ruin. The neat, gray flannel suit and silk shirt were a long way from how he felt, apparently. He dug, out of the bottom of the grip, a suit of workman's denim. They were the style for beachwear and maybe he had thought they'd have some time on the sand, as he looked at the cold, gray sea from time to time.

Slowly, he began to get dressed. The most recent denim men's styles required the material be torn, patched and grease-stained like true workmen's clothing. And although he might now be dressed in the beachwear height of fashion, my, didn't he appear a ragged wreck as he looked at himself in the mirror!

Then he sat for a long, long time, staring out the window at the cold, gray sea. What a treat for my eyes! Oh, how the mighty had fallen! He not only hadn't helped their precarious situation in New York, he had become the proud possessor of incalculable sums of utter ruin. I enjoyed it and enjoyed it. He was not only slowed down, he was going backwards!

He looked at his watch, at last. It registered nearly noon, Eastern Standard Time. I remembered that noon was the stated time of foreclosure. He looked at the door. Then he looked at the phone. I realized that he had been waiting around for news from Izzy.

He got up and went to the phone. He picked it up. No dial tone. Dead. He pushed some buttons for an outside line. Still dead.

Aha! I knew what had happened. The phones had been shut off

by the phone company! A surge of pleasure raced through me.

Heller put it back on the cradle. Then he looked at the bathroom. The lights there had been on a little earlier. He went in and threw the switch. He threw another switch. Nothing happened. No lights!

Oh, wonderful! The light company had shut off the lights!

He turned on a water tap. Nothing happened! Oho, I gloated. The water company had shut the water off!

He went over to a radiator and felt it. Evidently it was ice cold. The furnaces were off!

He was in a super-posh Atlantic City high-rise hotel-casino. He was, in fact, the proprietor. And all the utilities were shut down tight!

I gloated. Given time, even the pipes would freeze!

Glory, glory! Fate was driving misfortune in with a sledge-hammer!

He began to pace slowly back and forth, occasionally glancing at his watch and then at the door. Once he said, "Izzy, where are you?!"

Twelve-thirty came. The room must be getting cold, for he threw his trench coat over his shoulders.

He continued to pace. He continued to glance at his watch. Oh, I enjoyed every second of it!

One o'clock came. The Countess had not come back. No slightest sign of Izzy. Heller sank down in a chair. "Izzy, you have deserted me and I don't blame you one bit."

He saw some smoke rising from down the boardwalk, quite a distance away. He went to the window. He couldn't see it very well. Some sort of a burning vehicle. There was smoke drifting also from the direction of the beach. He didn't bother to go into the sitting room and look. I guessed that it might be rioting and looting.

One-ten. A knock on the door.

Heller raced across and opened it.

A very mournful Izzy stood there. He looked even shabbier than usual. The Salvation Army Good Will overcoat was faded and shiny with wear. His briefcase was a mottle of scuffs with paper tears showing through. And he looked far sadder and more slumped than usual, a feat which was nearly impossible. Heller let him in.

"Oh, Mr. Jet," said Izzy, "I told you not to do anything foolish. I have never heard of such a catastrophe in the whole history of business. I have told you and told you to keep your name off corporations. Now you're in it up to your skull top. You should leave business to me."

Heller sank into a chair and put his head in his hands. "I know that now."

"You should have known it yesterday. Business is one of the most treacherous tools of Fate. But it is my fault. I saw a gleam in your eye, and when you have it, you always go out and get people to shoot at you. And now they've used submachine guns, cannons and even a hydrogen bomb. Oy, what rubble and wreckage!"

Heller said, miserably, "I know. I know. What is the state of affairs now?"

Izzy said, "There is a little bit of nonpessimistic news which I don't trust and bad news which is reliable. So I will give you the bad news first."

"Probably," said Heller, "the good news is that they will feed me breakfast before they exterminate me. So go ahead."

"You should have been suspicious when they let you win so much for so long. In order to pay the bets you were placing with such wild abandon, they dragged down every casino's cash, every bank account the corporation had. They even wired money in from Las Vegas. They also collected in advance from all hotel guests. They exhausted every possible source of cash they could lay their hands on so it would flow back to them through you, laundered as corporation losses.

"The corporation cash-liquidity picture is minus millions and millions. And it also has to honor the IOU markers issued like an avalanche at the end of the night, and so we come to the nasty subject of debt.

"Money they should have paid for utilities—phone, lights, water—for months has been going into their pockets. So the service was cut off today on all these, and to it is added heating oil. It even includes gasoline charge accounts for the extensive corporation rolling stock.

"All staff of all the corporation's numerous businesses are unpaid and have been for some time. The government IRS withholding tax is also missing.

"The money which went into the staff pension funds was invested in businesses which mysteriously failed, and so the pension fund has to be made up.

"All state and local taxes, including sales tax, are owing for the past year.

"Most of the hotel equipment is on time-payment contracts and those companies want to take the equipment back, even the furnaces.

"It's winter and there is no yacht traffic for the marina and nothing is travelling on the Intracoastal Waterway.

"It's winter and there's nothing one can do with the amusement piers.

"It's winter and there are no vacationers to fill the hotels."

Heller shivered. "Is that all?"

"No," said Izzy. He was unfolding a newspaper. "That spaghetti-eating schlemazel Piegare must have talked to the press right away last night, the schmuck. Have you seen this?" He was holding the front page of the *New York Grimes* before Heller's eyes. It said:

WHIZ KID STEALS ATLANTIC CITY

The resort metropolis is the first American city to be stolen since the Indians ripped off Roanoke from Sir Walter Raleigh in A.D. 1590.

In a raging midnight gun battle which local police and the army did not stop, Jerome Terrance Wister, known as the "Whiz Kid," . . .

"Oh, my Gods," said Heller, reading no further.

"It's in every paper, local and national, that I spotted on the stands in New York," said Izzy. "Headlines!"

I really laughed. Izzy thought Piegare had talked to the press. But whether he had or not made no difference. Madison! Good old J. Walter Madison, priceless Madison: that marvel of PR had Rockecenter's Underworld Crime Computer Bank right at his fingertips. He had jumped onto the job, feeding a story to the media within minutes. What a genius!

Heller groaned, "Isn't there any good news at all?"

Izzy said, "I think you should come down to the auditorium. The employees are meeting there and they comprise about a quarter of the population of Atlantic City. I can't face that many people."

Heller opened his tattered beachwear denim jacket and buckled on his gun. He drew it and checked the load.

Izzy cried, "Oh, dear! This can't be solved by persuading more people to shoot at you! I only want you there when they start coming over the tops of the seats to tear me to pieces."

Heller threw his black leather trench coat over his shoulders, locked and hid his grip and then followed Izzy out into the dark passageway.

They had to walk down many flights of steps, as the elevators were not running. They came at last into the back of a vast auditorium. It was lit only with kerosene camping lights.

It was jammed with people, thousands of them. Waiters, cooks, maids, croupiers, doormen, marina sailors, clerks, janitors, drivers, pilots, carnival barkers, topless dancers and every other kind of riff-raff it takes to run casino-hotels, amusement piers, clubs, marinas and honky-tonks. Even security guards were there but they sure weren't on duty to keep things orderly. What a tough collection! They weren't the Mafia: they were the employees of all the enter-prises the Mafia had taken over and now dumped.

A low growl began to rise. Fingers began to point. Teeth began to show. And they were all directed at Heller as he walked down the aisle toward the auditorium stage. From those expressions, he was about as popular as a skunk with rabies. What an enjoyable moment for me!

Izzy cringed close to Heller. He whispered, "Don't fire them all at once. They'll riot and we'll have hospital bills. We have made no arrangements with them."

Heller whispered back, a little savagely, "Haven't you done *anything?*"

Izzy whispered, "It's an almost impossible business situation. I did file a name change for the corporation. Scalpello is too notorious. But that won't alter its debts."

They were walking up the steps to the stage. It was totally empty except for a set of trap drums. Izzy whispered, "I couldn't get any of my relatives to take over any director or officer posts. You own the shares, but I can't let you get involved any deeper. So I had to do the best I could."

Heller was about to turn and face the sullen audience but Izzy steered him further, pushing him off to the side of stage right. There was a little room there, probably a dressing room for performers. Izzy stopped Heller before they could enter. Heller peeked in.

The Countess Krak was sitting there with Mamie Boomp and Tom-Tom. The room was feebly lit by a single burning candle.

Heller whispered to Izzy, "What's that drummer doing there? He helped with the sacks last night but he can't count above four."

Izzy whispered, "I know. That's why I appointed him treasurer and secretary. He won't die of fright looking at the horrible corporation balance sheets."

I turned on Krak's viewer. By it, I could see Heller peering in, clothes looking ragged under his loose trench coat. My, his depressed expression was wonderful to see. It really exhilarated me. Oh, how the mighty had fallen!

Mamie Boomp said, "Hello, sailor. Would you mind loaning me that raggedy workman's jacket you've got on under your trench coat? It's freezing."

Heller looked at her. She was wearing a sequined blouse and a wide skirt. Gentleman that he was, he shrugged off the trench coat that lay loosely on his shoulders, took off the raggedy workman's jacket and held it for her to put on. She got into it and buttoned it up to her throat. My, but she looked weird. Like a plumber or something! Fat lot she really knew about clothes.

Izzy said, "Now, Mr. Jet, as you are the principal and only stockholder, we can waive the formalities of a shareholder meeting. Please sign these papers." He laid them on a small side table.

Heller bent over the papers poising a pen. He read the top lines. Mamie Boomp had been appointed president and general manager!

He looked up wide-eyed. Krak was looking at him very sternly. She made a small signing motion with her hand.

Heller signed.

At once, Mamie Boomp, Tom-Tom and the Countess Krak rose and started out onto the stage.

Heller also started to go with them. Mamie Boomp, with the flat of her hand, pushed him solidly backwards, making him sit down in a chair. She said, "You stay here, sailor, and act as marines if they land on us. But don't come out otherwise until I give you your cue."

They walked out on the stage and Tom-Tom absent-mindedly closed the dressing-room door behind them.

Heller turned to Izzy, "Why are we doing anything at all? The Grabbe-Manhattan Bank will padlock the doors."

Izzy said, "Oh, the bank. Well, when I called the Gambling Commission of New Jersey to tell them their order to Piegare to sell the corporation had been executed, they dropped the case and extended the corporation's license."

Heller said, "I'm talking about the Grabbe-Manhattan Bank!"

"Well, so am I," said Izzy. "You see, I could tell Grabbe-Manhattan that the corporation would continue to hold its gambling license. They thought they were at risk because the license was going to be revoked."

"Is that all?" said Heller.

"Not quite," said Izzy. "As the criminal charges they could have brought against Piegare no longer applied to the corporation —since it had been sold—I told them that if they didn't extend the loans, I would file bankruptcy and they'd lose everything. That's why I couldn't get here sooner. They have to have a bank directors' meeting on all matters that involve a billion dollars' worth of loans or more, and it took them until 10:00 A.M. trying to locate Rockecenter. But he and Bury are in China arranging peace and new oil monopolies and they had to go on without him. I'm sure he'll raise the roof when he gets back and finds out, but we got an extension on all corporation mortgages."

The Countess Krak opened the door and beckoned.

Izzy pushed Heller forward and cowered back. "You go," he said. "I'm too scared to face that howling mob!"

Heller walked out on the stage. Mamie Boomp was standing very tall and commanding. I suddenly understood her wearing a tattered workman's jacket. Sly psychology: it made her one of them. She had the audience dead silent. (Bleep) her performer's control of the house: Not a single jeer greeted Heller, only silent, grim faces. It spoiled the moment for me. No tomatoes!

Mamie Boomp, in a resonant voice, shouted, "May I introduce to you the principal stockholder of this corporation: This sterling, this remarkable naval officer, brought to you at great expense, who has come sailing up in his shore boat just to talk to you today. I give you, now, the star of stars, the friend of presidents, the one, the only, the real JEROME TERRANCE WISTER!"

Tom-Tom, sitting at the traps, had begun a drum roll. It was crescendoing up.

Mamie, voice covered by the roll, said in Heller's ear, "Just say 'Yes. I approve.' And bow. That's all. Nothing else!"

With a mighty cymbal crash, the drum roll ended.

Heller, probably shattered by the cymbal crash and stunned unthinking by the vast and silent crowd, in a loud voice said, "Yes! I approve!"

He bowed.

The hall exploded!

PANDEMONIUM!

Hats and caps went sailing into the air.

Yells burst from the thousands of throats!

Then, like a pack of hurtling animals, they came over the backs of chairs and up and onto the stage in a screaming mob.

They seized Heller. They lifted him high on their shoulders. They walked him all around the stage and then down the steps and all around the convention hall.

And all the time they were screaming, "Hail the chief!"

Abruptly the auditorium lights came on!

What must have been a stage electrician sprang up to a balcony platform and got a spotlight going. He threw it onto Heller and turned it blue and red and yellow and white. Then he must have heard a signal from Mamie for he swivelled it over onto her on the stage. She was holding her hands up to command attention. They lifted Heller up over the footlights and turned their faces to Mamie.

In a voice that would have made a Greek orator roll in his grave with envy, Mamie roared out, "Now, ladeeees and gentlemen, you proud employees of the newly named Lucky Bonanza Casino Corporation! Get the paddles chunking, the yachts flying! Get the boardwalk swept and the dice and wheels rolling in the dough. Tote that barge and lift that roll! In short, as your president and general manager, I advise you to get back to work! What do you say?"

The crowd cheered and rushed out of the auditorium, on its way.

Heller looked around at the deserted hall. He looked at Mamie and Tom-Tom and the Countess. He asked them, wonderingly, "What did I approve?"

The others had their minds on different things. Nobody answered.

Heller asked, "How did the lights come on?"

Tom-Tom stopped tightening a drumhead and looked at Heller timidly. He said, "I couldn't go to the utility-company offices myself. I know as treasurer I should handle them, but I wouldn't know if I was paying the right bank notes out, so I sent the band leader. The lights, phone, water and furnaces should all be on shortly, as he keeps good time."

Heller looked around. "But they can't start gambling in the casinos or even make change in the stores. There isn't any cash."

The Countess Krak was at his elbow. "I didn't tell you, dear, as you seemed so busy. But I put three sacks of that money in a ventilator shaft. It's about a million and a half, they guess. I gave it to Mamie so she could get your corporation going."

Mamie said, "And it is really appreciated, honey. It's enough to pay utilities, get money in the cashier's cages and fill up the slot machines so we can start pulling in some dough."

Heller asked them, "What did I approve?"

But he was being pushed out of the auditorium by Mamie. They got to the lobby.

It was jammed with newly arriving people! MOBS! There were four long lines at the desk where clerks were swiftly checking them in.

Heller looked out a side window. The parking lot was jammed with newly arrived cars. And more were strung out down the road, honking their way forward inch by inch. He said to Mamie, "Why are all those people coming in?"

She said, as she pushed him up some steps, "I guess it's to see the scene of the battle. It's all over national TV. Burning tanks, exploding landing craft, shot-down planes. The wrecks are all out there, real and authentic, too! The PR people did a great job on press-agenting your taking Atlantic City by storm. They even used some film clips of the Normandy D-day landing in World War II. It's been on every network since midmorning. But Atlantic City press agents have always been tops."

I snorted. Atlantic City press agents be (bleeped). That was Madison!

The Countess Krak said, "Was there a battle, dear? I was in the laundry room and corridors. I did hear shooting. But I didn't know you'd been down on the beach."

They had reached the former office of *Capo* Gobbo Piegare. Mamie inspected the place; she picked a beautifully sculpted black hand off the desk and dropped it in the wastebasket and dusted off her fingers. She then removed Heller's coat and sat down in the elegant yellow desk chair. From it she had a view of the boardwalk, which was getting noisier.

She tossed the jacket to Heller. "You sure are clever, sailor.

Having a stand-in doing autographs for you. It can be pretty tiring, as stars like me know only too well. But listen, sailor: when you choose a double, pick one that looks more like you. I can't abide buckteeth."

"Double?" said Heller. "Where is the double?"

Oh, my Gods. I certainly smelled Madison here in his relentless search for front page.

"Why," said Mamie, "he's out there now on the boardwalk, autographing like mad. Clever idea. Wears one out posing for TV crews. But the double is handling it well."

The Countess said, "So you don't have to go out, dear."

Heller peeked through the window down at the boardwalk. It was SWARMING with public and vendors and reporters and cameramen. The double, Madison's phoney "Whiz Kid"—glasses, big jaw, buckteeth and all—was standing on a wrecked army-surplus tank while some effects man rekindled the flames within it.

"I sure don't," said Heller, flinching. He turned back into the room. "Will somebody please, please tell me what I approved?"

Mamie sat up in the sumptuous desk chair. "Well, you see, none of the staff has been paid for ages. And they know the corporation can't pay them and it's winter and there are no jobs open." She looked at him questioningly as if to say, did he really want to know?

"Please tell me," begged Heller.

"Well, in short, sailor, I told them that if you approved it, they could have 100 percent of the profits of the whole corporation and all its holdings, after expenses, until all their back wages, withholding tax and pension fund was caught up. After that, you said they could only have 60 percent. However, that won't be for a long, long time."

Heller sat down suddenly in a chair. And well he might! For, to all intents and purposes, so far as income for an owner was concerned, Atlantic City again had just changed hands!

THE WHOLE ENTERPRISE HAD BEEN TAKEN OVER BY THE STAFF!

Mamie went on. "But I need an opinion from you on something very important."

Breathlessly, he said, "What?"

Mamie said, persuasively, "Don't you think I should order my name put up in lights on each casino-hotel? Real big: 'Mamie Boomp, President and General Manager.' How do you think that would go over?"

Very faintly, Heller said, "Wonderful." Then after a little he turned to Countess Krak, "Dear, I think it's time we went back to New York."

Oh, did I guffaw! Heller's venture to get Izzy out of debt had made exactly no progress at all! It had only brought more trouble. Moreover, he was now discouraged and of very low morale.

I decided then and there to stop worrying about him and let him sink. There was no slightest sign that he would do anything productive or active, and when the word came from Lombar, he and the Countess Krak would still be in the U.S. floundering around. They didn't have a prayer of completing before I could get the word and kill them both!

My euphoria revved right up to top-peak. It was I who was winning. Me, me, me!

Chapter 2

The next morning my beauty sleep was shattered by a shrieking sizzle at my bedside. It interrupted a beautiful dream: Heller and Krak were in a bread line in New York and a Manco Devil was standing there with a soup ladle, not only refusing them food but also banging them expertly over the head with the sharp edge.

The shrieking sizzle was the intercom. It was quite unusual for it to buzz, for Faht Bey never wanted any help from me if he could possibly escape it. So it must be an emergency.

I pushed the button.

It was!

Faht Bey said, "Come to the hangar quick! They're killing Doctor Crobe!"

I would have said, so what, why are you calling me? But he had closed the line.

It occurred to me that I should not be careless. Life is full of chances. I had learned from Bury to always have an alternate solution in case something went wrong. I might need Crobe in the event that Heller and Krak muddled through.

I got into some clothes. I armed myself very heavily. I went down the tunnel to the hangar to give Faht a piece of my mind. Things had changed and he had better find out about it.

He was waiting for me at the hangar end.

"Since when," I asked him acidly, "am I responsible for everyone on this base?"

"You sent for him!" said Faht Bey. "You had him brought from Voltar. And now look!"

Crobe was halfway up the hangar wall, hanging by his fingernails.

On the hangar floor, fifty feet below him, were the four assassin pilots and the five Antimancos. And they were furious!

They were yelling curse words up at Doctor Crobe, the like of which I had never heard before. Unprintable! An awful din!

"I won't let them shoot at him. He's only two feet away from an earthquake stability box," said Faht. "They might hit it and cave the whole place in."

True enough: the small box which kept an invisible bar beam going to brace two walls apart was right by his head.

I didn't want to go near the assassin pilots: They are pretty dangerous people to be around even when they're calm. And right then they were definitely not calm. They were howling and jumping up and down.

Faht Bey's hand pushing against my back propelled me into the scene.

"What's this?" I said.

A stream of vituperation sprayed at me from all sides. Only with difficulty could I piece together what had happened.

Doctor Crobe had lifted the detention-cell key off the guard. Sometime during the night he had crept out of the cell where he should have been studying English. An assassin pilot had awakened at the cut of a guard bayonet and had the bleeding slash to prove it.

Good Gods, Doctor Crobe sure did not have very good sense, to attack an assassin pilot!

Ploddingly, plugging away, I kept asking them if Crobe had volunteered any slightest explanation for this breach of good manners. Perhaps if I could get to the bottom of this, it could be handled.

No one at ground level had the necessary information. In fact, they were making such a din, I doubt they understood my line of interrogation.

There was only one thing for it, I realized in a spurt of genius: Ask Doctor Crobe.

I got a small bullhorn and focused it on him. "Why were you cutting on an assassin pilot?" I shouted up at him.

He had hold of the beam box itself now. He looked down with his wild, zealot eyes. His voice, coming from way up there on the wall, was pretty thin.

"I was just studying English!" he shouted down in his clumsy Voltarian. "I was only doing what you told me to do, Officer Gris."

That caused more smoke and profanity down where I was. Hastily, I yelled back, "I didn't tell you to cut anybody's throat!"

"You gave me texts on psychology and psychiatry as part of my reading assignment! They say man has a reptile brain in the lower middle of his skull. That was news to me, and I was only trying to find out! Why all this furor over somebody just trying to do his homework?"

Well, he had a point. The assassin pilots and the Antimancos didn't see it that way.

"You gave him some books that told him to do that?" snarled an assassin pilot.

I thought it prudent to change the subject. "If we can get him down from there, he can show you it is just a clinical matter."

They surged at me. I got my back to the wall and a blastick out. "Look," I said, "why don't you go someplace and have a conference and cool off. I'll get him down and we can discuss it like gentlemen."

They looked at the 800-kilovolt blastick. They looked up at Crobe.

"Later," said the assassin pilot.

They left, snarling considerably, leaving me and Faht Bey.

I yelled up at Crobe, "You can come down now."

"I can't. I am certain I will fall," he yelled back.

"We'll rig a safety net!" I yelled. "Hold on."

The hangar crew had been very inconspicuous during the argument. Faht Bey dug them out from behind things and made them get a net. They stretched it out below Crobe.

"You can jump now," I yelled up at him.

"My hands won't let go!" he yelled back.

I told Faht Bey and the hangar crew to wait right there. I went up the tunnel to my gun case. I selected out a needle stun rifle and came back.

Faht Bey took one look at it. "Don't shoot up there! You could hit that electronic-beam support box he's holding on to."

I told him icily, "You are questioning my marksmanship. I can hit a songbird at half a mile with this. How can I miss Crobe at fifty feet?"

I put the stun rifle on its lowest setting. The hangar crew around the safety net covered up their heads. Faht Bey ran all the way to the office and peeked back out.

Kneeling, I braced the weapon.

I took perfectly accurate aim. Right on Crobe's right hand as it clutched the box.

I fired!

CRASH!

The box exploded!

Down came Crobe!

Down came ten tons of rock!

Smoke and dust spiraled in the gloom.

Faht Bey hit the clanging general-emergency alarm button.

DEAFENING!

From all over the base people came streaming in to man the guns.

Faht Bey quickly redirected them into an emergency damage and rescue operation.

They began to dig the hangar crew out.

Crobe they found in the bottom of the net where he had landed safely, only to be at once bombarded by rock following him down.

Apparently the beam box had shorted and the beams had ceased to support the walls they proofed against the numerous earthquakes of the area, and slabs of rock had sheered away from old faults.

These people were making a lot of to-do about nothing. The

hangar walls were intact except for a few pockmark holes a yard or less in diameter. No equipment had been damaged unless you counted one safety net. There wasn't even anybody dead—only a fractured skull or two, and Prahd could patch those up.

But everybody passing me was giving me a most undeserved glare.

I had found what was wrong. The power pack in the needle stun rifle had not been recharged for two years and, low-powered, had missed his hand and shot low. My marksmanship was not in question. But nobody would stop long enough to hear the explanation.

They were very unappreciative. After all, I had gotten Crobe down. Not even Bugs Bunny could have done it any better.

Chapter 3

I had retired to my room after it became plain, by certain remarks, that I was in the way. They had to get the wounded to the hospital and the beam box repaired quick in case there was an earthquake, and the floor was pretty messy. After all, they were professionals and I was above all such menial work.

Thus it was that just while I was enjoying a delicious dinner of *cerkez tavugu*—which is boiled chicken, Circassian style, with a sauce of crushed walnuts and red pepper—served by a somewhat beat-up but very obsequious staff, Faht Bey had the effrontery to buzz me again.

"They're ready for your conference," he said.

"Some other time," I said.

"Then my vote is that we feed your Doctor Crobe to a disintegrator bin."

"Wait, wait," I said. I thought very rapidly. I was well aware of the havoc Crobe could wreak: He was a very valuable asset in any Apparatus operation. Heller was very sneaky and he might recover or get lucky and then my neck would be out. Reluctantly I said, "I will be right down."

The conference in the crews' quarters was attended by very grim faces. I walked in, blastick in my palm, taking no chances. I didn't sit down. It was not that I was invited to. It was simply very plain that the best place for a back was against a wall.

They had Doctor Crobe. Somewhat bandaged—most likely by

himself—he was crouched on the floor, and there were three guards with three guns pointing at his head.

"I vote death," said the first assassin pilot who had been cut.

"Seconded," said the second assassin pilot.

"That settles it," said Captain Stabb. "The verdict is hanged by the teeth until he falls in a pot of boiling electronic fire."

"Hold it," I said. "I haven't heard the evidence or voted."

"Do you wish to enter a plea for responsibility?" said Faht Bey.

These fellows were going a bit too fast for me. The green glow-plate didn't lend any cheer to the scene. I thought fast. Faht Bey had brought up an out for me but it was a tricky one. By Voltarian law, anyone who is knuckleheaded enough to take full responsibility for a prisoner, even when condemned, could have him. That was how the Apparatus could collect "executed" criminals. There was only one little hooker: If the person then, thereafter, committed any crime, the one who had taken responsibility—the claimant—could also be charged with that crime and if execution occurred could be executed with the criminal.

"It is quite certain," said the assassin pilot who had been cut and who seemed to be acting as the master of the conference, "that said Doctor Crobe *will* commit some other crime against base personnel, no matter how slight. In that event, the claimant can legally be executed. Therefore the conference entertains the plea. All those voting for it, raise your right index finger. The fingers have it. You are the claimant, Officer Gris. Conference adjourned."

"Wait!" I said.

They had all walked out, including the guards.

It was a frame-up!

Oh, what cunning (bleepards) they were! The probability of Doctor Crobe doing something else was an absolute certainty. I knew the man! What a murderous revenge that assassin pilot had taken. This could get me killed very dead in the most legal possible way. And right when I was in triumph everywhere. Low blow.

Crobe crouched there eyeing me with his glittery black eyes, probably wondering what to turn me into. I hoped it wasn't a spider. I dislike spiders.

I thought. Crobe crouched.

I remembered the expression on the assassin pilot's face when he glanced at me in leaving.

I saw a safety line in a coil, hanging above a bunk.

INSPIRATION!

I got the safety line. I wrapped it round and round Crobe's ankles. I wrapped it round and round his legs. I wrapped it round and round his body, pinning his arms to his sides. I wrapped it round and round his neck and head. I tied it with a triple knot and fused the ends. Not even a ghost could get out of that.

Speedily, I raced to my room.

From my safe I took fifty thousand Turkish lira, amounting to about five hundred U.S. dollars.

I raced back. I found the construction superintendent.

"I want to make a deal," I said. I showed him the money.

His eyes bugged, as I knew they would.

"You are going to build me a cell the like of which nobody ever heard of, and when you do, you get this."

He made a grab. I was too quick for him. "When done and when tested," I said.

"A few thousand on account," he said.

I peeled off ten thousand lira. I gave them to him. "The rest when you execute the plan."

He took the bills. "Where's the plan?"

A small detail I had overlooked. So we sat down near the cocooned Crobe and I drew the plan.

You can get carried away with these things. Once I began to draw I didn't really know when to stop. I kept thinking of other ways he could get out.

But finally we had it and, if I say so myself, it was a masterpiece.

At the very end of the detention corridor there was a big cell which had never been used. It was all the way back. Across the corridor, before you got to it, I would place a sheet of blastproof steel, heavily embedded in the stone of the walls. It would have a bulletproof viewport in it. The door through it would be openable only by combination lock.

Beyond that would be the normal cell bars and their door.

Between these two impenetrable barricades I would place a beam alarm system, so that if anybody got in it would ring and clang all over the place.

Now, there was a chance that Crobe might get persuasive to a guard, as he had already done. So I would leave no way whatever to communicate through these barriers. This required a new ventilation hole be drilled straight up to the air to come out, masked behind a rock, on the mountainside.

The possibility existed that Crobe might try to climb up it, so it would have spikes to gouge anyone who made such an attempt. And furthermore, it would have explosive charges in it, with crisscrossing trip wires, that would blow anyone to bits if they attempted to crawl up it. I would also put saw rays across the outside and inside entrances. In that way, Crobe could communicate to nobody in the cell block, would have air but couldn't get out.

Now for food. I designed a device which went through a maze with fifteen turnings. When you put something on a tray, it would float way up on antigravity pulses and then slide on antigravity rollers through all those turnings. More—it would have fifteen sealed doors that any tray would have to go through. Each door would have a living-presence detector on it and if anything live tried to squeeze through, the door would remain shut.

So far so good.

The light in the place would not hook up to any part of the base. Independent units, powered by the sun at the air-shaft entrance, would be the only power.

Now for the cell itself. It was pretty large, as it was designed to hold about fifteen prisoners. So these stone ledges would have to go. Crobe would have to be forced to study, so in their place I would put tables and shelves for books.

Crobe's sanitation was awful so I designed sprayers and a drain so the whole area could be washed down simply by tripping a remote button, only the bookshelves shutting automatically.

As long as I was designing, I also put in a toilet and running water, though I suspected Crobe would never touch it. However, he could not complain to the Voltar sanitation department that he had been left without facilities.

I then put in a bed. And that was the masterpiece. If Crobe got too active and went raging around, the next time he lay down, clamps would shut and hold him in bed until somebody could come in and gas him.

It was a true masterpiece, as I have said. I looked at it proudly.

"It's going to take about a week to build," said the construction superintendent.

I blinked. What was I going to do with Crobe for a week?

I could not bring myself to change a single line of the plan. "Four days," I said.

"Four days and an additional ten thousand lira," he said.

I groaned. No, I couldn't possibly change this plan. It was too good. Well, who cared. I could always draw more lira.

"Go ahead," I said. "Only start at once."

I dragged Crobe into one of the many unoccupied cells. I pushed him onto a ledge. I laid my weapons handy.

And amidst the buzzing of drills and the clang of metal in the cell block, for the next four days I stayed right there and guarded Crobe.

Oh, the arduousness of duty in the Apparatus!

All he did for four whole days was lie in his lashings and glare.

Chapter 4

Oh, was I glad when at last I could pay the construction superintendent his remaining money for a completed job. I almost parted with the lira with joy.

Four days of glares had gotten me down.

Getting four guards to stand with blastrifles pointed at the still-cocooned Doctor Crobe's head, I worked rapidly.

I got a huge case of spacecraft emergency rations—who knew how long he would be in there mucking about—and threw it into the middle of the cell floor.

Reviewing his language equipment, I made sure it was adequate to teach even an idiot English. I put it on the cell table.

Then, as I had before, I realized there still might be inadequate incentive for him to learn the language. He had exhibited interest in the first two texts. Accordingly, I unearthed whatever I could spare on the subjects of psychology and psychiatry. It was pretty juicy stuff: It included *Governmental Psychology*, all about man being a lousy stinking animal that was so depraved and writhing with unconscious passions he was totally incapable of rational thought and had to be policed with clubs at every turn; *Irrational Psychiatry*, all about how to cure people by killing them; *Psychology of Women, or How to Trick Your Wife and Mistress into Getting into the Bed of Your Best Friend*; *Child Psychology*, all about the techniques of turning children into perverts; *The Psychiatrist on the Couch*, giving seventy-seven unusual ways to engage in sex with animals; Dr. Kutzman's famous text, *Psychiatric Neurosurgery*, all about how to end every possible brain function; and *Psychiatric Stew*, which authoritatively told one what to do with people when they have been turned into vegetables by the latest techniques approved by the Food and Drug Administration. I included lots of other even more vital texts, all standard and accepted material of the professions. They could not fail to entice Crobe into reading English like mad.

I checked the cell carefully. There was no possible way to get out or to get in and there was no way anyone outside it could speak with anyone in it, and vice versa.

I went back, and with the guards standing ready, I burned the knot apart with a small disintegrator and began to unwind the safety line off his head. I got down to his mouth.

Crobe said, "I'll have the law on you for this!"

I was utterly amazed! Here I had saved his life. I had even become a claimant for him and put my own life at risk.

Then I understood: Crobe might be a doctor but he didn't know anything about law. He did not know, for instance, that I could now kill him without his thereafter being able to sue me. Further, if he knew so little about law, he didn't know ranks or how important I was. I recognized that I had better get a book and show him before I unwrapped anything else.

There was a crew library near to hand. I went in. I looked. There was a long shelf utterly covered with dust: Nobody had looked at these books for decades. I blew and when I was through coughing I read the titles.

It was all one series of volumes! More than forty of them, very thick. The title of the set was *Voltar Confederacy Combined Compendium Complete, including Space Codes, Penal Codes, Domestic Codes, Royal Proclamations, Royal Orders, Royal Procedures, Royal Precedence, Royal Successions Complete with Tables and Biographies, Court Customs, Court History, Royal Land Grants, Rights of Aristocracy, Planetary Districts of 110 Planets, Local Laws, Local Customs, Aristocratic Privileges and Various Other Matters.* Impressive!

I realized it would scare Crobe half to death. I promptly put the whole set on a cart and wheeled it to the new cell and stuffed it into the shelves. Why engage in chitchat? Let him find his own reasons he was being so ungrateful!

I went back to get Crobe. He was glaring so hard, I decided not to take a chance of completing the unwrap there. I dumped him on a cart and rolled it into the cell.

I said, "You will get out of here when you know English and decide to obey my orders!"

I picked up the loose end of the safety line and gave it a hefty yank.

He spun like a top!

Right across the floor.

His body even hummed, it was turning so fast.

I kicked the cart out of the cell.

I locked up the cell door.

I slammed the new armor-steel corridor door.

I spun the combination.

Only I knew that combination. Nobody could get in. Crobe couldn't get out.

My sigh of relief came with a gusty rush. In due time, if I needed it, I had a secret weapon I could send against Heller. At the least sign of resurgence or success in the U.S., I would launch the deadly Crobe.

Until then, he was safe and I was safe.

I looked in through the port. He had untangled himself. He was staring at the bookshelves. And just as I had hoped, his interest quickened. He was picking up *Psychiatric Stew.*

With a gay and jaunty step, I went upon my way.

Life had taken a new and pleasant upturn once again.

Chapter 5

After a marvelous breakfast served by Karagoz and a waiter, who crossed the floor only on their knees, it occurred to me that I had better check up on Heller and Krak just to make sure they were still failing.

With a pitcher of hot *sira*, I leaned back in a comfortable chair and watched the two viewers.

Heller was doing a whole bunch of figures at his desk in New York. All sorts of equations, mostly chemical. No threat there: he could do equations until the sky fell in and it wouldn't disturb the planet in the least.

I became interested in what the Countess Krak was doing. She was in the secretary boudoir and the door to the office itself was closed. The place was all festooned with cupids prancing around the wallpaper. But that wasn't what she was looking at directly. It was the cat.

She was down on her knees and she was teaching him to do backflips. He was working very hard to get them just right.

"Elegance is the watchword, Mister Calico," she was saying. "Now let's do it again. Saunter along—one, two, three, four—without a care in the world. Then FLIP! Takes the audience by surprise. Now here we go again: one, two, three, four . . ."

What a silly woman! She was still talking to it in Standard Voltarian and it was still an Earth cat! Couldn't possibly understand her.

And if this was all she was doing, it was certainly no threat to me.

The cat must have done a perfect flip. She petted it and Mister Calico purred.

"All right," said the Countess. "That's enough acrobatics for today. Now let's review yesterday's lesson. Go get a newspaper."

She opened the door a crack. That cat wasn't so smart after all. Had to have doors opened for it.

The cat went out into the office. It sprang up on a bar stool. A stack of newspapers was there. The cat caught the edge of one in its teeth and worked it off the bar. The paper hit the floor with a plop. The cat jumped down and again bit into the corner of it and, walking sideways, got it through the boudoir door.

The Countess closed the door. "That's fine." She knelt on the floor. "Now turn it over so I can read it."

The cat, with teeth and paws, turned the newspaper over.

It wasn't really a newspaper. It was the weekly news magazine, the *National Expirer.* I guess the cat liked spicy reading.

It didn't go smoothly. The Countess flinched back. She gave the cat an absent pat. She leaned forward, reading the front page story. It said:

IS MISS AMERICA SAFE FROM WHIZ KID RAPE?

This probing question is being passionately asked today by rape experts.

After his theft of Atlantic City, the thing has raised its ugly head: Is the reigning Miss America, only just crowned this autumn at Atlantic City, now safe from threatened Whiz Kid ravishment?

Many experts predict that the Whiz Kid will not be able to curtail his ardor now that Miss America is so easily in his clutches.

Others, reviewing the measurements of Miss America, agree that no oversexed normal male would be able to resist her charms.

No less an authority than the press agent of Miss America himself stated, "We have tried to hide her photographs from his view and we have her in a narrow bed that won't take two, but predictions of an early roll in the hay are rife."

The story was accompanied by a full-length, half-page picture of a gorgeous, half-naked blonde showing a yard of leg enticingly.

The Countess Krak sat back on her haunches. She was staring at the photograph. "Oh, dear," she muttered. "She *is* beautiful. Oh, dear, and we're not even married yet!"

She suddenly folded the paper and shoved it under the edge of the rug. She said, "Cat! Call Mamie!"

There was a phone on the side table of the couch. The cat jumped up beside it. I was amazed. A cat using a telephone? But then I saw it wasn't remarkable at all. The phone was a speaker phone and all you had to do was punch a button and it came on with a dial tone. Then it had a row of call buttons on a panel beside it and all you had to do was touch one button and it automatically dialed a whole number. Anybody can do that. Just two buttons.

"President and General Manager Boomp here," came out of the phone speaker.

"Meow," said the cat. Well, at least it didn't say "Hello" in Voltarian. That would have been a Code break for sure!

The Countess gave the cat a stroke and sat down on the couch. "Hello, dear. This is Joy. You know that dinner you were inviting us to attend this week? Well, I just called to say Jettero is very, very busy and can't possibly come down to Atlantic City."

"Oh, that's too bad."

Krak said, "How are things, dear?"

"Oh, just fine," said Mamie. "That (bleeped) Mafia had all the gambling devices rigged and they were paying off only to their own henchmen and shills, but we reversed the policy and only let popular people win—pretty girls we can get good pictures of and such. You should see them flocking in."

"Well, well," said the Countess Krak. "That confirms it. We won't be down, dear. Come up to New York any time. Bye-bye." To the cat she made a gesture and it punched the disconnect button.

"Hmm," said the Countess Krak. "This requires some heavy thinking, Mister Calico. That's the end of your training for today."

She sat there for a while, staring at nothing. Then she primped her hair, smoothed out her eyebrows, straightened up the expensive lounge suit she was wearing and went out into the office. She sat down in the chair across from Heller.

He became aware of her, looked up and smiled.

"Dear," said the Countess Krak, "exactly what are your plans for getting us home?"

I flinched. I knew what she had her mind on. Those "Royal" forgeries. Until they were presented and hers was signed, she thought she could not get married. The last thing I wanted was a push toward concluding Mission Earth! They could get me shot! I wished she realized that any effort to present those forgeries would also get her shot, but I dared not tell her.

"Oh, I'm sorry, darling," said Heller. "I guess I haven't been very exact in telling you about my planning. You see, I'm supposed to put this planet in a condition that will continue to support life.

"The first thing they need is a fuel that doesn't pollute. The oil companies are insisting that everyone burn chemical-fire fuels that smoke and get soot and poison gases into the atmosphere. Until they have and are using a better energy source, it's useless to do anything else to salvage the planet.

"Also, to do any real building or feed the populations, they need more fuel than is being made available. The inflation you run into is also because of the high cost of fuel, which monthly becomes more expensive.

"So (a) they are getting dirty and making fresh air scarce by using dirty fuel; (b) they are short on real fuel and can't build cheap sewage plants; and (c) they are unable to control their economy because they have such expensive fuel.

"So, whatever else needs fixing, they are going up in smoke unless they have and use proper technology."

"Very good," said the Countess Krak, "then what are your plans for getting us home?"

"Oh, you mean my immediate program? Well, it goes like this: (1) They won't listen to anybody who doesn't have a diploma. And in a very few months now, I should have that. (2) I am working on carburetors and fuels within this culture's own scientific-use-capability framework and should be able to produce these. (3) I need spores to clean up the particles and poison gases in the planet's atmosphere. I asked Gris for a cellologist and you say Crobe is learning English and will be here soon, so that's in train. (4) I have some other things to do to prevent continent immersion by floods. And (5) to set up anything as massive as planetary fuel conversion requires billions of dollars."

"Yes, dear," said the Countess Krak. "I find that all very interesting. But could you tell me *what* you are doing, *right now*, to get us home?"

Heller looked at her a bit defensively. "Just now, I was listing the contemporary content of atmospheric pollutants: carbon dioxide, carbon monoxide, sulfur dioxide, hydrocarbons, nitrogen oxides and particles from various burning and industrial sources. You see, aside from making it increasingly difficult to breathe, these block the sun out. They also hold reradiated solar reflection in. One gets a heating and a cooling factor at the same time. But the planet has been warming up gradually over the last century and this is connected to increased industrialization. The main danger, however, is that these particles do not permit adequately large water drops to form and so there is an increasing scarcity of rain. Aridity is a factor in reducing life-support capability. . . ."

"That is very fascinating, Jettero. And I am very glad to know it. However, looking at this head on, so to speak, what could you DO, RIGHT NOW, to speed up your program? Some VITAL point you could PUSH on."

"Well, I suppose I ought to be working on how to make some money. If Izzy doesn't come through, we'll even lose these offices."

"Oh, Jettero. I could buy what we need with my credit card."

"Oh, I'm afraid the finance required is way out of the range of a credit card. We need billions. We have to set up a spore-release plant. We have to get Chryster Motor Corporation out of the hands of IRS and get it producing carburetors. Such things really require billions and billions."

Krak looked very determined. She said, "No more Atlantic City!"

Heller looked shocked. "Oh, dear, no!"

She tapped the edge of the desk with her finger. "Plans get executed when they are at least worked on. Even a little bit at a time. You don't have to wait until you graduate to make billions." She wagged her finger emphatically at him. "I think you had better get very busy, Jettero, and make these billions right away. And do it in a manner that does NOT include ANY Miss Americas! Not a single *one!*"

I really had to laugh. She was pushing on him, yes. But after the fiasco he had just made I had no fears at all that he would suddenly come up with pots of money. All the money he had gotten so far was hit money put up to waste him that he, by luck, had gotten into his own hands. High finance is an entirely different variety of slaughter. The hit men there wear top hats and are very suave and clever and they do their shooting cunningly across desks. It was wholly out of his field. He didn't have, in my opinion, the ghost of a chance.

Billions, indeed!

What amateurs they were compared to me and the huge coup I had just pulled off.

I loaded the units with strips to record the signals. I dropped the blanket on them. Let them stew. I had my own high expectations. Madison was on the job. And I had Crobe in reserve.

And one day, when they had loafed around, Heller and Krak would be caught up with the order from Lombar that it was time to slay.

It was high time I took some air and saw what daylight looked like once more!

Chapter 6

It was bitter cold but for all that a bright and sunshiny day. The shrubs in the villa yard were all bound up for winter like corpses in shrouds and not a single songbird was in sight. Beautiful.

I stretched my arms and inhaled deeply.

I stopped right there.

I gaped.

Was that a locomotive in the yard?

The CAR!

I let out my breath in a swoosh. My Gods, but it was big!

There it stood, blocking the whole gate. Seen head on, the vertical chrome slats of the custom radiator grill looked like the cowcatcher on a train.

I sped forward, travelling to one side so that I could see it in profile.

Half a block long!

The black paint was a little dull but, oh, did that limousine have lines! Classic!

Blazoned on the door was the scarlet eagle, wings outstretched, wearing horns, wild-eyed and savage.

My, was I impressed!

I rushed around to the other side. Another eagle.

I opened the rear door. What space! All along the other side was a kind of bunk. The back of the front seat was a bar. A field radio-telephone was in a ledge. The interior upholstery was all new cloth and leatherette, a dark red.

I stood back. So this was a 1962 Daimler-Benz, specially built! I tapped a window. Bulletproof!

I stepped back further. Then I saw it. Below the huge, red eagle on the door they had painted my name in gold:

Sultan Bey

Magnificent!

The quiet of the day was marred by an evil laugh. I whirled. The toothless, beak-nosed old man was standing there. He was dressed in an olive-drab chauffeur's uniform much too big for him.

The taxi driver came out of the villa staff quarters. "You like it?" he beamed.

"What is that old man doing here?" I said.

"Oh, him? That's Ters. He comes with the car. He was the general's chauffeur, and unemployment being what it is, he hasn't had a job for more than a quarter of a century. He drove it down here from Istanbul."

Ters? That means "unlucky" or "unfortunate" in Turkish. I hoped it didn't combine with the taxi driver's Modon name, Deplor. Unfortunate Fate was something I didn't want anything to do with.

"But look at this great car!" said the taxi driver. "And didn't they do a great job of repairing it? A real Daimler-Benz, probably the only one of its kind left in the world. Distinctive! Fits you like a glove. Look, I even had them put your name on the door, real big, in gold. They'll know who is coming, believe you me!"

He jumped around to the other side and hit the horn. It almost blew the roof off the villa!

"Now," said the taxi driver, "I just told Karagoz to have a couple shrubs cut down so we can get it fully inside the gate and still get other cars in and out. So don't have any qualms about its size. Besides, you want people to SEE it. Makes you a big man! And if you park it right over there anyone can spot it going down the road. I tell you, it isn't everybody that has a car like this! Get in and try out the back seat!"

I did. The taxi driver got in the front seat. He shut the doors and turned to me confidentially. "Now we're in business. You wanted women. There isn't a woman in the world that could resist this car. Right?"

I allowed he must be correct. It sure was big and impressive.

"I have all this figured out. As this was a general's car, we ought to go about this like a military operation, a field campaign. That's what he used it for. That's why it has that ledge down the side you can sleep on. Now, in a military campaign, the timetable is everything, so let's synchronize our watches."

We did. I was getting excited.

"Now," he said, "I arrive at the villa here each evening at 6:00 in my taxi. I park it over there. I get in the limousine with Ters and he and I go out and get the woman. We'd be back around 8:30."

"Why so long?" I said.

"Finding the woman, time it takes to persuade her, time and distance to make the drive. We will have to go all over the Afyon plateau because we aren't going to repeat on women. You want them fresh every night."

"Go on," I said, my appetite whetting up.

"We don't come back through the gate, here. That would expose the woman to gossip. Instead, we park under that cedar tree just up the road. You know the place. Only a few hundred feet away. Then, when we're all ready, I blow the horn like this." He hit it and a chicken that was in the yard took off straight up.

"Now, the moment you hear that horn," said the taxi driver, "you come running. I introduce you to the woman. I come back here and get my cab and leave. You do what you want with the woman," and he leered, "and when you're through, you simply walk back here and the old man takes her home. Now synchronize our watches again just to make sure. The woman will be so hot for you, you mustn't keep her waiting. Promise?"

"Oh, I won't keep her waiting," I said and eagerly synchronized my watch again.

"One more thing," said the taxi driver. "Give me two hundred thousand lira so I can get a woman this very night."

"Two hundred thousand lira?" I said. "That's two thousand

dollars! In Istanbul brothels, that would be a whole year of women!"

"No, no. You don't understand the quality you are getting. These women aren't prostitutes, no sir! These are girls trying to earn their dowries, their bride money. If they have a big enough offer, even the hottest and most beautiful maiden will be slavering to get it. It means they can then marry a good husband. With that much, they'll come flocking! You'll have the best-looking women for miles around panting to tear their veils and robes off and get under you. Thin, plump, tall, short, a new one every night. Imagine it! A beautiful, passionate woman lying naked on that ledge, her hips twitching, stretching out her arms to you, begging, begging for it."

I ran into the house, opened my safe and got two hundred thousand lira and put it in a big sack and came back.

The taxi driver peeked in. He nodded.

The old chauffeur laughed an evil laugh.

"See you when I blow the horn!" yelled the taxi driver and drove off in his cab.

I could hardly wait.

Chapter 7

Eight-thirty came. No signal to come.

I was waiting in the patio, all steamed up to go. I looked at my watch. It was eight thirty-one and ten seconds.

The car had left on time, sliding smoothly out onto the road, running very quietly in the night.

Eight thirty-two. No signal to come.

I began to pace. I was very eager to get going, in no mind whatever to suffer through delay.

Eight thirty-six. No signal to come.

I paced faster.

This was cruel. I was beginning to ache.

Eight forty-six. No signal to come.

What could be keeping them? Had the girl said no? Oh, if she knew what Prahd had given me she would certainly never say no! Maybe I should have given Ahmed a portrait of it.

But never mind. After this once, word would get around!

Eight fifty-one. Still no signal to come!

I was beginning to perspire. My hands were shaking.

Eight fifty-nine. No call as yet!

Nine o'clock.

THE HORN!

It blasted hard as an earthquake!

I went out of there like a racehorse from the starting gate.

Racehorses, however, usually don't run into camel drivers, nor camels, or donkeys, either. I did. For some reason, the farmers along that road must have decided it was a superhighway. Caravan after caravan, lanterns bobbing in the moonlight, was choking the thoroughfare with slow-moving, evil-smelling traffic. Drivers fended me off with sticks and even a camel took a nip at me.

I dived into a ditch to avoid the lashing heels of a donkey and looked wildly about for the Daimler-Benz.

Anxiously, thrusting caravans out of my road with threatening yells, I rushed on.

Just short of the cedar tree, I ran into Ahmed. He stopped me. It was moonlight. The car was very visible from the road. You could even see the eagle on the door. The dome light showed there was somebody inside.

"What was this delay?" I said, trying to get away from him and to the car.

"She is a new girl. An untried maiden. She was shy. I had to convince her all over again when she got here. It took both old Ters and myself to keep her from bolting. But we convinced her. Let me introduce you."

He took me to the car.

I pushed an inquiring camel out of the way and got the door open.

Reclining on the ledge under her cloak, still veiled, dimly seen by the dome light, a woman lay.

"Blank Hanim," said Ahmed, "this is Sultan Bey." He pointed his finger at her. "Remember what I told you and be good. You please him, you hear me?"

Her eyes were big as saucers above the veil. I heard her swallow convulsively. A good sign.

I started to get in but a camel thought my coattail was edible and pulled me back.

I whirled to free myself. I cocked a fist, but a donkey was standing there. I thought better of it.

"Get in, get in!" said Ahmed. "Don't be shy. She's all yours!"

"Get these beasts out of here!" I yelled at him. "I don't want any (bleepety-bleep) audience! And you get out of here, too! I'm shy!"

"Oh, well, if you say so," Ahmed said. He helped me in and banged the door.

Unfortunately, when he slammed it, the side curtain rolled up. I turned to yell at him to be careful of the car and found I was staring at a camel's face. I tried to get the curtain down: the bottom snap had parted. After two tries, I gave up. To Hells with the camel. I had more interesting things to do!

The woman's great black eyes were pools of passion—or terror. I did not bother to decide which.

With a ripping yank, I got the veil off her face.

"O Allah," she said.

She was beautiful.

I started to get out of my clothes.

"O Allah!" she said.

There was a tap at the window. I faced it in a rage. A donkey was standing there, staring.

I rolled down the window.

I still held the veil. I hit him in the face with it!

He deafened me with a bray.

He didn't go away.

To Hells with him.

I grabbed the woman.

"O ALLAH!" she screamed.

The car springs began to rock.

"OOOO ALLLLLLLLAAAAAAAH!" screamed the woman.

The moonlit world went into a spin for me.

There was a hissing sound. I listened to it a while.

I looked up.

The donkey and two camels were looking in the window.

I yelled at them.

They raced away.

The hissing sound continued.

I realized a car tire was going flat.

To Hells with it!

Once more the car springs began to rock.

The sound of the woman's voice racketed clear to the road.

"I'm drowning! I'm drowning!" The caravans dodged.

A camel driver came up to the car. He saw the springs rocking. He stuck his head in the window.

"O Allah!" he said.

I was able to sit up again. I saw what the trouble was. The dome light was still on. I reached over and hit it savagely. It went off.

The camel driver raised his lantern up, flooding the interior again with light.

I grabbed the woman's cloak and threw it in his face.

I got busy again.

Above the squeak of car springs, I could hear him outside talking.

To Hells with them.

"O ALLLLLLLLLLLLLLLAAAAAAAAAAAAAAHH!" screamed the woman.

It was dark and it was quiet.

There seemed to be a chinking sound.

I looked out of the window.

A donkey and three camels were standing there. The chinking was from their bridles as they chewed the woman's cloak. An entirely different camel driver was trying to get it away from them. He succeeded, put it under his arm and walked off.

The donkey and three camels all tried to get their noses through the window.

I was too tired to argue with them. I climbed over the front seat back and got out of the other side of the car. I hadn't fastened my belt buckle and I tripped.

I stumbled around the car and tried to shoo the onlookers away. They ignored me. Then I shrugged. Let the animals gratify their voyeur tendencies: it had been great.

Ters appeared from somewhere and gave vent to his evil laugh.

Not even that phased me.

Ters saw that a tire was flat, got out a pressure can with goo and inflated it.

He got in the car, gave another evil laugh and drove off.

In the back window, lit by moonlight, I could see the woman staring back at me. She had a very beseeching look.

Ah, I thought triumphantly, there goes a VERY satisfied female!

Despite all the disturbance, it had been quite a night!

Chapter 8

The very next night was quite similar to the first. The half-hour delay was the same. This girl looked a little plumper and a little older. She seemed, however, strangely tired and wan when I arrived.

The caravan traffic was even more intense and its interest in the car was just as great, but I did not let little things bother me. I am the sort of man who stays right on course, regardless of minor disturbances, and gets the job done.

The only major difference between the first and second nights was that a donkey, since the window had stuck open, reached right in and nipped me. I got rid of him with a punch in the nose.

But Ters had at last driven the second woman away with her staring out the rear window, her eyes and gestures pleading. I felt I was really making a hit!

The third night had some variation. Some camel drivers had built a campfire near the car and were sitting around it. The red eagles and the gold letters of my name were really prominent in the leaping firelight.

Ahmed came to me where I eagerly waited, just outside the gate before he blew his horn.

"I've got to get rid of them first," he told me. "Give me a few lira and go back inside the villa compound: these rendezvous of yours are secret and you mustn't be seen."

I did as he told me. An awful lot of time passed: another half hour. Eventually the horn was sounded. I rushed out again.

The fire that had been flaming there was almost out: just a few sparks remained.

"What was the delay?" I demanded. "Those camel drivers are long gone!"

"It's the woman," Ahmed said. "She's a very virtuous girl, this one. Terrified of her reputation. When we arrived and she spotted the camel drivers and fire, she fainted. It took us until just now to bring her to!"

I was eager to get down to business and leaped into the car. But they hadn't done a very good job in bringing her around. She still seemed to be unconscious.

I yanked the veil off her face. This third one had a tawny complexion. She seemed to be quite young. Then I saw that tears were running out of her eyes.

I understood at once. She had just worn herself out in the eagerness of waiting.

Well, here was one that wasn't waiting!

The car springs began to rock.

"O Allah!" sobbed the girl.

After a while, I heard an evil laugh. I saw that Ters was standing, leaning against the tree, watching the road.

A passing caravan suddenly veered when the girl screamed "O ALLLLLLLLLAAAAAAAAH!"

A little later, I looked up and Ters was actually herding some camels and donkeys closer to the car!

"Get them away from here!" I screamed at him. "How can I concentrate!"

"The animals hide the car!" said Ters. "Ahmed said it must be secret." He gave his evil laugh.

But even so, despite the camels, the evening came off all right.

And once more Ters drove away with the girl looking out the back window, the moonlight plainly lighting the pleading look she was giving me.

Contented, I knew I was really a hit amongst hits! Every night, that same beseeching look. These women must be going absolutely insane over me!

What a beautiful idea, the car and the women!

All the third morning, I slept a dreamless sleep. I awoke and had a bounteous breakfast served by a cringing staff. Totally enjoyable.

Torgut, who was standing there with a club in his hand in case the waiter tried to get off his knees, asked, however, an unfortunate question. "Will it be the same schedule tonight, O Master?" he said.

I was about to say yes when a thought suddenly struck me. I must be almost out of money!

I rushed to my safe.

Fatality! I didn't have two hundred thousand lira left!

However, that was soon handled. I was a very rich Gris and had not drawn my million-lira allowance for the week.

I dressed in a purple silk shirt and a charcoal suit with purple pinstripes. I put on my bearskin coat and my karakul hat. Because I would be carrying money, I picked the FIE shotgun out of the case and checked its load.

Word had been taken to Ters. The Daimler-Benz was already warming up.

The back seat was all cleaned up. I got in. He closed the door. He got under the wheel. He gave his evil laugh. I shuddered at it a little bit but away we went.

We tore along the road remarkably fast. We spilled a camel load of opium and it cheered me greatly when the donkey who had been leading the camel bucked and brayed. It was a beautiful if bitterly cold day. And that little drama made it perfect. Nobody was going to argue with this huge, bulletproof limousine and its red eagles!

We blocked the traffic before the Piastre Branch Bank in Afyon and I went in.

The teller recognized me on sight. He called the manager. The manager beckoned me into his office and set a chair for me.

"Mudur Zengin in Istanbul asked for you to call when you came in," he said. "If you . . ."

"I don't want to talk to Zengin," I said. "I just want my million-lira allowance for the week. I can't send a messenger, you know. Only I can pick it up."

"Please," he said.

He got Mudur Zengin on the phone quite quickly for Turkey. I put the shotgun down on a chair and took the proffered instrument.

"Hello, Zengin," I said. "I trust there's no hanky-panky about my weekly allowance."

"No," said Mudur Zengin. "That is, not at the moment. I wanted to tell you personally and in confidence that your concubine is not following your orders completely. While all purchases have stopped elsewhere, they are still coming in from the Bonbucks Teller Central Purchasing agent on the Squeeza credit card. We've just gotten one here for nearly a hundred and eighty thousand dollars."

"Look at the date," I said. "I think you will find it predates my orders to her. They simply sent it in late." (Bleep) that Krak!

"Do you mind if I call Squeeza on the other phone? They did not give me the exact date of invoice at the store."

Go ahead, I thought. That's pretty ancient history.

He came back on. "You were right about the date of that one. But what they told me was correct. They have quite a few coming in since. They are small. But they exist. Your concubine has not obeyed your orders and is still purchasing, evidently by phone to New York." (Bleep), (bleep), (bleep) that Krak!

"I wanted to be sure you knew," said Zengin. "You see, this pulls down the amount of money I can invest from the sums you left me and if it keeps up, it will reduce the allowance. In fact, it already has. And I can only authorize eight hundred thousand this week to protect your capital here. Unless of course, you wish to drive up and give me further money, which I don't advise."

"(Bleep), (bleep), (bleep), (bleep), (bleep) that Krak!" I inadvertently said aloud.

"I beg your pardon?" said Zengin.

"It's just that I'm mad at the concubine," I said.

"Well, I would advise you to really get onto her about it," said Zengin.

I couldn't. And if I went to Istanbul I would miss a night of ecstasy. And I could see Zengin pulling down my deposit box to grains of dust.

"Authorize the eight hundred thousand," I snarled. I handed the phone to the manager and Zengin did.

I went home with my slightly lesser bale of lira. I put it in the safe. It was only four days' worth!

I tried to reason with the taxi driver when he came at six. "You've got to get a cheaper rate!" I said.

He stood there, staring at me. "Boss, I know for a fact that you have no complaints at all. That's because the merchandise is such top quality." He shook his head. "No, I cannot let you cheapen your delight."

"Listen," I said. "Those first three girls were over the wall about me. They were looking through the back window when they drove away. Why can't you persuade one of them to come back?"

"Alas," he said, "that parting glance you see is the look of forlorn, never-never again. They were taken back to their homes. They have their dowries now. And I know very well you don't want to marry one of them."

I turned ice-cold at the very thought of marriage. It sends shivers of horror through me any time I hear the word.

"Did you know that that first girl was married just today? To a fine young fellow. And the second girl is now going to go away to join her sweetheart who is an immigrant worker in Germany. That's what we're up against: prior commitments. That's the only type I can get. We could, however, cut it down to once a week. . . ."

"No!" I shouted. "Never! Here's a girl's two hundred thousand for tonight. And get one who is less tired to begin with. They are cheating me with the first go. The following ones are okay but that first one needs pepping up."

He rushed off in a blast of Citroen smoke.

And that night, again half an hour late, I was back under the cedar tree with a sloe-eyed creature, dusky in the dim light of the limousine. Tired out at the start but gathering energy as we engaged, she tried to claw my eyes out as we progressed. She screamed "Allah!" so loud that at the night's end I hardly heard the old man's evil laugh.

And so the nights flowed on. Woman after woman. All a half hour late. All different. All tired at the start. All soon desperate and clawing. All soon screaming "Allah." And all of them looking pleadingly out the window as they drove away.

My calls at the bank had to become more frequent. The allowance got reduced to six hundred and then to four hundred. And finally I was calling the bank every day.

"You're eating into your capital like a buzz saw," Zengin said. "You're spending one million four hundred thousand lira a week and the branch manager tells me you also have some local gasoline bills and other things you'll have to pay. That concubine keeps buying flowers and theater tickets in New York. You should take a whip to her!"

Oh Gods, if I only dared take a whip to Krak!

"Let it eat into the capital and be (bleeped) to it," I said. "I must have a minimum of two hundred thousand lira a night!"

"Then, as your banker," he said, "I advise you to come to Istanbul and open your box. If you give me another million dollars, I can get you an income like that and you won't be slicing capital away, which is the height of folly."

"I can't spare the time!" I said.

He hung up.

And so the days passed, with, oh, those lovely nights. A new woman every time! Fat and thin, tall and short, but all of them all woman! At first every one seemed totally limp, but soon enough they were frantic. All they ever said was "O Allah!" and "I'm drowning!" But not even curious animals could distract me from my duty.

And every night, without exception, when they were driven away by the evilly-laughing Ters, they had the same beseeching look.

I hadn't realized how the time was passing until I saw a bud on a shrub one day. Was it actually moving into spring?

But not for me. Suddenly, without any slightest forehint, my dearest dreams turned into horror, my connections disconnected into a tangle of terror and my whole life came unstuck. All in the torture of slow-motion like you see a proud building coming down to land at last in a heap of shuddering rubble.

Fate had only been toying with me. And with the planet.

PART FORTY
Chapter 1

It was midafternoon where I was. I had very little to do. I wandered into my secret room and was struck with the whim that, like Roman emperors of old, I might enjoy the suffering of those who were about to die in the arena.

I brushed off some webs from the blanket covering of the viewers and even killed a spider or two as a sort of hors d'oeuvre to the main bout. I threw back the cover and sat down.

For a moment I thought I had gotten the wrong station or something. It was a hall. People were rushing back and forth in mad streams, very busy. It was Heller's view of the world. He must be in some other building. Their half floor at the Empire State had never had that much traffic tearing around. But no, it was their floor all right. A nearby sign said:

Wonderful Oil for Maysabongo
Front Office

What on Earth was going on? They didn't ever have that much staff. Or did they?

He was now passing the Telex Communication Central. It was pretty jammed up. Machines were hammering away inside.

A man in white overalls stopped him. *New York Telephone Company, Lease Line Crew Chief, Alf Underwood* was on the badge Heller looked at.

"Hey, you," said the man to Heller, "you look like an executive. We got an order here to run three more lease lines from this floor to the Chryster Building. We dunno where you want the automatic-relay switchboard."

Heller looked into the communications room. Gods, there was an operator at every machine and they were working like crazy. Heller pointed to a young man at the end machine. "See him," he said to the crew chief, "the one in the lavender shirt. And if he can't tell you, see Mr. Epstein over at Multinational, third corridor to your right."

Heller went on. He was breasting quite a stream of clerks and callers. He arrived near the door of Multinational, marked with its big logo of an anarchist bomb.

So many people were rushing in and out that he was stalled. He finally got into a line of people waiting to go in.

It looked like he would take so long that I switched my attention to the other viewer. Krak was somewhere else. Looked like Fifth Avenue. She was going along, looking into shop windows. My attention was at once riveted. She must be going to buy something, and on my Squeeza credit card. The scene had such potential havoc in it that I didn't want to look. But just as one's eyes will rivet upon an imminent disaster, I could not tear my attention away.

She passed by Tiffany's with only a casual glance and I began to breathe once more. But the way she was staring at street numbers quickened my pulse. Then she saw something ahead. It was a banner sign in a window:

Grand Opening
Post Winter Sale

FURS!
They had racks of them, visible through the window.
She went in. A clerk bustled over.
"I wonder," said the Countess Krak, "if you have something suitable for a space voyage."
I felt the blood rushing to my head! It could only mean one thing. She was doing some sort of planning about going home! Maybe they had had a huge breakthrough!

"Space voyage, madam?"

"Yes. Something soft and warm and comfortable that can be worn instead of a pressure suit."

"Oh, I am sorry, madam," began the clerk.

A tall gentleman in a pinstripe tail coat had come up. "Please answer the phone, Beevertail," he said sharply to the clerk. "Madam, I could not help but overhear your request. Beevertail is a bit new: came in with our last shipment of pelts from Canada. He would not understand that you are from NASA. Now, it just happens that we have a mink jump suit that would be just the *very* thing you are looking for. This way, please."

Hastily, I turned to the other viewer. Maybe Heller was making enough money now to pay for such frills as mink jump suits. Such a thing would cost a fortune! I knew by experience!

Izzy just that moment spotted Heller in the line. He jumped up. He grabbed a young clerk and shoved him bodily into the chair to handle the callers and then grabbed Heller and pulled him out of the line into the hall.

"Oh, Mr. Jet. I do apologize for keeping you waiting. It's because I am so inefficient."

Heller got him out of there and into a vacant space in the hall. He had a sheet of paper and showed it to Izzy, speaking very low, like a conspirator. "It's your daily broker-order list. Chicago Board of Trade: Sell your 1,000 contracts of March wheat today; it is going down by market opening tomorrow by ten cents a bushel. At market opening tomorrow, sell short 1,000 contracts of corn; it is going to drop thirty cents before close. Chicago Mercantile Exchange: Get rid of all our feeder cattle today; they'll be going down to hoof level by tomorrow morning. New York Commodity Exchange: Buy 2,000 contracts of gold at market opening and place a sell order at $869.15 an ounce; that's what it will hit at 3:30 tomorrow afternoon. New York Cotton Exchange: offload every contract of cotton we have today, as the price has peaked. Got it?"

"Just a minute," said Izzy. He yelled for another clerk and gave him the list to rush to the brokers at once. Then he turned back to Heller. "Mr. Jet, I don't know how you get these lists. You must know some cow at the Chicago stockyards and some hog at the Federal Reserve. Oy! Such lists! You haven't failed once in thirty days of commodity trading. You know within two, twenty-four, thirty-six hours, exactly what the market will do! You never lose! You buy, sell. Always right on the money!"

"I'm trying to make a few billion," said Heller. "We need it for the spores plant, we need it to buy Chryster back from IRS and the government and you need it to get your plan to take over the world with corporations going."

"Yes, yes. I know that and we are already a half a billion on our way to it. But I'm scared to death. The quantities we buy are so big. If we ever missed, we'd be wiped out. I go have nightmares every night that this will turn into another Atlantic City!"

Oh, I hoped it would! This scene was giving me chills! Half a billion? That was almost twice what I had! Money is power and with enough money, Heller could succeed! All this had been going on, like an avalanche roaring at me down the mountainside, while I was just peacefully whistling.

"Be calm, Izzy," said Heller. "Be calm. Here, come with me. I've been meaning to show you because I can't be here all the time and you'll have to know how to do it."

They walked through the throng of hurrying people. Heller stopped before a blank door and took out a key. "This is the spare office I asked you to give me last month. Now, don't start screeching that I have ruined the decor or something, because I can patch up the holes in the wall and the floor and nobody will know the difference."

They went in. Heller locked the door behind him.

It was a very wide office now because some of the partitions or internal divisions had been removed and were stacked up over at the side.

A huge, long sheet of slate covered the entire far wall. It had white columns painted on it. At the tops of these columns were "Wheat," "Corn," "Soybeans," "Cattle," etc., etc.—all the various things sold on the commodity markets in terms of futures. Under each was a column of figures, very large. Over to the left were columns of times and months of contracts.

Along the far right wall, a set of ticker-tape machines stood chattering away, spewing out tape.

A stack of newspapers littered a desk.

Close to the wall opposite the huge slate stood a contraption that looked like it was built of armor steel. It had a padlock on the back and Heller unlocked it and opened the door.

The time-sight!

Heller stuck his eye to the eyepiece and twiddled a side knob. I couldn't make out the numbers but they seemed to be future numbers on the slate up to, perhaps, thirty hours. At least that was what the digital in the frame was spitting as time.

"Izzy," said Heller, "this is very confidential. The public must not get possession of these. It's a navigational time-sight."

"A what?"

"It reads the future," said Heller. "Right now, if that board is kept up daily, this device reads the future of that board. You can see what it will be reading this afternoon or tomorrow at specific times. It reads whatever is put on the board in the future."

"Magic!" said Izzy in tones of horror. "Divination! Oy!"

"No, no," said Heller. "It's just a machine, an invention. Look into the eyepiece."

"Never!" said Izzy. "Black magic! Necromancy! My mother would never forgive me. My rabbi would go into shock! He'd revoke my bar mitzvah! One must never touch magic! Moses would roll in his grave fast enough to turn the Red Sea into buttermilk!"

"Izzy," said Heller, "it has nothing to do with magic. It's just that time is the dominant factor in this universe and forms the positions of matter in space. The machine simply operates on a feedback."

Izzy was shuddering back, afraid of his future chances in Heaven.

Heller said, "All it's reading right now is future dollar marks."

"Dollar marks?" said Izzy.

"Correct and direct," said Heller.

"Well, that puts a different value on it," said Izzy.

Heller said, "Izzy, I have to come in here twice a day and chalk up the whole board, using the data from those machines. If I get busy on something else, we lose out. I also have to read the sight and figure out what to buy and sell. And you, with your business-administration knowledge, would be much better at it than I am. You could probably make the setup grind out twice as much as I do."

"You mean we would make a billion a month?"

"Whatever you say," said Heller.

"How do you operate the machine?" said Izzy.

"Well, I can't demonstrate that until you take an Oath of State Secrecy. The Fleet is very touchy about these."

Izzy promptly raised his right hand.

"No," said Heller. "Put your hand on your heart."

Izzy did.

Heller said, "Repeat after me: 'I do hereby solemnly acknowledge that I have been entrusted . . .'"

Izzy did.

Heller continued, "'. . . with a secret of state and swear never hereafter to impart its portent or content in any way whatsoever. . . .'"

Izzy repeated it.

Heller went on, "'. . . to any unauthorized person, even under the threat or fact of torture or extinction.'"

Izzy repeated that with his eyes a bit round behind his glasses.

Heller continued, "'And should I violate this oath, I hereby surrender all my rights and privileges as a citizen, my rank as an officer and my name as an individual.'"

Looking a bit white, Izzy did so.

Heller concluded, "'Long live His Majesty!'"

Izzy looked at him, cocking his head over oddly. I knew what had happened. Heller was so used to simply spilling out the Oath of State Secrecy he had overrun it accidentally.

Izzy said, "Long live His Majesty?"

"Correct!" said Heller, hurriedly. "Now I can show you how to operate this."

"His Majesty?" said Izzy. "Then it *is* black magic after all. You made me take an oath to Satan, the King of the Nether Regions!"

I hurriedly grabbed a pen. Heller was skidding right on into an outright Code break. He'd have to tell Izzy now that he was an extraterrestrial, a Royal officer of the Voltar Fleet and a subject of the Emperor, Cling the Lofty.

But instead, Heller replied, "Of course. Isn't it said that money is the root of all evil?"

Izzy thought that over. He nodded. "How do you run the sight?" he said.

I threw down my pen in disgust. Heller was getting too knowledgeable about this planet!

Heller was showing him, in some detail. Izzy, looking through the eyepiece, said, "Wait. Look at those pork bellies! The March contract will go down to thirty-four, the lowest I've ever seen them. Hurry, Mr. Jet. Finish showing me. I can sell them short in the next half hour and make three hundred thousand dollars! Pork bellies will really get us out of the mud today!"

I mourned. Now, with Izzy's expertise on commodity futures, the money would *roll* in!

I turned my attention to the Countess Krak. With Heller making money absolutely at will with the time-sight on the commodity market, she mightn't use her credit card. MY credit card.

Yikes! She wasn't in the fur shop now. She was in an auto sales room—Porsche!

A huge sign said:

Who Cares About the Cost
When You Can Ride
in Foreign Luxury?

A salesman was bustling up to her. She was looking at a sparkling blue Porsche 1002 coupe.

"Do you have any disposable cars?" said the Countess Krak. "We won't be on the planet very long.'

The salesman caught his breath. He, however, was up to it, (bleep) him. He said, "Oh, yes, miss. Disposable cars? That one right there."

She regarded it thoughtfully.

"It's eighty-five thousand dollars," said the salesman. "It's turbocharged for track and street. It's the fastest thing in America. Its slalom is 8.0 seconds, five-speed box, overhead cams . . ."

"I'll take it," said the Countess Krak. "It matches the color of his eyes."

"Time payment?" said the salesman.

"Oh, no. He had a sort of birthday a month ago and the present was a bust. So I'll want the car right away. Tie a nice blue ribbon around it and send it over. And just put it on this Squeeza credit card."

Chapter 2

I was frantic.

I had to act.

In a blur of action, I made up my mind.

I would send Crobe!

Only Crobe could be counted upon to do Heller in!

Ters was in the yard. I flew into the car. With tensely pointing finger, I had him race me to the hospital.

A wild search through the Zanco shelves of the warehouse revealed a third audio and visio set, complete with an 831 Relayer, hidden under the other cases.

With this box under my arm, I sped into the hospital.

Prahd was in the basement operating room, working to alter the fingerprints of a newly arrived criminal. He was fortunately at a rest point and was just telling the hunted man he could go back to his cell.

Prahd looked up and saw me. "Ah," he said, "you've come to tell me my pay has started."

I gritted my teeth. I was in no mood for labor-relations conferences. "Grab whatever you need to install these you-know-whats," I said, "and come with me! You have a colleague in dire peril. There must be no delay."

"A cellologist?" he said, blinking his big green eyes.

"No, *me!*" I said. "Get going!"

He grabbed what he thought he would need. I even helped him carry it.

We got into the car and sped for the "archaeological workmen's barracks."

We hurried down the tunnel. We crossed the vast hangar floor. We went up the cell-block corridor.

I peered in. We were in luck! When there is no sun to watch going up and down, one can lose track of day and night. Obviously, this was the case with Crobe. He was lying in the bunk, sound asleep.

With a firm push on the remote-control button, I activated the bed clamps.

The metal arms swung over and pinned the body firmly to the mattress.

I undid the combination lock of the outer door. I turned the key on the inner door.

Crobe was looking around wildly, staring down at the metal arms and then at me and Prahd. "Wh . . . wh . . . wh . . . ?"

"Feed him the gas!" I said.

Prahd instantly had the mask ready. He clamped it on.

"Wh . . . wh . . . wh . . . ?" sputtered Crobe.

He was out.

I covered the viewport on the inside of the armored door. I thrust the box at Prahd.

"Install them quick," I said. "There is no time to lose."

"Wait a minute," said Prahd. "These are a different type. There are three units. Unit A alters the vision response of one eye so that it sees through solids like metal or clothes or bone, depending on where the person focuses his vision. Unit B is just the usual audio bug. Unit C registers the emotional response of the spy to what he sees."

I looked at the box. He was right. So Spurk had lied when he told me that he had only two units and then lied again when he said they didn't make any that monitored emotions. No wonder I felt justified in killing him and emptying his safe. Spurk was a crook.

"Details, details," I snapped. "Do they all operate as respondo-mitters? Do they have a two-hundred-mile activator-receiver? Is there an 831 Relayer for them?"

"Yes," he said.

"Well, put them in! What are we waiting for?"

Prahd set up some burners and catalysts on the desk. He sprayed the place with disinfectant—it was pretty filthy, as Crobe had not used the toilet to relieve himself—and shortly got to work.

I rushed out. I went to see Faht Bey. He sat at his desk and said icily that he was out.

"You've got to help me," I said.

"That would be a distant day," he said.

"No, no. This affects the security of the base. I have to ship Doctor Crobe to New York."

"You mean he'll be out of this base?"

"Yes."

"Never to return?"

"Yes."

"I'll give you all the help you need."

We made the arrangements at once. Crobe would be put in a Zanco restraint coat—something like a straitjacket they use on Earth, except it is held magnetically and has no ties. Two guards in plain clothes would accompany him to make sure he got there. The guards would have instant two-way-response radio contact with the base in case he got loose or anything went wrong.

While Faht Bey finalized those vital steps, I went back to the cell.

Prahd was working away, using a perpetual scowl mark to cover up the implanting of the bugs.

I looked at the library. Yes, he had been employing the language strips. But the things which showed wear were the psychiatric and psychological texts. Oh, I had been right—he had really been fascinated! He had read them all, several times it appeared! No wonder he didn't use the toilet!

That was what gave me my biggest idea. I went into the false I.D. department and we got to work.

Using I. G. Barben drug-runner blanks, we gave him a passport declaring him to be "Dr. Phetus P. Crobe, M.D." We made a beautiful certificate, making him a doctor of medicine and psychiatry from the Vienna Institute of Psychiatry. Using other blanks, we made him a graduate of the People's Medical Institute of Poland as a neurosurgeon. And we gave him a membership in the Royal British Medical Association as a Fellow.

It was a stroke of genius because I could not be sure he could speak English at all and any strange accent would be accounted for by the different nationalities of certificates. But more than that, psychiatrists always have a funny accent and nobody seems to be able to understand what they are talking about. Pure genius on my part.

We worked hard, for I was going to get him on the morrow's morning plane, come whatever. Heller was out of hand! Crobe would finish him!

I recalled vividly that day when Crobe had positively slavered at the thought of shortening Heller's bones.

Heller could not help but be stopped completely in his tracks!

Chapter 3

I sat at the viewer tensely.

All was going well.

At the Afyon airport I had given Crobe his final briefing. "You once wanted a chance to shorten a certain man's bones," I said. "He was too tall, remember?"

"Funny," said Crobe, "I can see right through you with my left eye. You must have altered the optical nerve."

"Yes, yes," I said impatiently. "Now, listen with care. The Countess Krak is not to know why you are there. You will tell her you are helping the man with a spore formula. But the moment you get him alone, you will handle his bones."

"I can see right through that girl's dress," said Crobe. "She has nice (bleeps). Easy to alter them to squirt semen."

"Pay heed," I insisted. "The man is drawing attention to himself because he is too tall. Cut him down to size."

"On the other hand," said Crobe, "it might be more interesting to change her tongue to a (bleep). That would cure her (bleep) envy."

"Do you hear what I am telling you?" I snarled.

"Very distinctly," he said. "Your stomach rumbles indicate you want a woman. Wouldn't a little boy do? I could fix up his behind so it looked like a goat's."

"You must follow instructions!" I threatened.

"Oh, I intend to," said Doctor Crobe, itching himself inside his restraint jacket as best he could. "Psychiatry is a wonderful subject."

I had to agree with that.

The viewer that had come with the set had only one face. But it had a set of electronic letters all across the bottom that registered the emotion of the person the bug was in. It was pretty hard for me to tell exactly where Crobe and the guards were as their flight progressed, because the viewer only registered the bugged eye that saw at different depths through things, according to what distance Doctor Crobe focused it.

Worn by a spy, it was supposed to be able to read through envelopes or enemy code-book covers and into gun breaches to identify the shell type. But Doctor Crobe wasn't using it for that.

By focus, he undressed every stewardess. The letters of emotion spelled:

DISSATISFACTION

I suppose when this unit was designed, it was thought that it would give a spy-master, ten thousand miles away, the opinion of the spy wearing it as to whether the spy thought the enemy invention was good or bad or to what degree. I wondered if it were just stuck on DISSATISFACTION. How could one visually undress stewardesses and not enjoy it? I know the sight of seeing them running up and down the aisles stark naked made it rather hard on me.

But when they changed planes at Istanbul, there was a shift. A fat man was sitting in a seat across the aisle and behind Crobe and the doctor began to examine the fat man's brain, seeing through the skin and bone. It sure was a weird-looking brain on my viewer!

Crobe seemed to have thought of some way to alter it. The letters flashed:

EXHILARATION
EXCELLENT

Satisfied that the third bug was working, I went out and had breakfast.

Something else was mildly disturbing me. I had missed my appointment with a woman the previous night—which shows how devoted an Apparatus officer must be to duty—and yet Ahmed the taxi driver had left no message today saying how he had handled it.

I had Musef, who was standing guard, go find Ters and get the data.

Musef came back, "Ters said that Ahmed didn't appear yesterday evening."

"Tell Ters to call and make sure the taxi driver will be here tonight," I said.

"Ters," said Musef, "doesn't think he'll come."

"He didn't say why?"

"You can't get much out of him with that crazy laugh of his," said Musef.

That was true. I tried to call Ahmed on the phone. No answer.

Well, maybe he'd had trouble finding a woman to bring. Yes, that must be it. I'd get on to him later when things were less pressing.

Meal finished, I went back to my secret room and the viewer.

I must not miss any part of Crobe's arrival in New York. Too much depended upon it!

I hitched the two-way-response radio close to me, ready to give the guards coaching if anything went wrong.

If Crobe failed, my own life could be hanging by a thread. Heller must NOT succeed!

Chapter 4

It was predawn dark in a February New York.

After a six-hour delay in Paris that pushed my nerves to their limit, Crobe had finally arrived.

I looked at my other two viewers. No visio. Slow breathing. Aha! Both Heller and Krak were sound asleep. Crobe would catch them totally off guard!

His two security escorts got Crobe into an elevator in the Empire State Building. They got out on the right floor. The hall was empty of people and dim. One of them was carrying a big case with operating tools in it. The other one scouted ahead, apparently found the right corridor and door and came back.

They pushed Crobe forward. Then, before they turned the last corner, they got blasticks ready, took the restraint coat off Crobe, and while one stood by, the other took him up to the door with the jet plane on it. He knocked very loudly and then skipped back.

Crobe focused on the door. Then he focused on the inside office, seeing it through the door. He started to walk through it, bounced and recoiled. He probably would not have remained there if his eye had not focused on the cat. It had been asleep on Heller's desk, but had awakened now and was looking at the door to see what all the knocking and bumping was about. Crobe had probably never seen a cat before. Through the door, he was studying it. The digital letters said:

MYSTIFICATION

One of my other viewers had flashed at the first knock. I couldn't tell which one it was, Krak's or Heller's, until I looked at the letter on it: *K*. The Countess Krak had awakened.

She turned on a bedside lamp. She looked at an alarm clock: 5:39. She looked at the window and saw snow on the pane and behind it the greenish glow of the predawn city.

She got up, slid into some slippers, got into a red silk bathrobe and glanced at Heller. He was peacefully asleep, facing the wall.

My plans were not going quite right.

She went out of the "thinking room," closed the door behind her, turned on a light in the main office, crossed the snowy rug and opened the door.

Crobe got his attention off the cat. As the door sprang open before him, he stared.

"The Countess Krak!" he said. The digital-type letters said:

SURPRISE
FEAR

"Come in," said the Countess, in Voltarian.

He moved forward timidly. She closed the door behind him. She said, "Sssh." She moved Crobe over to the secretary-boudoir room, pushed him in and closed the door.

Crobe stood there, staring at her, eyes fixed on the surface of her face. Anyone who had worked in Spiteos was completely aware that the Countess Krak could kill on sight.

"Now, just what are you supposed to do here, Doctor Crobe?" said the Countess Krak.

On Crobe's screen, the letters flared:

TERROR

It was my fault. I accept all the blame. I had not specifically told him she was in New York. I had only told him what to tell her if he met her. Suddenly I realized that he was probably unaware of the relationship between "the man" he was supposed to handle and the Countess Krak. Would he remember what he was supposed to tell her? Or would he mess up and get himself stamped into the rug?

"I . . . I . . . I forget," he said.

"Hmmm," said the Countess Krak. I certainly did not like the sound of that "Hmmm." She knew Crobe's twist for messing up bodies; she had worked making trained acts while he made freaks. She knew very well what he was capable of. She might suspect I had sent him to physically cripple Heller. What she said now would tell all. "What," she said, "did Soltan tell you to do?"

My hair stood up! If Crobe spilled the real data, the Countess Krak would come looking for me and I was a dead man!

Oh, this wasn't going well at all.

Crobe was stammering. My life thread was getting frayed!

It is wonderful what the presence of death can do for the mind. Men have even been known to think.

"I'm supposed to help the man with the spore formula," blurted Crobe. He had remembered.

"Ah," said the Countess Krak. "Well, I am sure your help will be most welcome. Why don't you sit right there?" She pointed to a chair against the wall. "You must be very tired after your long journey."

My two-way-response radio crackled. A guard's voice. "I think he's there all right. We got his bag here. What do we do? Just shove it in the office and come back?"

I said into it, "No, no. You wait right there out of sight. I don't like the way this is going."

"He must have the place bugged," said one guard to the other. "We're supposed to wait."

The Countess Krak was fishing into the upper shelf of the secretary's closet. She was getting down a box. "We'll just refresh you, Doctor Crobe. Relax you so you can get some sleep." She was taking something out of the box.

A hypnohelmet!

I suddenly began to pray. Under that, he might give up the real orders he had. And that would be the end of me.

On Crobe's head went the hypnohelmet. The letters on the screen flared:

DOUBLE TERROR

The click of the helmet switch as it went on.

The letters on the screen shifted:

PEACE

Then they shifted again:

HYPNOTIZED

There was no other vision on Crobe's screen.

Krak plugged in the hand microphone. She said, "Just sit there quietly now and wait."

She put the microphone down.

She went out the door, crossed the office, opened the "thinking room" door and closed it behind her.

She knelt on the bed and touched Heller's shoulder gently. "Dear, exactly what kind of spores did you want?"

He sat up suddenly, the way a man used to action does. "Spores? What's this? Is somebody here?"

"No, no, dear. I just got to wondering."

"I'll get up," said Heller.

"No, no, dear. You've been up half the night rebuilding the new carburetor for the Porsche, and in that drafty garage, too. Just scribble down what you want in the way of spores. I always like to keep up with what you are interested in."

She was handing him a big yellow tablet and pen from the bedside table. Heller yawned. He began to write. He filled up the sheet. She took it.

"It's got to be airborne," said Heller, pointing at the sheet. "It should be able to float in the stratosphere. It has to be able to live on those noxious gases and pollution particles and convert them to oxygen and perpetuate itself. Blown around by the winds of the world, it should be able to depollute the atmospheric envelope of the planet. I don't have the cellology formulas to synthesize it. Say, if you're so interested, maybe I ought to get up and explain it further."

"Oh, no, dear. It's the middle of the night. You just lie back there and get your sleep. Don't mind stupid old me puttering about."

He yawned again and lay back. He turned over and went to sleep.

The Countess Krak went out, closed the door, went to the boudoir and closed the door. She put the sheet in Crobe's hand.

"You will now feel a compulsion to develop the spore you are holding the requirements of. You will now develop the formula for synthesizing it."

She pushed a table in front of him. She laid a tablet on it. She pushed a pen into his fingers.

Mutterings from the helmet. Then, "I don't remember." The letters on the screen read:

CONFUSION

The Countess juggled the mike for a moment. Then she spoke into it again. "You are a young student again. You are sitting for your final examination. The test question is how to synthesize the exact spore required by the details on that sheet. If you do not write them down, you will fail the exam and never be permitted to cut up people again."

Cunning Countess Krak! She had appealed to his basic instincts. She had put him at a time when he did know.

Hastily, Doctor Crobe began to write. He filled up half the tablet. The Countess, watching the paper upside down, saw that he was giving the strains that must be interbred.

She slipped out of the room and went to Heller's desk. She found a book on Earth spores. She took it back.

"You will now look up in this book what you have written and see if they are there."

He did, with much thumbing. I knew what his trouble was. She had put him in a time before he knew any English. But the book had pictures and he was using those.

"They are all in the book," he said.

"You will now put down how to mix the cultures to put them in," said the Countess.

Crobe promptly did.

"You will now write everything else one has to know to accomplish this."

Crobe did. He was finished.

The Countess then said to him, "Will this pass the examination?"

"Indisputably," said Crobe.

"Good," said the Countess. "You are finished with that. Now, pay attention. You remember the man you saw in your laboratory in Spiteos: blond hair, blue eyes, Mancian. If you ever see this man you will become terrified. You will then run and run to be safe from him. You know that if you touch him, tentacles will spring out of your ears and strangle you. One contact with an electric knife or a fingertip upon that man will cause you to cease to breathe. Have you got that?"

"Yes," said the hypnotized Crobe.

"You will now forget everything that has happened here. You will walk out into the office. You will stand by the door to the hall. You will stand there and wait."

She put all the papers in the pocket of her dressing gown. She clicked off the switch and took the helmet back.

Crobe got up. He looked at her in a dazed fashion. The letters said:

FEAR

He went out of the room and into the main office and stood by the hall door.

The Countess went into the "thinking room." She touched Heller's shoulder. "Dear," she said, "why not get up and have a cup of coffee with me?"

Heller sat up, wide awake. He looked at her oddly. But he got up and slid into a white terry-cloth robe.

She held open the door and they went into the main office.

There was Crobe.

He saw Heller.

Crobe screamed!

He turned around, threw open the door and ran with all his might!

Heller turned to the Countess. "That was Doctor Crobe," he said. "What's he doing yelling and screaming and running?"

"The spearmint Bavarian Mocha is a new kind," said the Countess Krak.

"What was Crobe doing here?" said Heller. "Why did he run away?"

"Oh, Crobe? Well, he just brought these formulas to give you. He saw no need to stay. He had another appointment."

Heller looked at the open door to the hall. He took the papers from the Countess and glanced over them.

"Dear," he said, "you look like you've been up to something."

"*Me?* Jettero," she said.

Chapter 5

Doctor Crobe had gone by the guards so fast they had not been able to grab him.

He raced into a stairwell and instead of going down, went up!

The chief guard was on the radio as he ran. "What the blast happened?"

"He saw an enemy!" I cried. "After him, after him! Don't let him escape!"

"He's going down the stairs!" cried the guard.

"He's going UP the stairs!" I disputed. "UP, UP, man!"

Crobe burst out into a hall two floors above. An elevator was open. He dived in.

"He's in elevator number five!" I cried. "He's going down. No, he's going UP!"

The guards were invisible to me. But Crobe wasn't. His elevator stopped. The door opened. He raced out and got to the stairwell again. He was going UP once more. Good Gods, was he trying to get back to Voltar using the Empire State Building as a launching pad?

"Go up to the fiftieth floor, quick!" I told the guards. "And then start running down the stairs!"

They did.

But Crobe darted back into a hall, grabbed an elevator and went up again!

I sent the guards up again in an elevator. They got to the top floor. Another elevator door opened.

Crobe rushed out. And right into their waiting clutches!

"We got him," said the chief guard.

They had him all right. Crobe was looking wildly about. "They're after me, they're after me," he was saying in Voltarian.

The elevator operator, a girl, said, "I'll phone for the building police!"

I told the guard with the radio, "Tell her something, quick."

"It's all right, miss," the chief guard said. "He's just a nut that thinks he's from outer space."

"Oh, one of those," the operator said.

Crobe's screen letters were reading:

TRIPLE TERROR

He was struggling. His eye suddenly focused outside the building and he thought, apparently, he was falling, for he abruptly slumped. The letters shifted to:

OUT COLD

"What do we do?" the chief guard asked me.

THAT was the question. If they brought him back to the base in Turkey, Faht Bey would scream and rant and try to get me to pay for the wasted air passage and maybe even shoot Crobe. A destructive person like the doctor was far too valuable to be shot. In the Apparatus we value a planet-wrecker. Crobe must be saved!

Suddenly, inspiration came to me. There was only one other person I knew who was as potentially destructive as Crobe: Madison!

Only Madison would know how to use this lethal weapon in the war to destroy Heller.

I told the guards to collect Crobe's bag and get him to 42 Mess Street.

That (bleep), (bleep), (bleep) Krak had ruined my first plan but there was still hope.

It was early. There were only the remains of the night watch when they carried Crobe into 42 Mess. The reporter on duty offhandedly told them to wait in Mad's office. They went in and began to fan Crobe with press releases. He revived, possibly from the stink. One of the guards got some hot coffee from a machine, found a bottle of whiskey in Mad's desk and put some of it in the coffee. This further revived Crobe.

There was a roar outside—the Excalibur. J. Walter Madison had arrived.

"Now, put your radio to your ear and tell him what I say," I told the chief guard.

Crobe looked at Madison. The public-relations man was all groomed and sleek, the perfect example of the sincere, honest and appealing young American executive.

Repeating what I said, the chief guard addressed Madison. "Mr. Smith has sent us. We are here to present you with a perfect weapon in the war against the Whiz Kid."

"War?" said Madison. "Oh, no, you have it very wrong. We are engaged in the purest possible public relations and our motives are far beyond reproach."

Acting on my orders, the chief guard said, "May we introduce Doctor Phetus P. Crobe, the eminent psychiatrist."

"Who's talking on that radio?" said Madison, and before the guard could grab it back, he took it. "Hello. Who is this?"

"Smith," I said.

"You must be awfully nearby to be using such a little walkie-talkie," said Madison. "Why didn't you come in yourself?"

I realized I had to think fast. It was awfully close to a Code break. All he had to do was look at the nameplate on that radio to read Voltar Communications Industries. "I'm using Miss Peace's equipment," I said. "I have to be quick because it's in heavy demand. Look over the credentials of Doctor Crobe and I am sure you will be able to use him."

Madison sat down at his desk, laid the radio on his blotter and put out his hand for the credentials. He inspected them.

Unfortunately, Crobe got in the act. He reached across the desk and tapped Madison on the nose. He said, "Deed eet effer oggur to you dat you voot loook moch butter mit a libido instead of a nose dare? Or maybe a bellybutton? Unt your hands. Dey voot loook nicer mit fish flippers." And he got out an electric knife! A guard grabbed him from behind.

Madison stared at him, then snatched a telephone. He push-buttoned very fast.

I raised the sound volume on Crobe's viewer. The answering voice came through from the phone, "Bellevue Psychiatric Section," and then in a musical, lilting voice, "Good morning."

"This is J. Walter Madison, 42 Mess Street. Send a wagon quick."

The guard had retrieved his radio. But he wasn't listening to it. The other one was holding Crobe back from the desk, trying to get the electric knife away from him.

Madison pointed at the outer office with a quivering finger. "You hold him down at the foot of the stairs until the wagon comes!"

There was nothing I could do.

The Bellevue loony wagon shortly came, with all bells clanging. Two white-uniformed attendants leaped out and grabbed Crobe.

The guards, (bleep) them, handed Crobe's suitcase in. They pushed Crobe in. The doors closed.

In a terribly smug voice, the chief guard said into the radio, "Well, that's that, Officer Gris."

"Quick, quick," I said. "Follow that wagon! You've got to rescue him."

"As I was saying, Officer Gris. That's that. Those attendants looked pretty competent. One even had a blackjack handy. Our charge has been delivered into safe hands."

"WAIT!"

"I'll hand this radio over to Agent Raht at the office. If you want to discuss this further, you can talk to him. We're coming home. End of transmission." The radio gave a final emphatic click and went dead.

I mourned.

Chapter 6

Bitter in my defeat, I wandered out into the yard. The day was very cold. The sky was gray. A wind was snarling through the bleak shrubs like a hunting wolf. And it was after me.

I saw Ters. I walked over to him and said, "Where is the taxi driver?"

He gave his evil laugh. "I think he giving Utanc new car a test drive."

"New car?"

"Just deliver this noon. Mercedes-Benz. Brand-new. Very nice. Taxi driver have friend who sell."

I frowned. I suddenly realized that Utanc had *not* come crawling on her knees to me for money as expected. And here she was with a new Mercedes-Benz! They cost a double fortune! Where was *she* getting any money? Credit cards? A surge of rage raced through me. I would have it out with her!

"Where did they go?" I demanded. "Which way?"

"I think Agricultural Station." And he laughed his evil laugh.

I jumped into the car. "Take me there!" I demanded. The station contained Faht Bey's office. Was this some sort of plot to impoverish me?

We roared away. I was looking up and down the road, trying to spot Utanc and the new car. We pulled up at the station. No sign of that car.

I rushed into the hall just outside Faht Bey's office. I was on the brink of stepping through the door. Fortunately, my reflexes are very fast. Faht Bey was in some sort of a conference. I stopped. Several Turkish women and men were sitting around his desk, backs to me.

Faht Bey saw me. He made a motion with his hand, a sign to go away. I backed up quickly.

As I backed, one of the women looked toward the door.

Yikes! Even through the veil, I recognized her as one of the first women I had had in the car!

Faht Bey crossed the room. He came into the hall and closed the door behind him. "Listen," he said, "I wouldn't go in there right now if I were you."

"Some kind of trouble?" I said.

"I don't know yet," said Faht Bey. "In fact, I don't know what it is all about yet. About an hour ago, that woman of yours, Utanc, came by to tell me that some people wanted to see me, and they've just now arrived."

"Have they said anything?" I pleaded.

"Only something about pregnancy. Listen, why don't you come back later? I may know what it is by then."

"Pregnancy?" I said. "Listen, if there's any trouble with pregnancy, it can be handled. Don't promise anything! But it can be handled!"

I rushed out. I jumped into the car. "Take me to the hospital!" I demanded.

If one of those women was pregnant, the answer was very plain. I had not been a Rockecenter family "spi" without learning anything. You handled pregnancy with abortion every time! And Prahd was the man to see on this. I would get his agreement to do an abortion on that woman and everything would be all right.

I rushed into the hospital, through the lobby and to Prahd's office. I leaped in. He was sitting at his desk.

"Pregnancy!" I said. "You've got to handle it!"

Young Doctor Prahd Bittlestiffender looked at me. In a sad voice he said, "I am glad you have finally come to confess."

"I didn't mean to," I said. "It was an accident. She looked so beautiful lying there, I could not resist."

"And you took no precautions."

"How was I to know she would get pregnant just that one time! It was up to her to take precautions!"

"And you expect a young girl to know these things?" he said.

"She's not that young!" I disputed.

"She's young enough that her father is raving mad about it! And she isn't even of age."

A horrible thought struck me. "Who are we talking about?"

"Nurse Bildirjin," said Prahd. "Oh, Officer Gris, to think that you would contribute to the delinquency of a minor behind my back, to leap on her and rape her——"

"Hold it!" I cried. "If we're talking about Nurse Bildirjin, SHE raped *me!*"

"You just confessed that she was just lying there and you could not resist jumping on her!"

"No, no! That was somebody else!" My head was spinning. Suddenly I got a grip on it. "Wait, you sleep with Nurse Bildirjin all the time!"

"No, no," said Prahd. "I take the most careful precautions. You don't think a qualified cellologist would take a chance like that —she being a minor and all. Besides, I've made scope tests and examined the gene pattern, and just like the Widow Tayl's, it's indubitably yours. And now you infer there is some other woman, too! Officer Gris, you should control yourself! You can't just run around impregnating women left and right, day in and day out. And on two different planets, too!"

"Listen," I said. "As a cellologist you would have no trouble at all terminating these pregnancies. I tell you the planets are over-populated anyway. Just perform some abortions and that will be that."

"That would not be that," said young Doctor Prahd. "*That* would be murder. And murder is something not even you can make me do, Officer Gris. Unlike some I know, I have my own moral standards, to say nothing of the cellologist's code. Murder is out!"

"Then what can I do?" I cried, wringing my hands.

"You're asking me after you seduce my girl?"

"Prahd, remember that we are friends, and what is a girl between friends?"

"Trouble," said Prahd. "You see, it wouldn't be so bad if she had not been morning-sick. Her father is the leading doctor of the area and noticed it. And she told him. You probably know that his favorite sport is quail hunting. That's why he named his daughter Bildirjin, which means 'quail' in Turkish. He's one of the best shots in the country and he has one of the biggest shotguns. And as she is a minor, you could also go to prison. Have you ever seen the inside of a Turkish jail?"

I was beginning to moan.

He continued, "I think he has a thing about cutting off testicles, so possibly shooting off yours would be how his mind is running right now. However, if you would really take my suggestion . . ."

It was too much. I could no longer stand his sadistic chatter. It was obvious he, too, was after me!

I rushed out of his office. I looked up and down the corridor. Thank Gods, it was way past hours when the town doctors worked in the free clinic.

I sped to the car. I leaped in.

"Take me home, quick!" I pleaded. In the villa I would be able to fort up and defend myself!

In the yard, I was out of the car before it stopped moving. I raced across the patio and into my room. I barred the door and stood there with my back against it, breathing hard.

What a disaster! How was I going to get out of it?

There was a knock. For a moment I thought that Nurse Bildirjin's father had followed me up. Then I realized that the sound came from the secret tunnel door.

The father would not know about that. I opened it cautiously.

There stood Faht Bey.

He came in looking over his shoulder fearfully.

He spoke in a very low voice, "This is real trouble, Gris. I told you I would let you know when I had found out. Well, unfortunately, I have found out. It is pretty awful."

I got a grip on the bottom of the bed. I would take it like a man. "Tell me," I said.

Faht Bey shook his head sadly. "Are you sure that you can take this?"

"Go ahead," I said, bracing myself further.

"It's pretty bad news," he said.

"For Gods' sake, tell me," I pleaded.

"You know the taxi driver, Ahmed."

"Yes, I know the taxi driver, Ahmed!"

"He's going to testify that it was at your orders."

"WHAT was at my orders?" I screeched.

"And it very well could get him off."

"Testify to WHAT?" I begged.

"Maybe you better sit down in the chair there," said Faht Bey. "This is pretty awful."

I collapsed.

"Here," said Faht Bey, taking a bullet out of his shoulder gun and putting it between my teeth. "Bite on that and you won't break your molars when I tell you."

I bit on it.

"You know that the taxi driver they call Ahmed is really a convicted criminal from Modon."

I nodded.

"Did you know that the driver Ters is a Turkish communist who just served twenty-seven years in jail for murdering the general?"

I shook my head the other way. This was not going very well.

"For the past several weeks," said Faht Bey, "the taxi driver has been going out with this Turkish murderer in that car with your name all over it. The way they worked was to go to a farm and look over the women, and if they found a good-looking one, they would tell her husband and the family that it was at your orders that they burn the whole farm down unless the woman consented to spend an evening with you in your car. And that if anyone went to the police, that farm, nearby farms and the closest village would be put to the torch."

I bit on the bullet. The taxi driver had been keeping that fee for himself!

"That's not all," said Faht Bey. "They told the woman that if she hadn't pleased you, they would murder her husband."

I clamped down harder on the bullet. That explained those beseeching looks I had mistaken for a plea to be with me again in the future!

"This all came out because they thought I knew you and somebody suggested they come see me for advice."

Utanc! In a jealous rage, she had set them on me!

"But that's not all," said Faht Bey. "When the taxi driver and Ters came to the rendezvous, first Ahmed and then Ters raped the woman first."

My teeth were sinking deeper and deeper into the brass. No wonder the women had been so tired. No wonder they had always been so moist! Those (bleeped) (bleepards) had kept me waiting for half an hour while they both (bleeped) away and then they had called me to take their leavings! They must have been shrieking with laughter over it!

"One more thing," said Faht Bey. "This is adultery. In the *Qur'an* it states that the punishment shall be one hundred lashes for unmarried persons. But these women were married, so the punishment for you would be entirely different. The *Qur'an* states that in such a case the offender shall be stoned to death."

That settled it. The powder in the cartridge case spilled bitterly into my mouth as my teeth pierced it through.

I would have to leave Turkey.

There was no other way.

And I would have to leave Turkey AT ONCE!

Chapter 7

I grabbed a bag. I looked around wildly.

Where would I go?

What would I take?

Faht Bey said, "If you are leaving, I want to remind you that the *Blixo* will be in, in a day or so. They always have something for you. What do I tell them?"

My attention snapped painfully back to him. The *Blixo*? They were probably after me, too!

Faht Bey went on: "Those homo couriers you get always demand postcards for some reason. You better give me some."

Postcards? Postcards? I made my mind focus. He was talking about the magic mail cards. If they didn't get mailed on time, their mothers would be killed. That would make the couriers go after me, too!

I opened up the safe. I grabbed the whole pack of magic mail cards. I threw them at Faht Bey.

Where would I go?

What should I take?

I ran around the room looking under things.

Faht Bey was still there. He said, "If you're going to run out, there's nobody here can stamp cargos in. They have to be stamped in as received on Voltar before they leave. Why don't you give me your identoplate?"

I fished it out.

I threw it at him.

Enough was enough. "Get out! Get out! Get out!" I screamed at him. "Can't you see my sanity is on the ragged edge? STOP BOTHERING ME! I have to think!"

He gathered up the postcards and identoplate and left.

Only then could I begin to get my wits in order.

What should I take?

A tough problem when you don't know where you are going to go. The only destination I had was OUT!

Blind instinct saved me.

I opened the grip. Into it I packed guns and ammunition so I could defend myself. I packed the phoney Inkswitch federal I.D. so I could change my identity. I grabbed some instant gas pellets that would render any assailant unconscious and packed them. I snatched up the two-way-response radio and packed it. I stuffed in the three sets of viewers. I strapped the grip up. Then I realized I had forgotten to put in any clothes and unstrapped it. I put in a business suit, some shirts and ties and a combat camouflage dress. I strapped it up. I realized I had not put in any money. I unstrapped it. I looked in the safe and found I didn't have any money. I strapped the grip up once more. I wondered if I had forgotten anything and unstrapped it to look. I grabbed some things at random and threw them in, just in case. I strapped it up again.

It suddenly occurred to me I hadn't left yet. I had better get going. I started out the door. Then I realized I was not dressed for travel. I came back. I got into a business suit. I couldn't find any shoes so I put my military boots back on. I started out the door again and saw I had forgotten my bag. I went back. I needed something to discourage pursuit. I saw a pile of plunger time-fuse bombs in the gun case. I stuffed them in my pocket.

Wait a minute. My documents were in the grip. I needed a passport. The Achmed Ben Nutti diplomatic passport from the United Arab League was on top of the pile. It would get my guns and money through to wherever I was going. I put it in my pocket. Money. I didn't have any money. I must avoid Afyon: they would be waiting for me with a pile of lethal rocks and stones. I had it. I must get to Istanbul. Mudur Zengin would welcome the chance to give me money.

As an afterthought, working fast, I closed and locked my safe and secret compartments. I must get out of here. They might come for me at any minute.

I picked up my grip. I forced myself to stop shaking. I walked across the patio and into the yard.

With a surge of purest hate, I saw the taxi driver. He was polishing the new Mercedes-Benz.

Apparatus training makes one rise to any emergency. The hate distilled into the purest cunning. I determined then and there to kill two jailbirds with one bomb. They would learn in one last agonizing flash the penalty for grabbing women before I could get at them.

Cunning. Cunning. Cunning. I must concentrate on that. I went over and threw my bag carelessly into the Daimler-Benz. I did not even let my eyes dart under every bush to see if they were waiting for me, ready to spring out and stone me to death.

In an offhand voice, I called, "Oh, Ahmed. Would you like to come to the bank with me to get some money?"

He sprang gladly upright. I knew he would. He yelled for Ters and then raced around and got in the front seat of the big car. Ters ran out of the kitchen, putting on his old soldier's cap. He slid under the wheel.

We were off. I scrunched way down so nobody could see I was riding in the back.

We went tearing up the road to Afyon, scattering camels all over the place.

I could tell from the gay, insouciant manner of both Ahmed and Ters that they had no slightest inkling that this was their last day on Earth.

We entered Afyon and started down the street toward the Piastre Branch Bankasi.

"No, no," I said smoothly from the back. "You misunderstood me. I was talking about BIG money. I meant the Piastre Bankasi in Istanbul. Go there."

Happily, without the least suspicion they were driving their own hearse, they turned and we began to roar along the main highway to Istanbul.

Glancing backward from time to time, I detected no pursuit. I had been too fast for them. I might get away with this yet.

Several camels looked at us suspiciously, however, and some of my anxiety returned. Never trust a camel.

Ters was not driving very fast. But that was just as well. High speed would alert people that I was escaping.

The afternoon and the bleak February countryside moved along. Dusk came. We drove in the darkness. Our headlights flicked now and then upon the ruins of the ages. I was leaving Asia. Let it rot. It wasn't worth conquering anyway. Alexander's adventures had been but a waste of time.

We crossed the Bosporus into Europe about ten. We finally crossed the Galata Bridge over the Golden Horn and wove our way through the dying streets of Istanbul. We came at last to the Piastre Bankasi. The car came to a stop.

I intended to have the inevitable night watchman call Mudur Zengin. I had gotten this far and I was safe. But this was the end of the line for Ters and Ahmed. I slipped a time bomb with a plunger fuse under the cushion of the rear seat. I depressed the plunger. Ten minutes from now, this car and its villainous occupants would spatter all over the landscape in bits of dismayed and burning flame. Bye-bye, you woman grabbers.

I tossed my grip out onto the sidewalk. I got out. I said casually, "You can go home now. I won't be needing you."

"Don't you want us to take you to the airport?" said Ahmed.

"Airport?" I said. "What gave you the idea I was leaving Turkey? I'm just going to be in town three or four days, attending a convention of drug pushers at the Istanbul Hilton. You didn't think I would pay to keep you two in a hotel all that time, did you? So bye-bye. You're homeward bound," to whatever Hells they reserve for criminals who grab women first and then threaten to testify that it was all at my orders.

Ahmed shrugged. Ters gave his evil laugh. And away they went. I watched their taillights fade out of sight. It gave me a great deal of satisfaction. There wouldn't even be enough left of them to bury, for that was a Voltar maximum-destruction pocket bomb.

A moving shadow called my attention suddenly back to my own peril. But it was just the watchman.

"Phone Mudur Zengin for me," I ordered. "Have him come down to the bank. Say Sultan Bey wants to see him."

The watchman shined a flashlight in my face. Then he pointed to an upper window. It was lighted. "He's already here," the watchman said. "Came in half an hour ago and said he was expecting you."

A chill went through me. Then I realized it was true. The credit companies kept an accurate, to-the-minute check on the whereabouts of the paying man. They had told Zengin.

I must be fast. I raced inside. I entered his office.

Coldly, Mudur Zengin remained at his desk eyeing me. He did not rise. He did not even say hello. He just sat there and looked at me. I stopped in the middle of the room.

"I've been requested to detain you," Mudur Zengin said.

Terror surged through me. They knew. They were after me!

I went down on my knees. "Look, you were the boyhood friend of my father. Please don't turn me in! You've got to help me. I need money!"

"I can't give you any money. The vaults are closed."

"Then let me into the safe deposit boxes."

"I can't. They're closed tight. Nothing will be open until 9:00 A.M. tomorrow."

Too late. Too late! They would have dragged me halfway back to Afyon by then.

"I need dollars!" I begged.

"Dollars?" he said coldly. "Why don't you ask your concubine for dollars?"

"Mudur, please hear me. I need dollars and I need them right now. Tonight. FAST!"

He fixed me with his cold banker's eye. "The only dollars available at this time of night are not the bank's. They are my own. I keep some in my personal safe."

"Give them to me," I begged, my ear cocked for any sound of footsteps on the stairs. "Quick!"

"It would only be enough to tide you over," he said. "And it would have to be at regular terms: 30 percent interest per month."

He pushed a piece of paper at me. I swiftly signed it.

He went to his safe, opened it and took out some packets of U.S. dollars, counted off a hundred thousand and then tossed them on the floor and pushed them toward me with his foot.

I bent to grab them. I stuffed them in my pocket. Then I saw the contempt in his eyes. It struck me that he was certainly behaving in an unfriendly way. Rushed as I was, I still said, "What have I done?"

"What you have done," he said, "is between you and Allah. It is not given to a mere mortal to comprehend the actions of such as you."

He walked over and gave me a shove toward the door. "Good night and, I hope, good-bye."

Chapter 8

As I stole out of the bank, I knew my problem was threefold:

A. Get out of Turkey

B. Not get caught

C. Cover up my trail

In terms of pure theory, it seemed elementary. In fact, the Apparatus continually pounded *B* and *C* into one. They were the basis of practically every operating plan.

But theory is one thing and being in the middle of the night in Istanbul, Earth, surrounded by skulking enemies and pursued relentlessly by pitiless women who had noses like bloodhounds, was something else.

The minarets of a thousand mosques stood around me with pointing fingers. The very clouds were liable to open and drown the world with the voice of the Prophet hollowly commanding that the words in his *Qur'an* be followed: STONE THE ADULTERER TO DEATH!

Spooky. You can never tell about these primitive religions. They might come true suddenly. The very towers of the mosques might cave in on me to do just that.

I kept my wits. I had to. Nobody else would want them. Gods, how I had been taken in by those women!

Looking up and down the street I saw that Mudur must have miscalculated. He would want me under obligation on a note before he called the police. I would outwit him!

Running like a hare, clutching my bag to my chest, I got the blazes out of that district.

I ducked and dodged down numerous alleyways and streets. No pursuit yet. As I ran, I laid my careful plans to escape and cover my tracks.

Ahead I saw a small and mean hotel. I slowed to a sauntering gait. I had a cunning plan for the first stage. Police, when they want to trap a criminal they expect to be in a hotel, surround it. They would think I was inside when I was outside, and I would be able to detect them.

I went in. The clerk, if you could call him that, was sound asleep. I woke him up and told him I wanted a room. Without opening his eyes, he reached up, got a key and handed it to me.

Stealthily, I went up some stairs. I found the room. I went in and hid my bag. There was a drain pipe. I slid down it.

Through an alley I made my way up the hill to some always-open stalls around the Great Bazaar. There were no throngs at such an hour. Many shops were closed. But I soon found what I wanted: an Arab-and-Oriental-clothing shop. The place smelled suffocatingly of mothballs and camels. A single electric bulb shined down on racks of tangled merchandise. I pawed through them. I was looking for a *djellaba*, a hooded cloak. I wanted the kind that Arab chieftains wear. I found one. It was of soft, yellow wool. A bit ornate, since it had a border of embroidered gold thread, but it would have to do. I found a turban. I found some baggy pants. I found a gold-embroidered waistcoat and a shirt. I found a bandolier with lots of pouches.

The proprietor, suspecting thieves, woke up. He was very fat and yawning. He looked at me strangely. He began to add up the items I had selected. He yawned. "Eighteen thousand lira," he said.

"Nine thousand lira," I said.

Then he did something very suspicious. He shrugged and nodded! He did not try to bargain! I knew what that meant. He was hoping to lull my natural alarm.

I got out a bill. My Gods! Mudur Zengin had only given me thousand-dollar bills!

I had no choice. I had to give it to him.

"I'll have to wake up Muchmud the moneylender next door to

get the change," he said. My suspicions were confirmed! He was trying to detain me!

I was very cool, however. "Go ahead," I said.

He was gone for over five minutes! I knew he had called the police. He said, "Here is your change. Ninety-one thousand lira." It was an awful wad. It contained small bills. He thought I would delay long enough to count it. I would fool him. I didn't. I shoved it in the bundle.

He looked at me strangely. Then it hit me what this was really all about. He was making sure he would have my full description. He knew what clothes I had bought. He would tell the women what they were when they came to question him.

I was up to it. I executed item *C*. I would cover my trail.

While he was lying down again on his couch, I pretended to have trouble tying up my bundle. I bent over and slid a time bomb underneath a clothing rack. I pushed the plunger.

I walked out.

I went down the hill. I did not run.

Ten minutes went by.

KERUMPH! BLOWIE!

The shop and a lot of others around it flew into the sky in a pyre of orange flame. The concussion broke a window near me.

That part of the trail was covered. The women would never get my description out of him!

I felt reassured. But I remained very watchful. I approached the hotel. There were no police around it. My trap had not been sprung. Probably they were merely late. I had better be quick.

I scaled the drain pipe. It was only four feet long. I got back into the room.

Way off up the hill I could hear police and ambulance sirens going. A good diversion. Maybe that was why they had not come to the hotel. Clever of me.

I opened my suitcase. I took off my Western clothes. I got into the balloon pants and shirt and vest. I put the bandolier over my shoulder. I put my military boots back on. I tied the turban and got into the *djellaba*. Quite a change!

I transferred the remaining bombs and U.S. money to the pouches of the bandolier. I got my diplomatic passport and put that in a pouch. I stuffed the wads of Turkish money into my waistband: it was far too lumpy for the bandolier containers.

I repacked the suitcase with the clothes I had taken off. Then, with sudden decision, I took out a Beretta Model 81/84 .380 caliber. It was a lightweight pocket size and it held thirteen rounds in its magazine. I put it in the inside pocket of the *djellaba*. I looked around. I had left nothing in the room. I strapped my grip back up.

Now I would cover my trail.

I took a time bomb, put it under the mattress and pushed the plunger.

I went downstairs. The clerk did not fool me. He was pretending to be asleep. I would look very ordinary: I laid the key and a hundred-lira note on the desk. I sauntered out.

There were no police around. My distraction in the Great Bazaar had worked. Flames were really shooting up over there.

Not attracting attention to myself, I walked at normal pace through alleys in the direction of a thoroughfare.

I found a cab. I woke the driver up and got in. I would red-herring my trail. I said loudly, "Take me to the Istanbul Sheraton."

He drove off.

KERUMPH! BLOWIE!

The hotel went up!

I had covered that part of my trail.

Geysers of orange flame bulged into the sky.

The cab slued slightly with concussion.

"What was that?" the hacker said.

Aha. Trying to get information to tell the women later! I would handle that.

We drove along. He started into a shortcut up a narrow and deserted street. "Stop here a moment," I said.

He braked.

I hit him over the head with the Beretta butt. He fell sideways.

I got out. I pushed him onto the floor in front. I got in and started up the cab. I knew where I was going. It was not the

Istanbul Sheraton, Gods forbid! I had to get out of Turkey.

I knew where I was. I headed for a ferry pier on the Golden Horn.

I passed mosque after mosque. Istanbul is absolutely crowded with mosques. All ready to fall over and stone one to death at the command of the Prophet. Nerve-wracking. But I held on to my nerve.

The ferry pier was deserted at this time of night. I knew it would be. I got out. I removed my bag. I put the taxi in low gear. I walked beside it, steering. I stepped away.

Roar—SPLASH!

The waves raced outward in the dark.

Bubbles came up from the sinking cab.

I had covered one more part of my trail.

I ran back and got my grip. I knew exactly where I was bound now.

Speeding along the shore paths which ran perpendicular to the jutting piers, I came to a jammed fleet of fish boats.

I halted. There was enough ambient light from the city and enough paths of it across the water for me to make out exactly what I wanted.

At the end of the nest lay a vessel about ninety feet long. It had the exaggerated height of bow and stern compared to the waist that characterized the smaller ships which plied the Sea of Marmara. She had the high masts which permitted her to let out nets, and even sail on occasion. By the dock light I could see that she had a yellow and black triple stripe which ran the length of her gunwale, making an exaggerated curve. That she had been pushed out to the edge of this cluster told me that she was waiting there to go to sea at dawn.

I stepped down onto the nearest deck. I clambered from gunwale to gunwale, the boats rocking and groaning in the otherwise quiet night. I got to the edge of my choice. I saw the name. It was *Sanci.* That checked me for a moment. *Sanci,* in Turkish, means "stomachache." I don't like the sea any more than I like space.

But stern duty called.

I went aboard.

There was a little house toward the stern, sitting in the smell of fish. I pushed open a door.

A huge Turk was snoring on his back. He was the biggest Turk I had ever seen. So he must be the captain.

I fanned him awake. I did it very cleverly. A fistful of spread lira can make quite a breeze.

He woke up in midsnore. His eyes riveted on the lira.

"Sail now," I said, "and take me to the Greek mainland, and it is yours."

That brought him up, sitting, with only one scratch at his chest hair.

"How much?" he said.

"Forty thousand lira," I said.

"Eighty thousand lira," he said.

"Seventy thousand," I said, "if you shove off right this minute."

He got off his bunk and reached for his coat and cap. "I go to wake the crew now," he said, but he kept on standing there.

I took the hint. I counted out thirty thousand lira. "You get the other forty just before you put me on the beach."

He took it with a grunt and went to wake the crew.

Shortly the ship began to bob with activity. They were shortening up their lines, ready to cast off.

I looked at those other craft that I had walked across. One of them might have had a watchman who had seen me.

I could take no chances.

"Just a moment," I told the captain. "I think I left something on the dock."

I stepped swiftly across the intervening decks. I gained the pier. There was a small house there.

I took out a time bomb. I set it for long fuse, half an hour. I laid it under the edge of the hut door and pushed the plunger. I stepped back across the boats and to the ship.

They cast off.

The engine barked and sputtered and complained. The screw churned a wake. We sailed down the Golden Horn. We rounded Seraglio Point. The Ataturk Monument loomed in silhouette against a strangely illuminated sky.

KEROOMP! THUD!

Masked by the point and monument, the bomb flash painted an already blazing sky.

I looked back. I had covered my trail.

The sky above Istanbul was orange with continuing flames.

I was on my way!

There is nothing quite like Apparatus training to help you when you are in peril.

But I was not safe yet!

PART FORTY-ONE
Chapter 1

Down through the Sea of Marmara, down through the Dardanelles, twenty-one hours of retching, twenty-one hours of Hells.

I sat in the fish-stink cabin of a mate and puked my guts out into an evil-smelling bucket. The *Sanci* was well named! But no stomachache could compare with what I was experiencing. A bad head sea was being pushed along by a wind which originated in the Aegean and got worse tempered every mile.

More was against me than the wind. At first I had kept watch across the waters as the lights of Istanbul receded into a distant blur: It seemed inevitable that the Turkish navy would come roaring out to seize me, and I had made up my mind to sell my life at the highest possible cost. But then the pitching began to get me. In danger of going overboard as I vomited at the rail, I was pushed by the captain into the mate's cabin and given a bucket. The captain said he did not want to lose the balance of the payment.

At first I was so sick that I was afraid I was going to die. Then I became so much sicker that I was afraid I wouldn't.

Gradually, between retches, I began to ponder, as a man will, how I had gotten into this. Was there not some other way of life which would avoid wildly running spacecraft and madly pitching fish boats? Was it not possible that some sedentary vocation existed which steered wide of these things? I was simply not constitutionally adjusted to this lifestyle.

Hour by tortured hour I began to sort it out to certainty.

A dented, rusty bucket in which fish scales were sloshing around with vomit makes a remarkably good crystal ball. One can see quite clearly that much future of this kind was definitely hazardous to one's health.

So I began to wonder what had placed me in such a state. The threads of Fate, somewhere in the past, must have begun to weave this horrible tapestry.

As the gray day wore on and the gray wind whipped gray whitecaps out of the gray, polluted sea, the grayness of my mood condensed upon and added to a pure black certainty.

HELLER! If he had not undertaken the original survey of this planet, I would not be here. I would not be in this terrible plight—pursued by demon women, blown upon by malign and sneering winds, rocked and jolted about until my stomach no longer added anything to the bucket but noise.

HELLER! If it were not for his sense of duty as a combat engineer, the Widow Tayl would never have come back into my life. Nurse Bildirjin would not be now posing the menace of shotgun charges and marriage.

HELLER! If he had never appeared upon the scene, that fatal call from Lombar, so long ago, would not have interrupted my hunting trip, and right now, instead of watching anxiously for blood to spew into the bucket, I would be pleasantly shooting songbirds to my heart's delight in the Blike Mountains of Voltar.

HELLER! He had turned them all against me: Meeley, Ske, Bawtch, Mudur Zengin, Karagoz, Faht Bey. He had plotted, plotted and plotted some more to get me into trouble. Prahd, Krak, Ahmed, Ters and all this hellish crew of screaming demons would not be haunting me and sneering at me and standing with the Prophet in the clouds egging the women on to stone me to death.

HELLER! Oh, how very clearly I understood at last that it was all his fault!

HELLER! I vowed a holy vow upon the bail of the fish bucket that if it took the rest of my life, short though it might be, I would wreak vengeance upon him for all the suffering he was inflicting upon me with such sadistic glee.

When it became totally clear to me what had gone wrong with my life, I knew exactly what I must do.

I must go to New York. Regardless of any personal danger, regardless of any travail, I must end Heller once and for all. For the good of the Confederacy, for the good of Earth, for the good of all life everywhere, I must handle this menace to all the universe: HELLER!

Having come to that firm and dedicated conclusion, I felt easier.

It was a sign of Fate that at that moment the captain came in and told me we had arrived.

It totally confirmed my conclusion. The ship had ceased to pitch and I was no longer ill. It shows one what a completely right answer can do!

Chapter 2

We lay in the lee of the land. The black mass of a hill loomed in the luminescent dark of midnight. By a thin, cold sliver of a moon, a thin line of whitish beach showed about a mile away.

"Greece," the huge captain said, pointing. "When you pay, we put you ashore."

I knew what I had to do. Cover my trail.

I went into the cabin. I boosted my grip up on the bunk. Covering what I was doing by turning my back to the door, I got out a very flat stungun. I strapped my grip back up.

Using a dirty pillowcase, I stuffed in the Turkish lira. I put the stungun in the impromtu bag.

Turning to the door, I saw that the captain was still at the rail outside.

"I will pay you," I said, "when you have a boat in the water and have given orders for me to be rowed to the beach. Then you can have this." I hefted the pillowcase of money and then, with a handful, showed him what it contained.

The fool barked his orders. A rubber inflatable with an outboard was put over the side. Two crewmen got into it.

I beckoned the captain into the cabin. This captain and crew knew what I looked like. They would probably call the nearest Greek police. Even if there was no extradition treaty for adultery between Greece and Turkey, I could take no chances. This captain and crew might tell the women when they came to question them. I had to cover my trail. Besides, there was no use in throwing away money that could be converted back to dollars.

I edged around to the door so that I was closer to it than the captain. I closed it behind me as I held out the sack.

"There is something extra in it," I said. I reached in as though to take it out and show him.

He smiled broadly.

My hand closed around the stungun butt.

I shot him through the pillowcase.

The dull thud of the stungun was followed by the slap of the charge and then by the clatter as he fell into the bunk, knocked out.

My hands expertly went through his pockets. I found the thirty thousand under his belt. I put it back where it belonged: under mine.

I emptied the pillowcase and stuffed the rest of the money into the inside pockets of my cloak.

I set a half-hour delay on the plunger of a time bomb, put it under the mattress and pushed the thumb plate.

I picked up my grip. There was nothing here that I wanted now. I certainly did not want that awful fish bucket!

Stepping on deck, I closed the door behind me.

Two crewmen were in the inflatable. Others were standing at the rail. I went over to them.

I said, "He's counting the money. You men probably won't see much of it, and I so appreciate your trip that here's a gift."

I tossed a handful of lira into the group.

Madly they batted at the floating bills, trying to get them down.

The stungun was on broad beam. I fired rapidly.

They fell.

The two men in the boat tried to spring up. I shot them. They fell into the water.

From the deck, I picked up the bills I had thrown and put them under my belt.

I put my suitcase in the inflatable. I stepped down into it. I cast it off.

The outboard motor was some kind of a Balkan comedy of

levers and corroded bars. I tried to start it. I pulled the cord and pulled the cord and pulled the cord again. Nothing happened! It would not even cough!

The inflatable was drifting away from the dark bulk of the ship.

Suddenly there was a bustle aboard.

The engineers! I had forgotten there would be engineers below!

Swearing, Turkish and lurid, came from the ship.

Silhouetted in the moonlight, I saw a man with a rifle at the rail!

A bullet knifed a phosphorescent path in the water to my right. The explosion of the fired gun buffeted me.

I drew the stungun. I shot. It was on broad beam. It would not reach that range!

Another shot from the ship!

No phosphorescent path!

A sigh of escaping air!

The inflatable had been hit!

I threw the stungun lever to narrow beam. I aimed.

The rifle went off again!

I fired.

The man on the deck dropped.

Another one was trying to grab the rifle.

I aimed and fired again!

The other one dropped.

The inflatable was sinking!

I looked wildly for a paddle. None!

Hastily, I flung myself down in the bow of the collapsing craft. I dog-paddled in the water madly, getting back to the ship.

I caught a trailing line.

I started to get aboard the ship. I remembered my suitcase, stumbled back and grabbed it. I lost the line. I sprang with all my might, caught it again, and clambered on deck. I looked back. The inflatable completed its sinking.

The bomb! I had to get off this ship fast!

There was a rowboat in the waist of the ship. I cut its lashings and began to inch it to the rail. I got it there.

I looked about for oars. All I could find was the rifle.

I pushed the boat over the rail. I dropped the suitcase and the rifle in. I got in. I shoved myself away. That ship was going to explode!

Using the rifle stock for a paddle, I headed toward the beach. So slow, so slow! The boat behaved like a crazed thing. It went to the right and it went to the left. I had to switch paddling sides continually.

Foot by floundering foot, the rifle splashing wet and cold, I crawled at far too slow a pace toward the beach.

Each time I looked at it, the beach seemed to be no nearer. A crosscurrent seemed to be taking me parallel to the shore.

I valiantly redoubled my efforts. At last, progress! The beach was coming nearer.

Suddenly the whole sky behind me went orange!

Flame shot up a hundred feet in the black night!

BOOM!

The concussion hit me.

I thought I was all right.

Then the rowboat began to rise in the air!

A tidal wave!

The crest was breaking!

On the shoreward side of it, the rowboat and I plummeted toward the beach!

What speed!

Fast as a racing car rushing through the foam-white night!

Rocks were ahead! They came like speeding blobs of black straight at me!

Over the tops of them I went.

The rushing roar of water ended suddenly with a splintering crash!

I was stunned by the impact.

I did not know what had happened.

The water was going away but the rowboat and I weren't.

I was high up on a strip of beach. I was sitting in the shattered wreck of a rowboat which no longer had a bottom and only splinters for sides.

I looked back at the inky sea. I was through with it. No more sea for me! One more black mark against Heller!

A voice said, "Are you from that exploded boat out there?"

Chapter 3

He was a very old man. He had two dogs with him. He was peering at me in the thin moonlight.

Tragedy. My landing had been observed. My trail was not covered.

But I masked it. I said, "Where am I?"

"The island," he said.

Oh, treachery. I knew I never should have trusted that villainous captain. He had not landed me on the mainland as agreed, but upon an island.

Then a new horror hit me. The old man had spoken in Turkish! I do not speak Greek!

Oh, Gods, the women would find me yet. And the Prophet still must be sitting in the clouds above, ready to stone the Hells out of me.

I'd better make the best of this and find out which way to run. "What island?" I said.

"Limnos," said the old man.

I was too shaky on geography to be sure, but I had never heard of such an island as being part of Turkey. It didn't sound Turkish. My hope was dim but I asked, "What country?"

"Greece," he said.

"Then why are you talking Turkish?" I snapped at him.

He picked up a piece of the rowboat. Despite the paleness of the moon, one could clearly read *Sanci*. "This and your clothing." He pointed east. "Turkey is over there only twenty-five miles and my wife came from there."

He didn't fool me. He was just trying to detain me until he could call the police. If his wife was Turkish, she would know all about it. Women stick close together. And they are very treacherous.

"You better come up to my hut," he said. "Then I can call somebody to get you."

I played it very cunningly.

He saw my grip and picked it up and started to walk up the beach, beckoning me to follow. He was, of course, going to lead me into a trap. I followed him, knowing what I would do.

The two dogs kept sniffing at me. I knew that they had spotted who I was. I had to include them in my plans.

The hut was a very mean hut. There were some other buildings around. They all seemed deserted.

He sat me down at the table and got out a bottle of *ouzo*. That confirmed my suspicions. He was going to get me drunk so they could pick me up without a fight.

I, however, continued to remember my careful Apparatus training: Be clever and cunning when you are not safe, and as no one can ever be safe, be clever and cunning always.

"Where is your wife?" I asked.

"Dead for years," he said.

"And these other buildings? The people?"

"All moved to the cities. Gone now."

"How far to the nearest town?"

He pointed south. "Moudhros. Quite a ways."

"Nobody else around?"

"Just me. I retired years ago. I fish some. Drink your drink. You must be chilled to the bone. I'll have to walk over to the road and make a call."

I had everything I needed to know. And he was not going to detain me, drunk, while he brought the police. As he stepped out the door, I shot him with the stungun. It was on full power, narrow beam. It blew his head half off.

The dogs objected.

I shot them.

I dragged all three bodies down to the beach. I pushed the

remains of the rowboat down into the water. I put the bodies in it. I buried the fragment that had the ship's name on it.

People, if anyone ever came this way, would think they had been blown up by the exploding ship. And then cast ashore by the tidal wave.

I had covered my trail.

I went back to the hut. There wasn't much blood and what specks there were I obliterated.

The old man had had another suit of clothes. His Sunday clothes, I guessed. The Greeks wear Western things and white shirts without a tie, most usually.

I stripped. I dried out my clothes over the fire. And while they were drying I ate some biscuit I found and drank some water.

I opened my grip and packed my Arab things. I put on the old man's clothes. They did not fit very well so they looked very Greek.

It occurred to me that I would have trouble, not speaking the language. So I put a wad of cotton in my jaw and tied a rag under my chin and over my head. I could pretend I couldn't talk because I had a toothache.

Ready at last, I hefted my bag. It was quite heavy. But there was nothing I could spare from it.

I was on my way again, with vengeance in my heart for Heller!

Stumbling through the dark night, I made my way up a long path and came at last to a deserted road.

I walked south.

I walked and walked and walked.

It was very arduous but I had incentive. Whatever it took, I was going to get the man who had caused me to have to do this. And nothing was going to stop me!

In the dawn I came into a straggling town. It was not much.

Sitting at the end of a long pier was a small ship. A plume of smoke was coming out of the funnel. It was an interisland ferry such as ply the Aegean.

I flinched. Not more sea!

But what could I do? I had to get to the mainland. Unlike some they say once existed on this planet, I could not walk on water.

Only the sacred mission of final destruction on which I was engaged gave me the fortitude to set foot on that gangplank.

I went up it. Someone came out of a passageway and glanced down the gangway at the dock.

I looked behind me. A chill went through me. Several people were now walking up the dock. Some of them were women!

I tensed myself to run.

The man said something to me in Greek. He must be asking for money. Tight spot! I had no Greek money! I could not display Turkish money! It would open up the trail!

With great presence of mind, I reached to a pocket and fished out a U.S. thousand-dollar bill.

His eyes popped!

He grabbed the money and ran off. My hand tightened on the gun in my pocket.

He came back with another man!

More people were coming up the dock.

I was penned in!

There were too many! I did not have a machine cannon.

My lips formed a soundless prayer.

The new man had a box. He was chattering. It must be what they kept their electric cuffs in. I couldn't understand a word they were saying. He was opening it up. My hand felt hot and sticky on the gun butt in my pocket.

They had the box open. They were pointing at it. The first man waved the thousand-dollar bill. He pointed at the box again, chattering insanely all the while.

The word *Piraievs* kept occurring in his speech. Suddenly, I knew the word. Piraievs was the entry port of Athens, its seaport.

My knees almost buckled with relief. He was telling me, evidently, that he did not have enough change and would give it to me in Piraievs.

I nodded weakly.

The first man pushed a ticket in my hand.

I tottered into a lounge bar and unpried my sticky hand from the gun butt in my pocket. I looked at my palm, thinking it had never been that sweaty before. It was not sweat. It was blood from broken blisters formed in packing that (bleeped) grip. So I wasn't as nervous as I had thought.

I got into a corner seat where I could keep the whole room under surveillance. One part of me dreaded the moment the ship would sail, the other part of me couldn't wait to get it away from the dock. Was I turning into a schizophrenic, torn asunder by a split personality?

I began to itch. The itching got worse. I began to itch in several places at once. Nervous hives. According to psychology, when one is under an enormous strain, he tends to itch. If psychology said so, it must be totally true. But I didn't think I was nervous to the point of a nervous breakdown. I wondered how the crew would cope with me if I did have a nervous breakdown. I was sure a ferry didn't carry a doctor.

The itching grew worse and worse. Yes, it must be true that I was coming apart with a nervous breakdown.

Then something small and black was moving on my hand. I looked at it. Bubonic plague? Was I breaking out with bubonic plague spots? Oh, I hoped not. They would put me in quarantine and hold me until the Turkish women could find enough stones!

But wait. Bubonic plague spots don't move. They also don't jump.

I looked closely at the speck, which had leaped to my knee.

A FLEA!

Oh, Gods, the old man was getting his ghostly revenge! Associating daily with those two (bleeped) dogs, his clothes were full of fleas!

The things I was having to suffer because of Heller!

Only the grim determination to get him at the end of this tortured trail kept me going.

The ship had moved away from the dock. It began to pitch.

My stomach decided the old man's biscuits were too much.

I was shortly at the rail.

And each time I threw up again, I repeated my sacred vow.

Heller was going to pay for this. He was going to pay for it all!

It was the only reason now that I cared to bear all this and live.

VENGEANCE!

HELLER WOULD PAY!

I repeated it in every lull between the times that I threw up.

At least I knew who was responsible for my woe. And I was on my way to do something about it!

It was all that got me through that dreadful voyage.

Chapter 4

At Piraievs, where we arrived after an agonizing day and night, I found, with a shock, that I was out of bombs. I could not blow up the ship. It made me very nervous.

I would have to be more cunning and crafty than ever. Now that the ship was no longer moving, I had time to squeeze my brains for every scrap of Apparatus technique that I would need to get through this. At least I was out from under the Prophet in the clouds. The Greek Gods live at Mount Olympus and that was far to the north. So there was some hope they wouldn't notice me passing through.

Mingle with the crowd: that is an Apparatus must. The instant I started to do so and go down the gangplank I was accosted by someone rushing up.

He spotted me! I flinched. Due to the disembarking people I could not back up. I cringed as he reached out his hand.

He was holding a sack. He jabbered something as he shoved it into my hands. Expecting a bomb, I still thought it would look better if I glanced into the sack before I threw it in his face and ran.

I looked.

Drachma! A huge paper sack full of drachma, all in small bills. It was my change.

I rushed off the ship.

A bus carried me to Athens. But this was no time for cultural walks around the Parthenon. I had had quite enough history. What I needed was a change of clothes. It would help me to cover my trail.

A main street in Athens was very modern with shops. My purchases were very swift. A raincoat, a suit, socks, shirt, tie, hat. I paid for it all with drachma. It hardly made a dent in the bulk of the money. They were not expensive clothes.

I did not dare go to a hotel. They take your passport number and name. I took a cab to the airport. I bought a one-way to New York. I used drachma. It was a coach cut-rate fare. I still had plenty of drachma left.

The airport building provided a washroom. I went into a toilet. I put my suitcase on the seat. I got out of the old man's clothes. I didn't have any way to destroy them. I put them in my suitcase.

I brushed a couple of fleas off my skin and got dressed in the new clothes. I took off the bandage and removed the very saturated wad of cotton from my jaw.

I put my guns in the suitcase. It was too full now to put any of the money in. I had ninety-eight thousand U.S. dollars, ninety-one thousand Turkish lira, all in small bills, and twenty-nine thousand drachma left, also in small bills. What a wad! Enough to stuff a mattress.

My newly purchased clothes had been in a couple of large sacks. I stuffed the money in those. I would carry this money, my ticket and my diplomatic passport, and leave everything else in the grip. I strapped it up.

Back at the counter, I flashed my phoney United Arab League passport and had them put diplomatic tags on the bag to check it straight through to New York.

I had an hour to wait for my flight. As I crept across the airport waiting room, trying to be inconspicuous, one of the tattered sacks the money was in broke. I hastily snatched at it before it could reach the floor. A narrow escape! Turkish lira could have spilled out all over the waiting room. I shuddered at how that would open my trail.

With some drachma, I bought an oversized flight bag. I was cunning. It had *Air Israel* all over it. Nobody would expect anyone from the United Arab League to be travelling *Air Israel*. "Confuse the trail" is an Apparatus motto.

In a phone booth, I stuffed the money into the new flight bag. I crammed and crammed. It was awfully hard to get it in. When I finished, the zipper would only partly close. It was the best I could do.

With what relief did I hear my flight called!

And shortly I was aloft, leaving historic Asia, Troy, Athens and Olympus behind me. When you are in an airplane, you know who is overhead: Rockecenter. He owns most of the controlling stock in most of the world's airlines, and his bank, Grabbe-Manhattan, holds their mortgages, ready to foreclose if they even dare get out of line. As a Rockecenter family "spi," I was secure in my entrance to that Heaven.

But all told, it was a nerve-wracking trip. People on the plane around kept darting their hands this way and that, and for a bit I was sure they were reaching for guns. Even the stewardess began to make these sudden moves.

I studied them carefully. They were scratching themselves.

THE FLEAS!

Oh, I was so relieved to find it was only that. Because it seemed to be the growing fashion, I was even able to scratch myself without embarrassment.

There was only one other incident of note on the plane. The man in the seat beside me, scratching away, began to look at me suspiciously. I felt naked without my guns and no more bombs.

When they served a snack, I secretly stole a plastic fork off the tray. It was quite sharp. I hoped they did not detect the theft for it helped my morale enormously, there in my breast pocket, ready to stab if he recognized me and called the captain.

These one-way coach fares, economy, don't always get you there very fast. With long delays while they let the first-class planes go by, I finally arrived at John F. Kennedy Airport in New York.

On my diplomatic passport, I went through with a swish. The customs man for hand luggage—who sits just beyond the cooled corpse at Immigration—looked at me and then at the *Air Israel* bag a little oddly. But he pushed me through. I glanced back to see if the Federal police were massing up for a baton charge to grab me. But

behind me the embalmed officials were only scratching.
I had made it to U.S. soil!
Also, the God over the U.S. is Rockecenter. So I was safe.
Now to begin my retribution trail with a vengeance!

Chapter 5

I went out to the cab rank, followed by a porter carrying my grip.

The first cab in the line had a very squat and crumpled-looking driver, who actually got out to open the door for me. He didn't have any forehead and his eyebrows covered his eyes.

The porter threw the bag on the floor in back and stood there with his hand out. I knew I was in America.

I tried to get in the cab. The porter was in my road. I saw I was not going to make it. Not unless I bought him off. He could still call the airport police. They stay in constant communication through the Nazi Gestapo headquarters in Strasbourg, which operates under the name of Interpol. They have a huge radio station down in South America and use the lines of CIA to radio on ahead of planes and grab people they don't like or who aren't criminal enough to join their ranks. So I was not out of danger so long as I was on airport ground. I decided to tip him.

Because it would have been a dead giveaway to try to change the lira and drachma at the Grabbe-Manhattan airport-lobby bank, I had decided I would get driven into town to the Times Square area where they have lots of money-changing companies. That would be where I paid off the cab. So I didn't have any small dollars and I certainly wasn't going to tip him a thousand U.S. bucks—not for grabbing a grip out of my hand and tagging me out.

I gave him a drachma.

He pretended he didn't know what it was.

I gave him a lira.

He pretended he didn't know what that was.

I pretended to rummage around in the flight-bag money. I said, "I don't have anything else."

The taxi driver verified it. He tumbled the money about. He spotted the thousand-dollar U.S. notes at the bottom. But he kept his mouth shut. He turned to the porter and said, "That's all he's got in here. Buzz off."

The porter said something nasty and left.

We had a lot of trouble zipping the bag back up. With the taxi driver's help I finally made it.

"Take me to Times Square," I said.

I got in the cab. He drove a few feet out of the rank and stopped. "Just a minute," he said. "My radio is busted and I have to phone in to the dispatcher."

He was gone for five minutes. He came back. His radio came on, asking for Car 73. That was the number on the card hanging on the back of the driver's seat. "Dumb (bleepch)," he said. "I just told her my radio was busted." He shut the receiver off.

At a leisurely pace he drove out of the airport. He turned left. Some signs said Brooklyn and Floyd Bennett Field. We tooled along. Cold wind was blowing in the open window. I looked to my left and saw the ocean, or at least a bay.

"Hey," I called to the driver, "aren't you going the wrong way?"

"I'm taking you the scenic route," he said. "You being a foreigner, I thought you'd like to see the sights. I'm not even charging you an extra dime. See? The meter is off."

Some sights. Cold winter had not yet turned into spring. The gray, gray water was only visible from time to time.

We were on the Shore Parkway, according to the signs. We certainly were not moving very fast. Another sign said Spring Creek Park, Next Left. We came to a turnoff marked 14. The taxi turned.

It sure wasn't very scenic; the trees all dead with winter. There was even a sign that said Park Closed. But the taxi driver drove along the deserted winding roads. To the right and left were only desolation and leafless trees.

Suddenly a log came crashing across the road, dead in front of the cab!

The driver braked frantically.

There was a roar!

Three motorcycles leaped into view and stopped, two in front and one behind the cab!

The riders wore bandanas tied across their faces!

They had guns pointed at the cab!

"Throw down your guns!" the nearest rider said. "All passengers out! And don't try nothin' funny! We got the drop on you!" A stagecoach holdup! I knew! I had seen them in the films. The next order would be to throw down the Wells Fargo box! And I had no gun handy!

Gingerly, I moved out of the cab, holding my hands high.

The nearest rider stepped out of his saddle. He walked up to me. He gave me a push back. He reached into the cab and picked up the flight bag full of money!

He glanced into it.

He backed out and threw it to another rider. Then he turned to me. He reached into my pockets and got my wallet. He took it. He reached into another pocket and started to pull out my diplomatic passport. It was stuck crosswise.

"I will give it to you," I said. I reached up. But I didn't reach for the passport. I reached for my breast pocket.

Quick as a flash I pulled out the plastic fork.

I jabbed it into the back of his hand with all my might!

"He's armed!" he screamed.

I dived under the cab.

A gun exploded!

Something hit the cab.

Three bike motors were roaring.

They were gone!

The taxi driver was holding his shoulder. "The dirty (bleepards)!" he said.

Hastily, I dived back into the cab. I unstrapped my grip. I got out the Beretta.

The cab driver stared at it wide-eyed. It was pointed straight at him.

"Get after them!" I gritted. "And quick!"

"I can't drive!" he moaned. "I'm wounded!"

I leaped out and opened his door. I booted him sideways and got under the wheel.

All set to drive, I had no place to go. There was no motor sound anywhere. Only the wind.

"Where are they going?" I grated at the driver.

He crouched on the floor in the empty place they usually put luggage, beside the driver's seat. "I don't know," he moaned. And then he passed out.

No honor amongst thieves, a thing I knew too well. They had shot their confederate. They had probably also given him a false rendezvous.

On the run myself, I could not go to the police. If he told me anything at all, it would be just to lead me into another trap.

I sat there, hoping they would come back, now that I had a gun. But what would they come back for? They had the flight bag full of money. They had my wallet. They even had my diplomatic passport.

Any credit cards were in that wallet. But I could not use credit cards. The instant I presented one, the credit company would know exactly where I was. The full pack would come in on me from all over the world and stone me to death.

I dared not call Mudur Zengin.

The thought of going back to Istanbul made my forehead prickle with sweat.

If I called the New York office, they might turn me in.

I was in the U.S. without a penny to my name. I didn't even have anything valuable to sell. It was still cold winter and I had no idea whether I could survive sleeping in a park.

Wait a minute.

I knew where there was money.

A safe full of it.

It was early in the day.

Desperate and dangerous though it might be, I had only one place I could go.

Oh, it really put the chills up and down my spine to think of it. But not a soul would ever suspect I would go there.

I would complete my mission to end Heller's mission yet!

I started up the cab.

I headed out of Spring Creek Park. At Exit 14, I went away from Jamaica Bay and headed northwest. I worked myself on diverse streets, moving over toward the Manhattan Bridge. I crossed it, making the correct turn to the right, and got on Franklin D. Roosevelt Drive. I turned off to make my way toward Rockecenter Plaza.

My teeth gritting, but determined, I was heading stealthily for the apartment of Miss Pinch.

Chapter 6

I parked the cab in an alleyway three blocks from the apartment of Miss Pinch. It was early afternoon and I knew I had lots of time.

It seemed a shame not to cover the trail again with an explosion but lack of bombs had me stumped. The hacker was still lying on the floor. He had not bled very messily. He was breathing shallowly. Served him right.

I wiped off all the fingerprints from places I might have touched. It really seemed a shame not to properly cover the trail. It left a loose end. They train you in the Apparatus never to do that.

Then I had an inspiration. It seemed highly probable that his radio was in working order and that he had just been pretending.

Watchful that I left no fingerprints, I turned it on and pressed the mike switch. "Dispatcher," I said.

"Yes," she said.

Aha, he *had* been lying!

"Miss," I said, "this is Officer O'Grunty. Your cab Number 73 is blocking an alleyway," and I gave her the address. "Your driver is creating an awful scene. He's claiming he is part of a gang that is about to steal the Holy Sepulcher from Christ. He's even pretending he's been shot, complete with fake blood. Would you please call the Bellevue Psychiatric Section for us and have them send the wagon?"

"At once, Officer," she said. "I always suspected that (bleepard) was nuts."

I put the mike back on the hook. I picked up my bag and

walked away. It wasn't perfect, as nothing had been blown up. But if he tried to identify anybody, they wouldn't listen to a crazy. Maybe they'd even throw him in a cell with Doctor Crobe! I cheered up. I had covered my trail.

Now for the dangerous part: Miss Pinch. It would be untrue to say that as I approached that fatal place my skin did not crawl or that I could not taste mustard. But such was my dedication to the sacred trust of ruining Heller, I didn't even permit myself to flinch. Some things simply have to be done, come what may.

It was hours before either Miss Pinch or Candy would be home from work. I walked down the basement steps and past the garbage cans. I inspected the contents briefly: kleenex smeared with lipstick fresh as blood, beer cans that were still wet, a half-smoked joint and a newly broken rubber truncheon. That was all I needed to know. They still lived here and were up to their old tricks.

Masked from the street in the deep stairwell, I got out some picklocks and went to work. The iron grill was easy. The door had lately had a key jammed in it and was very abrased and stiff: it showed me they suspected nothing or they wouldn't have left a lock in that condition; it was very easy to pick.

When I opened the door I was hit with a blast of stale marijuana smoke and perfume. My hair tended to stand up but I smoothed it down, with iron control. I had my plans.

I took my bag inside. I checked to be sure there was no evidence of my entering. I closed and relocked both doors.

The main front room I would avoid. I knew it had a bank camera in it and if I guessed right that camera was keyed to the safe, and if anyone tampered with that safe the camera would start to take pictures. There even might be a connection to Miss Pinch's office. No, I would avoid that room. Just then I don't think I could have stood the sight of that bed and the shackles in there or the torture instruments, like cans of pepper and bottles of Tabasco sauce. I had been under strain lately.

I went down the hall that flanked the rooms. I looked out the rear door: The garden was just a mass of tin cans and leftover snow. The board fence around it prevented any view in.

I opened the hall door to Candy's room. Gingham everywhere, pink and white. Organdy curtains and a bedspread stained with lipstick.

Good. I would now get dressed for combat.

Something bit me. This had been going on for quite a while and I was getting tired of it. Here was my chance to get out of these clothes and get rid of some fleas.

I put my suitcase on the boudoir seat and opened it. I took out another gun, my Ruger Blackhawk .30 caliber. I laid it handy to the door with my Beretta. I could not be too careful. I knew exactly what I was dealing with. But also I knew I had to get the combination to that safe, which only Miss Pinch had. And I had the exact plan of how to do it.

But I had lots of time. There was a closet there. It was full of clothes, both Candy's and Miss Pinch's. I suddenly found something astonishingly apt for my plot.

It was a black silk kimono, very long and very big. It had an embroidered design upon the chest. I recognized it at once! It was a figure with two heads: At one end it was a horned dragon, at the other it was a fanged snake. The Ninja! They were a cult of outcast assassins, the most deadly secret executioners of Japan. How apt!

I promptly got out of my clothes. I went into the shower and let it run and run, washing off several fleas. It was a relief.

The towels were all lipstick stained so I dried myself with a wad of Candy's underwear.

I put on the Ninja kimono. Now I certainly looked the part. I grinned at myself in the boudoir mirror. If these two lesbians knew what horrible things awaited them today, they'd both collapse from shock and heart failure.

Oh, I would get that safe combination all right.

I took two objects out of my suitcase. I picked up a pillow off the bed.

I went out into the hall. I put the pillow down behind the front door so I could be comfortable. I sat on it and gently musing, grinning with glee from time to time, I waited.

Candy usually came home first. What a horrible shock was going to be hers today!

I wondered idly if there might not be something to the philosophy of one of Earth's truly great wise men, the Marquis de Sade, renowned propounder of sadism. When in Rome, do as the Romans do, they say. When in the apartment of Miss Pinch, the behavior pattern she set was almost impossible to attain. But I fully intended to go one better than even Miss Pinch's wildest nightmares.

I chuckled now and then, sitting there in the dark behind the door, savoring my plan. A master of Earth psychology was about to improve even upon the Marquis de Sade.

Chapter 7

The sound of footsteps coming down the basement entrance steps. The sound of a key being fitted in the iron grate. The groaning sound of hinges as the grill opened. The fumble of a key searching for the slot in the second lock.

I crouched back, waiting.

She came in the door.

Candy!

I gave her no chance to close it. I rose up with a smooth and stealthy spring!

My left arm went around her throat to shut off any scream.

My right hand quivered in front of her face. My thumb broke the capsule of five-minute knockout gas.

I let up on her throat.

She inhaled to cry out.

She didn't cry out. She went down like a pile of laundry, out cold.

I closed the doors.

I took hold of her foot and dragged her down the hall and into her bedroom.

I worked fast. I tore off her coat. Her shoes hit the floor. Her dress went flying to the back of a chair. One stocking went one way, the other soared up and draped over a chandelier.

I stood and looked down at the unconscious body with a triumphant grin.

She was really not a bad-looking woman.

But I had no time for any more scenic wonders today.

I put a wad of stockings in her mouth and gagged her with her own brassiere. I took down a piece of laundry line on which they hung their undies in the bathroom. I cut it and used the shorter piece to tie her hands behind her. I used the longer piece to strongly secure her ankles together. I had it all planned out.

I left her there on the floor. I closed the hall door to her room. I made sure there was no sign of struggle in the hall. I cat-footed back to my position behind the door. I laid out the Beretta and the Ruger just in case. The next one would be trickier, for it would be Miss Pinch. She was the vicious one.

I crouched down to wait. Sixteen minutes went by.

Footsteps on the basement entrance stairs. The crackle of paper as though someone were juggling a bundle. The sound of the bell. It rang but once. There was no one with her, then, for I knew the other signal.

Would she think Candy had not arrived yet? I held my breath.

Another rustle of paper.

Triumph! A key rattling in the grill lock. The groan of its opening. The rattle of another key in the door.

It opened!

"Candy?" called Miss Pinch as she stepped into the hall.

I sprang.

My left arm went around her throat.

She kicked backwards with her heel!

A bag of groceries crashed to the floor.

She was trying to turn.

My right hand was in front of her face. The second five-minute gas capsule burst under my thumb. I eased her throat. "God d . . ." I kicked her. An intake of breath.

Down she went to join the grocery sack!

I averted my face to avoid the dispersing gas.

I closed the grill and made sure it was locked. I checked for any telltale signs outside. I closed and barred the door. Then I pushed the second, padded door securely into place.

I was in a soundproof apartment with Candy and Miss Pinch.

Now I would show the Marquis de Sade a thing or two!

I grabbed Miss Pinch's right arm and dragged her into the front room. The place was much as I had seen it that agonizing last time. There were even some mustard and Tabasco smears on the huge bed. The torture implements were in their usual places but even more caked with dust. But it was no time for scenic tours.

I tore her mannish hat off her head. Her hair spilled out. I got her out of her topcoat and threw it aside. I stripped off her jacket. I unbuckled her belt, grabbed her pants cuffs and, taking her shoes with them, unshucked her out of her pants.

Her mannish shirt would not come off until I realized the tie was holding it on. I got rid of that. I pulled the shirttail over her head and got her out of it.

She was wearing men's shorts! But that wasn't the most astonishing thing. She had on a flesh-colored bra! I had never noticed it before. I thought she had been almost without breasts. It had no straps. It was sort of molded to her. I put my fingers under it and ripped. Off it came. It revealed perfectly normal female breasts! She had been wearing a breast compressor to make them appear flat! Well, well! The trouble some lesbian "husbands" will go to, to appear like men!

I yanked off her right sock and threw it in the air. I yanked off the left sock and it soared to impale itself upon a shield of swords. I stared at her. She was a far less masculine female than I had thought in my past deliriums.

But I would have to move fast. I only had those five minutes and after that the thin lips of Pinch were going to start their acid profanity again.

I had her ready now. I boosted her up on the huge, broad bed. I shackled her right wrist, I shackled her left wrist, I shackled her right ankle. I shackled her left ankle. And each to its nearest bedpost. Then I grabbed each chain in turn and tightened it taut so that she was spread-eagled face-up on that bed.

Ah, what a satisfactory sight! Turnabout is fair play and the worm had turned. Miss Pinch was at my mercy. And Gods, was she going to get a shock!

I went and got Candy. She was conscious now. Her eyes were shifting wildly. Tied though she was, she tried to cower away. Gagged as she was, she still tried to scream. Wonderful!

I picked her up and took her into the front room. I threw her down on the side couch. I stretched her out on her back. Working and holding her down at the same time, I lashed a third rope to her right ankle, which was nearest the couch back. I passed the rope through a slit where the back met the cushions. I passed the rope under the couch and tied her left ankle. Then I untied the original ankle rope. I spread her feet wide apart despite her kicks and lashed her there. When I finished she was spread-eagled on that sofa so thoroughly she couldn't even wobble away.

With considerable satisfaction, I stood back. I admired my handiwork. No Earth Boy Scout could have done better. I had earned my merit badge.

Very shortly now, Miss Pinch would be babbling the combination to that safe. I would have money. And I would be on my way to avenge myself on Heller.

The Apparatus had never had a better pupil than myself!

Today I was going to triumph! Marquis de Sade, pay attention!

Chapter 8

No psychiatrist ever gazed at the lacerated brain of a patient with more pleasure than I enjoyed when I saw the look in Miss Pinch's eyes after she came awake.

She had struggled up through the haze of gas into the horror of seeing her dear Candy, gagged and writhing, defenseless on that couch.

Miss Pinch had yanked at each chain in turn with no more result than a worm trying to lift the world. Less. She couldn't even flex her muscles!

You would have expected recriminations, revilement and vituperations. You would have expected things like "Inkswitch!" and "You (bleep)!" and "I'll have your (bleeps)!" I know I did. But nothing passed those deadly, compressed lips. Not one word. The eyes were saying it all!

I put my hands on the lapels of the Ninja kimono I was wearing. I rocked back and forth on my bare feet. I smiled at her in a deadly way. She was faced with a master psychologist about to outdo the Marquis de Sade. I was in no hurry. We had the whole night. No screams would penetrate these walls—that I knew too well. No sudden rescue would occur. But still, just looking at Miss Pinch, I had to cover up a feeling of ill ease. Act casual and relaxed. That was part of the plan. But don't forget for a moment, I whispered to myself, that you are looking at one of the most tricky and dangerous creatures alive: Not only was she a woman, she was also Miss Pinch!

I would be fair. Before I began on Chapter Two of the Apparatus field manual on torture, I would start with Chapter One: Pretend a friendly attitude at first, it increases the eventual shock of horror which is to come. But sometimes they break at once.

"Miss Pinch," I said, "I cannot tell you how glad I am to see you again. And to observe how healthy you are." Good stamina makes them last longer. "But I am a great admirer of yours. I have often thought of you for hours on end. So come, let us be friends right from the start, here. If you give me the combination to that safe, I will simply take my money out and be on my way. You've often said it yourself: It is my money. This isn't even robbery. So how about it? What is the combination?"

Her lips sealed even tighter.

Ah, well, there was no hurry. I went out into the hall and picked up the groceries so no caller, looking in, would see the disarray. I brought them back. I put the pizza in the freezer and the cans of beer in the Iron Maiden fridge to cool. A homey, domestic touch.

I looked at Candy. She was throwing her head from left to right, eyes wild, trying to spit out the gag. I trailed a finger down her throat and then made a mysterious circle with it before her face. Incomprehensible.

Miss Pinch lay there, tight-lipped, staring.

I loosened Candy's gag and took it off. She instantly screamed. Good.

I wandered casually around the room. Two sets of eyes followed me. Drag it out. Don't let them know what you're really going to do.

Candy stopped screaming. I got out a beer. I opened it. I extended it to her. "You usually have a beer this time of day, Miss Licorice? No? Well, you probably would rather have it in the usual place, now that you are screaming." I walked over and laid it against her foot. I moved it up and down a bit.

Candy screamed.

"You're really in good voice tonight," I said. "But come, dear Candy, you are in no danger at all. All Miss Pinch has to do is give me the combination to the safe and I will go away so peacefully, you'll never know I was here." I moved the beer can up and down.

"Pinchy!" cried Candy, looking beseechingly at the bed, "For God's sake, give him the combination to that safe."

Miss Pinch compressed her lips more tightly.

I pried open Candy's mouth and poured a small amount of beer in it. She choked. She spat it out. She turned her head to the bed again. "For God's sake, I don't know what this monster means to do! Please, please, Miss Pinchy! PLEASE!"

I put the flat of my hand on Candy's chin and began to rotate it gently. She stared at me in horror. She looked down and saw how naked she was. She strained at her bonds.

I moved my hand to her stomach and rotated it around. Then, circle by circle, I went lower and lower. Just before I touched between her legs, I stood back. I took a sip of beer.

Casually, I wandered over to the record cabinet. I put the beer down and began to go through the collection.

Two sets of eyes watched me, two birds staring at a snake.

I read record labels. I went further and further down the stacks. Then I saw a pile that was at the extreme bottom and the back, covered with dust. Aha! These must be records they hated and never played. In a cloud of dust, I took them out.

LOVE SONGS!

The very thing! How they must despise them, to bury them so deep! I slid them out of their jackets and stacked them on the automatic spindle. I dropped on the first platter.

"What are you going to do?" screamed Candy.

The music had begun. I gestured at the devil-mask speakers. "Let this be your theme song for tonight, Miss Candy Licorice."

The drum began a pound, pound, pound.

A tenor began to love-croon:

> *When I gaze into your eyes,*
> *I see love, love, love.*
> *When I try you on for size,*
> *I feel love, love, love.*

When I press your gushing breasts,
And I feel your thighs' caress,
I feel love, love, love.
Go into me!

Candy began to thresh about. Her eyes got wilder and wilder. She screamed. Then she turned her head sideways. She shouted, "For God's sakes, give him the combination! He's going to rape me!"

Miss Pinch compressed her lips tightly. I looked at her. I said, "She is absolutely correct."

I opened up the front of the Ninja robe and stood, facing Candy.

Candy stared at me. Then she screamed, "Jesus Christ!"

I walked over to her. I looked at Miss Pinch. I said, "You're the one that's making her suffer. All you have to do is give me the combination."

Miss Pinch's lips shut tighter. Her eyes fixed on me. It was a battle of wills.

I put a knee on Candy's couch. I looked again at Miss Pinch. Nothing but tight lips.

Candy was threshing her head from side to side, frantic!

I put my other knee on the couch.

Candy screamed!

I looked at Miss Pinch.

Tight, closed lips.

Suddenly something stopped me.

I stared at Candy in amazement.

She stared back at me in terror.

I had to keep my mind on the real business here. I looked at Miss Pinch. I said, "Your little wife here is a virgin! If I keep on, she isn't going to be a virgin anymore. One last chance. Tell me the combination to that safe or I open this one!"

Miss Pinch's lips were even tighter shut.

I said to Miss Pinch, "It's you that's doing this."

The devil-mask speaker grinned.

"Here goes!" I said.

Candy screamed louder than the music, by far!

She threw her head back and went unconscious.

The turntable went round and round.

Miss Pinch's eyes were unreadable.

The turntable went around and around.

Candy came to. She glanced sideways at Miss Pinch and then began to moan.

The beer can tipped over and gushed its foaming contents across the floor.

Candy screamed.

The legs of the sofa did a jumping waltz.

Candy's eyes rolled up into her head, leaving the whites showing. She slumped.

She was out cold.

Miss Pinch's eyes were unreadable. Her lips stayed sealed.

Candy's hair was trailing down to the floor. She was totally unconscious.

I stood up, pulling the robe around me.

I opened another can of beer. I took a sip. I walked over to the foot of Miss Pinch's bed. "You see what your stubbornness has done. You have caused poor Candy to break the most sacred Psychiatric Birth Control laws. You have caused her in your crass unfeelingness even to betray the holy name of Rockecenter. There she lies, no longer an innocent virgin." I pointed to her trailing hair, which flowed down from her unconscious face. "Alas, you forced her to be violated. She is a fallen woman!"

Miss Pinch said nothing through her compressed lips. Any reaction was utterly undetectable. What a heart of stone!

But I was not baffled very long. I knew what would frighten her. I said, "Even though you are a monster, Miss Pinch, I cannot help but feel compassion for you. Should you persist in this foolish attitude, I cannot answer for the dire consequences to you personally."

No change in the way she looked at me.

I felt some qualms. Good Gods, this woman must be made of solid brass!

I said, "More blood may still be spilled today. You better give me that combination before this gets out of hand."

Stony silence.

"Very well," I said, "you are reaping a whirlwind around your own head."

I walked over to the record player. I made sure the next record was ready to drop.

I took a sip of beer. Then I went over to the bed and got up on it on my knees. I held the beer can high and let the foamy liquid pour upon her stomach.

"You better give me that combination, Miss Pinch!"

No change in her eyes and lips at all. Not even a flinch!

The record dropped. Violins whined and sobbed.

I was opening up my robe. "Not much time left!" I said.

Miss Pinch looked at me. No change.

The devil mask grinned and a male crooner began to sing:

> *Sweet little woman,*
> *Please marry me.*
> *Man and wife together,*
> *How happy we will be.*
> *And then we'll have some kiddies,*
> *Maybe two or three.*
> *So here's the ring and there's the church,*
> *Oh, come, my honey be.*

She was trying to get some slack in the chains and lift herself higher on the bed.

The sock hung on the sword-rack points as I said, "If you don't speak, then here we go!"

Her hand was convulsively gripping the chain.

The turntable was suddenly stuck in a groove on a replay of the record:

> *How happy we will be . . .*
> *How happy we will be . . .*
> *How happy we will be.*

"Hey!" I said, "YOU'RE A VIRGIN TOO!"

Her eyes were wild. She was trying to fight upwards.

"Oh, to Hells with the combination!" I said. "This is too good!"

The devil mask grinned as she screamed.

Her eyes rolled all the way up in her head. She conked out.

The turntable went round and round. It had gotten off the groove now and had jumped to the rest of the song:

> *Oh, sweet woman,*
> *I am your guy,*
> *Sex with you and me,*
> *Is pie and ecstasy.*
> *Oh, sweet woman,*
> *Come to your man,*
> *You are my bed and butter,*
> *So drink me if you can!*

Miss Pinch had regained consciousness.

She was tugging at the chain with a hand that convulsed rhythmically.

The turntable shifted to a new song.

A woman's husky voice filled the room:

> *Long and slow,*
> *And up we go,*
> *The moanin' and the groanin'*
> *Is because I want you so.*
> *Long and slow,*
> *And down we go,*
> *The beggin' and the pleadin'*
> *Is to make you do it mo'!*
> *Long and slow . . .*

A beer can, teetering back and forth on the stereo, suddenly exploded. Foam flew all over the room.

The feet of the bed leaped up into the air and chattered back against the floor as Miss Pinch screamed in deafening crescendo.

The record player had shifted back to the first song:

> *Sweet little woman,*
> *Please marry me.*

I got up off the bed. I wrapped my robe around me.

The record player was crooning:

> *Man and wife together,*
> *How happy we will be.*
> *And then we'll have some kiddies,*
> *Maybe two . . .*

I batted the needle ferociously and it scratched off with a squawk.

I glared at the two unconscious women, out like lights.

"(Bleep) you, Pinch," I snarled. "Have you defeated me AGAIN?"

Chapter 9

I felt like shooting both of them. In fact, that was probably what it would come down to now.

I happened to look down at myself.

Blood!

I was in the peculiar situation of having to get rid of the evidence before I committed the crime. One maidenhead murder was bad enough, but two in a row had left enough evidence to convict me of the Jack the Ripper crimes. One forensic test and I'd be found guilty!

Normally, I am not considered a very fastidious person. In fact, there are those who would go so far as to infer that, like the Apparatus, I am downright dirty.

But there was no help for it: Prior to completing this slaughter, I had better establish my innocence. I'd better shower quick to cover up the tail—I mean trail.

I glared at the two still-unconscious females. I gave the Ninja robe a disgusted hitch. I marched into Candy's room and closed the door behind me.

There was lots of soap in the bathroom: I am no expert on the subject, but the American soaps, with their penny-a-barrel "perfume," stunk worse than I did. They use violent odors to cover up the even more violent odors of their questionable ingredients, like rancid hog fat. I finally found an "oatmeal health soap" that said it was for "that virgin look." I began my shower.

Lathering away, I thought this difficult situation over. I will admit that I was baffled.

My calculations had been out, somehow, no matter how deeply I thrust them in. Anyone would have thought that the cruelest possible thing you could do to a lesbian would be to make her witness natural sex.

The Marquis de Sade himself advocated, as the worst sadistic action possible, "anarchic sexual violence." I had only gone by the book. And he should know. He had been a man who practiced what he preached. Freud himself, a few decades later, would have been utterly spinning, had it not been for the earlier dedicated work of de Sade.

Somewhere I must have slipped. But enough of wondering. I was a man of the future, not the past. I toyed with the idea of simply killing them, disposing of the bodies, calling a moving company and having them take the safe to the manufacturer. I could tell them that I had forgotten the combination. But I discarded the notion, as they might get suspicious. I had to keep my trail covered.

I finished showering. I smelled disgustingly clean—or was that oatmeal?

I put on the Ninja robe. I picked up a gun. I was just putting my hand out to open the door when I heard them talking. They had come to! I listened. Maybe I could pick up a clue that would tell me what to do next.

Pinch's voice, "All right, then, you tell him."

Candy said, "No. *You* tell him. You're much better at tricky things."

"He won't believe me," said Pinch. "He doesn't trust me."

"He's got to believe you," said Candy.

"I don't think I can con him."

Candy said, "You've GOT to try! This is intolerable. He might do the most awful thing I can think of."

Pinch said, "God (bleep) it, he might at that. This is pretty desperate!"

Aha! They thought it was desperate, did they? My heart leaped with hope. There was something they were terrified of. I took a chance. I walked in, gun ready.

They were both staring at me, Candy tied up on the sofa, Pinch securely manacled on the bed. Was there fear in their eyes? Aha! There was! Unmistakable. They were terrified!

Miss Pinch took a deep breath. She said, "If you unchain me and leave the room, I will open the safe and give you your money."

Oh, man. I had accidentally hit upon something they were afraid I would do. I must pretend I knew what it was, even though I didn't.

But I knew Miss Pinch. She was, even more than other women, tricky to the last stab in the back. I would outsmart her. I would at least hear what this was before I murdered both of them.

I went around the room and collected every knife display and weapon in it. I even found the old dueling pistols of such painful memory. It took me three trips to Candy's room before I had the lot piled in there.

I ripped out the telephone cord. I ripped out the connections on the bank camera, after making sure it would not trip some remote. I looked in the cupboard and got all the pepper and mustard and Tabasco sauce and added them to the weapons pile.

With expert loops, I untied Candy's feet from the lashing under the couch and retied her ankles. She knew better than to fight: I was holding a knife in my teeth.

I held a pistol to her head and dragged her into her bedroom and tied her to the bureau.

I came back, and with the Ruger Blackhawk cocked in my left hand, I unshackled Miss Pinch and drew back hastily.

"One false move from you," I said, "and I will blow Candy's head off. Now open the safe."

"When you've left the room and closed the door," she said.

It was taking a terrible chance. But I needed that money in order to continue on my way to wreck the cause of all my woes, Heller.

I backed out of the door and closed it. I held the gun ready on Candy in case there was any treachery afoot.

Some small sounds in the other room. Believe me, this was one of the touchiest points in my whole career. I had to continue to look calm to them but it was very difficult.

I could almost hear my own heart trying to climb into my throat. Women are always dangerous and when they are lesbians they are doubly dangerous—and when they are Miss Pinch, watch it, man, for she was all three.

A voice from the other room. "You can come in now."

I was not to be taken unawares. I got hold of the naked Candy, still tied, and used her as a body shield. I kicked open the door.

Miss Pinch was kneeling, propitiative, in front of the safe. She had her hands behind her. Trickery! The safe was closed! I held the Ruger to Candy's temple, finger on the hair trigger.

"What treachery is this?" I demanded.

Miss Pinch took her hands from behind her back. She was holding a thousand-dollar bill. She said, "This is yours if you don't do it." Fear was in her eyes.

It was time I found out what they were terrified of. "If I don't do what?" I grated.

It was Candy that answered, all in a babble, the accents of sheer horror, "YOU MIGHT WALK OUT THAT DOOR AND *LEAVE!* WE MIGHT NEVER SEE YOU AGAIN!"

I blinked. A new kind of trick. They had a trap out there and were using the negative ploy, page two million and three of the Apparatus manual on hoodwinking.

Miss Pinch was talking. There was pleading in her voice. "Your money is still in the safe. By your signing a blank invoice I can even get you more. But this is all you can have right now. There are conditions."

"Yes?" I said suspiciously.

"You can have a thousand dollars every day if you will live here with us and promise to do that same thing every night."

"To both of us," said Candy. "Every night."

Oh, this was very suspicious. I said, "What about Psychiatric Birth Control?"

Miss Pinch said, "Anything that gets in the road of something that feels *that* wonderful can stuff it."

"To hell with Psychiatric Birth Control!" said Candy.

Miss Pinch said, "They have lied to us. We have been biting

and scratching and smearing lipstick in that back room for years. We have followed the Psychiatric Birth Control texts exactly. We have even had consultations with the psychiatrist in charge of it. And no one, not once, has ever told us the sensation was supposed to come from down THERE! Isn't that right, Candy?"

"That is correct," said Candy. "Not the faintest mention of it anywhere! I was almost to the breaking point of pretending, until I had that . . . that . . ."

"Orgasm?" I said.

"Oh, is THAT what an organism is?" said Candy.

"O-R-G-A-S-M," I spelled out for her. "Orgasm."

"Crikes, what a beautiful word," said Candy. "I know why people take up Christianity now, if that is going to Heaven."

"They lied to us," said Miss Pinch bitterly. "They simply told us that, to carry out Rockecenter's program to cut down the population of the world, we had to be lesbians. I was supposed to be the man-one and Candy was supposed to be my wife. We couldn't do anything else, as they've also turned all the males into gays and made it a crime to break up their marriages."

She stood up suddenly. It made me very nervous. She looked around. She couldn't find anything portable to throw so she slammed the whole Iron Maiden over frontwards on the floor. "(Bleep) them!" she gritted. "They've made us underprivileged! They have been depriving us of women's rights for all these years! I'm going to get my revenge!"

I was alarmed. "Wait a minute. This is treason," I said. "What about Rockecenter?"

She spat! She picked up a beer can and slammed it down on the floor. "Rockecenter can go (bleep) himself! Psychiatric Birth Control! I spit on Psychiatric Birth Control." She picked up another beer can and threw it down with a crash. "I spit on the Chief Psychiatrist! I spit on psychiatry! I spit on Rockecenter for promoting psychiatry! They've cost us years and years and years of a very beautiful thing!" She was looking around wildly for something else to throw down.

I knew how to stop this barrage. It might come my way in a

minute. It wasn't psychology, it was a sense of self-preservation. "You can't expect me to live here in the midst of all this mess—all this torture equipment. I'd have nightmares and walk out the door."

"No, no," said Candy hurriedly.

"No, no," said Miss Pinch in a sudden change of attitude. She dive-bombed straight down into propitiation. "Listen. We'll have it all moved out. We'll redecorate the place. You can have the back room. We'll have a lock put on the inside of the door. We'll have the garden cleaned up so you can have a nice view and sit and rest between times. You can come and go as you please. All you have to do is sleep with us in the front room every night and do it to us."

"Not in that bed," I said firmly. "And no shackles or mustard."

"We'll get a nice big bed to hold three," said Candy.

"No shackles, no mustard," said Miss Pinch. "Oh, please don't be a hard-hearted (bleepard), Inkswitch dear. Please, please, pretty please, say yes."

She looked like she was on the verge of honest tears. I said, "Yes."

"Oh!" screamed Candy, "untie me quick so I can kiss you, you dear man!"

I had trouble cutting her bonds off. Miss Pinch was hugging me and letting out little snarling sounds.

Candy got loose finally and kissed me.

Miss Pinch said, "You'll get your thousand bucks every day. And we'll fix up the place." Then she added, "And it's all settled?" as though she wanted to be reassured.

"Yes," I said again.

"Oh, goody!" cried Candy, clapping her hands. "Let's all get dressed and go to a restaurant and have a deflowering celebration."

"No," said Miss Pinch, looking at me with a cocked head, compressed mouth and hungry eye, "Let's stay right here and do it all over again. We've got the whole night. But I'm first this time, Candy. You can watch if you promise not to scream. I'M the one who gets to scream when I have another of those GORGEOUS orgasms. I'm getting breathless just thinking about it."

That was how I got the safe open. In fact, three safes. Well, not exactly as I planned, but one must learn to improvise. One must know how to go deeper into things than one might have, at first, intended.

One has to know when to take things lying down.

Alas, if it had only kept up on a level with that night.

Chapter 10

For more than sixty hours now, my best-laid plans were getting blocked. Stopping Heller was not making any progress, and it MUST, it MUST, it MUST!

In the back room of the apartment, I was fidgeting. Part of it was scratching fleas.

For two days a hellish din had been going on in the basement flat and garden. Redecoration and refurnishing were proceeding apace.

I had signed a couple of Octopus Oil blank petty-cash invoices with the name John Smith, and after that all Hades had come unstuck. Workmen in the front room, workmen in the back room, workmen in the garden. Plumbers, painters, electricians and even gays directing the new decor and furnishings. It was a very good lesson that one should never sign invoices!

But the main reason I was fidgeting (aside from scratching fleas) was my inability to raise Raht on the two-way-response radio. I knew he had it and I also knew he was refusing to answer it, just to spite me.

I did not dare phone the New York office, as I was on the run. Raht was different, because on the two-way I could fool him into thinking I was in Africa.

That I contact him was desperately crucial: The 831 Relayers were on and at this close range my viewers were just flared out. I did NOT know what was going on with my Target One: Heller! Without that data and without a check on that hellhound, the Countess Krak, I dared not act.

I was in a rage to get something—anything—done to begin the job of finishing him off.

I had money—three thousand dollars. Two of the bills were my regular pay. The third one was for overtime.

I stared disconsolately into a bucket of daffodil-yellow paint. A flea was swimming around in it, getting all yellow. I was about to push him under with a paint paddle when he jumped out and vanished. The incident sharpened my restless mood. I had to get out of this overrun place and think.

I wiped some yellow paint spatters off my trench coat and went out for a walk. The brisk and windy day should cool my fevered brow, calm me and let me concentrate.

All unsuspecting, I walked by a newsstand. And there on the front page of the *New York Grimes*, big as big, it said:

WOMEN'S BOMB RIGHTS COMING UP AT UN SECURITY COUNCIL

PETTICOAT PICKETING BEGINS

ANTINUCLEAR PROTEST MARCHERS HOLD RALLY AT EMPIRE UNIVERSITY

Heller again! They had put that headline there just to nag me.

Then the full import of it hit me. If that bill got through the Security Council now, Miss Simmons would be drooling all over Heller! Rather than flunk him out of Empire as she had promised, she would pass him! I would lose a vital ally I had counted on to block his villainous rehabilitation of this planet, a plot that would ruin me, Lombar and Rockecenter.

Oh, I knew an emergency when I saw one. What could I do?

I stood on the corner, almost frantic with the urgency of the emergency. I stared up into the sky, beseeching the Gods for an omen. I got it! Right in my line of view was the Octopus Oil Company Building! Rockecenter was in his heaven and all would soon be right with the world. I realized that Bury could not possibly know that "Wister" was behind this women's rights thing. Rockecenter, Bury and everyone who mattered knew how dangerous women were already. But completely aside from that, Rockecenter controlled the uranium supplies of the world, and the thermonuclear-bomb market would crash if there was no more war on the horizon! That bill, if passed, could bring about a devastating and disastrous peace! Rockecenter must be frantic!

No sooner realized than activated. I strode with swift stride to the Octopus building.

I walked straight in through the Benevolent Association door. I was in luck! There sat Bury! His little snap-brim hat was sitting on top of a cage of white mice on his desk. He looked up and the sides of his mouth twitched, as close to a smile as ever appeared on that prune face.

"Inkswitch!" he said. "Come in. Haven't seen you for a day or two." He waved a hand at the interview chair, "Take the stand. What have you been up to?"

I sat down. "I have to keep up my cover as a Federal agent," I said. "I just dropped in to see if you know about this Women's Thermonuclear Rights Bill."

"Women," he said. "I try stay away from those. Without much luck, I must say: They are as hard to escape as subpoena servers."

"Well, I thought you might like to know that this Wister is behind that bill right up to the hilt. He's a menace."

"Oh, Wister," he said. And the look came in his eyes that can only possibly appear in the hard orbs of a Wall Street lawyer. Then he tented his hands and sat back. "But I think we've got that case pretty well into due process. Madison is on it. And from the bills we're getting from F.F.B.O., I'd say he was pretty busy."

"Wister has got to be stopped," I said.

The "smile" twitched the sides of his mouth. "Well, you just wait, Inkswitch. Anything a public-relations man like J. Warbler Madman is onto is going to be stopped. You can count on it! By the time that maniac is through with Wister, the poor (bleep) will be absolutely begging for the electric chair and throwing anyone who tries to get a governor's reprieve straight out of his cell. Madison you can count on, Inkswitch. He tops every snake I ever met! When you combine the Madisons of this world with the media we have, even the Four Horsemen would plead for an out-of-court settlement. Worry not, Inkswitch. You can count on Madison to absolutely ruin Wister's life. The prosecution rests."

I saw I wasn't getting anywhere with Bury. I rose to go.

"Oh, by the way, Inkswitch," he said, "I just remembered, I had a present to send you the other day and my secretary told me he didn't have your current address."

"Snakes?" I said.

"No," he said. "They're pretty valuable. I picked up a set of acupuncture needles over in China and I thought you might like to try them out on Miss Agnes. If you put them in the wrong place, they raise hell. So what's your current address?"

"I'm undercover," I said.

"Oh, hell, Inkswitch, I know that. This is just for my own notebook."

I couldn't very well refuse and expose the fact that I'd never even met Miss Agnes. I gave him the basement-apartment address. He wrote it down in a little black book. Then he paused.

"I know this address," he said, prune wrinkles even more pronounced as he thought. "Yes, I was over there last month hushing up a murder. Somebody beaten to death. I have it! That's Miss Pinch's apartment!" He looked at me in real surprise. "Jesus," he exclaimed, "you're not living with Miss Pinch, are you?"

I said, "I got her under control."

"Jesus!" he said, admiringly. "Maybe I ought to turn you loose on my wife!"

Hastily, I shifted the subject on him. I was busy enough without another stud assignment. And I vividly remembered his wife's voice. Traumatic! "Please don't tell Miss Agnes I'm living with Miss Pinch," I said.

Bury shook his head. "Oh, no. You got a low opinion of me, Inkswitch, if you think I'd talk to Miss Agnes. I'm not crazy. At least, I'm not committed yet, in spite of this job."

"That's two of us," I said. But it was a lie. Being a Wall Street lawyer could not be anywhere near as tough as the job of an Apparatus officer. I left.

I was convinced that Bury didn't realize how serious this UN thing really was. I needed to get busy stopping Heller before he stopped everybody.

I found a cab and very soon was across town at 42 Mess Street.

Madison's Excalibur car was in the alley in front of the place, and an enterprising new reporter was polishing up its square yards of chrome.

I went upstairs into the loft pressroom. Just as I suspected, the place had gone slack. There were hardly any reporters there. Only half a dozen phones were ringing at once and over half of the fifty teletype machines were idle.

Madison was in his cluttered office, his feet on his desk, a complacent smile upon his youthful, sincere and earnest face.

"Smith!" he said. "Come in. Sit down. I haven't seen you all day."

It offended me. Wasn't anybody ever going to notice, when I'd been gone for weeks, months even?

I suddenly remembered I had a bone to pick with him. "You certainly weren't very smart sending Doctor Crobe away," I said sourly.

"Phetus P. Crobe?" he said, laughing.

"The doctor you had put away."

"*Put* away?" he said. "Why, where'd you get that idea, Smith?"

"You sent for the wagon," I said.

"Oh, I get it. Your men didn't come back and see me. Right after they carted him off, I was on the phone to the chief psychiatrist at Bellevue. Crobe seemed anxious to cut things, as all psychiatrists are, so they gave him his own laboratory and a top job on staff. You didn't think I'd overlook a valuable asset like that, did you? Heaven forbid. What would the media do for horror if it weren't for psychiatrists? But I've got to build him up before I can use him. You should keep track of things better, Smith. And I do wish you knew more about public relations than you do. It's hard to work with amateurs. That loony (bleep) could have killed me. You apparently don't know much about psychiatrists or you would have sent him directly to the hospital and not let him run around loose, slashing away at your colleagues. Psychiatry is for the *public,* Smith. Not for people who matter."

I saw I was in danger of being hectored. I said, "Don't land on me with all four feet. You're in no position to. There's a grave threat growing up around Wister and what are you doing about him? Next to nothing. The Atlantic City thing was weeks ago and by now has run its course. . . ."

Madison's feet came down off the desk. He sat forward in amazement. "Run its course? God deliver me from amateurs! It's been getting front page for weeks and weeks. It's setting an all-time record! The bulk of my staff is down at Trenton, New Jersey, stirring it up again!"

He grabbed a huge fistful of clippings. "Look! The New Jersey governor is having an absolute fit about the theft of Atlantic City still! He's continued to maintain that it is part of New Jersey even yet. But look at this, the riots we stirred up: The citizens there are refusing now to pay state taxes. We got a dreadful row going in the New Jersey legislature and the Whiz Kid was arrested by state police for stealing the town. And look at *this:* The Whiz Kid hauled before the legislature and the whole body throwing whisky bottles at him, trying to get him to promise he won't sell Atlantic City to Nevada."

He grabbed another sheet, "And look at tomorrow's headlines!"

I stared at the layout for the *New York Grimes.* It said:

WHIZ KID DECLARED AN ORIGINAL OWNER OF ALL NEW JERSEY

A shocked governor today was brutally brought face to face with the reality that not just Atlantic City but the entire state of New Jersey may belong to J. T. Wister, otherwise known as the "Whiz Kid" of recent notoriety.

No less an authority than Professor Stringer himself, the world's leading authority on genealogy and family history, has issued an authoritative warning that Wister is a direct descendent of Chief Rancocas, head of the Lenni Lenape branch of the Delaware tribe, the original owners of New Jersey.

The Indian name *Lenni Lenape* means "Original People." From this, according to Dr. Egghead, the State Historian, "it can be clearly seen that the word *original,* occurring in both instances, proves the claim."

"No deed of transfer or record of sale from Chief Rancocas or the Lenni Lenape Indians can be found in the Trenton Courthouse files or archives," said the State Recorder of Deeds at this fateful meeting last night. "Therefore it must be concluded that the entire state of New Jersey still belongs to the original owners."

Before I could finish reading, Madison slapped it on the desk. His eyes glowed. "The next day after that story, the Whiz Kid is going to order the original settlers out. After that we can get the Indian Bureau, Department of the Interior, on it and we can have another Battle of Wounded Knee and get a headline for every Indian shot and at least a back page for every Federal marshal killed. And next week the Whiz Kid will escape by robbing a train. . . ."

That startled me. I said, "Where does this train come from? What's it doing here?"

Madison sat back with a superior smile. Rather pitying. "Please see somebody about your memory, Smith. I distinctly told you a long time ago that I am trying to create the Jesse James image. Don't you recall? It's the best immortal one handy. You just don't understand public-relations work, Smith."

He had needled me too much. I said, "Listen, Madison. I came down to tell you that the Whiz Kid is behind this women's-right-to-not-be-thermonuclear-bombed bill. It's coming right up before the UN Security Council. He got it through the General Assembly using whores to lobby for it."

"Is that a fact?" said Madison, idly.

I put a bite in my voice. "Yes, it is! And you better get to work on it!"

"Nope," said Madison. "It doesn't fit the image."

"But my Gods!" I said. "It's the TRUTH!"

Madison gave an amused laugh. "Truth? What does PR have to do with truth, Smith? News today is *entertainment*. Ask NBC, CBS, ABC, ask all the major papers. They'll tell you. News is the biggest entertainment draw in the world. Now let me ask you, how can you entertain anybody by telling the truth? Preposterous! No, Smith, you just don't understand the modern media *at all*. Let's leave this sort of thing up to me, shall we? And then we'll have 18-point MADISON SCORES AGAIN exclamation point unquote."

Acidly, I said, "You forgot the front quote."

He said, "So I did. Rewrite: 18-point quote get the hell out of here, Smith, and let me do my job!"

It was no wonder they called him J. Warbler Madman. I left before he started frothing at the mouth. Even rabies was tame compared to the bite of PR men and the media.

But I was worried. None of them really seemed to get the danger in that UN bill. If the Security Council passed it, Rockecenter would lose all his thermonuclear profit. The Octopus Oil monopoly on uranium claims would be worthless. Lombar would be raving. And even worse, that Miss Simmons would be slobbering all over Heller as a prize hero.

I was worried!

I paced.

Then INSPIRATION!

I would go and see Miss Simmons!

PART FORTY-TWO
Chapter 1

I leaped aboard an AA train and soon was speeding north. My rendezvous with destiny would set off a chain reaction even Heller would be powerless to stop.

The roar, roar, roar of the pounding wheels carried me relentlessly forward, oblivious of the churning crowd. At last I was in action. My mission of vengeance would be fulfilled. Blood, red blood, would pay the awful price of putting me through the agonies which had spent my energies and lacerated my soul.

At 116th Street I sprang off. With stern and unrelenting face I made my way to Empire University.

I found Miss Simmons in the Puppet Building of the Teachers' College. She was sitting at a classroom desk. She had a wild look in her eyes—as well she might, haunted and destroyed by that villain Heller.

She didn't have her glasses on and I knew very well she couldn't see without them. They lay upon her desk and I covertly laid a book upon them as I sat down.

"I'm from the *Morning Press*," I said. "I've come to interview you about the Antinuclear Protest Marchers' reaction to the UN bill on women's thermonuclear rights."

She peered at me. She said, "If they don't pass it, we're going to blow the UN up, New York Police Tactical Police Force or no New York Police Tactical Police Force. I am president of the marchers now and what I say GOES!" She looked for her glasses, couldn't find them. Then she added, "And you can quote me."

"There are black forces at work behind that bill," I said.

"I'll hear no talk against minority groups," she said. "The Harlem 'I Will Arise' Burial Society is right behind us to the grave." She patted around, still looking for her glasses. "Haven't I seen you someplace before? In the psychiatric ward, maybe?"

"You have indeed," I said. "We're fellow revolutionaries. I am from the PLO, actually. The *Morning Press* is just my agent cover."

"Then we can talk freely," said Miss Simmons. "Thermonuclear bombing has got to stop even if we destroy the whole world to do it. Didn't I meet you in Psychology 13?"

"You did indeed," I said. "I sat right behind you and cheered you on all the way."

"Then your name is Throgapple," she said. "I always remember my classmates."

"Correct," I said.

She was patting around trying to find her glasses again so I thought I had better distract her. "What are you teaching here?" I said, pretending to indicate the book, but actually moving it so her glasses dropped off the desk into my hand.

"Postgraduate deportment," she said. "These young teachers go out into secondary schools and foul up. So we preindoctrinate them to be calm and controlled, even cold, at all times. Spare the child and spoil the rod is never used today. Hysterical conduct by the teacher is frowned upon, even when she finds a can of worms in her purse. Where the *hell* did I put my glasses? Do you see my glasses around anywhere, Throgapple?"

"No," I said—which was true, as they were now in my pocket. "But to get back to the Antinuclear Protest Marchers, what will be your statement if that UN bill does not pass the Security Council?"

I recoiled. She had leaped up and began to pound on her desk and rave and rant in four-letter words that even I had never heard. "And you can quote me!" she screamed. She sat back down pretty spent. "But of course their failure to pass it is unthinkable. All the women of the world would tear them into little bits with their fingernails, laughing all the while!"

I don't like to see women get upset. It recoils on one. I decided

I had better calm her down, put her mind on gentle hills and chuckling brooks. I had to dim down that insane glare which still made caldrons of her eyes. I said, "I understand you also teach Nature Appreciation."

The glare got worse! "Throgapple, there was once a time when I enjoyed those little Sunday rambles in the woods. I could cheerily chatter to the rabbits and smile upon the daffodils. But last year, Throgapple, an awful thing happened. It changed my life!"

"Tell," I said.

"Throgapple, in a moment when my poor motherly heart swelled chokingly up in my breast with pity, I took into my class that vilest, that most awful, that most vicious species of malignant fauna ever devised by the devil. . . ." She was breaking down. Her lips were twitching to disclose clenched teeth. Her breath was coming faster.

"I understand," I said gently. "A nuclear physicist named Wister."

She leaped out of her seat. She grabbed student chair after student chair, stacked them in a high tower and agilely scrambled to the top and sat there teetering. She was glaring blindly all about.

"He isn't here," I said reassuringly.

"Thank God for that!" she cried.

Two students, probably for her next class, were standing in the door with their mouths open.

"I take it," I said, "that you do not like him."

She began to scream. It hurt my ears.

The two students thought I must be baiting her. One of them ran off. The other, a brawny youth, stood there glaring at me.

Miss Simmons, apparently having run out of breath, stopped screaming.

More students were gathering at the door. The original one was whispering to the others and pointing first at me and then at Miss Simmons, sitting clear up to the ceiling on the rickety tower of chairs.

"Miss Simmons," I said, speaking upward, "please let's get on with the interview. Incontrovertible evidence has come into our office that there is a mammoth, elephantine cabal on the prowl to defeat that UN bill, and the editor ordered me to come and get your reaction."

She was looking way down at me. I was probably just a gray blur below.

I had her attention so I continued. I had worked it all out after that original flash. I knew exactly what to say. "You can understand completely, I am sure, that certain parties would give their very lives to stop that bill from passing."

The tower gave a shake. Then she stared blindly down at me, her mouth poised to start screaming again.

I went on. "Working day and night, slaving into the tiniest hours before dawn, creeping out of the woodwork like a vile serpent, praying at black masses and enlisting all his friends, working secretly with a slyness only he is capable of, one person alone is seeking to corrupt the delegates with women and drugs, blackmail and threat, to crush that bill so thoroughly that it will never raise its head again."

I knew I had her attention. I had the attention of the mob of male students, too. It was a dramatic moment. I dragged out the suspense.

When I was sure Miss Simmons' every brain cell was glued to my speech, I added the death blow.

"The secret enemy's name," I said, "is Wister."

She jerked upright in a dreadful spasm beyond any possible control.

The pile of chairs started sideways.

In slow motion the lofty tower fell, faster and faster.

The chairs came all apart.

Miss Simmons hit the floor!

CRASH!

There was a spatter of splinters and debris and then, with a mighty roar, the gang of students rushed on me.

"He pushed her!" screamed one.

"Get him!" screamed another.

"Kill the (bleepard)!" howled a third.

I had made a mistake. I had not realized that going amongst a gang of students was not dissimilar, today, to entering the hangar in Afyon. I had not come armed!

Pummelling me and tearing at me, they bore me out. They got me to the top of a stairs.

One ambitious soul plunged a hand into my ripping coat and got my wallet.

"A FED!" he screamed. "A dirty, stinking, rotten FED!"

That was all it took.

They threw me over the stairwell.

I hit with a thud.

Outraged, they threw my hat and wallet at me.

I outsmarted them. Before a single one could get down those stairs, I grabbed hat and wallet and sped like a leopard out of the building.

The roars behind me diminished behind the drive of my General Service Officer boots.

I got to 116th Street. I was just in time to catch an express train.

As it closed its doors, only then did I start to laugh.

I had done it! Actually, it had worked perfectly.

If that bill passed now, she would jeer at Heller that it had gone through despite his most villainous plots. And if it didn't pass I could certainly guarantee that his life from there on out would be a hell not even he could live through.

Riding along in the lurching, roaring train, I sucked my hand cuts quite contentedly.

What is a little battering, after all? They tell you you have to be tough in the Apparatus. I was. And in a moment of triumph like this, the pain was almost nice.

I had struck a blow that Heller would not soon forget and certainly could not possibly recover from.

I had seen my duty. And I had done it. It was the Apparatus way.

Chapter 2

As the deadline approached for the UN Security Council meeting—2:00 P.M. on Friday—I was frankly getting frantic.

Four days I had been in New York, four days I had been buzzing and hissing on the two-way-response radio, and no Raht.

Workmen were still everywhere, trying to finish the whole job before the weekend cost the contractors overtime, and the apartment was a madhouse.

I would make one last try. I scrunched down in the back of a closet that had been completed and, surrounded suffocatingly by wet paint, once more began to push and pull at the radio controls. I had not brought its manual and it was mostly hit or miss. There was a needle under glass on top of it and a red button there which should light. Trying to get more comfortable and avoid the paint, I accidentally touched it. It lit up! That was the first time that had happened. Had it been on when I had used these things before? Such radios came only in pairs. They were very simple rigs. The Department of the Army used them between generals so they had to be very elementary.

I shook it to see if anything was loose.

"Yes?" Raht's voice!

"You've been sleeping on the job!" I railed at him. "And this proves it!"

"Officer Gris? Where are you?"

"I'm in Africa, you idiot! Where did you think I was?"

"You sound awfully loud to be in Africa, Officer Gris. You

almost blew my ear out. But now I've turned my volume almost down to nothing."

"It must be a skip wave," I said. "I'm still in Africa and don't you forget it. I can barely hear you! But this is no time to argue. Turn all three 831 Relayers off right away!"

"If you want them off," said Raht, "that must mean you are within two hundred miles of me. The direction needle . . ."

I clicked the radio off hastily. He wasn't going to trick me into telling him where I was and open up the trail. No indeed!

I went into the chaos of the back room and got my three viewers and a portable TV. I went back into the closet. It was pretty uncomfortable, what with paint fumes and scratching fleas. But I knew I had to do my duty. The way of an Apparatus officer was hard, especially in this apartment.

The viewers were still flared out, as it would take him a while to scale those antennas on the Empire State Building. But the TV set was live. All three networks were giving heavy coverage to the event.

Some political commentator was giving a long rundown on the background of the measure and all the national battling that had gone on around the world. I smiled a superior smile: Those national battlings had been done in bed at the Gracious Palms!

After half an hour of suffocating and scratching, my viewers stopped flaring out and steadied down.

Crobe's came on first. He had some woman on a couch and was apparently psychoanalyzing her, for she was saying over and over how her three-year-old brother had raped her when she was sixteen. Crobe might or might not have been listening but his vision was exploring her genitalia in depth. He looked up once and, my, they had given him a beautiful office: whole shelves full of skulls and his psychiatric diploma framed in gold. But beyond noting that he was far from a lost resource and that Bellevue seemed to be providing him with its best facilities, I had no interest today in Crobe. I turned his viewer off so it wouldn't distract me.

The Countess Krak was sitting in Heller's Empire State main office. No, correction. She was lying on the floor, chin propped up with her hands, reading a book, *The Food of Many Lands*, according to the print across the page top. She was going over all the recipes of India. Then she made a clicking sound and the page turned. It startled me. Then I saw that it was just the cat. She started on the recipes of Indonesia.

Heller's viewer was showing the same TV program that I had on my portable TV, only Heller's viewer was much clearer and the colors were better. Wise fellow. He had not gone in person this day. The women of the Gracious Palms would have been there and he would have had a bad time trying to explain all this to Krak.

She looked sideways at Heller, sitting there in a chair. "You looked worried, dear. Is something wrong?"

"It's this UN thing," said Heller. "I don't like the lay of the land. From what the commentators say, it looks sticky. The measure I'm interested in passed the General Assembly. But to go into force it now has to pass the Security Council. The Security Council has fifteen members, but a single veto from one of the great powers can kill the bill."

"Great powers?" said Krak.

"United States, France, United Kingdom, Russia and China. Even if nine members vote for it and just one of those five vetoes it, it's finished."

"What is the measure, dear?"

"Women's rights," said Heller.

"Hmm," said the Countess. She got up and sat down on a sofa near him. "I don't really understand why they have to have a law to give women rights. Women make their own rights. Why are you so interested in this, dear?"

"It's important," said Heller.

"Hmm," said the Countess Krak.

At that moment some crowd shots came on. There were mobs of women around the UN, carrying placards on poles, waving flags, singing, being cheer-leadered.

The camera focused on one group with huge placards and Heller gave a small laugh. The Countess looked at him sharply. He was smiling at the screen.

One huge placard read:

The UN Security Council
Will Be Boycotted
at the Gracious Palms
if They Do Not Pass
UN Resolution
678-546-452

The Countess looked back at the screen. The camera focused in on one huge poster this group was carrying. It said:

In Memory of Pretty Boy

The picture was a poor one but it certainly looked like Heller!

The Countess said, "Who are those ladies, dear?"

"Where?" said Heller.

"Hmm," said the Countess Krak.

The cameras were working inside the Security Council room. A pan along the mural picked up the symbols of Peace and Liberty, Equality and Fraternity. Then the view travelled along the member representatives. They were getting busy.

The president of the Security Council this month was Russian. He had a big, square face and Mongolian eyes. He brought the meeting to order by banging his fist on his desk. Through the translator who was putting it out on the networks in English, the Russian said, "I call this waste-of-time meeting to order."

"Oh, oh," said Heller.

"I had to come all the way back from Yakut in Siberia," continued the Russian, "just to attend this special meeting. And all because the silly General Assembly passed some silly nonsense."

"Oh, oh, oh!" said Heller.

"So I read it," said the Russian. " 'UN Resolution'—which is not resolved and if it is resolved I go back to Siberia— '678-546-452.' Hereas, et cetera, to wit: 'RESOLVED: WOMEN HAVE THE RIGHT NOT TO BE THERMONUCLEAR BOMBED

AND NOT TO BE FORCED TO SHUT UP BY SLAPPING OR TORTURE.' "

"That's a good resolution," said the Countess Krak. "It's the first sensible law I've heard on this planet. I'm amazed it isn't in force already. But you seem very interested, dear. Did you have something to do with it?"

"It's a political matter," said Heller.

"Hmm," said the Countess Krak.

The Russian was talking again. "We will now have the debate. I will be the first one to debate. So listen, Comrades: It is well known that the only workers who can be made to do any work are women. If the women did not do all the work, men would have no time to sit around and drink vodka. But," and he fixed the other members with a ferocious glare, "you know and I know and everybody knows and Karl Marx who had an awful married life knew, too, that if you don't slap women they talk all the time, day and night. And if they talk, talk, talk, where goes the Five Year Plans then, right? And if they make the Five Year Plans fail they are counter-revolutionaries and ought to be thermonuclear bombed once and for all so we could have some peace. And that's all there is to it, Comrades. This resolution would undermine the already-undermined theory of Marxist Leninism. Russia votes against it—*nyet, nyet, nyet*—and spits on it, too. So there is no point in debating further or even voting, as a great power has vetoed it. Meeting adjourned!" And he got up and put on his fur coat and stamped out of the hall where a regiment of KGB guards got him into a helicopter and away.

"Oh, blast, blast those Russians!" said Heller. "The girls will be SO disappointed after all their hard work!"

"What girls?" said the Countess Krak, very alert.

"And there goes any chance I had with Miss Simmons!" said Heller. "Confound those Russians!"

The Countess Krak said, very loudly, "WHO is Miss Simmons?"

Heller came out of it. He looked at the Countess. "What?"

"I said, 'WHO is Miss Simmons?' "

"My teacher in Nature Appreciation. That's the class I have to personally attend each Sunday."

"Oh, is that what you have been doing Sundays? I notice that you use the words '*have* to attend.' However, I have been told personally by Izzy that you are going to the university just wonderfully, and all without attending any classes whatever. Bang-Bang tells me that you are just doing splendidly in the ROTC, and yet you don't have to attend any drills or ROTC classes. Now, WHY, Jettero, do you *have* to attend the Sunday class of this Miss Simmons?"

Heller said, "She forced me into it."

The Countess Krak said, "Jettero, I can understand completely why she is infatuated with you, but I cannot for the life of me see why you are infatuated with her."

"I'M NOT!"

"Jettero, you need not be defensive. You are not being accused of anything. I just want to know why you are infatuated with her."

"I HATE the hussy!" said Heller.

"Oh," said the Countess Krak, "be very careful of hate. The poet says it is the closest neighbor of love."

"Oh, Gods, he didn't know Miss Simmons! Listen, that woman is working day and night to wreck my plans. She is not only going to fail me, she is tearing around demanding that others flunk me!"

"Jettero," said the Countess Krak, "maybe you had better tell me about this very exactly."

Heller told her about needing a diploma so people would listen to him and how he had signed up for a major in nuclear physics. Miss Simmons hated nuclear physicists and had forced him to take an optional on Nature Appreciation, which she herself taught. Then he drew a long breath and told her in detail about following her into Van Cortlandt Park, finishing off the attackers and taking Miss Simmons to the hospital. And how, in the new term, they had released her from the psychiatric ward so she could resume teaching.

The Countess Krak nodded gravely. "I understand it completely now. She walked into that park well knowing there were unscrupulous men about and lured you after her. She is the kind of woman who craves to be raped. Oh, I am afraid this has gone far enough, Jettero. I knew all the beautiful women on this planet would be after you and I now know that my worst fears have been realized. I could forgive that Miss America thing, but this has gone on and on right under my nose every Sunday."

"Please," begged Heller. "If I take you to the theater and buy you a dozen roses and get up first every morning for a week and get the room warm, will you, in return, stop talking about Miss Simmons?"

"Hmm," said the Countess Krak. She got up and went into the secretary boudoir.

She paced up and down. Then she suddenly sat on the edge of the couch and punched a button and had Mamie on the phone promptly.

"Mamie," she said, "it has happened. I've got to have your advice."

"Certainly, dearie. You just tell Mama Mamie."

"He is so disturbed that I am absolutely certain he has become infatuated with another woman and it may hold him on this planet. We are not married yet. I MUST get him away. What should I do?"

"Scratch her eyes out," said Mamie, promptly.

"Hmm," said the Countess Krak. "Well, thank you. I was just checking to see how it was done on this planet. How is business?"

"Just fine, dear. Now that my name is up in lights, we're playing to a full house every night. Don't you worry your pretty head about this place, dear. I've got these stage-door Johnnies shovelling out the diamonds like a rainstorm. That's a mighty cute sailor you got there. You just get that (bleepch) under your fingernails and rip away. And give her a kick in the slats for me. Never let a good man get away, dear. They're (bleeped) hard to find!"

I went into alarm. This was not coming out the way I had expected. And although I had always suspected that when women talked privately together they plotted things, I had never understood their conversation was that bloodthirsty.

Oh, I would have to watch this carefully.

And then I experienced a surge of hope. Maybe I could get the Countess Krak for murder!

Chapter 3

She was on the phone again. She got the number of Empire University and asked for Miss Simmons.

Of course they didn't know which "Miss Simmons" amongst all their 18,005 students and 5,002 faculty. The young man said so with some asperity.

"This is a life-and-death matter about one of her students," said the Countess.

"Then she must be a teacher," said the young man's voice. "What does she teach?"

"Nature Appreciation," said Krak.

"Wait a minute, please." Then he came back on the line. "You must mean Jane Simmons, Ph.D., D.Ed., Teachers' College. She teaches Nature Appreciation 101 and 104 also."

"Does she have a student named Jerome Terrance Wister?"

"Thank God for computers. Yes, ma'am. But it says here that she's recommending he be expelled."

"Dangerous stuff, hate," said the Countess.

"I beg pardon?"

"I said, what is her home address so I can advise the next of kin?"

"It's that bad, is it?" said the young man. And he gave it to her very promptly. It was in Morningside Heights.

The Countess Krak opened up the wardrobe. She looked over her clothes. She chose a scarlet suit with an enormous pearl button holding the jacket closed. She got out some red gloves and red Moroccan-leather boots.

Murder. She obviously planned murder!

Over it all she draped a black sable short cape. That confirmed it. She looked just like an assassin pilot to me. Visions of her red heels stamping that yellow-man into the floor back at Spiteos swam around me. Frantically, I wondered what I could do.

The sickening realization that I was about to lose an ally made me feel faint. And I had so carefully prepared it all, too.

Then I realized I could call my friend Police Inspector Bulldog Grafferty. I knew where the murder would occur. Maybe I could get her walked in on red-handed, with the corpse of Miss Simmons still quivering in its pools of mangled blood.

The Countess then got down a shopping case, a black plastic one, of a kind that had lately come in fashion. She grabbed several items off a shelf so quickly I could not see what they were. And then she did a thing which shot my alarm right up to fascinated horror.

She got down a hypnohelmet and put it in! Deoxygenated as I was from lack of air in that closet, dizzy from paint fumes and plagued with fleas, I did not gather in the first moments the full import of this action. Then I understood completely because it was exactly what I would do.

She was going to get Miss Simmons, under hypnosis, to write a suicide note and then she was going to stamp her into the rug!

My hair stood on end! The Countess Krak was going to commit murder and then get off scot-free! Only if she were caught in the act could the crime be detected! Here was a convicted murderess waltzing about New York, slaughtering at will! And only I knew about it!

I suddenly realized that I COULD act. That helmet she had wouldn't operate at all if I were within a mile or two of the place. The relay breaker switch in my head would make it inoperative. I didn't have to come close to Krak, only within a mile or so. And meanwhile I could call Grafferty and get him there, if not in time to save Simmons, at least in time to catch Krak in the act.

But that address was more than four miles away from where I was, near Rockecenter Plaza. I must hurry!

I rose up and thrust against the closet door.

IT DIDN'T OPEN!

I pounded on it.

The awful pounding that was going on in the apartment was drowning all my hammering from within the closet. I pounded louder. They pounded louder. I yelled. They started yelling at each other to be heard above the din.

I put my shoulder to the door and pushed with all my might. All I got was some wet paint on me. I realized they must have piled all the furniture against the door.

I was TRAPPED!

The nausea of claustrophobia gripped me. The only thing I hate worse than space is no space. I got all confused. The naked electric light bulb hanging there began to look like a sun trying to suck me in.

I covered up my eyes. I knew I would have to get a grip on myself. My world was coming to pieces but that didn't mean I had to come to pieces, too. Or did it?

Gradually I managed to choke back the screams rising in my throat until they were only faint yips. That was better.

Think! I must THINK!

I peered at her viewer. More time had gone by than I had thought. She was riding on a subway train. It made her seem magical. How had she gotten from the secretary's boudoir onto a subway train so quick? Then I remembered that the station was right in the basement of the Empire State Building.

I beat my head with my fist. That helped.

THE RADIO!

I had that radio in here! This time I remembered to push the top button.

Raht answered.

"Get on the phone at once," I said. "Call Police Inspector Bulldog Grafferty and tell him there's going to be a woman murdered in Apartment 21, 352 Bogg Street, Morningside Heights, within the next hour. Tell him to be there!"

"Is this urgent?"

Oh, I could have killed him! "You slip up on this and I'll give your name to Madison as a client!"

"Who is going to murder whom?" said Raht. "How can you tell all the way out there in Africa?"

"Are you going to make that phone call or aren't you?" I seethed. "The assassin pilot is on the way right this minute! The murdered woman will be found stamped into the rug!"

"You seem a little overwrought, Officer Gris."

"Not as overwrought as you'll be if I put a Colt .44 Magnum through your worthless skull!"

"Oh, you're down near Rockecenter Plaza."

(Bleep) him! He'd been holding me on the line to be able to read the distance and direction meter on the radio top! "Repeat that message!" I screamed at him.

He repeated it all back very precisely, the way spies are trained to do.

"Now listen, you bulge-brained (bleepard), if police don't appear there to catch that murderer with the corpse within the hour, you'll be turning in your head."

"Oh, I'll take care of it, Officer Gris. I'm on my way."

I hunched down on the floor. I watched Krak's viewer with horrible fascination as she rode the subway to her appointment with doom. Hers.

There was every chance that I would soon be rid of that vicious female, the murderous Countess Krak.

Chapter 4

The neighborhood in Morningside Heights was not too bad. It was full of winter-dead trees and peopled with rather well-dressed but sullen kids, who watched the Countess Krak go by in total conviction that she was a truant officer in disguise and was about to blow the whistle on them all. And Krak's purposeful progress could not have done otherwise than give that impression. Gods, I thought, how they would have screamed and run had they known they watched a murderer on the brink of bloody slaughter. Even the streetwise kids of north Manhattan would not have been able to stomach what I was sure was about to occur.

The grim pound of her boots halted before an apartment house that bore the number 352. It was not a shabby apartment house: Miss Simmons must have some income of her own. There was no doorman, but the brass mailboxes shone. And there it was, right there on number 21, the nameplate:

Miss Jane Simmons

It meant she lived alone! Gods, wasn't anything going to stand between the Countess Krak and this awful crime? Ah, yes, there was. Police Inspector Grafferty would soon be on his way.

Unsuspecting of the trap I had set for her, the Countess Krak pushed the buzzer. I was torn between hoping Miss Simmons, who must have been at the UN, had not yet returned home and savagely hoping that she was, so Grafferty could catch this Manco Devil in the very act of mangling.

The brass grate spoke up. "Yes?"

The Countess Krak said, "I am a fellow teacher, from Atalanta University, Manco, and I want to talk to you about a student of yours."

The voice came back, "It's about time somebody listened to me! Come right up!"

Oh, blind, blind Simmons! You just invited yourself to murder!

I punched the radio button.

"Go ahead," said Raht.

"Have you done your duty?" I said.

"Police Inspector Grafferty was quivering like a bloodhound. I talked it up as a private inside tip. He said he could smell the headlines already. Eager. I caught him at the Civic Center and he's just now locating squad cars. He won't fail you."

"Good," I said and clicked off. Oh, Countess Krak, you've been outsmarted for once and you won't even be able to trace it to me! Grafferty the glory hound was going to do this one himself! It's a long ways from the Civic Center to Morningside Heights, but the police drive over everybody.

The Countess Krak regarded the foyer door. It kept clicking and she didn't know you were supposed to push it when it clicked. It stopped clicking. She gave it a shove, a very impatient gesture. The lock was faulty. It swung right open.

She strode past a fountain and between two statues. She saw the elevator was in use and went up the stairs. She turned down a carpeted hall and stopped before apartment 21.

The door opened without her even knocking. Never was a woman so anxious to be done in. Simmons was already talking. No hello or who are you. She looked dishevelled and very wild of eye. She said, "You know what he did today? He sabotaged the UN bill! He's got to blow everything up, even women's rights! He's a frothing fiend! We teachers must gang together in a solid phalanx of fury and stop him, even before we blow up the UN! Nobody is safe with him on the loose. And the college thinks that just because I was in a psychiatric ward, they don't have to listen to me. They think I'm paranoid about him. And just to make matters worse, the New York Tactical Police Force is after me again."

Miss Simmons was having trouble locating the Countess to talk to her. The Countess must have seen that she was speaking to someone who was as blind as a bat.

"The police!" said the Countess. "Then you need head protection." She kicked the door shut behind her and right in front of Simmons took the hypnohelmet out of the square shopping bag.

I suddenly realized that I still had Simmons' glasses in my pocket. Unwittingly, I had made it very easy for Krak.

The Countess simply turned the helmet on and dropped it over Simmons' head! Just like that!

Krak looked around the rather large and well-furnished living room. Looking for a place to stamp, I thought. A radio seemed to be playing in the next apartment. The Countess Krak saw that a corridor led to a bedroom. She pushed Simmons toward it.

Like a sleepwalker, my favorite ally went down the hall toward her doom.

There was a wide bed, a boudoir table and an easy chair, all decorated in frilly white organdy. The Countess Krak closed the bedroom door. She lowered Simmons onto the bed. She arranged the pillow so it would support the helmet properly. She plugged in her microphone and then sat down in the easy chair.

Simmons had evidently been changing out of her street clothes when the door buzzer went, for they were lying on the floor. She had tossed on a dressing gown. It had opened now as she sprawled there. Not a bad-looking body.

Krak apparently didn't care for that. She moved out of the chair again and pulled the dressing gown together to make Simmons decent. Then she laid her sable cape aside and took off her own jacket, the equivalent of rolling up her sleeves to get to work.

The Countess spoke into her microphone. "Be calm, relax. You are quite safe." Oh, what a liar, I thought. "Sleep, sleep, pretty sleep. Can you hear me?"

Muffled, "Yes."

"What were those eight men going to do to you in Van Cort-landt Park?" said the Countess, leaning back in her chair.

Muffled, "Rape me. All eight of them. They were going to rape me hour after hour."

The Countess lowered her mike and pushed it into her shoulder. "I thought so," she muttered in Voltarian. "A real rape-crazy slut. The whole thing has been just a pose to steal Jettero!" She raised the mike and reverted to English. "When was the first time you saw Wister?"

Miss Simmons flung out her arms, throwing the robe wide open. Her hands extended down, straight out, so rigid they were quivering. Her feet jerked down. She looked like she'd been put on an electric rack. A faint scream came, muffled, from under the helmet.

"Answer me!" snapped the Countess Krak.

Simmons said, "Registration Hall last September." The quivers increased.

Krak said, "You are there at that moment. You see Wister. What do you *really* think?"

Simmons let out a faint scream. The vibrations of her body increased as the rigidity grew.

"Answer me!"

Simmons said, "He is too good-looking."

The Countess lowered the mike into her shoulder and muttered in Voltarian, "Just as I thought. Love at first sight." In English she said into the mike, "Anything else?"

The answer was a muffled scream, "That it was awful that he was a nuclear physicist major and had to be stopped."

"Why?" said the Countess.

Miss Simmons looked to be in torment. She shouted, "THERE MUST BE NO EXPLOSIONS!" Then in lower volume, muffled by the helmet, "My father held the chair of psychology at Brooklyn University. He said explosions were substitutions for sexual (bleepu-lations) and a girl must be frigid, frigid, frigid to protect herself." She was stiff, stretched out now like hard marble, totally rigid.

Krak spoke into the mike, "When did he say that?"

"When he caught me putting firecrackers in the dog's (bleep)."

The Countess dropped the mike. In Voltarian she muttered, "What a *weird* planet!" She sat there a bit and then picked it up and said in English, "The real incident was different. Your father made a mistake. You get NO pleasure out of hurting animals. You were feeding the dog milk and petting it. That is really what you were doing and what really happened. Your father was totally wrong. Accept it."

Simmons suddenly relaxed. She whispered, "I accept it. Oh, I am SO glad that was really what happened. Then my father must have been wrong about everything."

"Right," said the Countess Krak, villainously undoing in a breath what that poor, laboring psychologist father had devoted his whole life to build up. What a destructive Manco Devil that Krak was!

The Countess took a firmer grip on the microphone. She was obviously through playing around. Now she was going to get down to business. She said, "Now we're back to the first time you saw Wister. What you really thought was that you were not good enough for him. Correct?"

Simmons said, under the helmet, "Correct."

Krak said, "Now it is the time of the first Nature Appreciation class last fall. You are alone, you are leaving the UN. You do not want Wister to follow you because you know you are not good enough for him. You feel very sad about it, right?"

Simmons said, "Right."

Aha, here it came. I knew that Krak was going to order her, now, to write a suicide note. For that is exactly what I would have done. Simmons was finished!

The doorbell rang.

I let out a wheeze of relief for Simmons. She had been saved by the bell. Grafferty! All was not lost. He was just a little early, for there was no corpse there yet. But he would see at once what this was all about: He would find Simmons in a hypnotic trance and know that murder was in the air.

Krak said into the mike, "You will lie there quietly for the moment and ignore anything you hear until I get back."

She put down the mike. She went out of the bedroom and closed its door behind her. She went into the living room. She peeled off her gloves, threw them aside and fluffed her hair. She opened the door.

DOCTOR KUTZBRAIN!

He was standing there in a bowler hat and black overcoat. He lifted up his inch-thick glasses and stared at Krak. "Well, well! Lizzie Borden!" Then he smiled like a hungry wolf and pushed his way in and banged the door shut behind him.

As soon as he was in, he said, "I just stopped by to tear off a little (bleep). I always visit my patients in times of stress, namely mine."

In a disgusted voice the Countess Krak said, "Really."

Kutzbrain was taking off his overcoat. He said, "Nothing like a little psychiatric therapy to cheer one up."

The Countess said, "Do you live with Miss Simmons?"

"Oh, no, no. I'm Doctor Kutzbrain, her psychiatrist at the University Hospital. But I'm impartial. I spread my professional skills around. I don't think you've been an inmate of my ward yet, Borden, but you're a real looker so I'll make sure you soon will be. So just lie down on that sofa and pull up your skirt and we'll get into the preliminary professional psychiatric examination. If it feels good enough, I can get you into the ward instantly. Those look like nice (bleeps) under your shirt. But they need a (bleep) erection test."

My hair rose. The Countess Krak had killed three men just for extending a hand toward her sexually. This dumb (bleepard) was about to be stamped to jelly! And then I really laughed with glee. Grafferty was going to find a real corpse!

The Countess Krak was reaching into the plastic shopping bag. I knew it was for some lethal weapon. It was a roll of something black. She tore one of the perforated bits from it.

The doctor's hand was still reaching. She put the small black square in it. "Hold this," she said icily.

He took it and stared at it.

She reached into the black plastic bag. There was a little dynamo in there. She touched a plunger which started it.

Doctor Kutzbrain stood straight up. He went utterly rigid. His face went blank. He was fixed in place like an awkward statue!

Oh, my Gods! One of the Eyes and Ears of Voltar devices she had filched from the Afyon hospital! I remembered it. It was a remote-control rig. When one had one of those black patches planted on him and the device was activated by the tiny dynamo, the person went rigid and blank and stayed that way as long as the dynamo ran, and when it was cut off the person returned to motion without being aware of the halt. According to the directions I had fleetingly seen, they used it to obtain evidence photographs in low-level light conditions. But she was simply using it to immobilize Doctor Kutzbrain.

Probably she would kill him later. Grafferty still had a chance to get his corpse, so necessary to headlines and to my plans for finally wrecking the Countess Krak. Still, even if Grafferty came early, there was quite enough to cook her goose: a leading psychiatrist of the city standing like a catatonic statue in the middle of the living room and a very pathetic victim hypnotized in the back bedroom. Whichever way the cards fell, the Countess Krak was for it! New York City would give her Hells, to mention nothing of Voltar penalties for Code breaks.

She made sure that Doctor Kutzbrain was remaining statuized. Then she went back into the bedroom to finish off Simmons, all unaware that the police were howling on their way. I knew that she could never get out of there in time.

Chapter 5

The Countess Krak closed the bedroom door behind her. Miss Simmons was sprawled on the bed—breasts, belly and thighs bare. The Countess reached over and pulled the bathrobe closed: I could not figure why she was doing that; I myself thought Simmons' nakedness pretty stimulating.

Krak sat down in the chair and again took up the microphone. "It is just after the first Nature Appreciation class last fall. You have left the UN and are now entering Van Cortlandt Park. Where are you?"

"Just entering Van Cortlandt Park," said Simmons, very muffled under the helmet. Her body started to stiffen.

"You see that Wister is following you. You know you are not good enough for him. You plead with him to go away."

From under the helmet, "Please go away, Wister."

"Good. Now he has gone away. You walk further into the park. You see eight men following you. Look back at them. What do you see?"

Miss Simmons' body went more rigid and began to twitch.

"I see eight men following me."

Krak said, "You are looking for a secluded place. You find one. What does it look like?"

Miss Simmons went more tense. She said, "A hollow with a high bank all around. The path comes down from the hill into it. The grass is green, there is a brook."

"Good," said the Countess Krak. "One of the men is closer

-328-

than the rest. What would you really want him to do."

"Like it says in Krafft-Ebing."

"What is Krafft-Ebing?" asked Krak in a puzzled voice.

"The books like *Psychopathia Sexualis*. Like Havelock Ellis' books or Sigmund Freud's. My father used to read them to me every night at bedtime. As a psychologist he said that all those nasty fairy tales were full of phallic symbols. Like putting thumbs in pies. And he said his daughter must read the same things they teach in kindergarten today because psychology is the best arousal-depressant for children as it pounds into them all the horrible things they must not do. He did it to help my natural frigidity so I could be normal like the other children in my class."

The Countess Krak lowered the microphone into her shoulder. "Good Heavens!" she muttered in Voltarian. Then she raised the mike and said in English, "So what did you want the first man to do?"

"Like Krafft-Ebing. To knock me down in the mud and . . ." mumble . . . mumble . . . mumble . . . "just like it says in Kra . . . mmmmmmmm! Oh, yes. Oh, my, YES!" Her words had been more and more choked and her breathing was short and heavy. "Come on . . ." mumble, mumble . . . "Put . . ." mumble . . . mumble. "AH!"

The Countess Krak was staring at her. She covered the microphone. In Voltarian, she muttered, "Well, there's no stopping her now." In English she said into the mike, "That's exactly what is happening. You can see it, feel it, you are right there. Go ahead."

Miss Simmons got more rigid. Then she threw her arms and legs wide. She arched her back. Her hands impatiently ripped the robe even further away so she was totally uncovered. "Ah, ah . . . the mud . . . so beautiful . . . so dirty . . . ah. MORE! . . . MORE!" Her back was arched like a bow.

Some clothing on a hanger began to dance. Mumble . . . mumble, panted Miss Simmons.

"My word," said the startled Countess Krak.

The clothes blew off the hanger with the violence of Miss Simmons' scream.

The Countess Krak stared at her, stunned.

Miss Simmons was now lying there, spent, her tongue hanging out the side of her mouth.

The Countess Krak raised the microphone up. But she didn't get a chance to say anything. "Now YOU!" cried Miss Simmons.

Both Miss Simmons feet rose into the air and began to kick jerkily. Mumble . . . mumble . . . mumble.

The items on the makeup bureau began to jump and quiver.

"Good Lords," said the Countess Krak.

"NOW!" screamed Miss Simmons. "NOW! NOW! NOW!"

The makeup bureau implements cascaded to the floor, battered by Miss Simmons' piercing screech.

Then Miss Simmons was lying there, tongue lolling out of the side of her mouth, panting.

The Countess Krak raised the microphone to speak. She didn't get a chance. "Two, two, two!" cried Miss Simmons. "Both . . ." mumble . . . mumble . . . "GOT TO!"

Miss Simmons was sitting up. She began to bounce up and down on the bed.

The Countess Krak was watching her, very puzzled.

A piece of plaster in the ceiling began to shake and splinter.

"Yowee!" cried Miss Simmons.

A piercing scream hit the plaster and it came crashing down.

Miss Simmons was lying back again, tongue lolling.

The Countess Krak raised her microphone once more. "Miss Simmons," she said, "I think . . ."

Miss Simmons was now on her hands and knees. "Oh, no!" she shouted, "Don't do that! AHHHH!"

A floor lamp beside the chair of the Countess Krak began to dance. She put out an alarmed hand to steady it. The lamp just jiggled worse.

"MORE! MORE! MORE!" cried Miss Simmons.

The closet door slammed shut as she let out a piercing scream.

Miss Simmons was lying there again with her tongue lolling out, panting.

The Countess Krak looked relieved. She composed herself and, in a business-like way, once more raised the microphone to speak.

But the voice of Miss Simmons interrupted her, "Now three!"

Miss Simmons had a pillow. She was tearing at it. She got it under her, then turned over and seized it. Mumble . . . mumble . . . mumble! she said.

The floor lamp again began to rock.

Miss Simmons' hand tore a wad of feathers from the pillow.

The Countess Krak stared. She couldn't make it out.

Miss Simmons' housecoat flew up into the air. "Mmm! Mmm! Mmm! Yippeee!" she cried.

Then Miss Simmons was lying there again, panting.

The Countess Krak retrieved the housecoat and then stood staring. In a perfectly natural voice, Miss Simmons was saying, "We will now take up page 92 of Krafft-Ebing. I am certain that your psychology teacher called it to your attention. Six of you form a ring. The other two . . ."

The lamp had begun to rock. The Countess Krak grabbed it to keep it from falling down.

"Mmm! Mmm! Mmm!" crooned Miss Simmons.

Suddenly the spilled makeup implements on the floor bounced as a shuddering shriek came from Miss Simmons.

The whole pillow-load of feathers shot into the air.

The Countess Krak tried to bat the flying feathers off her face.

The floor lamp came down with a splintering crash.

Miss Simmons lay back, relaxed, smiling under the helmet. She was drenched with sweat and so was the bed around her. She looked totally exhausted. She stretched lazily.

The Countess Krak shook her head. In Voltarian she muttered, "Well, I hope she got her fill! The slut!" Then she raised her microphone and said in English, "The men are all going away now. They are waving good-bye. You see them walk up the trail and vanish. They were all very happy. Are you happy?"

"Oh, yes," came the muffled voice of Miss Simmons from the helmet.

"Anything worrying you?"

"I'm nice and lovely dirty with the mud. But my leg feels a little strange."

"You broke it dancing for joy," said the Countess Krak.

"Oh, that's all right, then."

The Countess Krak now took a firm grip on her microphone. She said, "The incident you have just been through is the right one, the correct one, the one that happened. All other memories of that time and place are false and are gone. You have just been through the true one. Do you understand?"

"Yes," said Miss Simmons.

At that instant there were some shouts and car-door slams outside.

Somebody shouted, "Get up there to apartment 21!"

I tingled! Grafferty!

Chapter 6

The Countess Krak said into the microphone, "You will lie there and think of nothing until I come back."

She put down the microphone, stepped out of the bedroom and closed the door behind her. Doctor Kutzbrain was still standing like an awkward statue.

Feet were pounding up the stairs.

The crash of a boot against the apartment door!

Lock flying into fragments, the door smashed open.

Grafferty and three policemen sprang into the room!

Grafferty stared at the immobile Doctor Kutzbrain. "Where's the rape-murder?" he roared.

The Countess Krak had reached the black bag. She hit the dynamo plunger, turning it off. But she drew out a small object that looked like a thumbtack. I caught the briefest glimpse of the tag on it.

Doctor Kutzbrain went into motion, drawing all eyes.

The Countess Krak stepped across the room to him. She had that tack held in her fingers. She grabbed Kutzbrain by the shoulder with that same hand. At the instant of contact, Kutzbrain let out a yell.

Krak said, "If it's a rapist you're looking for, here's your man!" She stood away.

Grafferty shouted at Kutzbrain, "Where's the murder?"

Doctor Kutzbrain inhaled a lung-full of air. He shouted, "I hate you! I'll tear you to bits! Answer me!"

Oh, Gods, that (bleeped) Krak had used an interrogator dart on him, the one that made a questioner so furious and overwrought he could not ask sensible questions!

Grafferty waved a gun. He roared, "Who the hell do you think you are, talking to police that way?"

Kutzbrain shouted, "You must answer up! I'll kill you if you don't! I'll tear you to bits!"

Grafferty signalled to two policemen. "Take him along, men. And bring this girl as a material witness. And you," he said to the third cop, "look around here and make sure there isn't a corpse in one of these rooms. We need evidence!"

Krak said, "I've got the evidence. It's right here!" She reached into the black case and tore four tabs off the black roll.

She reached out her hand to Grafferty and the cops, using a magician's forcer gesture, the way they make people feel they have to grab something.

They each took a tab, looking at it.

The Countess Krak pushed the dynamo plunger.

Grafferty and the three cops went into rigid statue stances!

So did Kutzbrain!!

Krak went over and closed the apartment door and put the chain on it.

She stood back and inspected the five statues. They were unseeing, paralyzed into awkward stances.

The Countess Krak went back into the bedroom.

She neatly covered up the naked body of Miss Simmons again. She picked up the microphone and sat down in the chair.

Miss Simmons was sprawled out, relaxed and smiling under the helmet.

"Now," said the Countess Krak, "we will take up how you really feel about Wister. You know you are not good enough for him. But you are eternally grateful to him for not having you himself but letting you be raped. Your gratitude amounts to the worship you would give a saint and you know you would defile him if he so much as touched your body parts. You understand that, don't you?"

"Yes," said Miss Simmons.

"Therefore," said the Countess Krak, "the very next time he comes to class, you will tell him that he has been such a good student you are passing him with the highest grade for the whole remainder of the course. You will tell him that he does not have to attend your class further, does not have to take any examinations for Nature Appreciation, that he is unconditionally complete, and you will mark your records accordingly so there is no slip-up. Have you got that?"

"Yes."

"You will also tell other teachers what a fine student he has been and will believe it yourself. Got that?"

"Yes."

"At the very next class he attends, you will promptly send him away. You will never have to see him again. Isn't that nice?"

"Very nice."

The Countess Krak fingered the mike. Then she took a deep breath. She said, "After you have sent Wister away, you can please yourself. It will be your life that you are living and I have no wish to take control of it, but I want to give you some very sound advice. Stop running around with this Krafft-Ebing fellow. He and his pals Havelock Ellis and Sigmund Freud are a crummy crowd. My suggestion to you is that you find a nice young man—NOT Wister —and get married. It's your life, but you should consider settling down and doing things in a more normal way."

"A normal way," muttered Simmons.

"Exactly," said the Countess Krak. "You'll find it is much more fun."

"More fun," muttered Simmons.

"Sex without love," said the Countess Krak, "is a waste of time. Do you understand?"

"Waste of time," said Simmons.

"Good," said the Countess Krak. "Are you confused or worried about anything?"

"Oh, no!"

"Good. You will now forget I have ever been here. When I remove the helmet you will go quietly to bed without leaving this room. You will ignore anything you hear or see until tomorrow. You will have a nice night's sleep. You will awake fully tomorrow to a new world. Anything you find or that happens in this apartment or the living room tomorrow, you will disregard, invent a reasonable explanation for, and will refuse to be troubled about. Okay?"

"Okay," said Miss Simmons.

The Countess Krak turned off the helmet and removed it. Miss Simmons promptly crawled under the bedcovers and was instantly asleep.

I flinched now as the Countess Krak went out of the bedroom and closed the door behind her. I knew what I would do: kill the witnesses. My only question was *how* she would do it. I was losing allies right and left and could only sit there in that closet, trapped, and watch, powerless to prevent the inexorable, crushing wheels of fate.

Chapter 7

Police Inspector Grafferty was standing in a silly pose, immobile, staring at his hand. The three policemen remained in different stages of arrest, one looking at the ceiling, another at the floor, the third twisted halfway 'round, staring blankly at his chief.

Kutzbrain had his mouth open, stopped in midflight of overwrought fury.

The Countess walked up to Kutzbrain and recovered her dart. She put it in the black container.

Then she went to each policeman, took his gun away, unloaded it, took his spare shells and dumped them in the shopping bag. She put their guns back in their holsters. She pried Grafferty's from his fingers and did the same and then holstered it for him. How had she learned to do that? I was puzzled until I recalled that Bang-Bang was always around the office. What had that mad car-bomber been teaching her? Goose pimples broke out on my arms despite the closet heat. I did not like this! What would she do now? Something diabolical, I was certain.

She then got on her jacket. She threw her black sable short cape over her shoulders. She stepped to a mirror and arranged her blond, fluffy hair. Then she recovered and drew on her scarlet gloves.

She went over to a window and opened it an inch. It was dusk but the sound of neighborhood children shouting and yelling came from the street.

She wound up the microphone cord very neatly and packed the

hypnohelmet in the shopping bag. She looked around to see if she had left anything.

Then she drew out a very tiny object.

I froze.

A BOMB!

Oh, my worst fears were realized.

The Countess Krak looked at the five men. It was like a waxworks where they show famous figures in the middle of a notorious crime. But this crime was not something of the past, exhibited for historical edification, it was here and now! It was about to happen in all its hideous awfulness!

Those poor devils were about to feel the full fury of the remorseless Countess Krak.

Poor Kutzbrain. If only somebody had thought to warn him that she had slaughtered three men for simply making an innocent pass at her! I knew she would never forgive that. She had simply put it off because she had other things to do. Now the world of psychiatry was about to feel the full degradation of one of its leading lights. I wondered if in his final moments he would trace his downfall to the cheery words inviting her to lie down on the couch for a jolly romp? How, in his profession, could he possibly suspect he had been dealing with worse than death itself? Alas, poor Kutzbrain's professional habits—nay, his professional duty to rape women and wives—had not included a subcourse in dealing with a Manco Devil incarnate, like the vicious Countess Krak.

She placed the bomb a bit closer to Kutzbrain than the rest. She looked around one last time. Her gaze lingered on Kutzbrain.

Then she pushed the plunger!

The bomb was set to go on time!

She picked up her shopping bag. She walked to the door. She left it wide open.

She walked sedately down the stairs.

She went out the front door of the apartment and into the dusky street.

She crossed it. A side alley was directly across from the apartment building.

She lurked like a lepertige beside the trail, hidden and waiting to enjoy the death agonies of its prey.

She had a hand in the shopping bag. She checked the position of her thumb. It was resting on the trigger of the dynamo that immobilized the men.

She was watching the apartment window intently as though expecting something to happen. It happened!

A FLASH!

Smoke began to roll out the window slit she had left open.

She pressed the trigger of the dynamo, releasing the men.

INSTANT SCREAMS!

The sounds they were emitting must have been tearing out their throats!

They were deafening even across the street.

The thunder of feet!

More screams of terror!

Police Inspector Grafferty came tearing out of the apartment house.

He leaped into a squad car at the curb. He was frantically trying to find the keys. He was screaming, screaming, screaming the whole while!

Two more police burst out. They were howling with panicked horror.

They sprang into the second squad car. It started up instantly. Its wheels screeched and smoked as it sped a weaving course away.

The third cop had fallen down the stairs. Howling, he finished rolling across the foyer and leaped as though shot from a rocket into the squad car.

Grafferty and the cop wrestled for the wheel, both screaming.

The third cop got the engine started.

With both of them trying to drive and knocking the other aside, the squad car raced away.

Just as it went, Kutzbrain finally got a window open in the apartment. But he didn't jump through the opening. He went through the glass, screaming.

He landed in a privet hedge, screaming.

He got up and ran in a circle, screaming!

"They're after me, they're after me," shrieked Kutzbrain. And only then did I understand what she had used. It was an emotion bomb from the Eyes and Ears of Voltar, and from all the assorted emotions available she had chosen horror.

But the Countess Krak, that insidious female fiend, was not through with poor Kutzbrain.

I understood now why she had lingered.

She had a little package in her hand. It was a one-time disposable dart gun. She stepped forward. She aimed. The piteous spinning figure of Kutzbrain came in the sight.

She fired!

Kutzbrain was still running in a circle.

Suddenly the pitch of his screams changed.

Leaping up and down, he tore off his jacket.

Still screaming, he suddenly began to run on a course that would take him squarely into a mob of children who had stopped to stare at the pandemonium.

Kutzbrain was tearing off his shirt.

Kutzbrain, still screaming, was tearing off his pants.

"They're after me!" he shrieked, and got rid of his undershirt and shorts!

Then he began to run in earnest.

Krak, that Devil, had shot him with a dart that causes people to get warm and itch so violently that they shed their clothes.

What terrible revenge!

The children, like the tail of a speeding comet, were racing after Kutzbrain shouting, "A streaker! A streaker!" It was a dreadful din. The whole neighborhood was turning out to join the chase.

The Countess Krak tidied up her shopping bag. She fluffed her hair.

Sedately she strolled off in the direction of the subway. She was thinking, no doubt—the sadistic female monster—that this was a day's work well done. She even bought a Milky Way at the subway stand and munched on it quite happily as she rode triumphantly home.

My state was not one that could be described as victorious.

I couldn't get out of the closet.

I had to call on the radio and beg Raht to phone Miss Pinch and plead with her to move the furniture away so I could open the door.

It was not that Raht had had a sneering tone in his voice on the radio, it was not that Candy and Miss Pinch laughed at me for getting myself locked in the closet "like a naughty boy," it was not that the redecorators had not finished after all and the place was still a screaming mess, and it was not the fleas. It was the smug manner in which the Countess Krak had been eating that Milky Way!

Fury can sometimes open the door as often as it closes it. And fury opened it now.

INSPIRATION!

Miss Simmons was a doctor of psychology as well as education. Her father was a psychologist. She would know very well what hypnotism was!

I would tell her she had been hypnotized and blow the whole implant!

And then we would see who had the last laugh!

Chapter 8

What with one thing and then the other and then the first thing again, it took me the better part of the night to write the letter. Written so the calligraphy could not be traced, it said:

> *Dear Miss Simmons,*
>
> *I herewith return your glasses so you will know I am a friend.*
>
> *I have to inform you that a dastardly deed has been perpetrated upon you.*
>
> *You were hypnotized and lied to by the foulest fiend who ever existed between Hells and Heavens. You were told a pack of lies while in hypnotic trance. DON'T BELIEVE THEM!*
>
> *The things you were told were utter hogwash and you should cast them utterly from your mind. You have been absolutely right all along about him.*
>
> *Just realize that your future and that of this planet depend utterly upon your exposing that (bleepard) for what he is.*
>
> *Don't let the firm hue of resolution be sickled o'er by the pale cast of hypnotism. ACT. ACT. ACT! Your true friend.*
>
> *X*

Shortly after sunup, I woke Raht with the radio. I made an appointment to meet him at the Slime-Tripe Building at 8:30 A.M.

When the time came I was there, standing on the wavy terrazzo paving. Raht arrived. (Bleep) him, he had let his mustache grow despite orders and it bristled on both sides. But I had no time to upbraid him. Besides, we might be being watched.

I gave him the letter. "On your life, make sure that this is personally delivered to Miss Simmons at 352 Bogg Street, Apartment 21, Morningside Heights. As soon as you have done that, meet me at the west side of that building just to the south of us, at the tables in Gruffaw-Spill Park."

"Why not just meet you at Miss Pinch's apartment?" said this insolent ruffian.

"You stay away from there. And if you breathe a word of where I am to anyone, I'll shoot you in hot blood, gallons of it."

"I believe you would," he said. But despite the insolence, trained as he was, he sped away.

I went to the Gruffaw-Spill Building. Down on the concourse it has the only walk-under waterfall in New York. You walk straight through it. I was using it because it covered the trail.

Inside was a refreshment stand and tables. It is very nice. I had some coffee and a hot dog, feeling pretty cheerful about things, really. The waterfall was splashing away, and since this was Saturday, there was hardly anyone around. Quite peaceful. No riffraff.

Two hours later, it did not seem so restful. I was drinking too much coffee.

Five hours from the time I had sent Raht off, it wasn't peaceful at all. I was getting worried. I blamed myself. I should have taken the message there personally: I had been deterred by the positive conviction she would recognize my voice after our first interview. Or some of her students might drop in and take a swing at me.

I was nervous now, so that my hands were shaking and the man at the refreshment stand was eyeing me, no doubt trying to make up his mind to call the police, Raht showed up.

He was nervous and furtive, white of face and shaky of hand. He looked apprehensive. I knew he was hiding something.

In answer to my furious demand as to what had detained him, he said, evasively, "Oh, she wasn't up. Her cleaning service was, and some people putting a new glass pane in the window were, though. How come the place got so wrecked? Do apartments you have anything to do with always get wrecked, Officer Gris?"

I kept my voice down. The man at the counter had his eye on me. "Did you or did you not deliver the message?"

"I didn't want to leave it with the cleaners," he said nervously. "They didn't seem reliable. You learn not to trust people in our line of business. And with a threat of buckets of blood . . ."

"Gallons," I corrected him sharply.

". . . I wouldn't hand it over to the glass company. So I waited for her to get up. And she did about half an hour later."

"Wait a minute. That was over four and a half hours ago! What in the name of Hells detained you?"

"Gently, gently," he said anxiously. He leaned forward. "Those two little girls over there and the proprietor are watching. You're talking Voltarian."

"Raht, I have a gun in my pocket. It is pointed straight at your stomach under this table, Raht. If you don't tell me what happened, Raht, I am going to pull the trigger, Raht."

That got to him. "I bet you would," he said. "And cops would instantly be all over the place." He gave me a glaring look. But he got down to business. "So she got up. She was wearing a housecoat that was pretty wrinkled and she didn't seem to be bothering to keep it closed. She sure is built. Breasts nice and firm. Brown pubic hair. Nice legs . . ."

I made a threatening gesture with my hand in my pocket.

He got on very hurriedly. "She looked at the cleaning-service people and said, 'It must be Saturday.' Then she looked at the glaziers that were fixing the window and said, 'That's nice of the owner. It's been drafty. . . .' "

"The letter, Raht," I snarled.

". . . and then she saw me standing there and she said, 'Oh, an early-morning caller. How nice.' And I said, 'No, ma'am. I am acting as a courier, even though that isn't my proper job designation. But I've been improperly sent so here I am.' I gave her the glasses. She put them down on a walnut sideboard about three inches from the edge. I gave her the letter. She opened it with a hairpin. She read it."

"Wait a minute," I said. "She can't see anything at all without her glasses. You may have given it to the wrong woman. Describe her."

He did. Brown hair, hazel eyes, wart on the back of her left hand. It was Miss Simmons. "And then?" I said.

"And then all Hells broke loose," said Raht. "And that's why I've been delaying telling you because you're liable to get excited and shoot somebody. Promise me you won't shoot. You might hit those two little girls over there."

Excitedly, I said, "Go on! Go on! I won't shoot you! This is good news, you idiot!"

"Well, she read the letter and she stood there, going white and red. And then she read it again. And she kind of began to yelp. Officer Gris, why would you write a letter that would upset the poor woman so? I don't like acting as a courier. And especially NOT of your letters! I thought she was going to have a stroke. Why would you want to upset her so? She seems a nice girl. But upset people seem to be good news to you."

I was glowing with eagerness. "Go on! Go on! Exactly what did she do or say?"

"She screamed, 'I knew it! I knew it! The moment I woke up, I knew it but I wouldn't admit it to myself!' And she rushed into the bedroom and I heard her getting dressed and she came back into the living room. I hoped she would write something really nasty back so I said, 'Is there any answer?' And she said, 'Wait right there until I return and I'll give you one. This is a matter for the police!' And she went tearing out of the apartment."

I was ecstatic. She knew what Krak looked like. She could put it together on an identokit. Better, Grafferty, the three policemen and Kutzbrain could identify the woman. They even had her fingerprints on their guns. They knew it connected to Wister and when they questioned him they would probably run right into the Countess Krak. Perfect!

Raht was still talking. "Finally, I tailed her but lost her in a downtown express, so I came back to Bogg Street. I found a place where I could keep the apartment under surveillance without being noticed and I waited. On the one hand, I thought maybe if she came back with the police, I could give them your address, but on the other hand, if this got rough, it could compromise Voltarian presence on the planet. I decided I should find out more. If she came back with police, I could disappear. But if there were no police with her, maybe I could find out more information—which is, after all, my proper job, no matter how many times certain people seek to drive me off it, doing incorrect functions."

"Get on with it," I ordered him.

"She was gone for hours and when she came back she was alone so I walked with her. She was smug beyond belief. She seemed all happy and cheerful, but smug. These Earth women are that way. They're happiest when they've got something on somebody, and that's the way she looked."

"Beautiful," I said.

"Yes, I would say she did look more beautiful. But smug. We got clear up to her apartment and went in and then she did the weirdest thing. She kissed me on the cheek and she said, 'Tell your friend, thank you, thank you, thank you! It is totally true. His or her letter has practically saved my life.' So I got out of there real fast. Women don't kiss you without some covert reason and I think she was just trying to keep you from taking flight until the police could come. So I recommend, knowing you, that you sort of lie low."

"No, no, you idiot. She wasn't covering anything up. She was being absolutely honest. I did save her life."

I was so enthralled, I didn't even notice when he left.

I could hardly wait for Sunday. Wow, was this going to go in the most unexpected direction Krak could ever imagine. (Bleep) her! Her and all her fancy, stupid tricks!

Chapter 9

It was late morning of the day that would long live in my memory as Simmons' Sunday.

Crouched in the closet again, this time with the door plainly marked "Occupied," I eagerly watched events begin to unfold.

Heller, at his office desk, had been working on some calculations for quantities and volumes of spores. He now stood up and went to the window. Lower Manhattan spread out before his gaze under the mantle of sun-illuminated smog.

The Countess Krak was lying in the middle of the room on the rug going over museum programs, the cat dragging them off a pile for her.

"What's the matter, dear?" she said to Heller. "You seem rather agitated."

"Me? Agitated? Well, yes, but that's a pretty strong word. Bang-Bang phoned about an hour ago and said the Nature Appreciation class location had been changed to Van Cortlandt Park today. It was to have been the Bronx Zoo. I was wondering why."

"That's that Miss Simmons, isn't it, dear?"

"I wish you'd forget about this Miss Simmons thing. She hates me like poison. My only interest in her is that she could cost me my diploma and nobody will listen to me when I make my proposals."

"I shouldn't be counting on proposing to Miss Simmons, dear."

"Please, can't we call a truce on . . ."

"Dear, what is the weather like?"

"A warm, spring day," said Heller. "If it weren't for the smog, it would be beautiful. In a lot of ways, you know, this is a very nice planet."

"Well, that's probably why they changed the class location," said the Countess Krak. "Who'd want to be penned up in some stuffy zoo? Are you driving, dear?"

"Well, yes. That's a good idea," said Heller. "I put the new carburetor on the Porsche and I haven't had a chance to give it a good spin."

"You do that," said the Countess Krak. "I have some exhibits I want to see, so if you don't mind, dear, I'll just run along."

She was up like a shot. She had her blue suede topcoat, purse, shopping bag and hat right by the door. She gathered them up in one scoop and was gone.

Heller glanced out of the window again. Then he got into a white silk trench coat, found some papers and a notebook and put them in his pocket. He glanced down at his feet. He was wearing ankle-high walking boots and not his spikes. It gave me a nice feeling: If the police were waiting for him up there, he had no cleats to battle with. He was getting satisfactorily careless.

The Countess Krak had plummeted down in an elevator. She came out of the building on 34th Street, walked swiftly up the block and sped into a new, multistory, spiral-roadway garage. The attendant waved at her, she got into an elevator and shot upwards.

She was fishing in her purse. She stepped out into the ranks of cars. She spotted the blue Porsche. She opened the door, entered, closed and relocked it from within, and then, as only a trained magician's assistant can do, curled herself up in the big luggage compartment behind the front seat and dropped the luggage canvas over her.

It made me nervous. I had forgotten to fill the strip well in her viewer and had no way to check back on what she had packed in that shopping bag. I had not counted on her presence at the next class. Maybe Bang-Bang, (bleep) him, had gotten her a demountable sniper rifle. These stupid men around her didn't seem to realize what they were dealing with: a killer! The Countess Krak would have made top Mafia hit men look like kids shooting marbles.

I knew her for what she was: a dangerous fiend with a thirst for blood unequalled by even Dracula of Earth fame.

Heller came trotting along shortly. He noted that the springs seemed a bit lower, for he gave the car a cursory exterior and motor check, probably for bombs. Then he gave an "Oh, well," and started the car up, possibly believing all the monkeying he was doing with it had changed its balance or weight.

He sent it spinning down the ramp and shot it out onto the street. It was Sunday and New York, doubtlessly recovering from a Saturday night hangover, had about as much traffic on the streets as a cemetery.

He was shifting up and down through the gears like a rally driver. The purring Porsche was shortly onto the West Side Elevated Highway and in no time at all was on the Henry Hudson Parkway. The river was blue and sparkling in the spring sun. The George Washington Bridge flicked by.

It worried me. He was driving by the tachometer, not the speedometer, and while he could have outdistanced a cop with that Porsche like the squad car was standing still, I yet was afraid he would get arrested for speeding and his appointment with destiny would be interrupted. But there just plain wasn't any traffic. Those leaving for the country were gone and they had not yet begun to create the traffic jams of return. For once I was glad the police were asleep where Heller was concerned. Nothing must interfere with the coming catastrophe.

He had the stereo going and a song came over:

> *Fatal Woman,*
> *Cherchez la femme.*
> *Fatal Woman,*
> *So drenched in sin.*
> *Fatal Woman,*
> *The Devil's twin.*
> *Fatal Woman,*
> *You done me in.*
> *And that's why I shall die.*

I smiled so broadly, I almost tore my lip. It went double for Heller: the one riding just behind him and the one waiting in that park ahead with scissors across his fate line, all ready to snip.

I almost felt sorry for the poor (bleepard). There he was, driving along so gay in his hopped-up Porsche, enjoying the early spring day, little suspecting the bomb that had been planted by the woman hidden behind him—and neither of them aware at all of the fuse sizzling up ahead, lit by me.

It's bad enough to face one woman. But he was absolutely surrounded with the treacherous species.

He continued on the highway into Van Cortlandt Park and shortly took a branch to the right. He was now driving through a vast expanse of golf course. He found a turnoff and a parking lot. He stopped, got out and locked his car. He went swinging off past some golfers and onto a woods trail.

The Countess Krak waited. Then she rose up and looked around. All was clear. She got out and locked the car. Then, with the aid of a side mirror, she adjusted her black beret and put on a set of very dark glasses, for all the world as though they would disguise her, and set off after Heller, shopping bag on her arm.

I was puzzled. I was getting two sets of footsteps in the Countess Krak's audio. I couldn't make it out. I turned Heller's off for a moment. Yes, two sets of footsteps from the Countess Krak's speaker.

Very difficult to understand how this was happening.

She was going along the path at least two hundred yards behind Heller, completely out of his view.

He was walking along briskly.

The Countess Krak did not seem to be the least bit concerned about losing him.

Heller came to a high point in the trail. I recognized it. It was the same place he had stood months before when he had been stopped by the gang. This time he looked behind the trees to right and left. Nobody hiding there. But a bullet scar was visible.

He looked down into the vale. New grass was just beginning to spring up. The trees round about were in bud.

Several students were down there, sitting around on broken trunks and stones.

Miss Simmons was standing behind a large, flat stump. It made a sort of an altar facing the class. A sacrificial altar, I trusted.

Heller, unarmed and unsuspecting, walked down the path to the group. Miss Simmons had spotted him from some distance away. When he came up, he would have taken a place back of the other students, a bit off to himself.

Miss Simmons fixed him with a cold eye. She pointed to a white stone near the altar to her right. She said, firmly, "Wister, sit there."

It was like putting somebody in the dock reserved for the accused. Or, I hoped, the spot where they put the condemned to hear sentence.

Miss Simmons looked to be in the grip of considerable tension. She had on a black topcoat and black slouch hat. She was not wearing her glasses and her hazel eyes were narrow and unreadable as she scanned the approach trail.

Several more students drifted in. A boy said, "Jesus, this ain't easy to find, Miss Simmons. I almost got lost."

"Sit down right over there, Roger," said Miss Simmons in a firm, uncompromising teacher's voice. She was pointing toward the others.

A bit more time passed. Three more students straggled in. A bit of wind stirred the upper branches of the large trees.

Miss Simmons was counting students aloud.

The Countess Krak was just to the side of the path as it started down into the vale. She stepped behind a large tree, looking down at the people in the hollow.

The counting was also sounding in the Countess Krak's audio speaker. I wondered how this possibly could be. She was too far away for Miss Simmons' voice to reach her.

Then the Countess Krak reached up and touched something and the sound came in louder.

THE GLASSES!

She was wearing an Eyes and Ears of Voltar device, disguised as sunglasses, that amplified distant sound. No wonder she could follow Heller. She had had these focused on his footsteps.

She reached up her hand again to the side of the tinted spectacles and suddenly the image of Miss Simmons leaped into close-up. Those things were also telephoto! And they looked like any other pair of sunglasses.

"The hussy," said the Countess Krak.

"Twenty-nine," said Miss Simmons, in a cold voice. "And thirty if you count Wister. There are some surprises in store for all of you. We can begin."

How ominous!

I expected Grafferty or at least police to be waiting around that wood. I hugged myself. If they were, they would catch the Countess Krak! Maybe even arrest Heller for the original eight murders!

Chapter 10

Miss Simmons lifted up a sack and placed it on the tree-stump altar. She wrapped her hand around a broken stick and pointed it at Heller.

"You sit right there, Wister, and don't you move an inch. For you are in for the biggest surprise of all."

She rapped upon the tree stump with the stick. She fixed them with a baleful eye. She said, "Gather round here, students—closer, for I have just made a terrible discovery."

They shifted forward and sat in a tighter semicircle before her.

The Countess Krak muttered, "What on Earth is this slut up to now? She wasn't told to do that."

I laughed aloud in glee. The Countess had not allowed for my contribution to this day.

Miss Simmons spoke, "As all you students know, my life has been a sort of hell." She looked at Wister. Then back at the small crowd. "I have been burdened by a demon, a fiend so merciless as to defy all the annals of Hell." The students clucked in sympathy. She turned to Heller, "Sit right there, Wister."

Miss Simmons sighed and looked back at her class. "Now, students, a vile, foul trick has been played on me. You have all had basic psychology from kindergarten up, so you know about HYPNOTISM!"

A shudder went through the Countess Krak that made her glasses wobble.

Miss Simmons was going on. "In unscrupulous and vicious

hands it is a despicable and awful weapon against an innocent and unsuspecting pawn.

"Students," she continued, "I have been told, under hypnosis, the most disgusting lies you ever could imagine!

"Undiscovered, they could have ruined the remainder of my poor life.

"But, just yesterday, a hidden and unknown friend opened my eyes suddenly to the TRUTH!"

"My Gods," whispered the Countess Krak.

Miss Simmons went on in ringing tones. "Now listen to this, Wister. Listen to this, students. Listen carefully. I received this letter. It told me I had been hypnotized! Instantly there occurred to me the only possible reason—to undermine my sex life, to leave me open to an awful fate."

The Countess Krak whispered, "That orgy was your own craven appetite, you false tart!"

Miss Simmons brought the stick down on the stump with a thud. "I went to the police. They told me I could only act if I had the evidence." She leaned forward confidentially, "I obtained it with another's help. And I am sitting on it, ready to take an awful vengeance. It is in a secret place, ready to be mailed if there is any effort to do away with me."

She stepped back proudly. "Oh, I have friends! You should understand that, Wister. You should know that, students. And they will support me in this amongst the highest university faculties."

Miss Simmons leaned forward impressively again. "You may or may not know that my father holds the chair of psychology at Brooklyn University. Ever since I was a child he has warned me of designing males." She looked at Heller sitting separately upon his rock. Then she looked back at the class. "My father taught me every night at bedtime that men were no good and only wanted vile gratification of their base desires."

Miss Simmons looked at Heller. Then back at the twenty-nine other young men and women of her class. They were gazing at her intently, utterly absorbed.

Miss Simmons plunged on. "So when I got that invaluable

letter, I realized at once that when it said I had been subjected to hypnotism, it was TRUE!"

She rapped again with her club. "When I had been told by the police I needed evidence, I went directly home. I told my mother and she looked very sad. We went to see my father. He was downcast, for it is an awful thing!"

Miss Simmons stood up straight. "My mother, God bless her, forced him to tell me!"

She leaned forward and spoke in a hissing voice. "My father, that vile fiend, had hypnotized me as a child. Not just once but repeatedly!"

Her face contorted in disgust. "He confessed that he had told me again and again under trance that I was FRIGID! He told me that if I had a man or experienced an orgasm I would go BLIND!"

She banged the stick upon the stump. "He is a craven traitor to psychology! It is supposed to (bleep) everybody, not make them frigid! And I am the living proof that he was mistaken. Look at my eyes! No glasses! Standing here, I can see every pimple on your dear faces!"

Miss Simmons stood back triumphantly. And then she stood in a humbled pose. "But who do I have to thank for this?" She turned to Wister and went over to him and knelt before him. "Oh, Wister, thank you, thank you, thank you. I am eternally grateful to you for letting me be raped. The orgasms were GLORIOUS! Time after time and right here on this very hallowed spot. I never dreamed such joy and ecstasy could exist. And TIME after TIME!"

She tenderly took Heller's hand. The Countess Krak flinched.

"Oh, dear Wister," said Miss Simmons. "I know I am not good enough for you. But my gratitude knows no bounds. You have been such an excellent student that I now declare you fully passed for the whole course. I will mark you A+ in Nature Appreciation for you appreciated nature even far better than I."

Simmons, kneeling, pressed his hand to her lips. She gazed upward into his eyes. "So, dear Wister, you are excused from all further classes, and even though it breaks my heart, you must leave this very minute. My gratitude walks with you forever for letting me be raped. So good-bye, my dearest, beautiful man. Good-bye."

Heller stood up, looking a little dazed. Then he waved a hand to the rest of the class and walked on up the hill.

Miss Simmons was a bit overcome. She knelt there for a little. Tears were dripping from her eyes. Then she rose and went back to the stump. She stood there, mastering her grief before she talked again.

Heller reached the top of the path. A very alert man of action, he instantly saw a flick of motion behind a tree. Alertly, he stepped over to it.

THE COUNTESS KRAK!

"What are you doing here?" said Heller.

"Just visiting the classroom to see how the pupils were getting on," said the Countess Krak.

"I'm excused from these classes for the rest of the year," said Heller. "And even after the UN loss. People knew I was pushing that. I don't understand it. I think she must have scrambled her main drives." He was looking back down the trail at the group in the vale. "Maybe I better go back and see if she's all right."

The Countess Krak bristled. She said, "Come along, Jettero."

"No," he said, "she sort of looked wild in the eye." He stepped back down the hill a few feet and stopped behind a tree, watching.

Chapter 11

Miss Simmons had regained her aplomb. Standing behind the stump, she spoke to the attentive students in clear and educated tones. "So, class, you will be very glad to know that I am no longer under the influence of that traitor to psychology, my father. He was mistaken. I can do what I please with my life.

"I am at last free to teach you what I subconsciously wanted to teach you in Nature Appreciation. Now, Nature Appreciation is really about the birds and bees. So there will be a substantive change in course material.

"We will not use the texts of Krafft-Ebing, Havelock Ellis and Freud, for they are crummy fellows to run around with. Such sources are bad, because they do not have any love in them. Instead, the text we will now use for this class is a classic Persian book, *The Seventy and Seven Variations in the Act of Love* by Hammer Hammer, translated by the respectable Chinese scholar Hoo Chu Longdong, with beautiful illustrations and diagrams by Phullup Cummings. I was able to get these at the college bookstore last night."

She flipped open the sack on the stump and began to pass them around. The students took them with great interest. "Now, girls, open your books to Chapter One, 'The Essentials of Orgasm.' But the boys should open theirs to Chapter Thirteen, 'Variations of Gang Rape.'"

The Countess Krak, able to see those pages with her sunglasses, muttered, "Now I know for sure why he was so tired Sunday nights.

The slut! Jettero," she said in a louder voice, "I think we better be going."

He couldn't hear what Miss Simmons had been saying. He shook his head. "I think that it's material I didn't get on the course."

The Countess Krak drummed her fingernails against the tree she was behind but she said nothing.

Miss Simmons said, "Now, students, I know the text is in Chinese, but the diagrams are very explicit, so simply notice the details for now. You can go over it more thoroughly in your homework. The point I am now trying to make is that nothing serves to teach better than experience. So I am going to lie down on this nice grass behind me here and you, Roger, are going to take my coat off."

Roger, a gangling youth, bounded to her side.

Heller, looking down into the glade, shook his head.

Miss Simmons' coat went flying through the air.

Miss Simmons' voice was coming over the Countess Krak's speaker. The tones were heavy with emotion. "For classwork during the remainder of the term, each boy of the class must first handle me and then each female classmate."

Heller, who had no speaker, turned to Krak. "She's saying something about classwork. I'm afraid I'm not going to get the whole subject."

"I'll say you're not," said the Countess Krak in a deadly voice.

Roger's coat hit the ground.

Heller stared. He looked back at the Countess Krak. "Why are they stripping? That brook isn't deep enough to swim in."

"Jettero," called the Countess Krak. "It's getting late."

Heller was staring down into the vale. Some cries were coming from there. "What on Earth?" he muttered.

A stack of schoolbooks lying on a bank slid down. One fell open at the bottom. A splash of mud hit it, *splat.*

"The hussy!" gritted the Countess Krak. "No wonder his clothing was all muddy every Sunday when he came home!"

"What did you say, dear?" said Heller. "I think they've gone crazy down there!"

The Countess Krak was fuming. Through her speaker came Miss Simmons' voice. "Now, Roger, we'll call that a pass. Thompson and Oswald, you come over here at once. The rest of you get busy. BUSY! BUSY!"

A boot landed in the brook with a tremendous splash!

Three girls' jackets went flying up in the air!

The very trees were shaking!

The Countess Krak had a leafy willow in her hand. Miss Simmons' strained voice came through the speaker. "Remember, it's no good without love. So I love you and you love me. OH, OSWALD!" The Countess snapped the willow with a furious jerk.

Heller was standing there, utterly flabbergasted.

The Countess Krak came up behind him, tugging at his sleeve to pull him away.

He shook his head as though trying to wake up. Then he turned and started back toward the car. "Blazes," he said, "am I glad to be out of *that* course! Teaching on this planet can get rough!"

"You mean," said the Countess Krak, "that some people on this planet can't even get the simplest lessons straight. The tart!"

Heller looked at her. She was taking off the glasses. She put them in a case.

He was gazing at her very suspiciously. "Did you have something to do with that?"

Her look was very bland and guileless. The very soul of innocence. She said, "Me? Jettero!"

That did it so far as I was concerned. The whole thing had gone wronger than wrong. Who would ever have suspected that Simmons' father, a renowned psychologist, would go against his whole profession and try to suppress promiscuous sex, the very backbone of Earth psychiatric treatment.

But I had only overlooked two minor points: In her hypnotic commands the Countess Krak quite accidentally had told her her father was mistaken, so no credit for the eyesight recovery was due to the Countess Krak. The other point was the order to Miss Simmons to disregard anything that happened in the living room the next day and to find a reasonable explanation for it. The latter unfortunately had included my letter. And that, too, was pure accident on Krak's part.

Oh, she was no genius. She was just lucky in a crude female way. Women simply do not have the brains to anticipate trouble like that. All they have is the ability to make vicious and cruel trouble for men. I knew by bitter experience this was their foremost skill. Look at the trouble she was causing me! Costing me priceless allies like Simmons, burning up my cash reserves by throwing around that credit card.

In a brilliant flash, as clear as lightning itself, I understood something utterly: In order to thoroughly wreck Heller, I would first and foremost have to get rid of the Countess Krak!

And then another lightning bolt. Whereas I could not slaughter Heller until I got the word from Lombar that the former's communication line to the Grand Council no longer mattered, there was NO restraint of ANY kind WHATEVER in removing the Countess Krak. She could be dropped off buildings or ground to mush under the heavy wheels of trains and I would suffer not the blink of an eye about it from Lombar.

AHA! I knew now what I had to do.

Concentrate on that deadly female.

She was expendable! She was the major barrier!

Unlike Heller, she was not trained in avoiding snipers. She knew nothing about car bombs. She had no war experience with booby traps or mines.

I could do it! I *would* do it!

And my eyes slitted with firm resolve.

GET RID OF THE COUNTESS KRAK!

*What crazy plan
will Gris use now?
Does this finish the
Countess Krak?*

Read
*MISSION EARTH
Volume 6
DEATH QUEST*

About the Author
L. Ron Hubbard

Born in 1911, the son of a U.S. naval officer, the legendary L. Ron Hubbard grew up in the great American West and was acquainted early with a rugged outdoor life before he took to the sea. The cowboys, Indians and mountains of Montana were balanced with an open sea, temples and the throngs of the Orient as Hubbard journeyed through the Far East as a teenager. By the time he was nineteen, he had travelled over a quarter of a million sea miles and thousands on land, recording his experiences in a series of diaries, mixed with story ideas.

When Hubbard returned to the U.S., his insatiable curiosity and demand for excitement sent him into the sky as a barnstormer where he quickly earned a reputation for his skill and daring. Then he turned his attention to the sea again. This time it was four-masted schooners and voyages into the Caribbean, where he found the adventure and experience that was to serve him later at the typewriter.

Drawing from his travels, he produced an amazing plethora of stories, from adventure and westerns to mystery and detective.

By 1938, Hubbard was already established and recognized as one of the top-selling authors, when a major new magazine, Street and Smith's *Astounding Science Fiction*, called for new blood. Hubbard was urged to try his hand at science fiction. The red-headed author protested that he did not write about "machines and machinery" but that he wrote about people. "That's just what we want," he was told.

The result was a barrage of stories from Hubbard that expanded the scope and changed the face of the genre, gaining Hubbard a repute, along with Robert Heinlein, as one of the "founding fathers" of the great Golden Age of Science Fiction.

Then as now he excited intense critical comparison with the best of H. G. Wells and Edgar Allan Poe. His prodigious creative output of more than a hundred novels and novelettes and more than two hundred short stories, with over twenty-two million copies of fiction in a dozen languages sold throughout the world, is a true publishing phenomenon.

But perhaps most important is that as time went on, Hubbard's work and style developed to masterful proportions. The 1982 blockbuster *Battlefield Earth*, celebrating Hubbard's 50th year as a pro writer, remained for 32 weeks on the nation's bestseller lists and received the highest critical acclaim.

"A superlative storyteller with total mastery of plot and pacing."—*Publishers Weekly*

"A huge (800+ pages) slugfest. Mr. Hubbard celebrates fifty years as a pro writer with tight plotting, furious action, and have-at-'em entertainment."—*Kirkus Review*

But the final *magnum opus* was yet to come. L. Ron Hubbard, after completing *Battlefield Earth,* sat down and did what few writers have dared contemplate—let alone achieve. He wrote the ten-volume space adventure satire *Mission Earth.*

Filled with a dazzling array of other-world weaponry and systems, *Mission Earth* is a spectacular cavalcade of battles, of stunning plot reversals, with heroes and heroines, villains and villainesses, caught up in a superbly imaginative, intricately plotted invasion of Earth—as seen entirely and uniquely through the eyes of the aliens that already walk among us.

With the distinctive pace, artistry and humor that is the inimitable hallmark of L. Ron Hubbard, *Mission Earth* weaves a hilarious, fast-paced adventure tale of ingenious alien intrigue, told with biting social commentary in the great classic tradition of Swift, Wells and Orwell.

So unprecedented is this work, that a new term—dekalogy

(meaning ten books)—had to be coined just to describe its breadth and scope.

With the manuscript completed and in the hands of the publisher and all of his other work done, L. Ron Hubbard departed his body on January 24, 1986. He left behind a timeless legacy of unparalleled story-telling richness for you the reader to enjoy, as other readers have, time and again, over the past half century.

We the publishers are proud to present L. Ron Hubbard's dazzling tour de force: the *Mission Earth* dekalogy.

"I AM ALWAYS HAPPY TO HEAR FROM MY READERS."

L. Ron Hubbard

These were the words of L. Ron Hubbard, who was always very interested in hearing from his friends, readers and followers. He made a point of staying in communication with everyone he came in contact with over his fifty-year career as a professional writer, and he had thousands of fans and friends that he corresponded with all over the world.

The publishers of L. Ron Hubbard's literary works wish to continue this tradition and would very much welcome letters and comments from you, his readers, both old and new.

Any message addressed to the Author's Affairs Director at New Era Publications will be given prompt and full attention.

NEW ERA PUBLICATIONS U.K. LTD
Dowgate, Douglas Road,
Tonbridge, Kent, TN9 2TS, U.K.